C000130828

Dawn Brett lives and works in Orpington, Kent and is happily married with two amazing children and a lurcher dog. She is extremely fortunate to have a great network of family and friends who live nearby. Her passion is shoes and she has an enviable collection.

Dedication

To my amazing family and loyal fantastic friends; without you this would
not have been possible.
Thanks to you all. ☺

D B Brett

WHATEVER YOU CAN COPE WITH

AUSTIN MACAULEY PUBLISHERS™

LONDON • CAMBRIDGE • NEW YORK • SHARJAH

Copyright © Dawn B Brett (2017)

The right of Dawn B Brett to be identified as author of this work has been asserted by her in accordance with section 77 and 78 of the Copyright, Designs and Patents Act 1988.

All rights reserved. No part of this publication may be reproduced, stored in a retrieval system, or transmitted in any form or by any means, electronic, mechanical, photocopying, recording, or otherwise, without the prior permission of the publishers.

Any person who commits any unauthorised act in relation to this publication may be liable to criminal prosecution and civil claims for damages.

A CIP catalogue record for this title is available from the British Library.

ISBN 978-1-78823-057-5 (Paperback)
ISBN 978-1-78823-058-2 (E-Book)

www.austinmacauley.com

First Published (2017)
Austin Macauley Publishers Ltd.
25 Canada Square
Canary Wharf
London
E14 5LQ

Acknowledgements

Thank you to my family for everything; without you
I would not have been able to create.
Thank you to my friends for everything; without you
I wouldn't be the person I am today.
I love you all unconditionally!

Love…………..
A misunderstanding between many fools!

Chapter 1

Katie looked at the clothes hanging in her wardrobe. "What do I wear for a first date?" she said out loud to herself.

She had been very excited since Steve had phoned on Sunday afternoon to confirm their date. He was taking her to Partners, the extremely expensive cocktail bar in town. She had been dying to go there but hadn't as yet had the opportunity and cocktails were her favourite, although they were so moreish and got her drunk quite quickly. She must ensure that she paced herself on Wednesday so as not to make a show of herself or Steve.

There wasn't a lot that was suitable, she thought; most of her clothes were extremely tightfitting and short and she didn't want to let him see everything she had on a first date, she needed things to be left to the imagination. Not something Katie was bothered about normally but this felt different somehow.

She decided that she had nothing that was suitable and no time or money to go and buy anything so she went into her flatmate's room; Lexi will have exactly what I am looking for. The soft pinks and creams of the room made it feel warm and cosy. Lexi was such a tidy arse, never had anything out of place and all her clothes were colour coordinated. Katie ran her fingers along the clothes; Ted Baker jackets, Reiss dresses, Jimmy Choo shoes. There was so much here, Lexi wouldn't mind.

Money was not Katie's strong point and she found herself wishing she was more like her flatmate; the perfect Lexi, she thought with a huge sigh, with her savings account and never spending beyond her means! She always had great designer clothes too, how did she do it? She had been meaning to ask her if she could borrow her cream Ted Baker jacket.

She found a Julien Two wrap dress in a soft berry that complemented her complexion, touched her curves in all the right places and came down to just below the knee. If she wore one of her normal bras, rather than the plunge type that she usually went for, then her ample breasts would have some control within the confines of the dress and wouldn't just spill out over the low neck line. She also never remembered seeing Lexi in this dress.

She decided to wear her hair coiled up in a high bun. Her makeup had been done to perfection with tinted moisturiser and smoky eyes and a lot of mascara; Katie didn't think false lashes would be appropriate for tonight.

She had small diamond hoop earrings to match the bling on her wrist and her favourite pair of Louboutin heels to add a touch of glamour to her outfit. They had made a serious dent in her already failing bank balance when she bought the six hundred and fifty pound shoes but she just had to have them.

Katie went back into her room and looked at herself in the full length mirror that adorned her feature wall.

The Eaton stripe dove grey Laura Ashley wallpaper complemented her cream Paris antique furniture well and a cream wrought iron king-size bed dominated the room, with soft lilac and cream bed linen. The cushions stood to attention against the intricate flower design bed posts. She had made her bedroom a place of peace and tranquillity, which sometimes doubled up as a den of iniquity, she thought, and laughed out loud! It was never as tidy and organised as Lexi's but she loved her space and was happy that she had managed to bag the en suite.

Katie Fox was five foot six, slim build with large, almond-shaped green eyes, a small button nose and full, rosebud pink lips. She was a natural beauty with a wicked sense of humour and a very dirty mind!

She had long shapely legs on which sat her pert bottom. Her natural 32D breasts were quite large for someone with such a small frame but they were high and firm and she loved them. She had often been complimented on her large nipples, which men seemed to be very turned on by and said they were perfect for sucking. She had smooth, silky, pale skin, which was why she got through a fair amount of fake tan, as she preferred the bronze look. Her long, almost white blonde hair shone down her back and sat just above her small waist. Katie Fox was very satisfied with what she had been given and knew that her face and body were an instant attraction for the opposite sex.

She thought back to some of the men who she had brought back to their apartment, much to Lexi's disgust. "Do you have to keep bringing your conquests back home?" Lexi had shrieked at her, one Sunday afternoon when her shag of the moment had just left.

"Oh, get over yourself, Lexi!" Katie had shouted back. "What is your problem these days?" Lexi had given her one of her nasty stares.

"My problem, as you put it, is that I don't want your fuck buddies coming back to our apartment. They could be anybody and I am not happy with you doing that, not to mention the noises you make. I have hardly slept a wink all night. I thought we had an agreement!"

Katie had turned on her heels and walked back into her bedroom, slamming the door loudly. "Fuck off, Lexi, just because you're not getting any at the moment!" she had shouted.

They had both agreed when they moved in together they wouldn't bring people back if they weren't mutual friends, but lately Katie had been bringing all sorts of undesirables back, which Lexi was not at all happy with.

She had walked in on Katie one night when she was back later than usual from work, as she was out to dinner with her work friends. She arrived in the apartment to a piercing scream coming from Katie's bedroom. She dropped her bags and rushed in there, wondering what on earth was going on, only to find two naked men and Katie, also naked, spread eagled on her bed. One of them was thrusting his large cock in and out of her whilst the other was sucking on her nipples and she was giving him a blow job!

Lexi was totally embarrassed and couldn't believe Katie would do this, especially in their apartment, especially without warning her first!

Katie had made a mental note whilst climaxing to get a lock put on her door.

Lexi had not spoken to her for days after that until Katie had promised never to bring guys back to the apartment.

She must make a conscious effort to stop annoying Lexi who, after all, was her best friend, some would say only friend, who she could confide in with anything. The last thing she wanted to do was piss her off.

She really needed a good shag herself, she thought. That was Lexi's problem; she didn't have enough sex. Katie should think about hooking her up with a few men. A threesome would sort her right out and might stop her being such a miserable cow!

Chapter 2

Lexi was an only child and had grown up in Cornwall, in a rundown chocolate box cottage by the sea, having had an idyllic childhood with two very loving parents. When she was ten, her father was killed in a car accident. Coming home from London on the M3 motorway, a lorry had ploughed into his vehicle after jack knifing due to the heavy rain. Her father had died instantly and Lexi was always thankful knowing that he wasn't really aware of what had happened. The police had told her mum that and Lexi had overheard.

Her mother, who had been totally distraught at losing her husband, came back to Kent to live with her brother and his wife, but never really got over the loss and Lexi was mainly brought up by her uncle, who instilled the same values as her parents had done.

Lexi and Katie had met at college. They were complete opposites, which is probably why they had become friends. She was as dark as Katie was blonde, with a shoulder length bob hairstyle that showed off her turquoise blue eyes to perfection. She was slightly smaller than Katie at five foot four but her curves were in all the right places and she had an enviably flat stomach from working out three to four times a week. She had darker skin than Katie, which bronzed as soon as she looked at the sun. Katie was envious of this, as she had to continually apply fake tan and factor fifty when out in the sun to stop getting heat rash, something she constantly moaned about.

Lexi had always completed her assignments on time, sometimes earlier than expected, whereas Katie left everything to the last minute and always relied on Lexi to help her out.

Lexi would ensure that she was at every lecture, enabling her coursework to be thorough and precise, where Katie was always late or sometimes didn't turn up at all and wanted to copy Lexi's notes. Lexi found this extremely frustrating but Katie always managed to bring her round.

That was what Katie was good at, communication. If she had put as much effort into her studies as she had in getting her own way continuously she would have graduated with flying colours, thought Lexi. As it was Katie just scraped through, and that was due to Lexi's help, but still getting nothing above a C, which her tutor said was an absolute miracle. Although she could not prove it the word 'cheating' was often branded around within Katie's earshot.

Katie wasn't at all bothered what anyone thought of her, especially after realising that her body and looks were a great asset that got her everything she required in life, especially from the opposite sex.

They had decided to flat share after they'd finished their studies and both had secured full-time jobs. Katie couldn't wait to leave home. She was an only child and her parents had split up early in her life; her mum couldn't be bothered with Katie so left her to get on with it herself. She grew up very quickly and after one of her mum's boyfriends had tried to make a pass at her she knew it was time to go. Lexi had come into her life at the right time and for that she was thankful.

The two bedroom, two bathroom apartment Katie and Lexi shared was on the top floor of a smart period building half an hour's walk from the centre of town, where there were ample shops, bars and restaurants that couples often frequented for intimate dinners and good, reasonably priced food.

They were lucky to have secured such a great place with two bathrooms. Katie had insisted on the en suite; no surprise to Lexi, as she had whined that it took her longer to get ready.

They had a large lounge/diner with double doors that led onto a balcony that was big enough for a table and four chairs overlooking green fields as far as the eye could see. The kitchen was well equipped and had a breakfast bar for late night chats and early morning coffee. The only downside to the apartment was that it was on the top floor and had no lift, but walking up the eight flights of stairs each day was the only exercise that Katie seemed to get. Although she and Lexi had joined the fitness centre in town some months previously she could never find the time or inclination to go, unlike her flat mate. "More wasted cash," as Lexi would often point out to her, a little envious that Katie had a washboard stomach without even bothering to exercise.

The landlord, who was short, balding and three stone overweight, had taken a shine to Katie when she and Lexi had viewed the apartment, as she had turned on her sexiest charm that day. Although it was slightly above their budget and they had fierce competition for it, Katie had flirted outrageously to secure the apartment, having assured the landlord that they both had good full-time jobs with great prospects and a budding career ahead of them. This wasn't strictly true in Katie's case but Lexi was definitely going to be making something of herself in the not too distant future.

Lexi wore a pale blue shift dress and navy suede pumps for work that morning. She was pleased that she had been to the gym the evening before as she knew she had a very busy day ahead of her. Meeting and greeting lots of new clients, she doubted there would be time to get a work out today.

She enjoyed her role as office manager and was extremely organised and efficient. She was good with her money and had a savings account that she called her 'rainy day' fund, just in case she ever needed it.

Lexi believed in living within her means and always budgeted her money well, never going overdrawn or relying on credit cards, although she did have one for emergencies.

She was a hardworking individual, outshining her peers; she had been promoted within six months at Prospect Law, as they saw the potential in her quickly and fast tracked her up the ladder into a junior management position. She was now working in the main office alongside the lawyers, and they thought extremely highly of her as a team player and a person whom they could completely trust to run a busy efficient office. Her main role was meeting the clients; she was a great ambassador for the company as she dealt with people well.

She had a great work ethic and was able to multitask. She was kind, considerate and extremely good at what she did, which showed in both fast track promotion and her salary.

Although Lexi often turned heads she didn't rely on her looks to get her up the promotional ladder. She had got where she was at Prospect Law through hard work and sheer determination and her peers would totally agree with that fact.

Men had come and gone in her life, without making too much of an impact, and although she had an enviable body, that she had worked hard to achieve, she didn't ever feel the need to flaunt it with tight, tarty clothes, unlike Katie.

Lexi had not found that 'someone special' that she wanted to have a long-term relationship with. Many of the men in her life had wanted more from her but she found it hard to commit and was happy to go on random dates, which she was frequently asked, rather than stick with one person. She was after the bells and whistles and that had not yet come her way.

There was a guy at the gym, whom she had sometimes said hello to in passing. She had heard others call him Frank and he seemed a nice genuine person, very tall at six foot four and looked like he spent most of his life working out. His body was ripped and he had dark grey eyes that Lexi thought extremely sexy.

They had not got past the "hello" stage but Lexi thought it would be nice to go out for a drink with him. As yet he hadn't asked her and she wasn't bothered either way. She was happy with her job and had quite a few other friends, apart from Katie, who she went out with.

Lexi was a kind, considerate human being, which was why she had always stuck by Katie, even though she annoyed the fuck out of her most of the time. She was getting fed up with Katie always bringing random men back to the apartment. It had to stop, and she had decided that a proper chat with her was the only thing for it. Her selfish flatmate had to be told that this couldn't go on any longer; if it did then Lexi would find someone else to flat share with.

Chapter 3

Steve couldn't believe his luck when Katie had agreed to a date.

He had first seen her in a coffee shop across the road from his gym. He had had an early work out and decided to treat himself to a cappuccino.

She had gone into the shop to get out of the rain that was bucketing down, suffering from a severe hangover.

She was wearing a little black dress that just about covered her pert bottom, with six inch heels that made her bronzed legs look even longer, and was on her way home from a party that she had been invited to by Gary in the accounts department at work. Her attire was completely out of place for the time of day and weather conditions and she had received many odd glances walking along the street.

Who said people in finance were boring? She had had an amazing night and got extremely drunk on homemade punch that Gary's flatmate had provided. The kick it had was like no drink she had ever tasted and was also extremely moreish.

She had drunk so much of the stuff that her last memory was playing a hilarious game of strip spin the bottle; that's all of the evening Katie could remember. She had passed out from the amount of alcohol she had consumed and woken up in her thong and nothing else, with mascara all down her face and Gary snoring loudly next to her on the sofa, his hand cupping one of her breasts.

She moved his hand and got up quickly and felt a rush to her head. She waited for the dizziness to subside and looked around the room for her clothes.

After finding her dress on the armchair and her shoes across the other side of the room, she washed her face in the downstairs loo, tidied herself up and made a very quick exit.

She hoped that she hadn't done anything she shouldn't have with Gary, or any of his friends for that matter, as some of their girlfriends had been at the party and she knew she would live to regret it when she went to work on Monday morning.

The last thing Katie needed was to be the talk of the office yet again after her drunken antics, as she was already on borrowed time with her manager, Miss Dawson, who Katie had felt had taken an instant dislike to her when she had started at the company a couple of years previously.

She was sure she only got the job as the two guys that interviewed her had taken a fancy to her. They were no longer at the company, which was a shame; it was one of the best interviews she had ever had with lots of flirting and innuendo, very unprofessional but who cares about that, she got the job.

Katie practically fell into the coffee shop due to the height of her heels, nearly knocking over two people that were about to leave. She apologised and made her way to the counter. She had received mixed glances from the people that were in the busy shop.

Steve had been sitting at a table nearest the door. He had looked up from his newspaper, seen her make an entrance and began to give her one of his slow smiles, that she found totally sexy, and she couldn't take her eyes off him.

He was extremely handsome, wearing a tight T-shirt showing his muscles off to perfection. She could see he liked to work out, which was an attraction Katie was always turned on by, along with a set of good white teeth and a healthy bank account; oh and of course they had to make her laugh and be very good in bed. Sex was extremely important, as were the right tools, she grinned.

She had smiled to herself at her list; this guy was ticking all the boxes.

She knew she didn't look her best but his piercing blue eyes and his dark short cropped hair with the long fringe were enough to send a single girl wild at that time of the morning. She had given him one of her killer smiles, arranged herself and strolled up to the counter and ordered a medium skinny latte. The coffee shop was very busy and all the tables were full.

Katie had decided to take the bull by the horns and, after being handed her well needed coffee by the woman behind the counter, she went over to Steve's table and asked if anyone was sitting in the chair opposite. He pushed the chair out with his foot, gave her a long hard stare with his baby blue eyes and said, "Be my guest."

Steve smiled to himself, wondering what she was up to last night, looking her up and down and liking what he saw; a very sexy smile plastered over her face and her ample breasts spilling out of that killer dress.

"Hello, I'm Katie."

"Hi, I'm Steve."

The pair of them just stared into each other's eyes for a full minute before the coffee shop door opened, bringing them back to reality.

"You look like you've been out all night," said Steve.

Looking a little embarrassed Katie tucked a strand of hair that had come loose from her ponytail behind her ear. "Er, yes I have, some guy at work was throwing a house party and I stayed longer than I intended." She had a big wide grin on her face.

Steve grinned back. "How's your coffee?"

"It's hot," said Katie, and started to blow the top of it to cool it down.

"You most certainly are," said Steve. Katie smiled, wow, she thought.

She got her mobile out of her bag to check the time. It was only nine a.m. "What brings you out this early on a Saturday morning?" she asked, unable to stop grinning.

"I had an early workout and decided to treat myself to a well-deserved cappuccino after," he advised, still looking straight into what he deemed to be the most amazing green eyes he had ever seen, regardless of the stunning body that went with them. He felt his groin stir and moved his leg so she wouldn't realise. Katie never missed anything.

They both finished off their coffee and he started to get his bag together. Steve thought he should strike while the iron was hot. "Can I get your number?" he asked, with a lot more force than he intended.

Katie looked at him, pleased that he had asked. She stared him directly in the eyes and reeled off her number. He picked up his phone from the table and tapped her number in. "Great," he said, "I may give you a call some time."

"I look forward to your maybe doing that," she said, leaning in nearer to him so he had the full view of her ample breasts, knowing that he would definitely be calling her.

Steve left the coffee shop, wondering what on earth had just happened. It was unlike him to be so flirty but she was absolutely gorgeous and he couldn't take his eyes off her. His cock stirred again, what is she doing to me?

It had been a couple of months since he'd had sex. The memory was a good one; Jemma, whom he had known for a while, was always willing to accommodate with no strings attached. Their relationship worked well as they both had needs without the complications that go with a full-on relationship, but she was away travelling for six months and he wasn't the type of guy to have random sex with just anyone. Things may change, he thought, as he was in definite need of a woman's body and touch.

The rain had eased off and was a slight drizzle so he decided to jog home, happy with how he was feeling and wondering when was best to call the stunning Katie for a date. He put his bag over his shoulder and took a slow run to his apartment.

When he was putting his key into the lock his phone started to ring. Martha's name showed on his screen. He pressed the accept button and said a friendly, "Howdy, sis," down the phone.

"You're in a good mood," said Martha. "What's happened?"

Steve smiled. "Oh nothing much, sis, just the possibility of a hot date on the cards with a very fit young lady," he laughed into the phone.

Martha was Steve's slightly older sister and was used to her brother's 'hot dates'. He had many of them and was never short of friends or women in his life. He was a good person from within and without and she had a good relationship with him as well as her parents, which she was happy about.

"I was wondering if you fancied taking me to see that new scary movie that's out at the cinema? You know, that none of my friends like, and you're the only one that I can rely on to go with me."

He laughed. "When were you thinking?" Martha laughed back. "Wednesday evening? I could meet you from work and we could get an early dinner and see the eight p.m. showing."

They had always been very close as siblings and liked to spend time with each other as they had common interests. Scary movies was one, as was a love of Italian food.

"Sounds like a plan, I look forward to it. Wednesday it is." They both hung up, pleased with their short conversation and looking forward to Wednesday.

Steve had made arrangements to see his best friend Toby that evening. He called him to discuss timings and ask if they were going to their usual haunt, The Feathers, a pub in town that sometimes had a late licence. He also wanted to tell him about the sexy Katie!

Toby picked up on the fourth ring. "Take your time," said Steve. Toby apologised. "Sorry, mate, just got out of the shower, still on for later?"

"Yeah," said Steve. "Feathers?"

"Yep, eight-ish," said Toby.

"See you there," said Steve. Both were men of few words.

Steve pottered about his apartment for the rest of the day.

He was twenty-five years old and had been in a serious relationship, that ended suddenly when he had found out that his girlfriend, Grace, had been cheating on him with her boss.

He was devastated at the time but after a year he had begun to think how lucky he was that it had ended, as the arguments were continual and the relationship had run its course. The sex was boring and he just wanted to live his life. Maybe if he had tried to make the sex more interesting Grace wouldn't have had to play away, but it takes two to tango and no point in dwelling on the past.

He was not looking for anything serious, he was happy with his life at this present time. He had no shortage of dates if he wanted them, but commitment was not on his radar.

He lived alone in an old Victorian building, that had been renovated and made into five two bedroom open plan apartments, on the outskirts of town with an inherited cat called Ralph, who was the laziest, friendliest, docile cat that Steve had ever known; which was why he had agreed to take ownership of him when his neighbour Andy moved to New York after being offered a once in a lifetime job opportunity.

Steve had moved out of his parents' house when he was nineteen, determined to get his own space and live his life. He still allowed his mum to clean his apartment and paid her the going rate, which worked out for both of them.

She still cooked him his meals and left them on the side for when he came home with sticky notes advising what they were, stocked his fridge with the essentials and did any other shopping that he needed when she was doing her own shopping for the family. She always made sure that she left the apartment by four p.m. so that she was not around when he came home from work, or met whoever he came home with when out with his friends. She was aware of her son's good looks and that women and some men were attracted to him. He'll settle down when he is ready, she told herself, and it will be with the right person this time. She was never keen on his ex but would never have told him so.

She had often witnessed the sultry looks that women gave him when they were out. He was a definite catch and whatever girl he landed up with would be a very lucky one, his mother was always telling him. He towered above her at six foot two. She was glad that Steve had been lucky enough to have the genes of his father in the height department.

His father always said, "You spoil that boy too much, Linda, he needs to fend for himself." She would always brush this off and ensure that he was not left out either. Steve's father, Ted, always had home cooked meals, beers in the fridge and they still enjoyed a full healthy sex life. They were a strong close family with the utmost respect for one another and all enjoyed spending time together.

Steve put on a pair of navy skinny chinos, a light blue Ralph Lauren shirt that brought out the blue in his eyes, and a pair of smart tan leather brogues to go out that night. Although it was only their local bar he felt like he wanted to make the effort rather than wear his normal attire of faded jeans and a T-shirt. He had had a good work out that morning and time to himself and was feeling in good spirits.

The pub was extremely busy when he arrived. The music was very loud. A DJ had been booked and the lights were dimmed to create an ambiance. There were a lot more women than men at the Feathers that evening and he saw Toby at the bar ordering the beers.

The Feathers was a trendy bar that had a rustic feel about the place. It had old wooden floors and large wooden tables to sit around. It also had comfy sofas and armchairs around the edge and a small dance floor over to the right of the bar where they often had a resident DJ playing music to suit all tastes. It had a mixed range of ages and a lot of people used it as their local before going on elsewhere to late night clubs to finish off the evening. They sometimes had a late licence for special occasions. Valentine's Day was a particular special evening as were Christmas Eve and New Year's Eve, where they sold tickets so as not to attract the wrong type of clientele.

"Hey mate, good shout, it's so busy in here," said Steve when he reached Toby, looking around at the fit women.

"Yeah," said Toby, "some hen night going on and this is their first stop so hopefully it'll quieten down later."

The hen party had been in full swing since early afternoon and they were all extremely drunk and falling about on the dance floor with their pink feather boas and sparkly Stetson hats.

A short blonde with enormous breasts had tried on numerous occasions to get Toby to dance with her but he kept declining, advising her he was waiting for his friend and needed a chance to catch up with the copious amounts of alcohol she had consumed before he could even think about getting up to dance.

She finally got the message and made her way over to another crowd of men and managed to get a couple of them on the dance floor. She turned round and stuck her tongue out at Toby; he smiled and raised his glass to her.

They picked up their drinks and made their way to the nearest table. "How has your week been?" said Steve. "Work busy?" Toby looked around whilst taking a sip of his beer. "Hectic, mate, so much to do but makes the time go quickly."

As he took a sip of his beer he nearly spat it out. There through the crowd was a girl with the blondest hair he had ever seen wearing the shortest skirt and a skimpy white vest top. Her breasts were spilling over the top, her nipples could be seen through the sheer of the material and her legs seemed to go on forever due to the very high black patent heels that she was wearing.

"Wow," he said to Steve, "look at that girl over there." Steve turned to look and his eyes widened as he saw the blonde coming towards them.

"That's the girl I met this morning in the coffee shop on the high street," said Steve. "She gave me her number and I said I would call her for a date. Actually, I said I might call her for a date." Toby looked at his friend. "Might, mate, why only might?"

Toby looked at Steve. "Are you kidding me?" he said with amazement, as Katie continued to walk in their direction, her breasts bouncing up and down. Steve laughed. "No, her name is Katie." He stood up. Katie was on her way to the ladies when she noticed Steve in front of her. A big grin appeared on her face as she saw him and his good-looking friend staring at her.

"Well, hello, twice in one day," Katie said in a very sexy drawl, as she leaned in to kiss Steve on both cheeks, her chest squashed against his.

Steve smiled as he stepped back. "This is my friend Toby. We just came down for a quiet drink, didn't realise that it was going to be quite so busy."

Toby looked at Katie and held his hand out. "Pleasure to meet you both," he said, grinning at her very large breasts. Katie turned to look at Steve. "Is your friend always this rude?" she asked, smiling, lapping up the attention these two gorgeous men were giving her.

"Oh, don't mind him, he's harmless. He's my closest friend and doesn't mean anything by it." Katie smiled. "I haven't heard from you yet," she said, giving him a killer brilliant white smile. "Have you decided if you're going to call me?"

Steve was a bit taken aback by her forwardness. "I only got your number this morning and have had a busy day," he lied. Katie looked straight at him. "It's fine, if you're not interested, I am sure your friend is." She looked at Toby, who seemed to be drooling at Katie's toned body; she put her hand on his chest.

Steve was caught completely off guard by this and although he sensed total danger he saw Katie as a challenging prospect and definitely wanted to take her on a date.

"I was going to give you a call to ask if you wanted to meet next week sometime?" he found himself saying. Katie looked straight at him. "Well, why didn't you?" She had had a few to drink and found herself totally confident and loving the attention she was receiving. She got aroused when she saw good-looking men staring at her body.

Steve pushed his hand through his hair. "Well, what night are you free?" He wanted to say any day but Wednesday but thought that sounded silly. "Wednesday," she said. It was not a question, more a statement.

He looked at Toby. "Is there a problem with Wednesday?" she asked through the silence. "No!" he blurted out. "Wednesday is good, what do you fancy doing?"

"Surprise me," she drawled, leaning in towards him and pressing her ample breasts against his chest once again.

Steve could feel himself get hard. Katie noticed this too and she pulled away and smiled slowly. "Call me tomorrow to arrange where," she said, and walked off in the direction of the ladies' toilets.

Steve looked at Toby, trying to adjust himself to make it less obvious. Toby laughed out loud. "Wow, what happened there?" Steve looked a little sheepish. "I don't know, mate, but you need to do me a big favour and take Martha to see this scary movie on Wednesday, as I have a very hot date lined up."

Chapter 4

Toby Green had always been an athletic child. He was good at every sport imaginable and his many medals and trophies adorned a whole wall in the lounge of his parents' three bedroom semi; he was a strapping six foot three and had blonde hair and blue eyes.

They were extremely proud of their only son and had spent their life ferrying him around from one sports event to another. Charlie and Beth Green had put all of their energies and hard-earned money into ensuring that their child had everything he needed to succeed; the right kit for each event, from football boots to basketball shirts.

Toby's younger sister Ava sometimes felt like screaming with the amount of travelling that she was forced to attend to accommodate the wonderful Toby!

"Don't be so miserable," his mother would often say to Ava, "be thankful that your brother is good at sports and wants to take part." Ava would scowl when her mother berated her for complaining but Ava had wanted to spend more time with her friends and listen to music and dance around her room, dressing up in short skirts and high heels. Boys were what Ava was in to and she wanted to attract as much attention as possible from them, something her parents were not too happy about.

"Why can't you be more like Toby? Get a hobby, stick to something that you are good at. You'll have plenty of time for boys when you are a lot older," her mother had told her on numerous occasions, so much so that Ava was sick of hearing it!

Ava, a stick thin lanky child who wore braces on her teeth and had long straight mousy blonde hair, was not at all sporty like her brother and couldn't think of anything worse than getting in her PE kit at school and having to parade around the playing field to take part in hockey or netball games; something Ava detested with a passion.

Ava liked the boys but the boys were not at all interested in Ava, not when Isabelle Morton was on the playing field that's for sure! Isabelle was everything Ava was not and everything Ava aspired to be. Golden curly hair cascading down past her pert bottom, long toned legs, a curvy figure and breasts that jutted out of her polo shirt, giving Isabelle her hour glass figure that Ava so craved to have and the boys loved to stare at, and huddle together and make lewd comments in her direction.

As Ava got older and more mature she became a swan. The braces left her with enviable straight pearly white teeth, her hair had thickened out and was long and luscious down past her toned bottom. She had a regular cut and colour at the hair salon and they would coo over the thickness and strength of her blonde locks. Although still thin she had new-found curves and her 32C breasts, which had come along a lot later than most of her friends', gave her the body she had craved all through secondary school. At twenty-two Ava was a stunning-looking woman who turned heads wherever she went, much to her parents' concern.

Ava and Toby had a close relationship despite her always resenting him when growing up. They enjoyed each other's company and he was always there to protect her when men leered at her and photographers handed her their card inviting her to attend their studio with promises of getting her a modelling contract. Ava was not interested at all in the modelling world; Ava was only interested in one thing, having the biggest most lavish wedding possible and settling down and becoming a wife.

Finding Mr Right was what Ava craved; her friends thought she was ridiculous, that she should see some of the world. They had tried to get her to take a year out and go to Thailand and India, backpacking, but Ava couldn't think of anything worse. She enjoyed the comfort of her home far too much, still living with her parents, and had her bedroom just how she wanted it, pink, fluffy and very girly. Travelling to some third world country and living out of a rucksack was Ava's idea of hell.

She wanted to find the right man and eventually have his children and live happily ever after with Mr Prince Charming and there was no question in Ava's mind that he didn't exist.

"There is someone for everyone," she could often be heard saying to her friends when they were all out together. "You just have to wait until the right one comes along."

Ava had got through a lot of frogs in her short lifetime but she had never let anyone go past third base and was still a virgin, and intended to save herself for her prince. She was very vocal about this and her parents were grateful that she had a good head on her shoulders. She was a stunning-looking woman and they worried about her.

Toby Green was not exactly happy about having to take Martha to the cinema. Although he had practically grown up with Steve's family, he always thought of Martha as a bit immature for her age; he was also gutted that Steve had met the gorgeous Katie earlier that morning, as he had had every intention of asking her out on a date and then hopefully taking off what little clothes she had on back at his flat. But that ship had now sailed as there was the 'man code' to think about and he would not go there after his friend had.

Toby, unlike his sister, was definitely not looking for Mrs Right. After his encounter with his ex, Penelope, and the embarrassing situation he had got himself into, that was the very last thing on his mind.

Toby was single like his friend, although not by choice, as he had fallen hard for Penelope whom he had met at work while she was temping. Penelope wanted to see the world and didn't want her wings clipped by any man.

Toby had proposed to her one summer's evening, after they had been going out for six months, in a top restaurant overlooking the river. The waiter had put the single solitaire diamond ring in her napkin and as she picked the napkin up the ring had fallen onto her lap.

Toby had gone down on one knee in a packed restaurant and asked her to marry him, with a glass of Cristal in his hand which had cost a hundred and thirty-eight pounds for the bottle.

Penelope was shocked, as she hadn't seen this coming and also had no intention of settling down, lovely as Toby was. She had the whole world to see and it wasn't going to be as Mrs Toby Green. As much as she would have loved him to go with her she was a free spirit and wasn't ready to be tied down to one man.

Toby was devastated and bolted for the door with embarrassment, leaving Penelope sitting there alone and the waiter coughing at the table with the bill, something she was not at all happy about.

On Monday morning she walked into his office and told him exactly what she thought of him for leaving her alone in the restaurant and then proceeded to storm into the office of Toby's boss, Malcolm Watson, screaming that she could no longer work for his company due to the disrespect of one of his employees!

Toby was totally embarrassed and it took a while for all the whispers and sneers from the ladies in the coffee room and by the photo copier to die down. It did eventually, but Toby vowed he would never, ever date anyone at work nor would he ever ask another girl to marry him.

Although Malcolm was not at all happy with the scene caused in the workplace he did see the funny side of the situation but kept that to himself as he didn't want another episode happening with any other members of his staff in the future. He also thought Penelope was a little too stuck up and wasn't bothered that she didn't want to work there anymore.

He liked Toby and their mutual respect for one another went a long way. Toby was an extremely valued member of staff. He was not about to make his life difficult over one minor indiscretion; he thought he had had a lucky escape from Penelope anyway.

Toby spent most of his time with his friends after that, nursing a broken embarrassed heart. He went on a lads' holiday with Steve to Tenerife for two weeks, just engrossed in the sports programme that the hotel had to offer for the whole time, despite many advances from a whole bunch of women, but he was not at all interested, much to their disappointment.

When he returned home to the UK he made a promise to himself to never propose to another woman, and although he still enjoys the ladies he never sees the same woman more than a couple of times for fear of getting too close, even though a few have tried to tie him down.

Steve, like Toby's boss, would never have said it to his face but felt that Toby had had a very lucky escape and didn't think Penelope was right for his friend.

Chapter 5

Steve sat up in bed on Sunday morning, his cock stirring at the thought of Katie in her short skirt and barely there top. Not normally the type of girl he went for but he saw her as somewhat of a challenge. I had better call Martha first and explain the situation; hopefully she'll be okay with Toby taking her and then I'll call Katie to arrange a time and place. Where was he going to take her?

Ralph was purring beside him, happy to have his owner all to himself. "Where should I take the sexy lady, Ralphy?" He found himself talking to his cat, something he did frequently but still thought a little odd.

Ralph looked at his owner and purred louder. "You want breakfast?" Steve asked and pulled the duvet back, revealing that his cock was still hard. Oh my God, he thought, what is she doing to me? He climbed out of bed and went straight into the shower. It was eleven a.m. and he had had a good beer with Toby last night. The hen crowd had left around ten p.m. leaving the pub a little quieter than it was. The DJ lowered the sound of the music slightly and Steve and Toby had a chat about football and how their team was doing, work and Katie. She was always cropping up in their conversation throughout the night, Toby still pissed that he hadn't met her first. Not that she was his type either, but he thought of the fun that Steve was about to have as he was sure she was a very dirty girl.

He telephoned Martha and explained the situation. She was quite a bit put out and said they could go another night, but when Steve had explained that Toby would be taking her he could tell she was secretly pleased, although she did have a right go at him. After ending the call with Martha he decided to call Katie. She picked up on the third ring. She was standing naked in front of her bedroom mirror, looking intently at her body, something she did a lot.

"Hello, is that Katie?"

"Yes, who is this?"

"Hi, it's Steve." He hoped she wasn't going to play hard to get as he wanted to see her.

"Hi Steve, how are you?" She cupped her breast.

"I'm good, how are you fixed for Wednesday, say eight p.m.?"

"I can make that, where?"

"Do you know Partner's Cocktail Bar in town?"

"I do," she drawled, smiling. Her thumb started to stroke her nipple, which immediately went hard.

"Great, I'll book a booth for eight p.m. and meet you there if that's okay, as I have a late meeting not far away."

"Sounds good," she purred, already starting to feel moist down below.

Steve smiled. "It's a date," he said. "I look forward to seeing you on Wednesday at eight p.m."

"I look forward to it too," she said, as her hand reached for her wetness.

Chapter 6

Katie was pleased Steve had rung. She threw her phone down on the bed and continued to look at her naked body in front of the full length mirror in her bedroom.

"I think Steve will like what he sees," she said, turning her body round to look at her pert bottom.

She was aroused after the phone call, her breasts had swelled and her nipples hardened at the thought of Steve.

She went to her bedside drawer and pulled out her favourite vibrator. "A little me time," she said out loud, and lay down on the bed and started to caress her nipples.

She was still moist down below and started stroking herself, closing her eyes and immediately thinking of Steve in the room watching her.

She opened her legs wide and quickly rubbed her fingers against her clit, spreading the lips of her pussy open, feeling the sensation that her expert fingers were giving her.

She felt her left breast, imagining Steve sucking her nipple, his strong hands on her right breast rubbing it roughly; she moaned.

Katie reached for the vibrator and thrust it deep inside of her, wanting it to be Steve's cock. Before long her juices flowed out of her, thrashing around the bed, the vibrator being forcefully pushed in and out of her wet pussy, pulling at her nipples hard.

Finally her orgasm ended and she opened her eyes and stared up at the ceiling, breathless.

I needed that, she thought, I needed that a lot.

She reached for the tissues on her bedside table, still feeling the full effect of her orgasm, her nipples still rock hard.

She turned back to her full length mirror to stare again at her body. She knew she looked good and that men loved her ample breasts and her large nipples, ripe for sucking. She laughed out loud as she walked slowly towards her shower, still glowing from the aftermath of her orgasm.

Katie loved to pleasure herself; it had always been a release for her and her body tingled for hours afterwards. She stood under the warm jets and let the water cascade over her, still caressing her nipples and letting the soap wash away her juices, still enjoying the feeling of arousal. She sighed. Wednesday couldn't come quick enough!

Chapter 7

Steve hung up, pleased with himself for his bar choice. She seemed to be happy with it and he was looking forward to the date. His cock stirred again. Down boy, he smiled, she is doing things to me that I seem to have no control over, as he pushed his hands through his hair.

Would it be bad of me to ask her back to my apartment after, he thought. Let's see how the evening progresses, not something Steve often did, but she seemed to be doing untold things to his groin area which he had not had in a while. The sexual heat that Kate radiated from her very sexy toned body was immense.

Monday morning came round all too quickly. His alarm shrilled in his ear as he groaned at the thought of getting up. The weather had gone from bad to worse and the rain lashed against the window in his bedroom. More shit weather, he thought, and jumped out of bed to get in the shower. "Babies will be born with webbed feet at this rate," he said, laughing at talking out loud.

The next few days flew by.

Wednesday came around and Steve arrived at work earlier than usual. He was in an exceptionally good mood and Debbie, the receptionist, noticed this.

"Morning Steve, you seem happy," she said, staring at her handsome boss. "I am feeling good, Debbie, thank you for noticing." He smiled. "How was your evening?"

He had kept his distance from Debbie ever since his first Christmas party at the firm, when she had cornered him. She was extremely drunk and had untied her sparkly halter neck dress in front of him to reveal her small round breasts, asking if he wanted to suck them. Steve was horrified. Debbie was a nice girl and great at her job but Steve had never looked at her in that way. Work should not interfere with your private life, it doesn't pay to date your work colleagues. The two definitely don't mix as it gets too messy when it goes sour; he had learnt from Toby's mistakes.

Women were odd and females he would never understand. Doesn't mean I don't like them or get turned on by them but they are not to be messed with, and Steve liked keeping work and play separate.

Debbie's voice brought him back out of his thoughts. "I had a fabulous evening thanks, Steve," she said, with a definite twinkle in her eye while pushing her chest out. Steve walked towards the kitchen to make himself a coffee. Debbie had never made a secret of the fact that she fancied him, something that was definitely not reciprocated and he had no intention of ever going there and had made it quite clear to her and others in the office.

He didn't think it was something she ever remembered, as she was never any different towards him, always flirty and sticking her small chest out whenever he was around her. He was embarrassed at first, for her rather than himself, but he didn't dwell on it too much.

He entered his spacious office that he had been given after he had secured a promotion six months previously. It had a black desk in the corner and a large window that overlooked smaller buildings below; he enjoyed being on the fifteenth floor as he had a great view across the whole of town.

There was a television screen on the wall and two leather chairs with a small table under it where he held any informal meetings or one to ones with his staff. He was proud to be the buying director and had worked extremely hard to secure this position.

He sat at his computer and started going through his emails. It had been an extremely busy couple of days which he had found challenging. He was looking forward to this evening and going out with Katie and was on top of his workload.

He had stayed very late the last couple of nights to ensure that he had an easy day ahead, although he had a late meeting with clients. His mum had fed Ralph and left him meals.

His cock stirred again at the thought of the evening ahead. If she was here now I could happily bend her over my desk, he thought. "What the hell," he said out loud. "Steve, mate, get a grip!"

Chapter 8

Katie took one last glance in the mirror. She looked very sexy in her outfit and showed just enough cleavage without being tarty. The cut of the dress skimmed her curves and showed off her sexy figure to perfection. Katie licked her lips and tasted the strawberry lip gloss; very nice, she thought, as she saw her nipples harden in the reflection of the mirror. She was extremely excited about tonight in more ways than one and was hoping that Steve was feeling the same.

Katie heard the buzzer. That's my cab, she thought, and ran out of the apartment and down the eight flights of stairs, nearly knocking Wilbur, her neighbour's cat, off the step where he was preening. "Stupid cat!" she shrieked, and carried on running down the stairs. Wilbur looked up and meowed and went back to cleaning his paws.

The cab driver looked at Katie with definite appreciation. "Off anywhere nice, love?" he asked, as she got into the cab and put her seat belt on.

"Hot date," she smiled.

"Lucky guy," said the cab driver, and started the engine. "Where to then, pretty lady?" he asked.

"Partners on West Street," she said with a beaming smile.

"Very nice," said the driver, and sped away towards the centre of town.

Katie arrived at the wine bar twenty minutes later. The traffic was a nightmare but the cabbie knew a few short cuts and she arrived only five minutes late.

Steve was already there at the bar with a bottle of beer. She walked slowly up to him to admiring glances from men sitting at the various tables around the bar area.

He turned round as she approached, looked her up and down appreciatively and gave a slow whistle. "Wow, you look amazing." She beamed at him. "Thank you, you don't look bad yourself." He too had made an effort; he had chosen a soft lilac shirt, blue trousers and loafers. He looked extremely smart and enjoyed making an effort for the ladies. Steve was not a huge fan of shopping, he tended to buy online.

He leaned in for a kiss which she happily accepted. Her heart fluttered at the touch of his soft lips on her cheek.

"What would you like to drink?" he asked, unable to take his eyes off her.

She looked at him shyly. "I'd love a champagne cocktail, please," she said in her low sexy voice. She was mesmerised by his stunning blue eyes and didn't know how she was going to get through the whole evening without ripping that shirt off his back!

He ordered her drink and another beer for himself. He felt a stirring in his groin. She was stunning and that dress looked a million dollars on her. He felt other eyes looking at her from around the bar area, even the waiter lingered longer than he should have done taking in her beauty and sexy curves.

Steve smiled. "You have made quite an impression on the bar staff," he said, looking straight into her eyes, "not to mention the other people in the bar."

"It's not the bar staff I am here for," she said, as he handed the cocktail to her. Their fingers touched and she could feel the mutual electricity between them. She noticed movement in his groin area and was very pleased that he was feeling the same as her, very sexually charged.

She could feel the wetness of her crotch already and was glad that she had worn a dress. She had a lacy black bra with matching thong that was now rubbing against her sex. She was extremely aroused and had not had sex with anyone for over a week.

She wasn't counting the party she had attended on Saturday night. She couldn't remember a thing about it although not many of the girls were speaking to her in the office, as she had apparently given a lap dance to Michelle Ford's boyfriend in the bathroom whilst he sat on the edge of the bath drooling over her amazing body. Katie did not remember that at all and was adamant to them that he had been flirting with her for ages when she had seen him out a couple of times, and it was him Michelle should be angry with!

Michelle Ford was heartbroken and not one of the girls in the office were on speaking terms with her. Miss Dawson, Katie's boss, was quietly gloating as she loved nothing more than seeing Katie being given a hard time. Katie was a definite shirker in the workplace and had a knack of getting away with doing as little as possible while her work colleagues always took up the slack.

Was she saving herself for this gorgeous man, she wondered, as she licked her lips?

The evening continued to go with the full sexual tension that they were both feeling. They had moved to the private booth that he had booked and were having polite small talk about friends, family and work which was taking up most of the conversation, but the real question Katie wanted to ask was "Your place or mine?"

She didn't want to come across as forward and decided that, for now, it was right that he made all the moves, as she would be stupid to take the reins, and didn't want a great evening ruined with him thinking she was a sure thing; and there was the possibility of a second date hanging in the air, which she wanted.

They had consumed quite a few drinks by the time the bar was starting to close. Steve had been extremely attentive all night, a great quality in a man that sent a shiver of delight up her spine. Katie craved attention; what a catch, she thought.

He leant over, taking his glass to finish the last of his drink and his arm brushed her nipple, which immediately became hard. He smiled at her. "Shall we go?" he asked in a low voice. She looked at him. "Go where?" she asked, as innocently as she could, but wanting desperately for him to take her there and then.

"I ordered a cab to take you home when you were in the ladies."

"Oh," she said, unable to hide her disappointment and annoyance.

"I'm really sorry, I have a very early start in the morning," he said, "but I've had the most enjoyable evening and would like to take you out again, maybe to dinner next time. Are you free on Saturday evening?"

As much as Steve wanted to take her back to his and slowly slide that dress from her amazing body he also wanted to keep the excitement going and didn't think she would put out on a first date anyway; he clearly didn't know Miss Fox!

"That would be lovely," again trying to keep the disappointment from her voice. This one was a keeper, she thought. She didn't want him to think she didn't respect herself, and also didn't want to piss him off.

He leaned over and kissed her very softly on her mouth. She parted her lips slightly and she could feel his tongue snake its way into her mouth. She reciprocated with the softest of motions and heard him quietly moan.

He eventually slowly pulled away and said, "I would love to take this further but maybe next time."

They both got up and walked to the door. He had one hand on her back; she could feel the heat radiating through and she got a tingle down her spine. There was no doubt she would definitely be getting one of her toys out when she got home as the whole evening had sent her into sexual overdrive. What a shame he had to be a complete gentleman.

She got into the taxi and he waved her off, shouting that he would call her. She told the cab driver her address and she turned to see him waiting until the taxi was out of view. That was sweet, she thought, but the whole evening had left her completely aroused; she wasn't at all ready to go home yet.

Lexi had been staying at her uncle's house for a few days as her mother had been unwell, and she felt bad at having not seen her for a while. Katie wasn't sure what time she was due back and knew Lexi would be tired from her trip and probably in bed now anyway. Katie needed her friend to discuss every second of the evening's events but where was Lexi in her hour of need; tut, how fucking annoying!

Katie was completely hyper and couldn't face the prospect of going back to an apartment with no one to talk to. She told the cab driver that she had changed her mind and gave him an address of a club just outside town that she knew would be open late, where she could get a well needed drink and maybe something or someone else to combat her frustration. She knew it wasn't the appropriate thing to do but it's not as if they were exclusive, they had only had one date; she wasn't tied to him yet.

She let out a slow cackle. When she and Steve finally did get down and dirty she knew it would be an orgasm that she wouldn't forget in a hurry, but for now...

Chapter 9

Martha was fuming that Steve had cancelled their arrangement so he could take out the 'stunning blonde' as he had described her.

"I am so sorry, sis," he had said over the phone, "but this one is just too gorgeous to mess around with. You know Toby, he loves scary movies just like you do. I am sure you will have a great time."

Martha had huffed down the phone, "It's not the point, Steve, we had made an arrangement and you have now gone and cancelled on me and got your mate Toby to replace you. He must think I can't get a date or something!"

"No, no, it's not like that, Toby loves the bones of you, he wouldn't think that way, he is happy to take you out," Steve had said, running his hand through his hair.

Martha thought differently and was embarrassed that Steve had asked Toby before asking her if it was okay. "Why couldn't you have asked me first before asking Toby?"

"Sorry, I thought you wouldn't mind as you still get to see the film."

"Well, I fucking do mind, Steve, but it's done now so I have no choice but to accept it!"

She had slammed the phone down and refused to answer his continuous calls.

When Toby had arrived to pick Martha up he was impressed with her smart new house and how stunning she looked. She had greeted him at the door with a beaming smile. She had had a couple of days to get used to the idea of going the cinema with Toby and it had gradually grown on her. He had got her number from Steve a few days previously and had rung her to make arrangements and they had got on well on the phone. Toby was a funny guy.

Martha had been employed at Poole's Estate Agents since leaving school. She had bedded in well and was very happy there. David Poole drip fed her the reins and she ran the office with expert precision. She had been headhunted a couple of times but had no plans to move from her current position. She loved the familiarity of her working environment and had built up a good client base as well as having a great team to work with. She enjoyed taking people on viewings to look at houses and flats within the area that were up for sale or rent and had no intention of ever leaving. She was well thought of at Poole's and the owner David was a great person to work for. He had mentored her from the beginning and brought her up to the position she now held, head of sales/lettings, or God as David sometimes referred to her. Martha was always finding her family and friends houses or flats to rent or buy; she had never yet had any complaints.

Martha had bought her off plan two bedroomed two bathroom house six months ago in a smart area a few streets away from Steve, and was enjoying the freedom of living on her own. She knew that she had waited too long to move out but she hadn't been ready before and had managed to save a huge deposit, which is why she had decided to buy rather than rent. Something that she could call her own and decorate to her style. Her parents' house wasn't by any means old-fashioned but she was happy to have put her own stamp on her new build, and had been buying furniture for a few years which had been stored in their garage. By buying off plan she was able to watch the house be built from scratch and personalise her choices throughout. From the black granite worktops in the kitchen and the style and colour of the kitchen units along with making decisions on the floor and tile choices available.

The house had a small garden at the back and a drive where she could keep her beloved black VW Golf convertible that she had bought some years earlier. She had named it Miss Ellie, having been an avid Dallas fan many years ago, and had remembered JR Ewing's mother, Miss Ellie, having had a white one. This had always been a family joke and they had all roared with laughter when she had told them one evening after a family dinner.

Martha was happy to be going to the cinema to see her long awaited scary movie but would rather have gone with her brother as planned. She thought maybe Toby had been forced into taking her in order that Steve could go on his date, which she wasn't at all impressed with, and certainly didn't want Toby to feel like he had to chaperone his friend's older sister.

Although Steve and Toby had been friends since school their paths had never really crossed due to the age gap. Two years was quite a difference when you were a teenager, and Martha always thought of herself as much more mature than her brother and his spotty mates.

Whenever she had seen him he seemed quite shy and always hung his head down. Sarah Cunningham, one of her closest friends at the time, always used to fancy them both and was constantly asking if Martha could arrange a date with one of them. Martha didn't want her best friend going out with her brother, or any of his friends for that matter, and constantly made up excuses as to why this would not be a good idea. "You'll be the laughing stock of our year," she would say to Sarah. "Can you imagine going out with someone that young!" Sarah wasn't bothered about the age gap. She thought both boys were totally hot but Martha couldn't see this and always changed the subject whenever she asked, much to Sarah's annoyance.

The weather had been quite warm that day. The paper had announced that it was the first day of summer and we should all look forward to some warmer temperatures and sunshine. Yeah, right, thought Martha, a couple of days' sun and then that would be our lot until next year.

She decided she should look casual for the cinema, so she had chosen skinny blue jeans and a white cropped top that showed her slim figure off to its best. Her long light brown hair was tied into a neat ponytail and she looked much younger than her twenty-seven years. She had the same blue eyes as Steve but was quite a lot shorter than her brother at only five foot five inches. Her genes must be from her mother's side, as Linda was only five foot two. She was wearing red wedges and looked surprisingly beautiful, thought Toby, when she opened the door to greet him.

Toby had also opted to go casual in jeans and a Lacoste polo shirt and had thrown his soft leather jacket on the back seat for when it got colder later in the evening. Martha was surprised at how good-looking he was and became suddenly pleased that her brother couldn't make it.

"Come in, come in," she said to Toby, and showed him through to her lounge, that had the kitchen at one end.

It was a large bright airy space with a huge fifty inch TV on one wall, with a cream leather corner sofa that dominated most of the room, but Martha had added finishing touches which made it feel soft and warm. There were long grey curtains that fell to the floor at the large window to the left and a soft cream roman blind with slight flecks of grey running through it which she closed at night to make the room feel cosy.

Martha loved flowers and there were two vases with her favourite cream tulips in one and pink roses with jip in another. She had collected a few ornaments along the way that were tasteful and stylish and complemented the room. She had a large bookshelf to the left of the television that housed Martha's beloved collection. She was an avid reader and had bought herself a leather reclining chair where she would sit and read for hours on end. Her books were mostly romantic fiction, in which she could lose herself on Saturday afternoons if she wasn't working, draping the soft grey fur throw around her body. That was how Martha liked to relax.

The room led into her kitchen, which was large and bright and had double doors that could be closed, which Martha rarely did as she liked the open plan space. She had purchased four pink bar stools that sat around her kitchen island. Martha loved to sit here with her friends, drinking wine and having a gossip. The house was perfect. Her friends were very envious and wished they had waited to save a big deposit so they could buy the house they had wanted, rather than the one within their budgets.

For some reason Toby felt instantly at home in Martha's house. "This is lovely, Martha, you have really made it look great."

Martha gave Toby a beaming smile. "Thanks," she said awkwardly, but loving the compliment. "Would you like a drink before we head off?"

"Do you have a beer?" asked Toby, enjoying his surroundings.

"I do," said Martha, and went to the fridge to get him a bottle.

Martha poured herself a small glass of Pinot Grigio. She didn't want to have too much to drink before the evening had even started. She didn't have Steve's stamina when it came to alcohol and she was always slightly pissed after two glasses.

She handed him the beer and took a sip of her wine. They sat at the bar stools and Toby looked straight at her. "You look lovely, Martha," he said, as he took a gulp of his beer. Martha blushed. "Thank you," she said, feeling her face redden.

Toby and Martha had obviously known each other for years but they had never socialised together. Sometimes there would be quick hello and goodbyes when she was meeting Steve and Toby had been around, but nothing more than that.

He was extremely tall at six foot one and very handsome, with deep blue eyes and light blonde hair that he had cut short. It suited him. She also loved what he was wearing. Her heart gave a flutter and she was starting to relax in Toby's company.

"We will have this and go," said Toby, "we don't want to miss the film."

Martha drank her wine and took Toby's empty bottle and put it in the pink recycling bin that was at the end of her kitchen units. Martha liked to keep her home tidy and recycle everything she could. She grabbed her short leather jacket and they headed for the door.

Toby was a gentleman and held the door open for her. She stepped through and smiled. Chivalry is not dead, she thought, how lovely.

Chapter 10

Frank Boyle was abandoned as a child by his mother.

She was an alcoholic. Frank was conceived at the back of a seedy club in a dark cold wet alley from a random guy his mother had met at the bar one hour earlier and she had never seen again; she didn't even know his name. By the time she had found out she was pregnant it was too late. She didn't know how to look after a baby so instead of trying to get the help she needed found solace in the bottom of a glass. Frank was put into the care system at the age of four by the authorities, who deemed her unfit to bring up a child. She was glassy eyed and drunk the morning they came to collect him as he played naked on the dirty kitchen floor with a cockroach.

Growing up Frank felt completely let down by his mother and angry that she was unable to tell him who his father was. At the age of sixteen he left the care system, a cruel, heartless individual, who cared about no one and was mostly abusive and aggressive to anyone with whom he came into contact, angry with himself for still loving his mother, whom he still kept in contact with and was always asking him for money.

"Go on, Frank just fifty quid," she would slur at him. "You can afford it." He would look at her with disgust, as he knew that all the money would go on booze, but he felt sorry for her and he was 'putty in her hands'. Although he had never forgiven her for allowing the authorities to take him away and not try to get him back, he still loved her unconditionally.

He often dreamed of being in the perfect family where his mum would be baking in the kitchen waiting for his dad to come home from work and he would be playing with his cars at the table waiting for him too. He would wake up sweating and his heart pumping from the life he had always craved but had never been allowed to have.

He had managed to get through his life with a 'don't care' attitude. The only person who he had any thought for was his mother and was desperate for her love and approval. Anyone else just wasn't worth bothering with as far as he was concerned and so he didn't. He trusted no one and grew up quite a lonely soul. In school he had more enemies than friends. Teachers and carers alike constantly tried to make him into a better person but gave up in time and just let him get on with it.

He was always in trouble for something or another and they were pleased to see him leave when he was of the age, as he was nothing but a problem to the other children and teenagers around him. Constantly getting into fights, which he always won, putting his hands up girls' dresses, being rude to every adult he came into contact with and making many enemies along the way.

Frank didn't care what people thought of him, he could handle himself.

He had managed to avoid prison but was well known to the police, who had tried and failed continuously due to his 'legal aid' lawyer always managing to defend him adequately. The judges could only ever enforce a community service order rather than a custodial sentence, which was probably what Frank needed for him to mend his ways.

Frank would always leave court with a smug grin on his face and go to the nearest bar to find a woman to buy him drinks and celebrate. If she was lucky he would let her give him a blow job round the back of an alley or in the back seat of his car.

Frank worked at the local garage as a mechanic; that was one thing that he could do well, fix cars. His boss thought Frank was extremely talented as a mechanic but that was all he was good at. He had a tough exterior and his work mates were intimidated by him and gave him a wide berth. They didn't socialise with him outside of the garage either. Frank was known as a 'nasty piece of work', someone to be avoided at all costs, and was a bit of a loner.

He lived in a small bedsit which was about ten minutes walking distance from the centre of town and was a regular at Lloyds Bar. He knew the bar staff well and had made a few acquaintances there. Frank never got too close to anyone, which was how he liked it.

He was seeing a girl called Darcy who, he knew, wanted more from the relationship but there was no way he was going to commit to her, or to any other woman for that matter.

One thing that Frank did have going for him was his looks, which was what also got him through life. He was very tall at six foot four and had very light grey eyes with the darkest lashes set around them. He had been told his lashes were similar to a giraffe's, which apparently women would kill to have. He was a natural when it came to charm, which the opposite sex found endearing. They also referred to him as 'eye candy' and he had no problem getting what he needed out of them. He had an extremely high sex drive, probably due to having had no affection from his mother. He was also very well endowed, which he could see showed on faces of his conquests. He would tell anyone that wanted to listen, "The whores are putty in my hands."

That is how Frank saw women, only there to satisfy his sexual appetite.

Frank worked out a lot and had also joined the gym in town, which wasn't too far from the garage. He mainly went there after work before going into Lloyds. When Frank had seen Lexi working out one day he knew he had to have her; he had been watching her for a few weeks and liked what he saw, liked what he saw very much. She wasn't like the other women who immediately flirted and practically always offered themselves to him there and then; Lexi was different.

Her fit young body looked great in her tight Lycra shorts and crop top showing off her ample breasts and flat stomach. He could imagine her long toned legs wrapped round his neck whilst he was thrusting his hard cock deep inside of her pussy and hearing her moan and beg for him to fuck her harder.

He sometimes saw her arrive at the gym in her work clothes; very conservative but sexy, he thought. Underneath those pretty clothes he knew she had a body to die for, as he lifted the weights whilst watching her work out; often skulking behind pillars, getting sexually aroused while her large pert breasts were bobbing up and down as she ran on the treadmill with the sweat running down between them, delicious. He wanted some of that, he wanted all of that. He dreamt of hearing her beg him to fuck her while her tits were swinging in his face.

Not sure if I would forget this one in a hurry though, he thought. He needed an excuse to speak to her. He would use his charm that he knew the women loved; she couldn't possibly say no to a date.

He had to think of a plan of how to get her to go out with him. He felt it wouldn't be right to just randomly ask her, as he didn't want to give her the opportunity to say no.

He had followed her to work one morning when they had both been having an early work out. Frank had consumed a lot of beer the previous evening and wanted to sweat off some of the alcohol before he went in so his boss, who had the sharpest nose, couldn't smell him. He waited for her to change and when he saw her leave he trotted on behind her, keeping a safe distance so she wouldn't see him.

He watched her go into Prospect Law and wondered if she was a lawyer; great if she was, she could possibly help him out one day if he ever got into bother with the law again.

He liked that she worked in an office and imagined her naked in her heels bent over her desk with her pert arse in the air while he stood behind her, erect, waiting for her to beg him to thrust his huge cock deep inside her from behind. He licked his lips at the thought. She would love it and wouldn't be able to get enough of him!

Chapter 11

Katie paid the cab driver and walked into Horatio's, a small club playing jazz and soul, sounds that Katie needed to hear when she was feeling as sexually frustrated as she was.

The bouncer on the door recognised her and waved her through, looking her up and down. I must wear this outfit more often, she thought; she had definitely had quite a few admiring glances throughout the evening. She definitely needed to address her whole wardrobe and decided that the short skirts and revealing tops were so last year. Maybe she could raid Lexi's wardrobe, as she had some classic pieces that she knew she would look amazing in.

She walked through the throng of people straight to the bar; a good-looking waiter immediately came over.

"What can I get you?" he asked with a huge grin on his face, liking what he saw. Katie smiled back. "What would you recommend?" she asked sexily. The waiter held up his finger. "Wait right there," he flirted back. He was gone less than a minute and came back with an orange coloured concoction in a long straight glass with an orange segment hanging over the side. "Looks good," she smiled, "what is it?" The bartender looked straight into her eyes. "It's a slow comfortable screw against the wall!" he said seriously.

Katie was so used to men hitting on her that she wasn't at all fazed by him. She took a sip of the cocktail and could taste the large amount of alcohol he had put into it. It was also very cold, due to the crushed ice. "Wow, thank you," she said, not taking her eyes off him as the cold liquid slipped down her throat. She hadn't had anything to eat since breakfast and was feeling quite tipsy due to the amount of alcohol she had consumed that evening.

The bartender was tall and dark, almost foreign-looking, and had the darkest brown eyes she had ever seen, which Katie was drawn in by.

He was staring back at her too, and informed Katie that he got off at midnight and would love to go somewhere a bit more secluded, if she was up for it? She was feeling the effects of the cocktail taking over her body and needed to release the sexual frustration that had been going on all evening. "Sounds like a plan," she heard herself saying.

Feeling a little like Cinderella, she waited for the clock to strike midnight. The barman, whose name was Mario, sidled up beside her. "Ready," he whispered in her ear. She turned to look at him, their faces very close. "Where are we going?" She wanted to kiss him there and then but thought better of it. She jumped down off the bar stool. He was extremely tall, even for Katie, and she was wearing five inch heels. He took her hand. "Follow me," he smiled.

She followed him towards the back of the bar through a door which led to a flight of stairs.

"I live on the premises," he advised her.

"Handy," she said, still holding onto his hand.

He pulled her in front of him and pointed up the stairs. "I'm on the top floor, we won't be disturbed." His hands went round her waist and he squeezed her softly. She liked the feeling of his hands on her and she slowly started walking up the flight of stairs. There was another flight round the corner and he said, "Keep going," his hands still on her waist.

They reached the top and she stopped at the door. He pulled a key out of his pocket and put it in the lock, still with one hand on her waist. She liked the feel of his strong hands on her; she was going to enjoy this, she thought.

Chapter 12

Lexi was on the early train for work after visiting her mother, who hadn't been very well. She felt guilty that she hadn't seen much of her for a few months, but things had been so busy at work, and what with Katie driving her round the bend with her assortment of men through the apartment and their constant arguing she just hadn't had the time.

She had enjoyed her few days with her uncle and aunt, as well as her mother, who seemed to be on the mend although there was always something wrong with her these days.

It was just the break that Lexi needed and found herself waking up early and taking Jude, her uncle's dog, for long walks.

Jude loved it when Lexi came to stay as it was another person to snuggle up with. He was the most obedient dog she had ever known; with the softest of beige fur and a tail that never seemed to stop wagging he was a very happy contented dog and she loved to watch him run. He was so fast you could almost see him on a track with a number strapped to his back. Lexi enjoyed snuggling up with him on the sofa as much as Jude did when she went to stay. He was like a cat, he rarely left her side when she was there; as soon as she sat down he was beside her.

Her uncle had bought him when he was nine months old from a lady who had purchased him as a puppy for her son, but he had moved out to be with his girlfriend and she had four other dogs. Lurchers were a known breed for needing lots of love and attention so she felt it was cruel to keep him. Her uncle had seen a card in the local shop window and he had been wanting a dog for a while, so he rang the number to enquire. After speaking to the woman he had made arrangements to see the dog the next morning and had found himself immediately handing over the one hundred pounds that the woman was selling him for and taking him home.

Jude had immediately bonded with the family, especially Lexi's uncle, and they had been best friends ever since, following him around the house and going on long walks through the woods and fields together.

"Beats any man," Lexi would say to Jude, who would look at her with love in his eyes. She remembered seeing a sign once which said 'Dogs wag with their heart'. That was definitely true of Jude, he was always wagging and was so friendly; Lexi definitely loved him as much as the rest of her family did.

She was sad to leave but she had a lot of work to catch up with as she hadn't been there for two days and she hated being behind. She stepped off the train and walked the short journey to work, pulling her small case behind her.

"Morning," she shouted as she pushed open the double doors that led to her office.

"Morning," came a chorus of people. Everyone loved Lexi, she was a pleasure to work with and no one had a bad word to say about her. How she put up with that awful flatmate of hers they would never know but that was Lexi, always ready to be a friend to anyone.

Jo, Lexi's best friend in the office, came over to her.

"How is your mum?"

"She is on the mend, just a bad cold, nothing really to worry about, just Mum being Mum."

Jo looked at her friend. "You look tired, chick, that nasty flatmate been keeping you up again?"

Jo knew all about Katie's men. Lexi would confide in her over coffee and the odd doughnut at the local café when she had had a particularly bad argument with her.

"Remember Abbie is going away for six months in a couple of weeks, you are more than welcome to move in for a while."

Lexi smiled at her friend. "Thanks, Jo, you are a good mate, but you know how things are with Katie and I am not sure it would be right to leave her. I know I go on a bit about her but I'm not sure I could ever move out, although sometimes I could be tempted!" She walked into her office.

Lexi sat down at her desk, turned on her computer and saw that she had over a hundred emails to get through that she had been sent previously. She wanted to get through them all before she started her day.

"Coffee," she said out loud to herself. "Coffee, then I will sit down and start."

Her boss poked his head through the door. "Good break, Lex?" he enquired.

"Lovely to see the family, and Jude," she said warmly to her boss. "Loads of emails to get through though," pointing at her computer.

51

"Yeah, sorry, we've had a mad couple of days, no rush Lex. I think the majority are just to keep you in the loop. It's all under control, just sort yourself out. Come in and have a chat later if you fancy."

Lexi loved working at Prospect Law; all the people were fantastic and she had some great friends. Her boss, Michael, was one in a million and she was happy to work there; they were happy to have her and Lexi knew this. She settled down after making herself a coffee and got through her emails; she looked up at the clock.

"Blimey," she said out loud, "where has the morning gone?" It was two p.m. and she hadn't even stopped for a break. She stretched her arms over her head and yawned, reached in her bag for her mobile and saw that she had two missed calls from Katie and a text; she opened the text.

Where are you?

No, Hi Lex, how was your trip; Lexi decided to be just as rude back.

Work

She put down her phone and it immediately beeped.

What time r u home?

Lexi wasn't sure, as she wanted to go and have a workout straight from the office.

Not sure, want to go to the gym.

The phone beeped immediately again.

Don't go gym, come home, need to speak.

I won't be that late, thought Lexi. She decided she didn't want to be at Katie's beck and call and would speak to her later when she got home, whatever time that was.

She put the phone back into her bag and heard it beep again. She ignored it and left her desk to speak to someone in marketing.

The rest of the day went just as quickly as the morning had and Lexi saw that it was five thirty p.m. Time to pack up, she thought. I need to go and have a workout as I have eaten quite a bit at Uncle Sean's and even though I went on long walks with Jude I still need to get my heart pumping.

She picked up her bag and knocked on her boss's door. She went straight in, and Michael looked up over the rim of his glasses. "You've been a busy girl today," he said to her with a smile and warmth in his voice.

"I like to get on top of things." She smiled at him warmly.

"I know you do, Lexi, you off?"

"Yes, going to do a workout at the gym, get back into it."

He laughed. "Do you ever relax and just do nothing?"

"Not if I can help it," she laughed back. "Need anything before I go?" Lexi always said this to him before she left of an evening, he was used to it and missed it when she wasn't there.

"No, I'm fine," he said, "you enjoy your evening and we'll catch up tomorrow."

"Night then," she said, "have a good evening."

She closed the door behind her as she heard him say, "You too, Lexi, you too."

She picked up her bag and went into the outer office. Tracey, the receptionist, had left for the evening and there were only a handful of people at their desks. She shouted, "Good night," and they all said the same back. She made her way to the elevator down to the ground floor, thinking about what circuit she would do at the gym.

She didn't see Frank as the lift doors opened, as he was sat on the seat behind a large indoor plant in the reception area. He had followed her to the office one day a couple of weeks ago after she had had an early workout and had been planning to bump into her; he wanted to see her, all of her.

Lexi went out of the double doors and turned left towards the gym. He had an idea where she was going and so crossed over the road and ran towards the gym. He would accidentally bump into her and then the conversation could go from there; how could she resist, he chuckled to himself.

Lexi didn't see Frank until she literally bumped into him as she was going through the swing doors of the leisure centre.

The door had smacked him in the face and Lexi cried out, "Shit!" She saw that the door had knocked straight into him and he stepped back, holding onto his forehead. "Oh my God, I am so sorry," she said, with panic on her face. "Are you okay?"

Frank had let his foot take the force of the door and it hadn't hit him in the face at all. "Yeah, I'm fine, no thanks to you though," he shouted at her, still holding his forehead.

"I am so sorry," she said again. "I was miles away and didn't see you on the other side. Please let me help you." Frank looked at her and smiled. "I'm okay, honest, probably have a big bruise in the morning, maybe a black eye, but I'm okay."

Lexi felt awful. She could not believe she hadn't seen him. It wasn't as if he was small; he must be at least six foot four or more, what was she doing?

Frank went and sat down on one of the tub chairs in the foyer of the leisure centre. Lexi went to join him.

"Can I get you anything, cold compress maybe?" She still had a worried look on her face and Frank thought this could not have gone any better. "I'm fine," he said. "No need to fuss."

She looked at him and felt racked with guilt. He was a really good-looking bloke, his eyes were of the softest grey and he had lashes that any girl would kill to have; they were long and dark, almost like a giraffe's. His nose was a bit big for his face but it suited him and his hair was cropped short on both sides with a long bit in the centre. If he had gelled it back he could have a Mohican, she thought.

His strong muscular body looked great in his tight T-shirt and faded jeans. He really was total eye candy, she said to herself; get a grip, you have just nearly maimed this poor man by ramming a door in his face and now you are looking at him and ticking off your list!

She shook her head. "I feel awful," she said again to him. "Really, is there nothing I can do?"

Frank looked at her. She really was a beauty. Her eyes were the brightest of blue staring right into him; he almost felt like kissing her there and then. Her small nose and full lips had him mesmerised.

He took his hand away from his forehead. "Honestly," he said, "I'm fine, really, no harm done."

He stood up and Lexi stood up with him. He was quite a bit taller than her. She was wearing her flat ballet pumps but still even if she wore heels he would tower over her. Another tick she thought; Lexi, she berated herself. She touched him on the forearm. "I feel really awful," she said. He put his hand on hers and felt a frisson of excitement run through him. "I'm Frank, by the way," he said, still keeping his hand on hers. She smiled. "I'm Lexi." She looked at him shyly. "Don't you think you should sit back down?" He laughed out loud. "Are you a nurse, by any chance?" Lexi looked at him with a big grin on her face and laughed loudly. "No," she said, "I work in a lawyer's not far from here." Lexi thought that was funny that he should think she was a nurse; she knew he was only teasing but it made her laugh anyway.

The manager of the leisure centre came over. "Are you okay, sir? Can I get you anything?" Frank looked at him. "No, I'm fine, this gorgeous lady has been looking after me, thank you." Lexi blushed. She looked at the manager. "I was the one who caused the injury, so the least I can do is try to help." The manager asked if he needed any other assistance; he was a bit worried in case he wanted to make a claim. As he hadn't seen what had happened he was worried that it may have been a problem and he was going to have to deal with a health & safety issue. Frank sensed this and didn't want or need the manager hanging around. "It's all fine, really," said Frank.

The manager looked relieved. "Well, if you're sure," he said, and started to walk away.

Frank really did want to kiss her there and then but he knew if he did he may mess up his plan. It was all going far better than he could have ever expected and he wanted to ensure that she didn't leave without him at least securing a date with her. How could she resist, not when she thought she had really hurt him.

Lexi looked at him. "Are you sure you're okay?" she said, for the umpteenth time in the last ten minutes. He gave her one of his killer smiles. "I'm fine, I keep telling you." He looked at her seriously. "There is something you can do for me," he said intently.

Lexi's face went serious. "Anything," she said.

"Come for a drink with me tomorrow evening?"

Lexi let out her breath. She was thinking he was going to get her to take him to the hospital and she would have been upset to know that he was really hurt. "I think I can do that." She smiled at him.

"Great," he said, rubbing his forehead for effect. "How about I pick you up from work tomorrow, what time do you finish?"

Lexi looked at him. "If you're sure you are okay, I finish at five thirty p.m. but if we make it six then that will give me time to sort myself out," she said coyly.

"It's a date," he said, and gave her another one of his killer smiles.

He really does have the most gorgeous mouth, she thought. Lexi didn't feel like going to the gym now so she said her goodbyes and told Frank she looked forward to seeing him the following evening. She picked up her bag and left the leisure centre, still shocked as to what had just happened.

Frank punched his fist in the air. "Yes!" he shouted.

Chapter 13

Steve couldn't believe what he had just done; why the fuck did he not ask her back to his?

He was sure she had wanted it just as much as him, so why?

He got out of the cab he had seen dropping someone off just after putting Katie in hers and shook his head. Was he getting dumb in his old age? What was wrong with him?

He let himself into his apartment. It was eleven thirty p.m., he did have an early start tomorrow and he did have a meeting but nothing he couldn't handle. Mind you, he probably wouldn't have got any sleep so maybe it was for the best. His cock stirred again and he smiled.

He needed to call her tomorrow first thing to make another date, was Friday too soon?

He had nothing planned that evening but on Saturday he was taking his nan out for dinner with his parents and Martha, which would not be cool to cancel. Hopefully Friday would be good for her; hopefully he hadn't blown it.

Ralph was immediately purring round his legs. Steve bent down to pick him up and Ralph nuzzled into him. He walked through to the kitchen and put his beloved cat on the work top and got out his bowl; he would give him his favourite as a treat. He knew he had been fed that day as his mum had said but he felt like spoiling him. Ralph jumped down immediately at this unexpected meal and went to eat it straight away.

Steve walked into his bedroom, took off his clothes and got into bed. He stifled a huge yawn and wrapped the duvet over him. Tomorrow is another day, Stevie boy, and you will definitely have her in your bed come Friday. He smiled to himself; definitely.

He fell straight to sleep dreaming of peeling Katie's clothes from her amazing body.

He woke with the alarm shrilling in his ear and a raging hard on that he just had to do something about. He jumped in the shower and relieved himself thinking of her in the shower, all naked and slippery from the shower gel on her body. He imagined her large firm breasts against his chest and her warm inviting sex pulsating at his touch. He climaxed immediately.

Steve had wanted to call Katie as soon as he had finished his shower but it was only six a.m. That was a bit rude, he thought, not everyone was a morning person. He didn't know if he would wake her.

When he lived at home, even from a young age the whole family were extremely happy in the morning. None of them ever had any trouble getting up and there was always laughter and joviality at his parents' house from the start.

He felt so much better after having a shower. It had been a while since he had had sex, due to Gemma leaving the country for a while, so he was masturbating on a very regular basis. He wasn't a one night stand kind of a bloke and didn't like taking random women back to his apartment, or going to theirs for that matter.

Chapter 14

From across the bar Toby Green was ordering another round for himself and Martha. They had both enjoyed the film and he had asked her if she wanted to go for a drink at a club he knew that was open late.

She didn't want the evening to end and was thrilled to be asked. "That would be lovely." She smiled at him.

She had nearly jumped out of her skin a couple of times when the film reached a particularly tense moment. At one point she had held onto his arm for dear life, which he had found quite hilarious; but also he was surprised how much she made him laugh.

They got into a cab to take them to the club. Toby was being the perfect gentleman, something that Martha had never found in the men she had dated; opening doors, buying her popcorn and making sure she was okay. They walked straight in and up to the bar. Toby ordered beer and a glass of dry white wine for Martha.

His eyes were averted to the other side of the bar, where he saw a stunning blonde outrageously flirting with one of the many bar staff that worked there. He thought she looked familiar but wasn't sure where he'd seen her.

Katie, whose dress had slipped off her shoulders, showing a lot more of her breasts than earlier on in the evening, turned to look round the bar. She saw a guy staring at her and gave him one of her killer smiles. Toby then remembered who the girl was; Katie, who Steve was supposed to be taking on a date that night, which why he was with Martha. What was she doing here and where was Steve?

Martha caught his concerned expression and followed his eyes to the sexy blonde across the bar. She didn't know why but she was put out that he was looking at her and said, as casually as she could muster, "Who's that?"

Toby took his eyes from Katie and turned to Martha. "Oh, no one, just some girl I recognise." He didn't want to say anything to Martha about the flirty blonde being the reason her brother had cancelled.

"I've really enjoyed this evening, Martha, even though you were scared witless," he laughed. Martha went all coy and felt her face redden.

"Thank you for a fantastic evening," Martha said. "You are way more fun than Steve watching scary movies. He is always telling me to calm down and that I shouldn't get so worked up about them."

Toby gave Martha his full attention; he too had had a surprisingly good evening. Martha had certainly gone up in his estimation and he had enjoyed her company, although he couldn't stop wondering why Katie was at the club.

After a few more drinks and finding out that they had quite a lot in common, Toby said to Martha that he would escort her home. They finished off their drinks and were getting ready to leave when Toby noticed Katie and the barman heading through a door at the side of the club. Where the fuck were they going, he thought? He must speak to Steve tomorrow to find out exactly what went on with his date, if there ever was one!

When the taxi arrived at Martha's house there was an awkward silence between them. "Do you want to come in for coffee?" she asked, willing him to say yes.

As much as Toby really wanted to carry on the evening he thought better of it. "I would love to," he said. Getting out of the car and walking round to her side of the cab, he opened the door for her. "Sorry, Martha, I have a very early start in the morning." He looked at her disappointingly.

Martha took this as a knock back, went red with embarrassment and quickly got out of the cab. "No worries," she said. "Thank you so much for coming to see the film with me, I hope it didn't put you out too much." Toby noticed her embarrassment. "We should do it again sometime," he said, without wanting to look too enthusiastic. He definitely wanted to take her out again but thought he should run it past Steve first.

"That's fine," she said, as she started to walk up the path towards her door.

Toby shouted over to her. "Martha!" She turned to look at him as she was nearing her door. "Yes?" she said, bowing her head as she did. Toby looked at her intently. "You looked stunning tonight and I had a really great evening, thank you."

He got into the cab and the driver sped off to take Toby home. It was his last fare of the evening, he had done a ten hour shift and wanted to get his passenger home as quickly as possible so he could get his head down for some needed sleep.

Martha's heart skipped a beat and she opened her door, walked through and shut it quietly behind her. She had also had a really good evening and was surprised at how attracted she was to Toby. Who would have thought, after all these years, that their paths would cross. She knew it was early days but she was sure that they would go out again, maybe even on a proper date.

She walked into the kitchen and poured herself a small glass of wine. She was too wired to sleep and wanted to go over the entire evening in her head.

Chapter 15

Katie stood in the small room that was Mario's home. It was quite tidy for a man, she thought. A large king-size bed with lots of pillows and a blue throw at the end dominated the room. There was a small bedside table and another door to the left. "The bathroom," said Mario, as if reading her mind. Katie smiled, she could feel the sexual tension in the room. "Do you mind if I just go freshen up?" She was feeling a little lightheaded from all the alcohol she had consumed on an empty stomach and wanted to ensure that she was still looking good.

"Be my guest," he said making a hand movement towards the door. She moved straight away and opened the door into a tiny bathroom with a shower, toilet and sink. You couldn't swing a cat in here, thought Katie, but it was adequate for what she needed to do. There was a large mirror over the sink and she stared into it. Her wrap dress had become a little loose and she was showing her bra strap and the top of her left breast.

She looked at herself. Her makeup was still intact, as was her hair and she looked around for some toothpaste to put in her mouth.

Katie was feeling extremely sexual and started to remove her clothes. She stood in the tiny bathroom completely naked except for her heels and opened the door. Mario was standing over the far side of the bed. He looked up as the door opened and took a sharp intake of breath. "Wow," he said, not believing what he was seeing. "You look fucking amazing."

Katie knew she had a great body and was never embarrassed when she was naked. She walked over to him, slowly circling her nipples as she approached him.

Mario immediately became hard and started to unbutton his shirt. "Leave it," said Katie, "let me do it." Mario did as he was asked and she walked round and stood right beside him. She could hear him breathing heavily. "Do you like what you see?" she said, in a very low sexy voice, her fingers still circling her nipples.

Katie knew exactly what men liked. They enjoyed watching women play with their bodies, it was a definite turn on, and Katie enjoyed pleasuring herself in front of them.

Mario licked his lips. He really wanted to touch her but he liked her being in control and didn't want to break the charged electricity of sexual excitement that was filling the room. He had all night to play with that amazing body that stood so close to him with those suckable nipples.

Katie started to unbutton his shirt. He smiled and put his hands on her breasts, and his thumbs started to caress and knead her nipples. She looked up to him and smiled. "That feels good," she said. She pulled his shirt off from his body and started to unbutton his trousers. He had a six pack and Katie liked what she was seeing, hoping that he wouldn't disappoint when he was fully naked.

He was still playing with her nipples as she could feel his erection through his trousers that were still round his waist, and she could see that he wasn't wearing any underwear. "You like to go commando?" she said, looking up at him. Marco smiled.

His erect cock bounced out from his trousers. It was even bigger than she expected. It was rock hard and had a thick head as it jutted towards her. Katie could not resist dropping immediately to her knees. Marco moaned as she took his full erection in her mouth and began to suck, very slowly. Her tongue circled the tip of his penis, he was in heaven. She felt him get harder in her mouth as she took the full length of him deep inside her throat. He pulled her up and pushed her on the bed. She looked amazing.

He parted her legs wide and bent down to kiss her flat stomach and started to move downwards, stopping at the top of her sex and licking her, teasing her. Katie felt the need to spread her legs wider, wanting him to go to her most intimate body part. She was so wet and ached to feel his tongue on her as she arched her back.

Mario lifted her legs and put them on his shoulders and started sucking her clit as if his life depended on it. Katie had a very intense orgasm and shuddered as it ripped through her body. "You taste amazing," he cried as his tongue darted in and out of her pussy. Her fingers pulling at her nipples, "I love that," she groaned, as she felt her clitoris swelling and throbbing under his expert tongue, and she climaxed with a loud moan.

Mario stood up, his trousers still round his ankles, which he stepped out of, and looked at her lying on his bed spread eagled, totally naked and sated.

Her body was amazing, he thought. Her small waist and big breasts with those large nipples that she was touching so expertly made him moan with delight. He could see how much she was enjoying this as she was extremely vocal; that was a definite turn on, he thought.

He looked at her, his cock rigid at the sight of her beautiful body. He told her to turn over, which she did immediately. He smiled. Her pert bottom rose in the air and she knelt on all fours into the duvet. "I want you to fuck me hard," she said, moaning.

He parted her cheeks slowly letting his finger feel the top of her hole and then thrust his large erect cock deep inside her wet throbbing pussy. Katie let out a loud scream as he pushed his cock deep inside whilst fingering the tip of her anus. She could not remember feeling this good in a while; Mario was doing all the right things and she could feel the thickness of his cock inside her very wet pussy.

He continued to thrust in and out with force. Katie pushed herself into him as she felt him deep inside her. Her fingers reached down as she rubbed her throbbing clit, biting her lip and trying hard to not fully explode with the sheer heat that was radiating around her body. She didn't want this feeling to end, not just yet.

"You are so tight," said Mario, as he can feel the desire inside him. He cannot hold out any longer and explodes inside of her just as she comes herself. He is grunting loudly as he flops down beside her and his hands go straight for her nipples.

"Wow, Katie that was amazing," he says, softly caressing her breasts as she feels the full force of her orgasm. Her eyes are glazed and she is enjoying his hands on her.

She looked straight at Mario, breathless. The expression on his face is pure bliss as he smiled at her.

They lay for a while, both not speaking a word.

"See Steve, this is what you missed tonight," she said to herself with a smile, not feeling any guilt but just enjoying the moment.

Mario propped himself up on his elbow and looked at her. "You are such a sexy lady," he laughed. Katie turned to face him. "I know what and who I like," she said as her hands started to caress his rippling muscles. He leant down and kissed her hard on the lips, forcing her teeth apart and snaking his tongue around her mouth, exploring.

Katie moaned as she spread her legs, as he pinched her nipples, harder this time, with more force than before. She is amazed that he is able to go again.

He pulls her on top of him roughly and slips his cock inside her hard. Her large firm breasts were wriggling around in front of him and he pulled

63

her down so he can suck each one, biting them hard and teasing her nipples with his tongue.

Katie is loving the sensation that Mario is giving her. She loves the force with which he is thrusting inside of her and the painful pleasure as his teeth bite her nipples. "That feels so good, you are really turning me on, harder, harder, faster," she shouts at him and he does as he is told and explodes again inside of her, crying out louder this time, "You're so beautiful, you feel so good."

Katie loves the compliments he is giving her but still cannot get Steve out of her mind. Maybe it's because she was not used to being put in a cab at the end of a date without having sex, maybe it was the rejection she felt, something that she was not used to either, which was why even having a gorgeous man deep inside of her she still let her mind wander to Steve.

Mario fell asleep beside Katie but she was wide awake, her brain on overdrive and angry at Steve. It was him she should have been next to tonight, not some random barman!

She slipped out of bed quietly and went into the small bathroom to retrieve her clothes. She had to get out of here; she didn't want to stay the night in Mario's room. It was three a.m. She wiped his juices that were running down her leg with a tissue and cleaned herself up. Good job she was on the pill, there was never any mention of using a condom!

She opened the door quietly so as not to wake him and pulled out her mobile to call a cab.

After waiting outside the closed bar for ten minutes in the dark, her cab arrived to take her home, back to her own bed.

Chapter 16

Lexi heard the door open to the apartment. She looked at the clock; it was three thirty a.m. Katie was back late, hope she hasn't brought that Steve back with her, she thought, as she plumped her pillows.

I will definitely have a chat with her at the weekend. No point in bringing up anything up in the morning when she had to get to work, she didn't want her day ruined by having another argument with her.

Her thoughts went to what had happened earlier with Frank and how bad she felt smashing the glass doors of the leisure centre in his face! How awful; she cringed at the thought of it.

She was looking forward to their date that night and smiled to herself. What should she wear to work? Lexi believed in dressing smartly for work, not like some of the tarty outfits Katie wore; it's a wonder she got away with it, dressing as if she was going out clubbing. Michael, her boss, would definitely not appreciate that as Prospect Law had an image to uphold. Katie would not last one minute there with her continual sickness, lateness and very lazy attitude to work. How do they put up with it, she wondered.

She fell into a fitful sleep and woke up to the shrill of the alarm going off. It was six thirty and she wanted to ensure she was at her desk working by seven forty-five. She remembered about her date with Frank and dressed carefully.

She put on a cream shift dress that had a sweetheart neckline and came to just above the knee. The fitting of the dress was quite tight and showed off her ample breasts and curves, but if she wore her black Ted Baker jacket it wouldn't be too sexy for the office. She chose her flat cream leather Dune pumps and put her black patent Christian Louboutin heels in her bag, to change into later when she met Frank. He was so tall; she wanted to look good for her date and her heels gave her a little more confidence. She also wore a brightly-coloured scarf that set off the outfit to perfection and brought out the light blue of her eyes. Lexi stared at her reflection in the mirror and thought she looked smart for the day ahead. Secretly looking forward to meeting Frank later, she smiled and picked up her Michael Kors handbag.

She went into the kitchen area and Katie was propped up on one of the bar stools, looking like she had been dragged through a hedge backwards. She looked awful.

"How was your date?" she asked, turning on the kettle.

Katie looked up, happy to see her friend. "You look lovely, Lex," she said, with all the enthusiasm she could muster. She was feeling totally hung over and her body was sore from the previous night's sex marathon with Mario, but she couldn't afford to be late into the office again or she would be in serious trouble with Miss Dawson. Her work colleagues were still holding a grudge over Gary's party. Girls can be so bitchy, she thought. Katie wasn't too bothered about this; she had the men in the office to flirt with, as they didn't get involved with what the girls thought and showed Katie way more attention than they should have, considering most had girl-friends. She really didn't fancy any of them but loved their attentiveness.

Lexi made herself a coffee. She could see Katie already had one and was surprised that she was up so early. "How was your date with that Steve bloke?" Lexi wasn't sure she needed to ask, given the state of Katie and knew she had been out very late on a work night.

Katie's face lit up at the mention of Steve's name. "It was fab," she told Lexi. "He is horny as fuck and I can't wait to see him again." She hoped Steve would call her that day.

"Where did he take you, back to his?" said Lexi, with more of a sneer on her face than she intended.

"If you must know, Lexi, he was the perfect gentleman. He put me in a cab at eleven thirty and said he would call me for another date." She looked smugly at Lexi.

"How come you didn't get in until three thirty this morning? Where had you been?"

Katie didn't realise Lexi knew what time she had got home. Bollocks to it, she thought, what have I got to hide, and decided to tell her the truth about what had happened.

"Well, I wasn't in the least bit interested in coming home, the night had been so good but Steve had to get up early so didn't want a late one and I thought it better not to try and seduce him," she laughed. "For some reason I really would like to see him again, Lex, so I was a good little girl and got in the cab he had ordered me without saying too much." She was proud of herself and thought Lexi would be too.

Lexi wasn't; what on earth was wrong with coming home?

"I got the cab driver to take me to Horatio's."

"On your own?" enquired Lexi.

"Well, I met a friend there, we had a few drinks and you know."

"No, Katie, I don't know, what friend? Oh my God, don't tell me the friend was male and you had sex with him? You just said you liked Steve, you have been banging on about nothing else!"

"I do like Steve!" Katie shrieked, "But I wasn't ready to come home and you know, one thing led to another and we ended up in his room."

Lexi was horrified. "Katie, what the fuck is wrong with you?"

Katie looked annoyed. "Nothing is wrong with me actually, I had one date with Steve, am I supposed to be a nun now?"

Lexi was flabbergasted. "You could have waited until another night to shag someone else, not straight after the date with him!" Lexi was disgusted at her friend, she was going from bad to worse and had the morals of an alley cat!

"Oh, go fuck yourself, Miss Prim and Proper!" she shouted at Lexi.

Lexi didn't want this argument. She had a full day ahead of her and then an evening with Frank, and Katie was not going to spoil her day!

"I'm off to work, Katie," she said, with venom in her voice. "I think you should go too, as you don't want to be late again!"

"You sound like my fucking mother!" screamed Katie.

Lexi put her cup down, picked up her bag and went to walk out. "I'm not sure about your movements later but just to let you know I'll be late in tonight."

"Why?" said Katie. "Where are you going?"

Lexi didn't want to tell Katie about Frank. She wasn't sure if anything would become of it anyway and it was only a drink after work. Nice as he was, Lexi never fell in love instantly, unlike her flatmate.

"Just out with the work girls," she lied, "a spur of the moment drink we arranged yesterday."

"Have fun, Lex, don't mind me."

Lexi looked at her flatmate. "What's that supposed to mean?"

"Just go to work, Lex," said Katie, walking out of the kitchen.

"You need to seriously get a grip, Katie, you're going off the rails. How many men have you slept with in the last six months?"

"Here we go," said Katie. "How is that any business of yours what I get up to? If you bothered to make time for me instead of always going out with your work mates or going to the gym then I wouldn't have to go out on my own, would I?"

"I am not your only friend, Katie, surely?" Lexi felt a little bad at hearing this. She and Katie had not spent much time together lately but that's because Katie was always going on 'hot dates' and constantly banging on about one conquest or another. Lexi was bored with hearing about them. They also hadn't been getting on great; whenever they were in each other's company it always turned into an argument. Lexi was not a confrontational person and hated arguing with anyone, especially her flatmate.

Katie was not happy about letting her guard down with Lexi. She didn't want her thinking she was needy or felt left out, and she was the tough one of the two, the one who didn't care what others thought. How was it her fault if all these men found her attractive and wanted to explore her body? There was plenty of time for settling down with someone, they were both only twenty-four years old. What's wrong with having a bit of fun? Just because Lexi was such a prude and was waiting for 'the one' to come along; Katie was too busy enjoying herself, although Steve had made an impression on her and she was thinking about him far too much for just a first date. The sex with Mario had been amazing but it was Steve she wished she had been lying on top of that night.

Lexi had to get to work. "Look, how about we have a girly night in on Friday?"

"If you can manage to spare the time, that would be lovely, Lex," Katie said, pouting.

Lexi ignored her sarcastic comment. "How about if I go shopping after work tomorrow and get some good food and a nice bottle of Barolo and we can have a catch up like we used to?"

Katie thought this was a great idea. She had nothing planned for Friday. Although she hoped Steve would call and arrange another date she could go out with him on Saturday night, maybe even stay over at his place; she felt a sensation in her crotch and her nipples immediately became hard and protruded through the thin material of her dressing gown. She smiled at her body's reaction to the thought of Steve.

"That would be lovely, Lexi." Katie went over to her friend and wrapped her arms around her. "Sorry for being such a cow and shouting at you all the time." Katie did love her flatmate; they just sometimes had a difference of opinion.

Lexi hugged Katie back, glad that they could go to work as friends rather than keep attacking each other.

"I must go to work now as I don't want to be late. Go get yourself ready too and get in early and surprise that Miss Dawson." Katie grinned. "Yes, Miss," she said, standing up straight and giving Lexi a salute.

Lexi laughed and headed for the door.

"Might catch up later, if not we will definitely see each other tomorrow," she called out.

"Look forward to it, take care of you," Katie called back.

Chapter 17

Toby was in work early. He hadn't been able to sleep much; one for thinking about how much he had enjoyed the evening with Martha but also the fact that he had seen Katie leave the bar with the guy.

He felt something wasn't right and wanted to know why Steve hadn't met her for a date. He wasn't complaining at all that he had asked him to take Martha to the cinema, as he had really enjoyed her company and thought she had looked gorgeous in those tight-fitting jeans, but it just didn't make sense to him.

He had never really looked at Martha before last night. She was always Steve's older sister, nothing more than that. Their paths had never really crossed in the past, apart from the odd hello and seeing each other at a few Christmas parties that his parents or Steve had organised.

"Why was Katie with that guy though?" he said out loud to himself in his office. There was a slight knock at the door and in walked Anabel the office secretary.

"Hi Toby, Malcolm is wanting to see you in his office. Do you want me to bring you a coffee through?"

Toby got up from his chair and walked around his desk. "Thanks, Ana, that would be lovely if you don't mind."

"No problem," she said.

Toby walked the short walk from his office to his boss's and knocked politely on the door.

"Ah, Toby, come in," said his boss, smiling. "Ana found you, thanks for coming straight away."

Toby and Malcolm had been at the company for a few years and had a great working relationship. Toby was very good at his job and Malcolm was happy to have him on his team.

"What can I do for you, Mal?" said Toby, smiling back.

"I have a client who is keen to put quite a lot of business our way and I feel he should be given the star treatment. Wine and dine him, that sort of thing."

"Yeah, no problem" said Toby who was always taking clients out to lunch or dinner depending on their preference.

"Thing is, he lives in New York and is flying in at the weekend to spend three of four days here and he is bringing his wife. I thought you could take them to dinner and maybe one of your lady friends could accompany you so as to not make the wife feel out of place?"

Toby felt like he had been put on the spot. He didn't normally mix business with pleasure and wasn't sure who he could take.

"No problem, Mal," he said. Toby always thought on his feet and didn't want Malcolm to see he was a tad uncomfortable with this situation; something would come up, and it always did.

Toby left the office at five that evening, a lot earlier than he usually did, but he was in early and he had been busy all day without a break. He decided to go into the bar at the end of the street,; he needed a cold beer to think about what Malcolm had said.

This was definitely an unusual situation. This client must be very important for me to have to take the wife too, he thought.

He walked into Lloyds, not somewhere he usually frequented as it was a bit of a dive, but he needed a beer and didn't think too much about his surroundings.

"Bottle of Budweiser, please," he said to the barman, who put down the glass he was cleaning and went to serve Toby.

He handed him the bottle and a glass and Toby immediately poured the golden liquid down his throat, ignoring the glass.

"Looks like you needed that," the barman said, smiling at Toby.

"Helps me think," Toby said, smiling back.

A long-haired brunette in a short skirt and blouse, that was unbuttoned so her bra was visible, went and stood next to Toby at the bar. He glanced at her and smiled and took another swig of his drink.

The girl licked her lips, liking what she saw. Toby was wearing a navy suit with a pale blue shirt and multi-coloured navy tie. The girl, whose name was Darcy, loved a man in a suit and thought Toby looked very smart. She was waiting for 'a friend' but couldn't resist going up to Toby.

"You look really nice," she said to him.

"Er, thank you," said Toby, thinking how random that was.

"I'm Darcy, by the way," said the brunette, moving in a little closer to him.

"Hi, I'm Toby. I've just come in for a quiet drink," he said to her, not wanting to be rude but wondering why a girl would just start talking to a complete stranger at the bar. He wasn't in the mood to make small talk, he

71

wanted to have this beer and think who he could take with him to dinner with the Americans.

"You do look really smart," she said again.

The door to Lloyds opened and a tall, good-looking guy walked in. He went straight up to Darcy and Toby.

"What the fuck do you think you're doing, Darc?" said the tall man.

Darcy's eyes darted from one to the other. "Nothing, Frank," she said. "I was just saying how smart Toby looked in his suit." She started to step a little further away from Toby.

"Sorry," said Darcy to Toby, "this is Frank, my boyfriend. He doesn't like me talking to other men."

Toby thought this strange; why can't she speak to other men? He didn't say anything. Frank looked a little too menacing for Toby's liking and the last thing he needed was to be involved in a bar brawl.

He picked up his bag that he had put down beside his feet. "I'm off now anyway," said Toby, finishing the last of his beer. "So no harm done," Toby said to them both.

"Well, hands off!" Frank said to Toby, with menacing eyes.

"Easy, mate," said Toby. "I've just come in for a quiet drink and your girlfriend came up to me, and it wasn't me hitting on her at all!"

"Well, make sure you don't," said Frank. "Get me a beer, Darc!" he said, shouting at her. She was now looking quite frightened by him.

Darcy asked the barman for a pint and Toby picked up his bag.

"Nice to meet you, Darcy," said Toby, "but in future I wouldn't just go up to random men and start speaking to them; you don't know what kind of trouble you can land yourself in." He looked at Frank. He smiled at them both and went to walk out the door.

Frank stepped in his way. "Next time you feel like speaking to a lady, make sure she isn't spoken for. Fucking office types are all the same, thinking you can speak to anyone."

Toby looked at Frank. What the fuck, he thought, but held his hands up in front of Frank. "Whatever you say, mate," he said, and sidestepped round Frank towards the door. It just wasn't worth it.

He saw Frank grab Darcy by the arm roughly while taking his pint in the other.

Lucky escape there, thought Toby, what on earth did she see in that moron? He made a mental note to choose another bar next time.

He still didn't want to go straight home and decided to call Steve.

Steve's phone went to voicemail. Toby left a brief message, not something either of them did, and asked Steve to call him, and put his phone back in his pocket. It then hit him as to who he could ask to go to dinner with his clients. Martha.

He was sure she would be up for it as they'd had a great evening the previous night and he was going to call her anyway, so this would be the perfect excuse.

He decided to go to another bar and call Martha from there. He hoped she was available and would accept the invitation. Could it be construed as a second date; was last night a first date?

He wasn't sure what either of them were but he knew he had enjoyed Martha's company and he hoped she felt the same. She would be perfect to meet his clients, without reading too much into it, although she had been lingering on his mind ever since he had said goodbye to her.

He could always take her out a third time to say thank you for agreeing. Must run that past Steve, though, he thought, if he was going to take Martha on a proper date.

He decided to go into Partners. It was more expensive than a lot of the bars in town but the customers were definitely not of the same calibre as Lloyds; he still couldn't believe what had just happened.

There were quite a few people at the bar area already and it was only five fifteen. Thursday nights were the new Fridays, he thought.

He ordered another beer and decided to sit at one of the tall tables that surrounded the bar area, that had comfortable black leather bar stools to sit at. There were candles on each table that made the lighting very soft and the bar had a good vibe. Toby looked around and thought the staff were in for a busy night.

He pulled out his phone and found Martha's number. She picked up immediately. "Hello Martha, it's Toby."

"Hi," she said, wishing she had let it ring for a while, but thrilled to see his name come up.

"I really enjoyed last night, hope you did too?"

"I did, Toby, thank you," said Martha, whose voice was a little more high-pitched than she intended.

"I was wondering if you fancied coming out to dinner with me? I have to take a couple of clients out, who are over from New York, one being his wife. My boss thought it would be a good idea if I took someone, too, and I thought of you."

"Oh," said Martha, taken aback a little. "When were you thinking?"

"Not sure yet," he said. "They are flying in at the weekend so it will probably be early next week, if you are free? It won't cost you a penny and

I'll make sure you have cabs to and from the restaurant; in fact, I will pick you up in the cab myself."

Martha was pleased that Toby had called, but would have preferred it if it was just the two of them going to dinner. She would rather see him than not and she felt like she couldn't refuse such a generous offer.

"I have nothing planned at the moment for the early part of next week but if you could let me know details as soon as possible I would love to accompany you."

She wanted to keep it light and didn't want him hearing her disappointment at them not going out on their own.

"Great!" said Toby. "Well, as soon as I have more information I'll be back in touch."

"Okay," said Martha. "I'll wait to hear from you."

She was just about to put the phone down when she heard him say, "Thank you, Martha, you have done me a right favour."

"No problem," she said, and hung up.

Toby was pleased with his choice; Martha was a professional herself. She knew how to conduct herself in business and he was sure that she wouldn't be an embarrassment to him or his client.

Some of his other female friends may think this was Toby wanting more from them, which was certainly not the case, although Martha seemed to be lingering in his head a lot longer than most had in a while.

He took a sip of his beer as a woman with long blonde hair passed by him with a much shorter man by her side. Nice, he thought, what a body. The girl was wearing a very short suede skirt and thigh high suede boots; her legs seemed to go on forever. Toby looked at the heels on the boots. How on earth do women walk in them, their feet must be killing them at the end of the evening, they must be at least six inches, he thought, taking another sip of his beer.

The blonde went and sat at a table, her skirt riding up even higher as she sat down, whilst her short companion went to the bar. Toby looked at her face. Katie!

The man walked over to the table where Katie was sitting, with a bottle of champagne in an ice bucket and two glasses. He sat down next to her and put his hand on her thigh, and she smiled at him and pointed to the champagne.

Toby couldn't believe that they were in the same bar again. It was not the same bloke he saw her with last night. How many men was she seeing?

He got out his phone to call Steve again. It went straight to voice mail. "Damn!" he said out loud. He really needed to speak to his friend to find out what went on last night.

He watched Katie and the guy, who had his arm around her now, talking intimately. He couldn't stop staring and watched her as she got her phone out. The guy looked extremely pissed off whilst Katie was speaking on the phone.

Chapter 18

Martha was very happy that Toby had rung. She would have preferred to go out alone with him but at least she was getting to see him next week.

She wondered what restaurant they would be meeting at and what on earth would she wear?

Men were so lucky, she thought, they just put on an expensive suit and hey presto, they're done! Women have to go into meltdown deciding on what outfit to wear, was it formal, informal, how to have their hair, make-up, what shoes, bag, the list was endless. She sighed.

She hadn't managed to speak to Steve to tell him that she had had a good time with Toby and to thank him for cancelling on her. She wasn't sure if Steve would like it if Toby and she became an item, but Martha didn't really think it was any of his business. She was also jumping the gun a little, too; it had only been one night. That couldn't even be classed as a date, as Toby had been doing Steve a favour. She blushed. He must think she can't get a date herself that she has to rely on her brother to take her out; that was not the case at all, thought Martha, still feeling embarrassed.

She had arranged to meet a couple of girlfriends in town, which was why she was home from work early. She had been putting in long hours over the last couple of months as the property market had gone through the roof. People were making lots of appointments to view houses and flats, and there weren't enough staff at Poole's for the sudden demand. She felt she deserved an early day.

David, her boss, never had a problem with anything that Martha wanted to do. She was a definite asset to the company and she was her own person and could come and go as she pleased. David would be lost without her and was always thankful for her loyalty, which was reflected in her pay.

Martha walked into her bedroom to decide what she would wear. She felt like being a little daring tonight for some reason and opted for a pair of black leather skinny trousers with a black sleeveless polo neck cotton jumper that showed off her toned arms to perfection.

She wore cream heels and gold jewellery that looked great with the black. She teamed all this with a small fur jacket that would keep her warm later in the evening when she went outside with the girls who wanted to smoke.

Martha had never understood smoking, all that wasted money, but worse, what it did to your health. She never preached to her friends about the disgusting habit and the health dangers, she was even happy to accompany them outside. She had had great conversations with 'the smokers' when she had been out and had even made a couple of good friends after meeting them randomly outside a club whilst they were having a well needed cigarette.

She looked at herself in her full length mirror and was happy with her outfit. She had been eating a little healthier the last couple of months and what with her frequent trips to the gym had found that her body had toned up nicely and there wasn't an ounce of fat on her. In fact, Martha felt very good about herself, and had been shopping to buy some new outfits to show off her new shapely body.

Her phone beeped. It was a text from Lauren, saying that she and Faye were on their way to her in a cab and would be with her in ten minutes.

She did a quick tidy round, put her make-up away and picked up her glass of wine that she had poured earlier. She drank the last drop and put the glass in the dishwasher. Her phone beeped again and she looked at it, thinking it was Lauren telling her they were outside. She saw Toby's name come up on her phone. She couldn't open the message quick enough.

*Hey Martha, so glad you agreed to coming to dinner with me and my clients next week. I'll let you know as soon as I can what day and the timings

T*

She read the text with a smile on her face. How cute, she thought, as she started to reply.

No problem, glad I could help, look forward to hearing from you M

She liked the way he ended the text with a 'T'. She was definitely looking forward to seeing him next week even if it meant she would have to share him with his American clients.

Her phone beeped again. It was Lauren, telling her they were outside. It was only six p.m. and still light outside, but she was happy to be going out early. This meant by ten thirty p.m. she could bid her goodbyes and be in bed by eleven. She had another busy day ahead tomorrow.

Friday was always extremely busy, arranging viewings for the Saturday and Sunday. It was her weekend off though, thankfully, and she was looking forward to having a lie in on Saturday morning. She was out to dinner with the family on the Saturday evening so she wanted to stay in bed as long as possible and potter about her house, not having to rush to get ready.

She set her house alarm and locked her front door and waved to Lauren and Faye as she got in the cab. Lauren was thrilled that Martha was coming out with them, not something she always did as she was so busy with work, but this time they had managed to persuade her.

They had all met each other through mutual friends but had immediately clicked as a group and they had made a strong bond throughout the years. All of them under thirty, they knew how to party hard when they had to, and had the utmost respect for each other.

Partners was extremely busy for a Thursday night, thought Martha, but was happy to be out with her friends. They ordered a couple of bottles of prosecco and five glasses. She was looking forward to seeing them all, as it had been a while since they had been able to get together in person; they were often texting or phoning each other but there was nothing like actually seeing each other in the flesh for a proper catch up.

Martha took the five glasses while Lauren and Faye took a bottle each. They found a high table in the middle of the wine bar and dragged two more high stools over, all ready for when Charlotte and Lucy arrived.

The waiter brought over a couple of ice buckets for them to put their fizz in. Martha and Lauren and Faye all said "Thank you" in unison and he smiled at them all, giving Martha a longer stare than was necessary before he left.

Lauren laughed. "Get you, being checked out by the bar staff," she said to her friend. Martha blushed. "Shut up, Lauren," she said, smiling. Martha had noticed this too and was chuffed that the handsome barman had lingered a little longer than necessary; she was loving her newfound attention from the opposite sex.

Lucy and Charlotte finally arrived. "All my best friends in one place," said Martha, beaming at the other four.

Lauren poured out the other two glasses and they all started chatting and laughing, catching up with various events in their lives. Charlotte had just come out of a long-term relationship and was still feeling very sad and unhappy. She still missed Ryan and found it hard not to call him. She had often had late night chats with one of the girls, crying down the phone, saying how hard it was being single and she didn't want to be 'out there' at her age! Martha always listened to her friend and felt very sorry for her. "If you want to call him just call him," she would say. "Don't listen to what everyone else tells you, you are the one going through the break up, not them. It's whatever you can cope with, Charl, just do whatever you have to do to get through the good days and bad." Charlotte loved Martha, who was always the most sensible and mature one of the group. She had a good head on her shoulders as well as a good heart and was always there for her friends.

Half an hour went by and the music was turned up a notch. The girls were happy with the tunes that were being played and swayed along whilst in deep conversation, singing loud to some of the words when one of their particular favourite songs was played.

The handsome barman appeared at their table with another bottle of prosecco in an ice bucket and five fresh glasses.

"We didn't order this," said Martha, looking confused.

"It's from the gentleman over there," said the barman, pointing towards Toby.

All five of them turned to look in Toby's direction.

Martha blushed. "Oh," she said, "how kind."

Toby raised his half-empty beer bottle towards the girls. They all did the same and Charlotte blew him a kiss.

"I won't be a moment," said Martha.

The girls looked at her. "Something you want to share with the group?" said Charlotte, laughing.

"I'll be back in a minute!" said Martha, getting off her stool and making her way over to Toby.

"Hello," she said.

"Hi," said Toby.

"That was kind of you," said Martha, leaning against the table.

He laughed. "I'm a kind person and wanted to come over, but saw you were all in deep conversation so I thought I would do the next best thing."

"Well, that was a lovely thing to do, thank you," she said, genuinely meaning it.

"I'm about to leave," he said, "so enjoy your evening."

Martha blushed. She was very happy to see Toby, and so unexpectedly, and the fact that he had sent a bottle of prosecco over made her feel all warm inside. What a great bloke, she thought.

"You are more than welcome to come over and have a drink with us," she said, "but I warn you, they are like dogs on heat and you may not be able to escape."

"Thanks," he said, laughing. "I think I'll leave you to enjoy your evening with your friends but I will text you." Toby picked up his jacket.

"I look forward to that," she said, with more confidence than she felt, and leant in to kiss him on the cheek.

Toby wasn't sure what she was doing when she leant over and turned his head, and her kiss landed on his lips.

"Very nice," said Toby, laughing.

Martha blushed bright red. "Oh my God! I am so sorry, I meant to kiss you on the cheek!" She was mortified.

"Well, it was rather unexpected and forward, you kissing me on the lips," he teased.

The girls all cheered. Martha was totally embarrassed and felt her whole body heat up; shit, she thought, what a nightmare!

Toby was slightly distracted when a blonde and her shorter male friend walked past his table. She saw him look at her and realised it was the same blonde from the other evening in Horatio's. Who was she, she thought, feeling a stab of jealousy. He obviously knew her and she seemed to be at the same places he went to. Had he just broken up with her, was she following him and trying to make him jealous by being with other men?

Toby quickly turned his attention back to Martha and reassured her that it was fine, and to stop her feeling even more embarrassed leant over and kissed her full on the lips.

Martha responded and they stood there kissing for longer than they had both intended. Her friends went wild.

"Put him down!" they shouted.

"Get a room!" said Lucy.

Martha pulled away. She blushed again and looked at Toby. "That was unexpected, too," she said shyly. She wondered if Toby was just doing that for the blonde's benefit; was he trying to show her that he had other women?

"I like the unexpected," he said. "I have to go but I will text you as soon as I can finalise things for next week."

He walked off towards the exit and Martha just stood there watching him go.

She put her fingers to her lips and was there for a full minute, thinking about what had just happened but still thinking about the stunning blonde. Who the fuck was she?

She was brought back out of her thoughts by Lauren coming over and taking her by the elbow and escorting her back to their table.

Her friends were going crazy.

"Who was that?" they asked.

"Where did you meet him?"

"Does he have a brother?"

Their questions made Martha laugh. "That's Toby," she said, "my brother's friend."

"Has he got any more friends like him?" said Faye.

They all thought Toby was total eye candy and were thrilled for Martha.

"It's very early days yet," said Martha, "and Steve has no idea so if you bump into him do not mention about me and Toby, whatever you do."

She started to tell them about their cinema date and about the dinner date with his American clients. They all listened intently and were delighted for their friend.

Martha was having such a good evening, and it had turned out much better than she could ever expect. They drank the bottle that Toby had sent over. It tasted different to Martha from the other two, much nicer for some reason; maybe because Toby had bought it, she thought, grinning like a Cheshire cat.

Martha and her friends had been chatting so much that she didn't even notice that the bar was closing. It was eleven p.m. and she knew that she would find it hard to get to sleep that night and get up for work in the morning!

They ordered three cabs to take them home. Charlotte and Lucy lived in the same area and Lauren and Faye shared a cab. Martha got in the cab on her own but she was happy to do this as she wanted to be alone with her thoughts. She couldn't wait to hear from Toby and was looking forward to their dinner date even more now.

"Make sure you call me to let me know how the date went," shouted Lauren, as her cab pulled away first.

Martha laughed. "I will but it's not really a date, how many times! Get home safe," she called out.

Her taxi pulled up and she got in, still smiling at the events of the evening.

Chapter 19

As soon as Steve walked into the office it was manic. They had pitched to a new client the month before and had advised his boss that they had won the business; it was worth a lot of money to the company.

His boss was ecstatic and put his arms around Steve as soon as he saw him.

"Well done," he said, "great job, Steve."

Steve was pleased that they had won this account as it had been a tough one to present. The client was extremely hard to please and had expected a lot of detail in the presentation and also asked a lot of questions on the day.

Steve and his colleagues had been working on this for over two months, and he was glad when they had finally walked out of the client's office. He could relax until the decision was made, which wouldn't be for a few weeks. He could get back to concentrating on other campaigns.

There were celebrations all round and he hadn't had a moment to himself all day. He wanted to phone Katie but there just hadn't been the time and he felt it would be rude to sneak off to make a call.

Finally at seven p.m. he left the office, saw that he had three missed calls from Toby and a text from Martha.

He decided they could wait and tapped in Katie's name. Her phone went straight to voicemail. He didn't know what to say so he put the phone down. "Damn!" he said out loud.

He was in the cab on the way home and wanted to speak to her to arrange another date. He tried her number again. She could have been on the phone, as it had gone straight to voicemail without ringing at all.

Katie picked up on the third ring. He could hear music in the background and wondered where she was.

"Hi Katie, it's Steve."

"Hi," she said, giggling.

"Are you okay to speak?" he asked, wondering if she was giggling at him or something else.

"Well, not really," she said, "but if you are quick," she replied.

"Oh," he felt a little put out but carried on, "I wondered if you were free tomorrow night, I could take you out to dinner?"

Katie giggled again. Clearly she was being distracted by something or someone, thought Steve; he waited for her to reply.

"That would be lovely, Steve," she said, still giggling and completely forgetting about the arrangements she had made with Lexi.

He was relieved. "Ok, great, give me your address and I will pick you up in a cab. Eight p.m. okay with you?"

"Ok, that sounds great," she said, and reeled off her address to him. He made a mental note.

"Be ready for eight p.m. and wear something sexy," he drooled down the phone.

"I always wear something sexy," she said, laughing out loud.

The phone went dead and Steve sat there staring at it. He was shaking his head as he couldn't believe he had just said that to her! Where the fuck did that come from, he thought, but was relieved that she had agreed to meet him.

He put a call in to Toby, and then Martha, but both their phones went to voicemail too. Not much luck tonight with phones, he thought.

He was home within the next ten minutes and opened his front door to quite a bit of mail on the mat. Ralph was there to greet him and purred around his legs. Leaving the post where it was he picked Ralph up and nuzzled into him. He was pleased he had him to come home to.

Steve suddenly came over feeling very tired. He let out a large yawn. It won't harm to have an early night, he thought, not when he had a hot date with the sexy Katie tomorrow and still had another day at work to get through. He felt his cock stir at the thought of Katie. "Down boy," he said out loud, shaking his head.

Chapter 20

Frank had got into work early himself that day. He was looking forward to seeing Lexi later and wanted to make sure he could leave a little earlier to clean himself up. Fixing cars was a dirty job and he was always full of grease and grime and would need to shower and change for his date.

He thought his little scam of letting Lexi think she had hurt him when she had walked through the doors of the leisure centre was brilliant. Women are so gullible, he thought, putty in my hands.

He returned his attention to the Mercedes that had been brought in that morning for an MOT. The lady owner had flirted with Frank outrageously and had practically been begging for it as she handed over the keys.

"What time will it be ready?" she had asked him, licking her lips after she had spoken and standing a little too close to him. She must have been at least forty and had on a short red skirt and very high black heels. Her black shirt was quite sheer; he could see that she wasn't wearing a bra and her nipples were rock hard through the material.

Horny fucker, he said to himself. He could see a large diamond on the third finger of her left hand and assumed she was married. Husband probably wasn't putting out, he thought, as he flirted back with her, they are all gagging for it. I could lift up her skirt and fuck her right now on the forecourt and she wouldn't put up a fight, he thought, giving her one of his killer smiles. "Come back around three and it will be ready for you," Frank said, as he looked her up and down.

"Your boss in the office has my number if you need to call," she said, smiling and showing him her pearly white teeth.

She handed him the keys and turned on her heels, swaying her body as she walked towards the exit.

I might just call her one day, he thought, as he stared after her, but for now I am concentrating on Sexy Lexi; he laughed at the name he had just made up for her.

He finished working on the Mercedes and went to get himself a coffee. As he walked towards the coffee machine his boss called him over. "Frank, got a minute?" he asked.

Frank and his boss got on okay. As long as Frank did what he was paid to do there wasn't a problem. His boss was also not frightened of Frank and that helped with the mutual respect.

Frank walked into his boss's office. There were papers everywhere, even on some of the chairs. Frank hated mess; he was an extremely tidy person, which came from being in care. The space you were given was minimal and it was one of the strict rules that was enforced on the children to always keep their belongings tidy or they would be confiscated. Frank grew up keeping what few belongings he had neat and tidy at all times but woe betide anyone who tried to take them away from him.

His boss beckoned him to one of the chairs that was not overflowing with paperwork, and Frank sat down. "What's up?" he asked, a little concerned as to why his boss wanted to speak with him.

"Nothing Frank, don't look so worried," his boss said. "I have been watching you lately and the speed and precision with which you fix those cars is excellent. I was wondering if you were up for a little promotion?"

Frank looked at his boss suspiciously. "What kind of promotion?" he asked.

"You know that Jim is leaving?"

Jim was the forecourt manager. Although Laura, the garage secretary, booked in all the jobs and answered a lot of the telephone calls regarding the appointments, Jim was the one that ran the garage. He also worked on most of the expensive cars that came in on a regular basis, including the classics.

"I had heard," said Frank.

"Well, I was wondering if you wanted to take over from him. I could get someone in from outside but I thought of you."

Frank was quite taken back by this. No one had really ever given Frank anything, and he had always pissed so many people off growing up that they had all washed their hands of him.

"Would I get to work on all the good cars that come in, even the classics?" he asked.

"You would," said his boss, "and it would also mean quite a good pay rise, too."

Frank smiled. "Ok, I'll take it," he said.

His boss was pleased that Frank had accepted. He knew that he was a good worker, maybe a little tricky with the other employees sometimes, but on the whole he was conscientious and took great pride in his work. There had never been any complaints from any customer with regard to the cars that Frank had worked on and the garage thrived on its repeat business.

"Great," said his boss. "We'll have another chat just before Jimmy goes, which is in about two weeks. That okay with you?"

"Cool," said Frank, and got up from his chair.

He leant over and shook his boss's hand. "Thank you," he said, with such sincerity that it took his boss by surprise.

"No problem, Frank," he said.

Frank walked out of the office and back to the car he was working on. He had forgotten he was going to get a coffee as his mind was suddenly elsewhere.

He punched the air. "Fucking awesome," he shouted, to no one in particular, and some of the guys looked up.

"You okay, Frank?" said Paul, who was working on a particularly tricky gear box.

"Mind your own business," he said. Paul went back to working on the gear box, knowing what a temper Frank had and not wanting to rile him.

Frank couldn't believe what had just happened. Must be my lucky day, he thought, as he pushed the lever of the car he was working on so he could look inside the bonnet.

Hot date with the sexy Lexi and now a promotion; Frankie boy, you are going places, he thought to himself, and laughed out loud. He looked at the clock. Two hours and he would be off home to get himself ready and looking good for his date.

Would she put out straight away? Should he play it a little cooler with her? Hopefully there would be a lot more dates to come, may even let her get serious with me, he thought.

Four thirty p.m. on the dot Frank stepped out of his overalls. He had been there since before seven a.m. that morning and he knew that there wouldn't be a problem with him leaving.

He jogged home in casual clothes that he always wore under his overalls and got straight in the shower.

Frank's bedsit was quite large. He had decorated it in white paint throughout and had brightly-coloured abstract canvasses that made his home feel light and airy. He had a small kitchen area to the left of the lounge, which was also used as his bedroom, with a pull down double bed against one wall. The other wall had his TV and music system on a black lacquered unit and a large comfy cream leather sofa in the middle of the room. There was also enough room for a small glass table with two Perspex chairs that Frank would often sit at when he was eating or using his laptop.

The bathroom was adequate enough for Frank's needs and had a bath and an inbuilt shower with a glass door to one end.

Frank was happy in his bedsit, which was cheap to rent and in a good area. He loved living on his own, as he had grown up with many children and never had the space and silence he always craved.

He stripped off his clothes and got straight in the warm shower. He washed thoroughly, making sure that he scrubbed his nails, as oil was always getting in them even though he wore latex gloves.

He wanted to make a good impression on Lexi, and wondered if he would have time for a quick pint in Lloyds before he had to meet her.

When he got out of the shower he looked at the clock. He still had two hours to kill.

He put on a white button down collared shirt with the faintest of blue stripes and navy trousers. He thought he would make an effort for her. She seemed like the person who would appreciate that and when women were appreciative they put out.

He put gel in his hair so the fringe flopped to one side. He had been told before by women how they liked his hair and how much it suited him, as they would put their hands through it and move it back from his forehead.

Lexi could do that whilst she was naked, straddling my cock, he thought, and I can suck on those gorgeous tits.

He couldn't believe he was going to so much trouble for someone. He never had any problems with the ladies. Whatever he wore, they seemed to want a piece of him, even in his overalls, but this felt different for some reason.

He took out his black leather blazer; he thought that would be smart. He didn't want to wear a suit, as that would be going over the top, and definitely not a tie. He wore black loafers to finish off his outfit and thought he looked very smart for his date with Lexi.

Frank had always been good with his money; whenever he had been given pocket money whilst in care he had spent it wisely, always managing to save a little each time. He believed that one day his mum would come and get him and he could buy her gifts to say thank you.

She never came to take him home. She would visit occasionally but she always took him back, even though he pleaded with her not to.

Frank lived within his means and never frittered money away. He felt safe knowing that his account was growing. He didn't know what he would use it for but some day he may be in need of it. It was his safety net if things didn't work out at the garage.

He also felt that it was he who would be paying for his mother's funeral one day, and funerals were not cheap. He wanted to ensure she had a good send-off; even though she hadn't been the mother that he had always dreamed of having she was still the one he was given and he would look after her.

All she ever seemed to want from him was money; he couldn't think of a time when he saw her that she didn't ask for cash. He was used to it and always handed it over eventually.

He called a cab to take him to Lloyds. It looked like it was drizzling outside and he didn't want to get wet.

He walked through the doors of the bar at five thirty p.m. and immediately saw Darcy speaking to a guy in a suit.

He went straight over to them. What the fuck was she doing practically shagging that bloke at the bar, he thought.

Darcy was always there for Frank's every need. She told him constantly how much she loved him although he had never said it back to her. This didn't seem to bother Darcy; she was there for him whenever he wanted her and hoped that one day he would say the three words she wanted to hear.

Darcy was getting very fed up with always doing what Frank wanted. He even had a go at her when she referred to him as her boyfriend. "I am not your fucking boyfriend," he would shout at her.

Darcy had spotted Toby as soon as he had walked in and knew that Frank may come in from work; she wasn't aware he was going on a date with another woman.

She decided to go straight up to Toby and start speaking to him. She knew she was being very forward but if Frank did walk in then he may get jealous and realise he didn't want to lose her.

Just as she was chatting to Toby she saw Frank striding towards her out of the corner of her eye. She immediately stepped back from Toby

She could see Frank wasn't happy and hoped that he would declare his undying love for her.

Frank was fuming and asked what the fuck Darcy was up to, he could see the bloke in the suit was looking scared.

"What are you up to, Darcy?" he said, when Toby had left.

"Nothing, I was just talking to him." She looked a little worried

"You were doing more than just speaking to him, your tongue was practically rammed down his throat!" he shouted at her.

"Don't be silly, Frank, I wasn't anywhere near him, not that you care."

88

Darcy then realised that Frank was dressed up and looking very smart in his shirt and leather jacket.

"How come you are all dressed up anyway?" she said suddenly.

Frank looked down at himself. "I have a business meeting, not that it's any of your business, Darcy!" he said, with venom in his voice as he took a couple of gulps of the beer she had bought him. He wasn't going to tell Darcy he was meeting the sexy Lexi, she didn't need to know that.

Darcy laughed. "A business meeting, you fix cars, Frank, what kind of a business meeting?"

"Well for your information I have just been promoted and my boss wants to discuss it with me over dinner!" he said, still shouting and angry that she was laughing at him. "I came in here to see if you were in here so I could have a drink with you but you were throwing yourself all over that suit so I wish I hadn't bothered."

He turned it all back on her, forgetting who he was meeting

Darcy was pleased that Frank wanted to come and have a drink with her before his meeting; her voice softened towards him and she put her hand on his chest.

"That's a nice thing to do, Frank, I didn't know you cared," she said, trying to get closer to him.

He pushed her hand away. "Get off me, and don't tell people I am your boyfriend. I have told you loads of times we are just fuck buddies, I am not your boyfriend," he said, still angry at her.

Frank didn't want to be Darcy's boyfriend, he didn't want to be any-one's boyfriend. Why do women have to label everything, why can't they just be happy without having to have a boyfriend. Random sex whenever he wanted it with Darcy was good. She had the most enormous tits and he loved burying his face in them. She also gave great head and he didn't want that to stop, she had such a way with her tongue that made him explode!

"I can hardly introduce you as my fuck buddy now, can I," she said, looking a little forlorn. "What on earth would people think?"

What was his problem, they had been having sex for months. Why on earth was it so hard for him to commit?

Frank laughed and downed his pint. He looked at the clock at the end of the bar; it was five forty-five and he needed to get going if he was to be at Lexi's office by six.

"I have to go," he said, putting his glass back on the bar.

She looked up to him, wanting him to kiss her. He bent down and snaked his tongue and pushed her teeth open with it. She responded as he

89

put his hands on her breasts. Darcy moaned. "Do you have to go?" she asked, putting her arms round his neck.

Frank felt his cock stir. "I do. I will see you tomorrow," he said, taking her hands away from his neck.

"Why tomorrow, why can't you meet me later?" she said, in her whiney voice that he hated.

Frank didn't want to commit to any timings later; he wasn't sure how things would go with Lexi. He was hoping to have her in bed by ten p.m. back at his bedsit, fully naked and ready for anything he wanted her to do to him. He had put the bed down and fluffed up the pillows earlier just in case the evening went the way he wanted it to.

"I am not sure how long this will take," he said, bending down and giving her a quick peck on the cheek. She did look good, he thought. He could see her nipples were hard through her bra; he loved to suck on them and make her moan.

"Sorry Darc," he said, looking again at the clock, "I have to go."

She gave him one of her pouts as he made for the door.

"I will see you tomorrow, okay?"

He didn't wait for an answer and opened the door of the bar. It was still drizzling outside and he had a five minute walk to her office.

Bollocks, he said, as he walked fast through the rain.

He arrived at her office at six p.m. on the dot. Lexi was waiting for him in the foyer

"Am I late?" he asked.

"No," said Lexi. "I just came down five minutes earlier, it's fine." She smiled at him. "How is your head?" she asked, with concern on her face.

She couldn't see any bruising. She thought he looked gorgeous in his jacket and shirt. She loved a man in a shirt, very sexy, and she blushed.

He noticed her blush. "Dirty thoughts," he laughed to himself, I bet she was thinking how long before she could take me to bed. He knew the effect he had on women. This one was no different, or was she?

"Where are we going?" she asked.

He hadn't thought about where to take her, shit, why hadn't he booked something?

"Er, I thought we would just go grab a bite to eat in this little Italian restaurant I know that's not too far from here." He was pleased he had thought on his feet and remembered Papa's.

Papa's was a typical Italian restaurant with lots of dark green and wood décor. An abundance of candles filled the walls and tables, on which sat crisp white table cloths. The staff were friendly and knowledgeable and always happy to help with regard to the specials of the day or what wine went best with what dish. There was a massive mural, that adorned one wall, of Lake Como that everyone always commented on at how stunning it was.

Frank had been taken there once or twice by one of his clients, an extremely attractive and wealthy thirty-something who had wanted to repay him for helping her when her Range Rover had got a puncture.

He had noticed her hazards on by the side of the road and stopped to ask if he could help. He had changed the tyre within ten minutes and she was so grateful. She explained that she had an important meeting to get to; by important she meant that she had to be at her hairdresser's by eight thirty a.m. as she had a party that evening to attend.

The woman, whose name was Francesca, was a very tall leggy blonde with large fake boobs, and had asked if he was free the following evening. Frank, never one to look a gift horse in the mouth, said he was and she had arranged to pick him up at his bedsit at seven thirty p.m. in the said Range Rover and took him to Papa's.

The sex back at her palatial home afterwards was something Frank had never indulged in. She was into being tied up and whipped until she bled and she also enjoyed sex in water; they had flooded the bathroom with all the thrusting about that had been going on in the large tub. Frank hadn't complained at all and was happy to indulge her in her fantasies. She also gave him a massage which was so erotic that he came all over her fake tits. Frank wasn't normally into anything surgically enhanced, he liked the real thing, but these had been done so well, she obviously had a good surgeon. It's amazing what you could get if you paid for it, he thought, as he sucked on one of her hard firm nipples while she massaged his erect cock with her special oils.

He had seen her again when her husband had been out of the country and she said she often took random men back to the house, as she was turned on by having sex with total strangers. "What he doesn't know doesn't hurt him," she said, over a glass of champagne at Papa's.

Frank had raised his glass and said, "Fine by me," as he could feel her bare foot pushing into his groin area under the table.

He hadn't had a chance to look at the bill as both times he had accompanied Francesca she had paid, but he remembered the dishes he had chosen were delicious and the restaurant was discreet and out of the way, with intimate tables dotted around the edges of the restaurant behind pillars and large plants.

The perfect place to take someone if you wanted to get in their knickers at the end of the evening; he laughed to himself for his quick thinking.

He hoped they had a table free at such short notice.

They got in a cab and arrived at Papa's a short while later and were greeted by Paolo the head waiter.

"Come in, come in," he said, in his Italian accent. Frank didn't think it was real but gave him the benefit of the doubt. They were happy to accommodate the striking couple and showed them to one of their best tables in the far corner of the room.

They were not too busy as it was early. They had quite a few covers for later on in the evening, as Thursdays seemed to be busier than Fridays for some reason.

The waiter, Paolo, offered to take their coats and they both accepted and handed them over.

"Can I get you a drink?" he asked, handing them large leather-bound menus that Frank remembered reminded him of a book. There was so much choice on there, each mouth-wateringly delicious. They were a very good-looking couple, Paolo thought.

Frank looked at Lexi. "What would you like to drink?"

"I'd love a glass of dry white wine, please," she answered, enjoying the feeling of being spoilt. It had been a while since she had gone out to dinner at such a nice place and wondered why she had never been here before.

Paolo asked if he should bring a bottle of Pinot Grigio, which he said was dry. Lexi looked at Frank. "I won't drink a whole bottle to myself," she said, "I have a busy day tomorrow." "Bring us the bottle anyway," said Frank. "I can always have a couple of glasses," he said. "Oh, and I'll have a bottle of Stella, too." Paolo nodded, Stella Artois coming right up, and left them to peruse the menu.

I am sure I can get her to drink a lot more than one glass of wine, he thought. Lexi looked very sexy tonight and he could hardly take his eyes off her. He wasn't going to let her go home without at least having a feel of those gorgeous tits, he thought. She had taken off her jacket and the shift dress hugged her body showing off her ample breasts and curves to perfection; Frank couldn't stop staring at her. She was having the desired effect on him; she was secretly pleased.

"What a gorgeous place," said Lexi, taking her napkin and placing it on her lap.

"Yeah," said Frank. "I have been here a couple of times and have always had a great meal."

Paolo returned with their drinks. "No rush to order," he said, "take your time. I will come back in a little while."

Lexi and Frank started to look at the menu. "Can you recommend anything?" she asked, looking up at Frank.

He thought she was beautiful and didn't know how he was going to get through the evening without touching her. He felt his groin stir; fuck, he thought, and put his napkin on his lap so he could hide his erection. He was imagining her lying naked on his bed, begging him to fuck her. Concentrate, Frankie boy, concentrate, he said to himself.

"I had the fillet steak, which was delicious," he said, still staring intently at her.

Lexi didn't fancy steak, it always sat heavy on her. She would either go for the fish or pasta, and she also didn't want a starter.

As if he read her mind he asked, "Are you having a starter?"

She looked up from the menu. "Not for me, thank you," she said politely. "I am happy with just a main course."

Frank was happy about this as he wasn't sure about the prices and also he could get her back to his place earlier.

Lexi decided on the linguine di mare which came with king prawns, clams, squid and garlic in a white wine sauce. She loved fish and they were all her favourites.

Frank went for the fillet steak medium rare which came with sautéed potatoes and green beans.

He wasn't very adventurous and always ordered what he knew he liked. Frank wasn't short of money but he liked to spend it wisely and hated waste so he ordered what he knew he would like.

Paolo came over after a time and took their order. "Good choice," he said to Lexi. "Chef has had many compliments over this dish."

Lexi was thrilled to know this and was very happy she had chosen it.

She took a sip of her wine that Paolo had poured moments earlier; the golden white liquid slid down her throat. "It's delicious," she said to Frank, "thanks for bringing me to such a lovely place." She hadn't eaten at all that day as she had been so busy at work and just hadn't had the time; she was also quite nervous about meeting Frank again so she hadn't felt hungry all day.

Frank picked up his beer and raised his glass to her. "You are beautiful, Lexi, thank you for agreeing to come out with me."

Lexi blushed bright red. "It's the least I could do after I nearly knocked you out yesterday," she said, enjoying his compliment.

"It's fine," he said, "look, see, no bruises," and he pushed his face over the table towards her.

They both took a few more sips of their drink. Lexi was feeling extremely nervous but the evening seemed to be going well so far and Frank was very attentive.

He really did have the most amazing grey eyes, she thought and stared into his face. Frank stared back and they sat like that for a full minute.

Paolo came over with their main courses and they both jumped. "Linguine for you, miss," he said, and put down the most enormous bowl of pasta in front of her with the most amazing smell. "And the fillet of steak medium rare for you, sir," he said, putting down an oval plate which was full of sauté potatoes and green beans that were cooked to perfection, just the right amount of crunch.

They thanked Paolo and took another sip of their drinks. "Cheers," said Lexi, and picked up her spoon and fork to dive into the delicious meal in front of her.

They spoke about work and their favourite movies and what kind of music they were into. Lexi was drinking much more than she intended and Frank had ordered another beer.

The linguine was delicious but she was feeling quite tipsy by the time they had finished.

Frank had noticed that she had become a lot more vocal and couldn't take his eyes off her rosebud lips; he thought about them sucking on his cock throughout her whole story about Jude and how her uncle came to buy him and how much she loved him. He was really mesmerised by her and couldn't wait to get the bill.

Paolo came over to take their plates and Frank immediately asked for the bill. "No coffees, sir?" he asked. "I'd love a coffee," said Lexi. She needed to sober up; she was feeling quite tipsy as she had just finished her third glass of wine.

Paolo lingered. "How about coffee back at mine?" Frank asked. "I have a great coffee machine that will make you whatever you want." He smiled, hoping she would want him.

Lexi felt she had been put on the spot; she had had such a lovely evening, which she didn't really want to end, but did have a full on busy day tomorrow.

"Er, I really should go home," she said. "I would love to but I have an early start and a very busy day tomorrow," she said politely.

Frank looked disappointed. "Coffee?" asked Paolo once again.

"Just the bill," said Frank, with a lot more force than he intended. Paolo left to get the bill. He was used to customers sometimes being rude, and it didn't bother him.

Lexi felt like she had upset Frank.

"Sorry, Frank. I have had such a lovely evening with gorgeous food and great company, maybe we could do it again next week and I'll pay?" she asked, feeling a little awkward.

Frank looked at her. This one was going to be a tough one to crack, he thought, but he was sure it would be worth it.

"It's fine, Lexi, I have really enjoyed your company and am not ready to say goodnight, that's all." He was more annoyed than he let on and as Paolo came over with the bill Lexi excused herself to go to the ladies.

"I'll be back in a minute," she said, and walked towards the toilets.

Frank paid the bill and was waiting for her just as she was coming out.

"There is a cab waiting outside for us," he said. "I'll take you home and take it on back to mine after."

"Thank you, Frank," she said, "that would be lovely."

What an absolute gentleman, she thought. She smiled at him.

The cab pulled up outside Lexi and Katie's apartment. Should I ask him in for a coffee and then he can call a cab from inside. She had enjoyed the evening so much she really didn't want it to end and one coffee would only be another half an hour. It was only nine thirty p.m., they had been in the restaurant for nearly three hours, and she really had enjoyed his company.

"Would you like to come up for a coffee?" she found herself asking.

Now you're talking, thought Frank, your bed, not mine. He smiled. "Love to," he said and paid the cab driver, leaving him a hefty tip.

The cabbie was shocked at how generous his passenger was, last fare of the night, too. He smiled and said "Thank you" as they got out of his car.

Lexi fished in her bag for the keys and opened the front door. "No lift, I'm afraid, so it's eight flights of stairs, we are at the top."

"We?" said Frank.

"Me and my flatmate, Katie." Lexi hoped that Katie wouldn't be in. She hadn't told her about Frank and as far as she knew she was out with her work colleagues.

They passed Wilbur sitting on the stairs, preening. "Yours?" asked Frank, pointing to Wilbur. Lexi laughed. "No, the neighbours'," she said, as she made her way to the top, giving Wilbur a little ruffle of his fur as she went.

They were both a little out of breath when they got to the top and were laughing. Lexi put her key in the lock and opened the door. Katie was stood there in nothing but a small towel, her hair and body still wet from the shower.

"Hello," she said, looking at Lexi and then looking at the gorgeous bloke that was behind her.

"I could hear you both coming up the stairs. How was your evening with your work colleagues?" Katie asked sarcastically.

Lexi ignored her question. "This is Katie, my flatmate," she said, looking at Frank, "who is just about to go and put some clothes on!"

"Don't mind me," said Frank, as he stared at this gorgeous green-eyed blonde in front of him.

Wow, he thought, very sexy!

Katie laughed as she watched Frank look at her up and down with his eyes bulging. Who the fuck was that, thought Katie, licking her lips. Lexi is a dark horse.

Frank caught her doing this and his groin stirred; fuck, two of them, how very cool that would be, he thought.

Katie could see exactly what Frank was thinking and she gave him one of her very sexy smiles and let her towel drop a little to reveal the top half of her breasts.

Lexi hadn't noticed as she was busy taking her jacket off and going through to the kitchen.

"Come through," she called to Frank. "I'll put the kettle on."

Frank did as she asked but wanted to see more of the lovely Katie and wondered, if he stood there any longer would she have dropped the towel altogether?

Katie also followed Frank into the kitchen, where Lexi had filled up the kettle and was getting out two mugs from the cupboard.

"I'll have a cup," said Katie.

Lexi was not at all happy with her. If she heard us coming up the stairs why didn't she go and put some clothes on?

Lexi reluctantly made all three coffees instead of two and Katie disappeared into her bedroom to do what her flatmate had asked.

She really was tempted to just drop the towel to really piss Lexi off but thought better of it. How horny was that Frank guy? How long had Lexi been seeing him, she wondered?

She came out with a tiny pink camisole top and matching shorts that revealed quite a lot of her body. She had no bra on and her nipples were erect and Frank nearly spat out his coffee when she walked back into the kitchen area.

"Katie!" shouted Lexi, "couldn't you have put a little more on?" She was so embarrassed and wanted to have coffee with Frank alone; she could see Frank drooling over her and she wasn't impressed.

Katie smiled. "Oh shut up, Frank doesn't mind, do you, Frank." It was a statement rather than a question.

Katie could see his erection in his trousers. My, my, she thought, what a catch.

They all finished their coffee and Lexi asked if Frank wanted her to call him a cab. He reluctantly agreed but would rather have stayed and got naked with these two stunning ladies.

Lexi went to find her bag so she could retrieve her mobile for the cab number, leaving Katie and Frank in the kitchen.

"It'll be here in five minutes," she said, as she walked back in the kitchen a few minutes later.

Katie and Frank had both moved to the sofa in the lounge. Lexi noticed they were sat quite close together.

Frank jumped up. "Okay, thanks," he said, looking a little awkward.

He walked over to Lexi. "I had a fabulous evening and wondered if we could do it again?" Lexi blushed. "I would love that," she said. "I'll give you my number and you can call me to make arrangements for a day next week."

She gave him her number and the buzzer went. "That'll be your cab," said Lexi, "I'll see you out."

Frank turned to Katie. "Nice to meet you," he said, and mimed the word 'both' which made Katie giggle loudly.

Lexi didn't know what was so funny and just ignored her flatmate.

Frank followed Lexi to the door and they both stood there awkwardly. He bent down to kiss her and she responded.

"Wow," thought Lexi, when their lips had parted.

Frank smiled. He could see she had enjoyed the kiss and was looking forward to calling her for a date next week.

"Thank you for dinner," she said. As Frank started to walk down the stairs, she shut the door behind her and went straight in to see Katie.

"What the fuck was that all about?" she shouted at her, "standing at the door in nothing but a towel and then going to put something as sexy as that on showing him practically all that you have!" Lexi was fuming with her.

"Will you get over yourself, Lex, he loved it," said Katie, laughing at her.

"Just fuck off, Katie," she shouted, as she walked towards her bedroom door.

She had really had enough of the selfish cow, how dare she, how fuck-ing dare she!

Lexi didn't say another word to Katie for the rest of the evening and got into bed as soon as she had taken her clothes and make-up off.

Katie fell asleep on the sofa with thoughts of Frank and Steve on her mind, dreaming of them both fucking and sucking her until she reached fever pitch orgasm. She woke up sweating and panting. She didn't realise where she was and lay there taking in her surroundings, feeling spent. "Wow, that was a delicious dream," she said out loud and sat up. She looked at the clock; it was four a.m. She would go to bed, she had a few hours before she had to be up and remembered she was meeting Steve that night, which put a big smile on her face.

Chapter 21

Katie arrived in the office on time; a few people clapped when they saw her and pointed to the clock.

She stuck her two fingers up to them and went to sit at her desk. She really could do without this today; she was still thinking about the argument with Lexi. She was pleased they had arranged a girly night in tomorrow, just them.

Miss Dawson came straight over to her. "Can I have a word in my office please, Miss Fox?" Katie groaned. "What now?"

Miss Dawson was not at all bothered by Miss Fox. She was an extremely lazy member of the team and the sooner she could get rid of her the better.

Katie walked into her manager's office.

Miss Dawson's desk sat in front of the window; on it just a telephone, computer and two trays, one saying 'in' and one saying 'out'. She had a straight-backed black chair and a foot rest under her desk. There were two more black chairs on the other side of the desk, where visitors to her office sat, normally those who were in trouble. She didn't like clutter and liked to see the top of her desk.

"Sit down," she commanded.

Katie did as she was told and started biting her thumb.

Miss Dawson looked at her with disgust at what she had chosen to wear today. The girl was always in a short skirt, barely there top; hardly the correct attire for the office, she thought. "Katie," she said with a sigh.

Katie looked at her with wide eyes, like a rabbit caught between headlights.

"Katie, how many warnings with regard to being late have I given you, not including your rudeness and your work attire?"

"But I wasn't late today," said Katie, trying to pull her skirt down as it had ridden up when she had sat on the chair.

"Not today, Katie, no, but your clothes are again not right for the office; you look like you are going clubbing."

99

Katie looked down at herself. She had chosen a very short black suede skirt with a black shirt that was quite sheer and a red bra underneath. She had worn her over-the-knee black suede boots and thought she looked quite cute.

She shrugged. "What's wrong with what I am wearing?" She looked straight at Miss Dawson, confused.

"Katie, if you don't think there is anything wrong with what you are wearing for the office then you are very sadly mistaken. I need to see a marked improvement in your attitude, work attire and time keeping. I am giving you a final warning," she said, rather smugly.

Katie really didn't care what Miss Dawson had to say, but she pretended she did. "No problem, Miss Dawson," she said, crossing her legs and showing her knickers.

"That skirt is far too short for the office, Katie. We have standards and you must wear the correct clothing for work!" She was nearly shouting at her.

"No see-through blouses, no high leg boots, no crop tops, no leggings," the list seemed endless.

"That's the majority of my wardrobe, Miss Dawson." Katie looked at her, annoyed. "Are you going to give me money to dress how you want me to dress?"

Miss Dawson was shocked she was asking such a question. "No Katie, that is up to you. All the other girls seem to abide by the rules, it's just you that doesn't. Hardly fair, is it?"

Katie wasn't at all bothered about any of the other girls in the office. They weren't exactly her friends, why should she care?

Miss Dawson had spent enough time with Miss Fox. "Do what I have told you or you will be fired, it's as simple as that!" She nearly spat the words out. "You have been warned, and I will follow this up in writing that you have by the end of the day."

Katie just stared at her. She really was a miserable old cow, she thought.

"Please get back to your desk and get on with some work." Miss Dawson looked at her computer. Katie made her blood curdle.

Katie got up and sauntered out of the door, not even shutting it. "Fucking bitch!" she said, loud enough for James Pickering, who was just coming out of the kitchen with two full cups of hot coffee in his hand. "Who is?" he asked, stopping to see if Katie was okay.

"Oh, Miss bloody Dawson!" said Katie, still fuming.

James had always fancied Katie, but knew he was totally out of her league. For one he was only five foot in height and two he had what she always described as a 'shifty' look about him. In fact she always referred to him as 'Shifty James", something he was well aware of; but he was always trying to get her to go for a drink with him so he could get her to see he wasn't shifty. He didn't know why she thought that and how he was going to convince her he wasn't.

"What's she done now?" he asked, immediately trying to show Katie he was on her side.

James was well aware of what the other girls said about Katie, how much they disliked her, as she never pulled her weight in the office, if she was ever actually there. Miss Dawson didn't have a good word to say about her.

"Always having a go at me. She is picking on me, as I haven't done anything wrong," she told him in a whiney voice.

James put the coffees down on the nearest table and went over to her, he thought he would strike while the iron was hot. "How about you and me having a drink later and you can tell me all about it?" he asked her, smiling and standing quite close to her.

Katie looked at him. He was always trying it on with her, but she didn't have any other offers and no one seemed to care that she was in trouble again with Miss Dawson.

"Yeah, that would be good," she said with a sigh. "I am going to get out of here at six p.m. on the dot."

"Okay," said James, unable to believe his luck. "It's a date," he said, smiling.

"It's a drink, James," said Katie, starting to walk towards her desk. "Just a drink."

James was happy to be going out with her. Maybe he would get her to change her mind about having just a drink with him.

The day dragged. Miss Dawson made her take far too many phone calls for her liking and she could hear the other girls sniggering. She didn't even bother going in the lunch room as she knew that none of the other girls would be speaking to her, and she didn't want to sit at a table on her own, so she just sat at her desk looking out the window.

As soon as it was six p.m. she picked up her bag and headed for the door.

"Wait for me," said James, running behind her.

Katie turned to look at him. "Why?" she asked. She had completely forgotten she had agreed to have a drink with him.

"We could go to Partners." He knew she would like it there. "Drinks are on me," he said, looking at her intently. She looked so sexy in that short skirt and he would love to get inside her top and take a look at those amazing tits.

Katie immediately perked up. "Okay," she said, smiling, never one to turn down free drinks.

She was totally broke and didn't want to go straight home as Lexi had said she was going out with her work mates. Katie wished she was going out with her work mates too.

They walked out together. He tried to put his arm around her but she shrugged it off.

It was a good fifteen minute walk to Partners but Katie didn't mind, she was looking forward to having a drink or two.

As they were walking he caught Katie's smile. "Why are you smiling?" James asked.

"I love it in this place, look at all the candles," she said, looking around her.

They walked past a few tables and James pointed to an empty one. "Go sit down and I'll get us some drinks." She didn't need telling twice.

He got back to the table with a bottle of champagne in an ice bucket with two glasses. "Very nice," said Katie.

"Only the best for the best," said James with a grin. Katie thought he was cute.

He sat down close to her and put his hand on her thigh. "Champagne would be nice," she said, pointing to the bottle and pushing his hand away. Cheeky bugger, she thought.

James poured the champagne and they chinked glasses. "To us," said James, as he put his arm around her.

She wanted to shrug it off but he looked like he needed a bone and he had bought champagne.

"Miss Dawson is such a cow!" she said, bringing up her day at the office. "She has turned all those girls against me; God knows what shit she has been saying."

James knew it wasn't Miss Dawson who had been talking about Katie and turning all the girls against her, but Michelle Ford. She had cried in the toilets about what Katie had done to her boyfriend at Gary's party and vowed she would get even with her one day!

He was pleased that she hadn't shrugged his arm away, and put it around her tighter, letting his hand rest over her shoulder near the top of her breast. "Poor you," he said, taking a large gulp of the champagne. He didn't like the stuff really but it had cost him fifty-eight pounds for the bottle, as he had picked the more expensive one that they had on sale, and he didn't want to fork out for a beer as well.

Katie was going on and on and downing the champagne like it was water.

Maybe she will get drunk and we can go back to her place, he thought, as he filled her glass up yet again.

They had finished the bottle quite quickly and were on their last glass when Katie's phone rang. She shrugged James's arm away as she saw Steve's name appear, and answered the call.

James seemed a little put out that Katie was on the phone, giggling to whoever was on the other end. He thought it quite rude of her when he had gone to the trouble of buying her the expensive drink!

She finished the call, with a big grin on her face.

"Who was that?" he asked in a sulky voice.

"My boyfriend," she said to him, as she took another large mouthful of her champagne.

She liked saying 'my boyfriend'. Katie hadn't had a boyfriend in a while and it just slipped out. She knew Steve wasn't her boyfriend but James didn't need to know this, and she always wanted to make it clear to him that they were just mates having a drink. She thought he was being very forward, touching her thigh and putting his arm around her, and she wasn't at all interested in him. She had no intention of having sex with this one, just interested in him buying her drinks, as she didn't have any money herself.

"I didn't know you had a boyfriend," James said, annoyed at her. "You never told me!"

"You never asked!" she said, downing the rest of the golden fizzy liquid. Katie loved champagne and this was a particularly good one. It tasted delicious and very moreish.

"You buying another bottle?" she asked him.

"It's your round," he said, still put out about her boyfriend.

Katie looked at him. "That's no way to treat a lady," she said, wondering what his problem was.

"I didn't realise you had a boyfriend," he said again.

"I thought we were mates having a drink together, James, you said you would buy."

"I did buy, I bought a very expensive bottle of champagne actually," he said, rather put out.

"Well, shall we go then?" she asked, not bothered either way but knowing that she didn't have the money to buy any drinks.

103

"Go where?" he asked. "Back to yours?" He had momentarily forgotten about her boyfriend.

"No!" said Katie, "what would my boyfriend think?" There, she had said it again, she liked saying it.

"Well, where are we going then?" he asked.

"I'm going home, James. Thank you for the drink, we must do it again soon." With that she got off the bar stool and picked up her bag. He walked alongside her out towards the doors.

She turned to him again when they got outside. "Sorry, James," she said, and walked off in the direction of the taxi rank and left him just staring after her.

Bitch! he thought, no wonder she has so many enemies; she treats people like shit!

Katie stood at the taxi rank waiting for a cab to turn up. She had just enough money on her to pay for one and was looking forward to getting home. The champagne had made her feel a little tipsy and she hadn't eaten all day. Her stomach was doing cartwheels and she didn't feel that great. She arrived home twenty minutes later. The apartment was in darkness and she was panting from running up the stairs.

She went into the kitchen and poured herself a glass of wine, feeling a little sorry for herself.

What is it about me that no one likes, she wondered, as she started to unzip her boots; her feet were killing her and she was glad to get them off.

She turned on the TV but there was nothing that was grabbing her attention, so started flicking through one of Lexi's magazines. Lexi always bought magazines, she said it was how she relaxed. Katie just skimmed the pages looking at the pictures, not really taking anything in; she was bored. It was only nine p.m. and she wasn't feeling at all tired, so she just lay on the sofa, still in her clothes, staring at the wall, her stomach still didn't feel great.

A while later she decided to get in the shower. The hot water over her body was heaven and she stayed in there for a long time, washing her hair and shaving everywhere. She liked to have a smooth body and she was looking forward to her second date with Steve the following evening. What should I wear for that, she thought.

She got out of the shower, put a small towel around her dripping wet body and padded into Lexi's room.

She opened her wardrobe. She did have some absolutely gorgeous stuff, she thought, as she put her hand up to feel a light suede jacket that Lexi had just purchased. That would look lovely with a skinny pair of leather trousers. Not bothering to wait to ask Lexi if she minded if she borrowed it, she took it out of Lexi's wardrobe and went to put it in her own room, ready for the following evening. She heard voices outside the front door of the apartment and went to see who was there.

Through the door came Lexi and the tallest, most handsome man she had seen in a while. She couldn't help but give him one of her sexiest smiles. She had also forgotten that she was in nothing but a small towel. Wow, she thought, as her eyes lit up; Lexi was a dark horse!

She could see Lexi was a little annoyed at her as she realised she only had a towel on but when he started flirting with her she couldn't help but let the towel drop a little.

She definitely didn't want to leave Lexi alone with this hunk so decided to gate crash the party. She hadn't had the best evening and thought things were looking up, as he was definitely enjoying looking at her. She thought it was best that she went to put some clothes on, just to please Lexi, so she opted for a silk camisole and shorts.

When she walked back in the kitchen she saw that Frank's eyes lit up at the sight of her; she blushed a little. She couldn't believe it when he beckoned her over to the sofa while Lexi went to find her bag to phone a taxi.

He had put his hand straight up her camisole and was fondling her breasts. Her nipples immediately became hard at his forceful touch. This bloke was a bad one. Lexi was better off without him, but he had definitely lit a fire inside of her and she managed to give him her number without Lexi noticing.

She went to bed with butterflies in her stomach from his touch and knew she would be seeing him again, with or without Lexi knowing.

Chapter 22

Lexi hadn't felt great when she woke up, she remembered the evening and how much Katie had annoyed her.

She was definitely going to speak to her about it later. She would go to the shops after work, and get the Barolo they had spoken about, and get a lasagne to go with it at the local deli round the corner from their apartment. It was quite an expensive shop but Lexi wanted decent food to go with the good bottle of red wine and didn't have the time to make it.

She got into work a little later than she normally would as it had taken her a lot longer than usual to get ready. She felt lethargic and her head was pounding. She hoped she wasn't coming down with something, Katie would not understand that!

I must take some headache pills when I get into the office, she thought. She always carried some in her bag.

Katie was still in bed when she left the apartment. She hadn't bothered waking her; if she was late she was late, her problem.

The morning went very slowly for Lexi. She just couldn't shift the pain in her head, that seemed to be getting a lot worse, and her body was aching too. She looked at the clock, it was almost one. She had done as much work as she possibly could, given the circumstances, and decided she really needed to go home.

She knocked on her boss's door and walked in.

"Mal, I am so sorry, but I feel absolutely awful. Would you mind if I went home?" Lexi had very rarely taken any time off sick but she still felt guilty.

"Sorry to hear that, Lexi," he said, "go straight away. Would you like me to call you a cab?" He knew she must be feeling unwell if she was asking to go home in the middle of the day, something Lexi never did.

She looked at him gratefully. "That would be so kind of you, I really don't feel great at all," she said, feeling very emotional. She hoped she wasn't coming down with something as she hated being ill; she was starting to feel dizzy.

"No problem, go and sit in your office and I'll let you know when it's arrived." Lexi didn't argue, she didn't have the strength.

She did as she was told and ten minutes later he came into her office. "Taxi is waiting downstairs for you."

"Thank you so much," she said, getting her bag and turning off her computer.

"Just get home and go straight to bed," Malcolm said to her with concern. He thought she looked extremely pale.

Lexi got into the taxi. The traffic was horrendous, it took half an hour to get home and it was gone two when she finally put her key in the door.

Straight away she heard a loud moaning noise, what on earth was that?

Lexi stopped and shut the door quietly behind her. The moaning came again, only louder, from the direction of Katie's bedroom.

Lexi thought there was something wrong and went straight to her door, which was open. There, tied to the bed spread eagled, was a very naked Katie with Frank on top of her sucking her nipples and thrusting his cock inside of her; she was screaming at this point.

Lexi stopped dead. She couldn't believe what she was seeing. Katie trussed up like a chicken, spread eagled on her own bed, and Frank pushing his cock deep inside of her with force. They were both too engrossed in their orgasms to notice her standing in the doorway. She was rooted to the spot before she found her voice.

"Oh my God," she screamed, "what the fuck do you think you are doing?"

Katie and Frank both looked at her. "Shit," said Katie, and told Frank to untie her, which he reluctantly did.

Lexi ran towards her bedroom and slammed the door shut, locking it from the inside.

Katie was outside the door. "Lex, let me explain," she called out. She felt awful that her friend had caught them.

Lexi was face down, sobbing on the bed, half from what she had just witnessed and half from the throbbing pain in her head. "Bitch!" she called out, and buried her head in her duvet.

"Why are you home?" asked Katie through the closed door.

Lexi couldn't believe the question Katie was asking. "I hate you!" she shouted back.

"Lex, Lex, open the door. I'm sorry, he asked for my number last night and so I gave it to him. I didn't know this was going to happen, he came on to me, honestly."

"So you thought you would reciprocate, did you?" she shouted again through the door. Her head was going to explode, she really wasn't well. "Have you ever said no in your entire life, Katie?"

"Just go away," she sobbed, into the duvet which was soaking wet from her tears.

Katie ran back into her bedroom. Frank was lying on her bed with his arms around the back of his head.

"Oops," he said, laughing, quite enjoying the fact that Lexi had caught them at it.

Katie felt awful. "Get your stuff and go," she said to Frank, as she bent down and started to get his clothes together.

"Can't we finish off?" said Frank, still laughing. "I loved you tied up and helpless."

"No, we fucking can't," said Katie, not believing what he was asking.

"You know you want to," said Frank with a wicked smile. He started to touch himself, not giving a moment's thought to Lexi. He would have had to work extremely hard and probably spent a shed load of cash to get Lexi to this stage of the game, he thought; lucky escape!

He was so sexy, thought Katie, she knew she had done wrong by giving him her number, but she could see Frank was a bad boy and would be no good for Lexi in the long run. She had done her a favour; he would have only broken her heart.

Katie had got the measure of Frank as soon as he walked through the door last night. The way he had looked at her up and down and lingered on her body for a few seconds too long told her all she needed to know. How was it her fault that he found her attractive? She had forgotten that she had greeted him in nothing but a very small towel.

When Lexi had gone to phone a cab Frank had beckoned Katie to the sofa and had immediately put his hands up her camisole and started to fondle her breasts. Katie had been a bit taken back but was loving his touch; he was very rough and she liked it rough.

They had sprung apart when they heard Lexi coming back in the room.

Frank had rung Katie first thing to ask when he could see her. She hadn't felt like going into work at all that day and Frank ringing so early gave her the excuse she needed to stay off. They had both agreed that Lexi didn't need to know.

I'm at home now, she had told him, come over when you are ready. Lexi had already left for work, so she knew she had the apartment to herself for the rest of the day.

Frank had rung in sick at the garage and had called a cab. He arrived at their apartment at ten fifteen a.m.

He had rung the bell and Katie had just got out of the shower. She didn't bother with a towel this time as she buzzed him up. That was the beauty of random sex, you didn't have to raid your wardrobe trying to find something to wear, she laughed to herself. When she opened the door to him she was standing there fully naked and dripping wet, making a puddle on the wooden floor.

Frank couldn't believe what he was seeing and shut the door quickly, taking in her beautiful body, her firm large round breasts and enormous nipples. He could tell they were not fake. He had felt enough of them in his time. Her flat stomach led down to her private area which was fully shaven, he loved a shaved pussy. He walked over to her and bent down to suck her right nipple, she moaned immediately and he started kneading the left one with his expert fingers. Katie just stood there enjoying the effect he was already having on her. He stopped what he was doing and started to undress himself without taking his eyes off her very sexy body.

Katie found it funny when he attempted to get out of his jeans, watching him hop around the hallway half naked. He chased her into the kitchen and bent her over the work top, removing the rest of his clothes.

"I'll teach you to laugh at me," he said, as he grabbed her and pushed his large erect cock deep inside her.

She squealed with delight at the sheer size of him. He touched all the right places and she was begging him to go deeper and harder as he pushed her body onto the cold work surface. Frank was thrusting in and out of her tight pussy, loving the feeling as he grabbed her nipples and fondled them roughly. "You are fucking awesome!" he said, breathless, feeling the full effect she was having on him. Katie didn't want him to climax just yet so she pulled away from him.

"You're a bit different from your flatmate," he said, panting and not able to take his eyes off her sexy body as she walked towards the fridge.

Katie laughed. "Lexi is great," she said, "but a bit too prudish and needs to loosen up a little."

"I could loosen her up," laughed Frank, "we both could!" He winked at Katie.

She reached in the fridge and pulled out a can of beer and a bottle of wine. She poured herself a very large glass and handed Frank the beer. They sat on the couch naked together, laughing, no real conversation taking place, just drinking and exploring each other's bodies. Frank thought this couldn't get any better. Women were always wanting to talk, trying to get him to 'open up', when all he wanted to do was fuck their brains out.

Frank was in his element and loved her large firm breasts with her big erect nipples. He couldn't stop sucking them and she was getting more and more aroused the harder he sucked.

She wanted him to go down to her pulsating sex and she spread her legs wide on the sofa. Frank got the message and immediately parted her lips and found her clit with his tongue. She moaned loudly as she felt his tongue on her most intimate place and he put his finger deep inside of her. She was touching her own breasts, which turned him on further. He loved watching women play with themselves and reaching orgasm. He could tell she was enjoying his touch as her pussy was soaking wet; he could taste her sweet juices. She finally couldn't hold it in anymore and exploded, screaming and writhing about, feeling the full force of her orgasm. Katie had not had an orgasm like that in a long time, well the night before, she thought, with a long sigh. Frank and Mario both knew what they were doing but it was Steve that kept coming back into her thoughts.

Katie's body tingled. She wanted to take Frank to bed where she could explore his body further. She got up from the sofa and took his hand. "Let's go to my room," she said, looking straight at him. Frank didn't need to be asked twice and followed her into her dimly lit room. He lay down on the bed. She bent down and started to take his cock in her mouth, slowly at first, moving her tongue up and down his shaft, and licking the tip of his penis that was bulging, teasing him before she took him fully in her mouth and began sucking with such vigour that he gave out a loud moan and exploded in her mouth almost immediately, unable to control himself. Katie smiled. She knew she gave great head and started to suck him dry. She was loving the effect she was having on him. His hand went to her arse and he put his finger inside her, making her gasp as she bit down and he moaned.

They had lain on the bed for a while, feeling spent. It wasn't long before he had become hard again, which was when he told Katie to lie down on the bed and spread her legs wide for him.

He looked around her room and left her spread eagled on the bed as he rifled through her drawers and found exactly what he was looking for; stockings. He went over and showed her them in his hand. Katie knew exactly what he was going to do and licked her lips. He took her left arm and pulled it up towards the bed head and tied her wrist to it. He went round and did the same with the other one. He also spread her legs open very wide and where she didn't reach the bottom of the bed the stockings were stretched. He tied them round both ankles. She was completely at his mercy, her full sex completely on show to him. He started exploring her whole body with his tongue and fingers and she moaned loudly, loving the sensation his touch was having on her. He bit her nipples very hard and watched her as juices came flowing out of her pussy; he could see her pulsating. The stockings were restricting her movement and her orgasms were coming in thick fast waves but her body was unable to move into them and he could see her straining from the depth of her climax. He couldn't resist a moment longer and jumped on top of her. She cried out when he went deep inside, her thrusting his cock in and out whilst he was sucking on her amazing hard nipples. She was moaning very loudly, enjoying the sensation she was feeling. They heard a scream and both stopped what they were doing immediately and looked towards the bedroom door to see Lexi standing there with her hands over her mouth

Chapter 23

Toby had stayed in Partners, still not being able to get hold of Steve and keeping an eye on Katie. She was in deep conversation with this guy and they were sitting extremely close to each other.

He could see that the man had his arm around her shoulder and she was leaning in quite close to him.

He had had enough and was just about to leave when he saw Martha and her friend walk in. She was engrossed in her conversation and she hadn't seen him.

He thought she looked absolutely gorgeous and wanted to go over but the two women seemed to be having a major catch up and he thought it might be rude to disturb them.

He didn't realise she was out tonight, not something he would know, he thought, feeling like he should.

He noticed there was a little lull in the conversation and was just about to go over when he saw another three females join them. All those females in one proximity was scary to Toby and he thought better of it so he sat back down. He was happy watching Martha and her friends laugh out loud and to him they seemed really close. His groin stirred. She looked stunning. He thought she had never looked so sexy.

Toby smiled. Watching Martha with her friends was endearing and he wanted to do something nice for her. He made his way to the bar and spoke to the barman. "Do you know what the ladies on the table over there are drinking?" he asked. The barman had served them when they had first come in and told Toby it was prosecco. "Can you send over a bottle in an ice bucket and five fresh glasses and I'll pay for it now, please, mate." The barman smiled and thought this was a nice gesture and wondered which of them Toby was interested in; they were all very attractive. "Sure mate, no problem."

Toby paid for the bottle and ordered another drink for himself and went back to the table where he had previously sat. He watched the barman take over the prosecco and glasses and tell them who it was from. They had all looked round at him and he blushed. He watched Martha coming towards him and he smiled. God, she looked sexy, he thought, as she stopped at his table.

As they were chatting he noticed Katie walk by with the man she was with and he couldn't help but glance in her direction.

What was she up to, he thought; probably taking that bloke back to hers to spend the night with him. I really need to speak to Steve, he thought, momentarily distracted.

He turned his full attention back to Martha. He would deal with it an-other time. Martha was in front of him and he couldn't help but be totally smitten with her.

He really did need to speak to Steve though, he thought.

Chapter 24

Steve was up early. His phone showed three missed calls from Toby; what on earth was that about?

He decided to put on his favourite Yves Saint Laurent navy suit and a crisp white Ralph Lauren button down shirt. He wanted to make a big effort with Katie tonight, as he felt bad about putting her in a cab on their first date, something he definitely wasn't going to do again.

He looked around his apartment. His mum had done a great job as usual, and it was clean and fresh. She must have had one of her spring cleaning days on, he thought, as he saw that everything was gleaming.

Ralph was curled up by the radiator and purred when Steve walked through. "You might be meeting a gorgeous new blonde tonight, Ralphy boy," he said, as he went to stroke his cat.

Steve's groin stirred in the confines of his trousers at the thought of Katie, he was definitely going to ask her back.

His phone started ringing, and he saw it was Toby.

"Hi, mate," he said. "Everything okay?"

"Yeah, why shouldn't it be?" asked Toby.

"Just had a few missed calls from you yesterday, wondered if anything was up?"

Toby didn't want to wade straight in about Katie, he needed to find out what went on.

"No, just wanted a catch up really, wondered how your date went with Katie, did you get to go?"

Steve smiled. "Yeah mate, it went really well. I was the perfect gentleman and put her in a cab at the end of the night without even touching her." He laughed.

"Oh right, so you did see her, then?"

"I did, mate, she is gorgeous, so fucking sexy, but I had an early start and clients to see and didn't want to go all night without any kip if you know what I mean." Steve laughed again down the phone.

"So you did see her but dropped her off early?" said Toby.

Steve was a little confused. "Yeah mate, you asked me that. What's going on, why all the questions?"

Toby quickly regained his composure. "Nothing at all, just wanted to know how it went, that's all, glad you had a good time."

"I really like this one, Tobes," said Steve, becoming serious. "I know we've only been on one date but we got on so well, and she is a proper lady. She didn't mind at all that I put her in a cab, in fact I think she wanted to keep the sexual tension going and knew there would be a second date."

Toby couldn't believe what Steve was saying but didn't want to mention about seeing Katie with not one but two blokes in the last forty-eight hours!

"I think I might even give up Jemma for this one," Steve said down the phone to his friend.

"Fuck mate, seriously?" said Toby, knowing that Steve meant business. Shit, his best friend was falling in love with someone he had only just met and from what Toby had seen was a right slapper!

The only thing Toby could think of to say was, "Well, mate, make sure you wear a condom."

Steve spluttered his coffee down the phone. "What!" he shouted, "what do you mean, wear a fucking condom?"

Steve pushed his hands through his hair. "Don't tell me you have fucked her?"

"No!" shouted Toby back to his friend, "why the fuck would you think that?"

"Because of what you just said, why would you say that?"

Toby pretended to laugh. "Oh, just some guy at work has the clap from some girl he had been seeing and he rode bare back, so it's been playing on my mind." He was pleased with himself for coming up with the white lie.

Steve gave a sigh of relief. "Fucking hell, mate, nasty." He shuddered.

Steve had always practiced safe sex and walked towards his bedroom to make sure there were supplies in his side drawer. He was relieved to see there were plenty, enough for a night of unbridled passion, he thought.

"Just so you know, Tobes, I have checked my stock and I am fine so don't go worrying about me," he laughed down the phone.

"That's good," said Toby, trying to laugh back, but feeling awful that he couldn't just come out with it and tell his friend what he had seen. Katie was definitely no lady, he thought.

"Look, I have to go," said Steve, "or I'm going to be late. I'll catch up with you at the weekend. Can't see you tomorrow night as I am out with the family for Nan's birthday, but maybe we can have a drink Sunday lunchtime, if you are up for it?"

Toby was relieved Steve hadn't seen through him. There was no way he was telling him anything over the phone, it had to be face to face. He also hadn't told him about Martha, but that was for another time as well.

"Is Martha going with you tomorrow night?" he asked, trying to sound blasé about it.

"Yeah, of course, why would you ask that?"

"No reason," said Toby, cringing that he had.

"You need to tell me something about my sister?" asked Steve, smiling, as he didn't think that Martha would be Toby's type and vice versa.

"No," said Toby, trying to lighten the mood, "just asking, as she made me laugh the other night when I took her to the film. I told you that we had a good night and was just wondering, making conversation, that's all."

Steve smiled. "Well, mate," he said, "that is a conversation for another time, as I need to go and do some work and make sure I am on top form for my hot date with the lovely Katie, so have a good day yourself and I will call you on Sunday to arrange timings."

They both said their goodbyes and Steve got his jacket and ran for the door. He really needed to get into work and start on a new campaign they were pitching for.

Chapter 25

Katie couldn't get rid of Frank fast enough. She felt awful Lexi had seen her tied up fully naked and having sex. She still felt like she had done Lexi a favour as he would only have treated her badly and she didn't want Lexi getting involved with a shit like Frank.

Lexi had now stopped crying and there was no sound at all coming from her room.

Frank reluctantly left but not before having another fondle of Katie's breasts whilst snaking his tongue in her mouth and hearing her moan. "You are so sexy," he told her, feeling himself getting aroused again.

"Frank, stop!" she told him. "I need to make sure Lexi is okay."

"She'll be fine," he told her, not really caring one way or another. What a stroke of luck Lexi had asked him up for a coffee, otherwise he wouldn't have met Katie and would have had to play the long game to get Lexi into bed. Katie was different altogether; they were kindred spirits, he thought.

He would definitely be giving her a call over the weekend for what he hoped would be a repeat performance. Her amazing body tied up on the bed like that with her legs spread wide made his cock stir. It would have to be back at his, obviously, as he couldn't be doing with emotional females such as Lexi; that one wouldn't be getting a call, not unless it was for a three-some. He smiled at the thought.

Katie shut the door behind her and went straight to Lexi's.

"Please talk to me, Lex," she said, pushing her ear to the door to see if there was any sound.

Lexi had fallen asleep. She was exhausted and felt really ill. She was disgusted with her friend for having sex with Frank. He seemed such a nice guy and she had had a really enjoyable evening with him.

She wondered if she hadn't gone home sick if they would have bothered telling her; if they would carry on betraying her until she did eventually catch them out. She had shuddered at what might have been and Katie's obvious betrayal.

Katie decided it was best to leave her and hoped that she would calm down, then they could speak about it properly and get back to being friends again. She suddenly remembered her date with Steve and felt her nipples harden.

"Shit!" she said out loud, "I won't be able to look in Lexi's wardrobe." She was thankful she had taken the suede jacket and put it in her room the previous day. I'll just have to wear my own clothes to go with it, she thought.

Katie went to her room and got out the suede jacket that she had put at the back of her wardrobe just in case Lexi went looking for something. She was always borrowing Lexi's clothes and never putting them back or getting them dry cleaned, which infuriated her.

"Why do you have to wear my clothes?" Lexi was continually shouting at her. "I wouldn't mind but not only do you never ask but you never bother having them dry cleaned either!"

Katie always shrugged, apologised and promised never to do it again; she always did though.

She pulled out some tight Lycra leggings and a figure-hugging black boob tube; both showed off her curves to perfection.

If I team this up with some high boots and a bit of jewellery Steve will go crazy and will definitely not put me in a cab at the end of the evening alone, she thought.

She went into the kitchen and looked at the clock; shit, she only had a couple of hours before Steve would be arriving in the cab. She needed to have a shower to get the smell of sex from her body and also his juices. She tingled at the thought of Frank; bad boy, she thought, very bad boy.

She was just about ready when her phone beeped and she saw Steve had sent her a text.

Hi Katie, it's Steve, I am on my way x

She wasn't sure where he lived so didn't know how long he would be but she knew it would be within the next fifteen minutes or so.

She liked that he had put a kiss at the end of his text, could be a night to remember, she thought, and replied,

I'll be ready! X

She laughed out loud at her reply. That should start the ball rolling, she thought.

She took one last look at herself in the mirror. The Lycra leggings showed off her slim toned legs, the thigh high boots always made her feel very sexy and she had put on a Lycra black boob tube that accentuated her curves and made her breasts look even bigger than they were. She wore no bra and was happy with how they looked under the top. It outlined them to perfection and she would definitely be taking off her jacket, correction, Lexi's jacket, when they got to whatever bar he had decided on. She smiled; there were no straps so he could get to her body with ease, she thought wickedly.

Lexi still hadn't come out of her room and Katie didn't hear any sound either. She was definitely not going to cancel her date with Steve; Lexi was probably going to stay in her room all night, what would be the point of putting him off.

She would speak to her at some point tomorrow, she wasn't sure what time she would be home, if at all.

She heard the buzzer go. "I'm going out, Lexi," she shouted from the front door. "I am sorry about Frank. We'll speak over the weekend."

She didn't wait for a reply and made her way down the stairs, again nearly running into Wilbur. "For fucks sake, cat, can you find somewhere else to preen," said Katie out loud, just about avoiding a nasty fall.

Katie was sorry about Frank, not about the amazing sex they had had but sorry that Lexi was upset. She hated it when that happened but when she got the chance to explain Lexi would see that she was crying over nothing, as Frank would be no good for her and wasn't ever going to be her Prince Charming.

Steve was waiting outside the cab when she opened the front door to her building.

"Wow," she thought, as she saw him in his navy suit.

He had the door of the cab open for her, standing waiting for her to get in.

"Fuck," he said out loud, not meaning to; she looked absolutely gorgeous and he was practically drooling at her thigh high boots.

This outfit was definitely different from the last one he had taken her out in; this one said "Fuck me".

He couldn't believe that he had actually got to go on another date with her. She was stunningly beautiful, her body was amazing and even the cab driver's eyes lit up.

She saw that he was bowled over by what she was wearing and smiled. Good choice, she said to herself as she got into the passenger seat in the back.

Steve got in after her. "You look gorgeous," he said, unable to stop looking at her breasts in the Lycra top.

"You look very dapper yourself," said Katie, looking forward to the evening ahead. "Where are we going?" she asked, in her sexiest voice.

"We are going to a little Italian restaurant I know called Papa's, on the other side of town." Steve had been to Papa's a couple of times and loved the ambiance in the place. The out of the way tables and the abundance of candles made the place feel very intimate.

Katie knew of Papa's but she had never been. One of the girls in the office was bragging one day that her boyfriend had taken her there and completely surprised her by getting down on one knee in front of the whole restaurant and had produced the most stunning diamond ring and proposed to her. Katie had said something nasty to her about how good he was in bed the other weekend and he was only doing it as he felt guilty. She was secretly jealous that no one had ever asked her. She had seen the girl running crying in the toilet, upset with Katie's harsh words. She had got quite a few nasty looks from the others that day too.

Steve opened the door for her and put his hand on the small of her back to guide her in; she felt the heat radiate and smiled.

As she walked in she was amazed at the amount of candles that were all around the restaurant. She could see small intimate tables with couples holding hands and speaking quietly and a few larger tables with families sat round. The smell of garlic and herbs was tantalising her nostrils and the sound of soft music could be heard all around her. The place was also filled with different sized plants dotted around the room, making for intimate corners and bringing the outdoors in. Katie loved it.

She immediately fell in love with the feeling she got from just walking into the restaurant. She turned to look at Steve. "What a gorgeous place," she said, in barely a whisper.

Steve smiled. "I thought you would like it," he said, whispering back, still keeping his hand on her back, pleased that he had brought her here.

He had been unable to think of anything or anyone else since their first date and was so pleased to be here with her now. He wasn't going to let her go quite as easily as he had before. She had definitely made an impression on him and was doing untold things to his groin area too!

The waiter showed them to their table, which was over in the far corner of the restaurant and was slightly hidden from view of the other customers by large plants that Katie was dying to ask about. She would love one in her apartment.

Their waiter introduced himself to them and advised his name was Roberto and he would be their waiter for the evening.

How lovely, thought Katie. "Can I ask what are these plants called? They are amazing."

Roberto smiled. Many people had often enquired about the plants. "They are called 'Mummie' plants," he said. "They are indoor plants that are harvested at their peak and retain their vibrant, natural colour and perfect condition for years without any intervention."

Katie was mesmerised, listening to him speak in his soft Italian accent. "So you don't ever have to water them?" she asked, liking what she was hearing. "No," said Roberto, "they require no water, supplements or pesticides, they are no maintenance at all, which was why we purchased them for the restaurant."

Katie loved hearing this. "I bet they cost a lot," she asked, smiling. "I love the large planters they are in too." Roberto thanked her and was glad she liked them.

"Can I get you a drink while you are looking at the menu?" he asked.

Steve ordered a bottle of beer and Katie went for a dry white wine. "Can I recommend the Peroni for you, sir, and an Italian Pinot Grigio blush for the lady?" he asked.

"Sounds delicious," said Katie, and put her napkin on her lap.

Steve was happy with the recommendation and nodded to Roberto. "Would you like a bottle or just a glass?" he asked regarding the wine. Steve thought a bottle would be better so he didn't have to keep asking her if she was okay for drinks. "A bottle would be great," he said, and Katie smiled. Roberto left to organise the drinks after leaving them with their menus.

"What an amazing place," said Katie looking around, once again unable to keep the excitement out of her voice.

Steve was thrilled that Papa's was a hit with her. She looked amazing and he was so glad he had thought of bringing her here.

It was warm in the restaurant and Katie decided to take off her jacket.

Steve couldn't believe how huge her breasts were. He could practically see them through the sheer of the top. She had the biggest nipples he had ever seen. He loved how pert they were. His crotch stirred, he was thankful he had the table cloth to hide his manhood which was straining in his trousers.

"You look so sexy, Katie," he said across the table, as Roberto returned and thought the same.

Lucky man, he will be having some fun tonight.

Roberto put down their drinks and poured Katie's wine for her to taste. "I'm sure it's fine," she said, "go ahead and just pour." She couldn't wait to get some of the alcohol down her as she was feeling quite dry and only had one large glass with Frank earlier in the day.

She put Frank to the back of her mind. This was much more interesting. Steve was gorgeous and was being a proper gentleman. She doubted Frank knew how to be but he did know how to get her to reach orgasm of the most gigantic proportions. She smiled at the memory.

Steve noticed her smile. "What are you thinking about?" he asked. Katie was brought back to the present. "Just how happy I am being here with you," she lied.

She was happy about being there with Steve but it wasn't what she had been thinking about a second earlier.

They ordered the most delicious meal. Steve went for the Dover sole and Katie chose the spaghetti alle vongole. She loved clams and cleared her plate, it was that delicious. They had shared a starter of fritto misto, which was lightly floured deep fried calamari rings, whitebait, prawns and a roasted pepper mayonnaise. It was also amazing.

"You have a healthy appetite," said Steve, as he poured her third glass of wine.

Katie gave him one of her very sexy looks. "I do indeed," she said, as she took a large gulp of her wine. It was starting to go to her head, which was unlike Katie as she could normally drink most men under the table. The fact that she had eaten as well didn't make sense. Maybe she was just heady at being here with Steve.

She could feel her nipples harden and he noticed this too.

"She is so coming onto me," he thought. "I am definitely going to ask her back to mine."

Roberto cleared away their plates and refilled Katie's glass. Steve was on his third beer. He didn't want to go too mad so stayed on the bottles rather than having a short.

Roberto asked if they wanted to see the dessert menu. "I am okay," said Steve, "but you go ahead, Katie, fill your sexy boots." They both laughed out loud. "I am okay for dessert," she said, "but I would love a Tia Maria with lots of ice, if that's okay?" She looked at Steve. "Have whatever you want," he smiled at her.

They spoke about their favourite films, books they have read, or not read in Katie's case, and thoroughly enjoyed the evening.

"Do you want a coffee here or back at my place?" he suddenly asked her, deciding that he couldn't wait any longer for the games to begin properly.

She couldn't believe what she had heard and shifted in her seat. She felt moist down below and smiled. "I'd love a coffee back at your place," she said, lifting her foot to rub his ankle.

He smiled back at her and was enjoying feeling her flesh touch him.

She finished the last of her drink and definitely felt light-headed. Steve rang for a cab and called Roberto over, asking for the bill.

Katie excused herself and made her way to the ladies. She had quite a few admiring glances from the men as she sashayed through the restaurant, much to the annoyance of the women they were with.

She felt good and she knew she looked it. She went to the toilet and was washing her hands, looking at her face in the mirror. She felt her nipples harden for the umpteenth time that evening and was excited about the night ahead.

She freshened herself up, taking out a small pack of wipes that she always carried in her handbag, ensuring she was smelling sweet down below.

She looked in the mirror and laughed. She couldn't wait to get Steve back to his place. She was extremely horny and wanted to relieve him of his clothes and hers and explore his muscly body. She pulled her top down further, showing the top half of her breasts, and walked out.

Steve had paid the bill and was waiting for her just outside the ladies.

"Ready?" he said.

"Very ready," she said, giving him a sexy smile.

He helped her with her jacket and noticed her breasts were now spilling out of that top. "Fuck," he said to himself, as they made their way outside to the cab that was waiting.

The air hit her like a ton of bricks and she was unsteady on her feet.

Steve grabbed her. "You okay?" he asked, thinking she may fall over.

Katie held onto him, enjoying the feel of his strong hands on her body. "I'm fine," she said, "just the effects of the alcohol."

He smiled. She had drunk the whole bottle to herself and Roberto had brought her over a double Tia Maria. Hope she isn't too drunk, he thought, his cock stirring again in his trousers.

The cab driver pulled up outside a red bricked Victorian mansion that had been renovated and made into five apartments. Steve was on the top floor and they walked up the stairs towards his door. He put the key in the lock and felt inside for the light switch.

Katie walked inside. Steve had a lovely apartment with very high ceilings. It was light and airy and spotlessly clean. He could teach her a thing or two, she thought. There were lots of period features; she especially liked the fireplaces and could imagine them lying naked on a fur rug while toasting marshmallows and drinking mulled wine in the winter. She laughed at the thought.

He showed her into the lounge, where two huge red leather sofas sat in the middle of the room and a large TV adorned one wall. He had a feature wall that was painted in bright red that matched the sofas and a kitchen with a glass table and four chairs off to the side.

"Wow," said Katie as she walked in. "This space is amazing," she said, looking all around, loving the colour scheme. "Where did you find this?" He had large sash windows that overlooked other buildings and black and white blinds that she knew would let in a great deal of light during the day-time,; hopefully she would be getting to see that in the morning.

He was pleased with her response over his apartment. He had enjoyed buying his furniture and he had opted for a modern look but still keeping the Victorian features. "My sister is an estate agent and she found it for me." He smiled as he walked over to her.

"Can I take your jacket?" he asked in a very low voice. Katie didn't hesitate and started removing her jacket, shrugging it off her shoulders so her breasts jiggled and her nipples hardened at his stare. His focus went straight to them.

"Looks like you are pleased to be here," he said, laughing.

"I am," she said, and he immediately kissed her full on the mouth, parting her lips with his tongue. She could feel his tongue exploring her open mouth and sliding against the inside of her upper lip. Katie felt her stomach contract as he did this and loved what he was doing to her down below.

She moaned. His cock stirred and he reached up with his hands to fondle her breasts, trapped within the confines of the Lycra top.

"These are amazing," he said, looking intently at her chest. Katie pulled down her boob tube for him, showing him her naked flesh and her large pert nipples.

He couldn't believe what she had just done but wasn't complaining in the slightest. His mouth went to lick her right nipple while his hand caressed her left one as he felt his cock straining in his trousers.

She moaned again. "That feels so good," she told him, looking down as his teeth bit her nipple.

"Harder," she said, and he did what she asked, taking her nipple in between his teeth and biting down as his thumb and fingers roughly played with the other one.

She immediately felt a rush down below. Loving the feel of his touch on her breasts, she wanted to get naked and started to pull her Lycra leggings down. She could see the bulge in his crutch and was very pleased with what he seemed to be packing.

He saw that she wanted to take her clothes off and started to help, unzipping both her boots as they fell towards her ankles. She held her foot out for him to take them off and became instantly shorter as his tallness became apparent.

He laughed. "You're a lot shorter without those sexy boots," he said, still staring at her ample breasts.

She loved the feeling of first time sex, it sent currents up and down her body and she started to breathe heavier.

She stood there with her leggings down to her knees and he saw that she wasn't wearing any knickers. "Commando, eh?" he said to her, still unable to take his eyes from her protruding nipples.

She pulled off her leggings and stood there with her top still around her waist. He loved the fact that she was clean shaven at her most intimate part.

His cock was raging now, fighting to get out of the confines of his trousers. He was still fully clothed, still wearing his jacket.

He was just about to take it off when his phone started ringing. He couldn't take in the sound for a minute, then realised. He reached in his jacket pocket and saw that it was his mum.

"Sorry," he said to Katie. "It's my mum, I have to take it." He walked away from her, leaving her standing there looking annoyed that he had answered his phone when they were about to have the best sex she had probably ever had. All the anticipation from the build-up of the evening was driving her crazy with sexual desire.

"Mum, hi, do you know what time it is?" Steve couldn't help the annoyance in his voice but was also worried as to why she had rung so late, it was so unlike her.

"Steve, sorry, it's your nan, she has had a fall and I thought you would want to know."

Steve pushed his hands through his hair. "Is she okay?"

"Well, the ambulance is here now and she will be taken to St Mary's." He could tell his mum was extremely upset. His nan was eighty-six but there was nothing frail about her. Steve and Martha had an extremely close relationship with their nan, and she had always been there when they were growing up. She still cooked the most amazing apple pie and they had never tasted anything else that could beat it, even though they had tried. It was a family joke that whenever they were all out together one of them would order the apple pie and see if it could beat their nan's. It had never been able to as yet and his nan was always grateful that they loved hers so much.

"Where's Dad, is he with you?"

Steve wanted to cry. The thought of his beloved nan in any pain brought tears to his eyes. He had been looking forward to seeing her tomorrow evening for her birthday. Martha and Steve had bought her a special present that they couldn't wait to see her open. It was a Teasmade that she could put on her bedside table and wake up to a lovely fresh brew in the morning without getting out of bed. She had had one years ago but it broke from old age, and she was always saying how much she missed having a cup of tea when she woke up.

They had made sure it was a top of the range one so she didn't have to do too much in order for the tea to be made. The shop assistant had assured them it was the best make.

"I'll get a cab to the hospital," said Steve. "Have you rung Martha?"

His mum gave out a loud sob. "Yes, she is on her way too."

Steve was beside himself as he put the phone down after saying goodbye. He put his hands once again through his hair, and Steve had completely forgotten Katie was standing there practically naked.

"Shit, I am so sorry, Katie, I am going to have to go. My nan has had a fall and they are taking her to hospital in an ambulance. I have to be with her."

Katie couldn't believe what she was hearing. "What?" she said. "Can't you go see her in the morning? You won't be able to do anything at this time of night. I doubt they'll let you see her."

Katie was extremely put out. There would be nothing he could do tonight, why on earth did they have to stop what they were doing?

Steve couldn't believe that Katie was happy to carry on, did she not hear him? "Maybe not," he said, "but at least I can be with my parents, and Martha, my sister, is on her way too."

"Well, if your sister is going why do you need to? Let's carry on with what we started," she said, her voice a little whiney as she pulled her top down over her bottom and stepped out of it.

She was standing in front of him fully naked and he was still aroused at the sight of her.

"I am sorry, Katie, it wouldn't be right. I doubt I would be able to do you justice. I need to get to the hospital."

Katie ignored what he was saying and went over to him, circling her nipples. "Come on, Steve, you know you want to," she heard herself saying.

Steve thought she looked awesome coming towards him but he couldn't have sex with her while his nan was on her way to the hospital. He would never forgive himself and he would feel extremely guilty if he didn't get there as soon as he could.

126

He called a cab from his phone. "What the fuck are you doing?" shouted Katie.

Steve was taken aback at the way she spoke to him. "I am calling a fucking cab," he shouted back, "to go and see my nan in hospital. Haven't you listened to what I have just said?"

She didn't like the way he shouted at her. "This is the second time that you have pushed me away, Steve!" she screamed.

"What are you on about?" He looked at her, confused.

"You put me in a cab last time we went out, remember?" She was still screaming.

"It was a first date," he said. "I wouldn't have thought you wanted to put out and I was being a gentleman!" He was not happy with what she was saying.

"Katie, put your clothes on. We can do this another time, maybe tomorrow, but at the moment I need to get to St Mary's to be with my family. I am sorry if that is not to your liking but that's how it is." He was very stern with his words; she felt like she had been slapped.

Katie was fuming with him. How fucking dare he, she thought, it's not as if they were alone; his mum, dad and sister were all going up the hospital. How many people did she want there, for fuck's sake!

Steve was running around his apartment calling for Ralph.

"Who the fuck is Ralph?" she shouted at him.

"He's my cat and I am surprised he wasn't here to greet us when we came home."

He was still calling his name.

"I'm not a fan of cats," she said, as she started to put her top and leggings back on, pissed off that she had to.

"Well, maybe he's not a fan of yours either!" said Steve, still angry at her. How fucking dare she, they could have sex another time, his family needed him and if she didn't like that then tough.

His intercom buzzed. "That'll be the cab, can I drop you somewhere?" he asked, hoping she would say no. He didn't want any detours as he wanted to get to the hospital as soon as possible. The traffic at this time of night would be virtually non-existent; he could be with his family within fifteen minutes.

Katie knew where St Mary's was and the taxi would have to go past the bottom of her road to get there. She was fucked if he thought she would be walking home, besides she had no money and felt he should pay anyway.

She told him that the cab would have to pass the bottom of her road so could she be dropped off. He was happy to do this but started to hurry her. "Get your boots on, the cab is waiting."

Katie was put out. How dare he start rushing her? He was quick to have a good look and feel of her body earlier, now he just wanted to discard her like some old toy.

"You forgot the sexy," she said, pouting her lips.

"What?" he asked. Clearly his mind was elsewhere as he pushed his hands through his hair.

"You called them sexy boots earlier," she said, still pouting.

"Sorry Katie," he said. "My mind is completely elsewhere," Steve said as he walked over to her. She was fully dressed now and ready to go. He kissed her on the lips. "I promise I will make this up to you but for now I really do need to get to the hospital."

She kissed him back. "You had better," she said, enjoying the feel of his lips on hers.

They got in the cab and she asked the driver to pull over when they were at the bottom of her road. "Promise you'll call me," she said, rubbing his arm.

"I promise, not sure when that will be, but I promise."

She felt like he couldn't get her out of the cab quick enough. It was midnight and Katie was far from tired, but seemed to have no choice but to go home.

She walked towards her apartment building, pissed off with the night's events. "Fucking clumsy Nan," she shouted out into the night air, and let herself into her apartment building.

Chapter 26

Martha was fast asleep in bed when she was dreaming that a phone was ringing. It just kept on ringing and ringing, she couldn't stop it.

She finally woke up and realised it was in fact her mobile going off, not her dream.

She saw 'Mum' on the screen and looked at the clock. It was eleven thirty p.m. What on earth was she calling for at this time?

A cold shiver went down her spine as she rubbed her eyes and reached for the phone.

"Mum, what's happened?"

Linda was just about to put the phone down and try Steve again.

"Oh Martha, thank God you have answered. I have been ringing for ages."

"Why, what's happened?" Martha said again, sitting up and putting her legs out of the bed.

"It's Nan. She's had a fall and we are taking her to St Mary's. I didn't know what to do so I just kept ringing you and Steve to tell you."

"How is she, is Steve there with you?"

"She is really poorly. She fell down the stairs in the dark. She wanted to make a cup of tea as she was thirsty, but forgot where the light was and thought she could get down them by feeling her way. She tripped and fell down half of them." Linda started to sob. "Oh Martha, she had a really nasty cut and bruise on her head and they think she may have broken her hip as well."

"Oh Mum, that's awful. I will get dressed and be right there. Have you told Steve, is he on his way?"

"No," she said. "I haven't managed to get hold of him." Linda started to sob louder. "Martha, if I lose her I will be devastated," she sobbed into the phone.

"I am sure she will be fine. Keep trying Steve and I will drive to the hospital. I had an early night so I haven't had anything to drink as I have work tomorrow."

"Okay," said Linda, thankful that Martha was on her way.

She dialled Steve's number and this time he eventually answered.

Linda wasn't normally emotional in a crisis. She was the strong woman of the family but this was her mum and she was so scared of losing her.

She put the phone down after speaking to her son and saw that the ambulance crew were ready to go.

"Can I come with her?" she asked.

"We can only take one," said one of the ambulance men.

"No problem," said Ted. "I'll follow the ambulance, you go with her, Linda."

Linda was grateful to be told what to do as she was all over the place.

The ambulance put its lights on with no sound, due to it being nearly midnight, and got to the hospital within ten minutes.

Ted was grateful there was no traffic. He could follow the ambulance and get to the hospital at the same time. Linda was in bits and she needed her family with her. He was pleased she had managed to get hold of Steve and Martha and they had agreed to come straight away.

Martha was waiting at the hospital Accident & Emergency when she saw an ambulance and her dad's car behind.

She was glad she left straight away. She just put on whatever was to hand, which turned out to be a pair of black leggings and a T-shirt with the words 'No Fear' emblazoned across the front, which she thought was quite apt given the situation. She had found a warm hoody that was bright pink. She hadn't worn it in a while, as she thought it was a bit young for her, but this was no fashion show and she needed to get to the hospital fast.

Linda followed them through to get checked in and the nurses asked if the three of them could go to the waiting area whilst they examined her.

As they were waiting Steve came through the doors. He immediately saw his family and went straight over to hug his mum. "Is she okay? Where have they taken her?" He shook his dad's hand and gave Martha a hug.

"You took your time," said Martha. She could smell the alcohol and garlic on him, and she knew he had been out. "Hot date, was it?" she said, looking at him up and down, and thought how smart her brother looked in his YSL suit.

Steve blushed. "You could say that," he said, running his fingers through his hair. Martha knew this was something he did when he was either embarrassed or worried; she guessed it might be both this time.

"It's okay, bro," she said, feeling a little sorry for him. "The nurses are examining her now. I'm sure it won't be long before we can see her."

Steve spoke to his mum and she told him what had happened.

"Shit," said Steve, looking at Martha. "We should have given her that Teasmade when we bought it, then this wouldn't have happened." He sat down heavily in the chair.

"Hindsight, eh?" said Ted. "It's not her birthday until tomorrow." He looked at the clock; it was past midnight. "Actually it's her birthday now," he said, "how ironic."

They waited about half an hour and then a doctor came out of the cubicle and walked over to the family.

"How is she?" said Linda, getting up from her seat.

"Well, she has been very lucky," said the doctor. "No broken bones at all. She will be badly bruised and sore for a while and we would like to keep her in for a few days just to keep an eye on her, but other than that she is just fine," he said, smiling to them all. "She is a very tough cookie for her age, but she will be fine."

Linda sat down in the chair and started to sob. Steve and Martha went over to her immediately and gave her a cuddle.

"Come on, Mum," said Martha. "You heard what the doctor said, she will be fine." A tear rolled down Martha's cheek. "Don't you start," said Steve, as he brushed his own tears away.

They all hugged one another and Ted and Steve shook the doctor's hand. "Thank you," they both said, "thank you so much."

Linda asked if they could see her. "You can for a minute," he said, "but we want to get her up on a ward to make her more comfortable."

"Thank you, doctor," said Linda, and went into the cubicle.

Her mum, Violet, looked so old and frail lying in the hospital bed. Linda let out a loud sob. "Oh Mum," she said, as she went over to kiss her. Violet had a big bruise on her forehead and one under her eye that was just starting to come out.

Vi, as she was known, looked at her daughter. "I'm fine," she chided, "don't fuss."

Violet was a strong woman. She had lost her husband, Linda's dad, very early on in Linda's life and brought up Linda, who was an only child, practically single-handed. Her own parents had died in the war and she had been taken in by a strict aunt, who gave her the values that Linda was brought up with and who instilled them in her own children.

Martha and Steve were very polite children and had family values instilled in them to this day.

The rest of the family walked in. "Anything for attention," Steve said, as he went to hug his nan gently. "I know you didn't really want to come out tomorrow night for your birthday but you didn't have to fall down the stairs to make your point, Nan."

They all laughed. Violet couldn't believe they were all there.

The nurse came in and said that Violet needed her rest and they could come and visit her in the morning. They didn't want to leave her but thought the nurses knew best and were so thankful she was okay.

They all kissed her and wished her well and promised they would be there first thing in the morning to visit her. Martha said she would drive back to her house and pick up some bits for her to make her stay more pleasant and they all left.

When Linda got in the car park she put her head in her hands and sobbed. Steve went over to her and put his arms around her. "She is in the best place, Mum, and she was lucky not to have broken anything."

Linda looked him. "I know, Steve, and I just keep thinking what could have happened."

Martha said she would take Steve home and would call her parents in the morning.

As they said their goodbyes Steve got in Martha's car.

"So," she said, looking at him with a smile on her face. "What were you up to earlier?"

Chapter 27

Frank was pissed off at having to leave Katie. He wanted to explore her body for the rest of the day, and had only taken Lexi out once, what was the problem?

He decided to go straight to Lloyds. He was still feeling aroused and wondered if Darcy would give him one of her amazing blow jobs, that would sort him right out.

He walked into the bar, looking around for Darcy. She wasn't in there but he decided to stay for a drink anyway.

Tony the barman came up to him. "Usual?" he asked, as Frank got to the bar.

"No," he said, "I'll have a vodka and coke, Tony, please. I feel like having a tart's drink," he laughed. Tony laughed with him.

He sat at the bar with his drink, thinking about the sex he had had with Katie that day. God, she was incredible, he thought. Those gorgeous tits were amazing. She looked awesome tied up; his cock started to stir at the memory of the day he had just had. Just as he took another sip he noticed a very pretty blonde at the other end of the bar.

"Who is the blonde?" Frank asked Tony.

"She's been in here for a while, I think she has been stood up," said Tony, looking at the beauty at the end of the bar.

"Get me whatever she is drinking," said Frank.

Toby gave Frank an orange juice. "No vodka in it?" said Frank, sniffing the juice.

"That's what she's drinking," said Tony, shrugging his shoulders.

"Put me a double vodka in it," he asked him.

Tony did as he was told. A paying customer was a paying customer and Frank was a good one, he thought.

Frank sidled up to the blonde. "Hello," he said, in his softest voice, as he knew the ladies liked a soft voice in a man. Until he had them between the sheets, that is, and then they all liked it rough; he laughed inwardly.

The blonde had already noticed Frank when he had walked in and thought how fit he was, not to mention his good looks, as she sipped her orange juice waiting for her date, so when he had walked over to her she was pleasantly surprised.

"My name is Frank," he said, handing her the vodka and orange.

"For me?" she said, taking the drink. "Thank you."

"Why are you in here alone? This is no place for a beautiful lady such as yourself," he said, giving her one of his friendly smiles.

The blonde blushed. "Actually," she said, "I was supposed to be meeting someone in here but it looks like I have been stood up." She took a sip of the drink Frank had bought her and immediately spluttered it all over the bar, coughing.

"That's not orange juice," she said, using a tissue to wipe the sticky liquid from her face.

Frank laughed. "I thought you needed cheering up so I got the barman to put a vodka in it."

The girl wasn't very happy about this as she wasn't really a drinker, but he looked so handsome and friendly she smiled. "Well, I am not really a drinker, I don't like the taste, but thank you for trying to cheer me up."

The girl went to get off the bar stool she had been sitting on. Frank noticed Darcy coming in through the doors at the far end of the bar. "Look," he said, "I can't really speak now but if you want I could take you out for a soft drink tomorrow night?"

The girl looked at him, her large blue eyes were like pools of the clearest water. "I'd like that," she said, giving him her whitest smile. He melted; she had the most beautiful face and the body was quite amazing too.

"What's your name?" he asked, as he saw Darcy was giving him daggers. She picked up her bag that had been on the floor. "It's Ava," she said, "Ava Green."

"Well, Ava Green, if you give me your number I will call you tomorrow afternoon and make arrangements to take you out tomorrow evening. How does that sound?"

"Sounds like a plan," said Ava, and she started to give him her number.

Darcy came over, wondering who the pretty girl was that Frank was speaking to. "Hello," she said, looking at Frank. "What the fuck happened to you last night? I thought you said you were coming back after your meeting with your boss?"

"Yeah, Darc, sorry, it all got a bit messy, you know how it is, and one thing led to another and before I knew it the pub was shutting and it would have been too late to come back here," he lied.

"There you go," said Ava, and passed him her number on a piece of paper that she had got out of her bag.

Darcy turned round to look at the girl. "Why the fuck are you giving him your number? I am his girlfriend, are you not aware of that?" Darcy spat the words out at Ava.

"Oh," said Ava, looking a little embarrassed. "I wasn't aware he had a girlfriend, I am so sorry." Ava didn't know what to do.

"Darcy!" Frank bellowed. "How many times do I have to tell you, you are not my fucking girlfriend!"

Ava didn't want to get caught up in an argument between these two formidable characters standing before her. "I'm going," she said, looking rather sheepishly at them both. "I didn't mean to cause any problems."

Frank's heart melted, not something that happened very often. An angel sent down from the skies just for me, he thought.

Darcy was fuming. "You turn me on and turn me off at your conven-ience, Frank!" she shouted so the whole bar could hear. "I have had enough of you treating me like some whore!" She walked away, out of the bar.

Frank wanted to shout "that's because you are a fucking whore" but thought better of it as he noticed Ava's face.

Ava was looking a little scared; last thing she wanted to do was upset anyone. "Sorry again," she said. "I think I should go now."

Frank was so angry with Darcy for telling people he was her boyfriend. He wasn't anyone's boyfriend and that was the way it was going to stay.

"I'll ring you," he said, still holding onto the piece of paper with her number on it. "Don't mind her, she is delusional!"

"Not sure your girlfriend would like that," she said, looking towards the door. "I think you had better go after her, don't you?"

Ava picked up her bag and made for the exit too. She really didn't need this. She had already been stood up by one man tonight, she didn't want to get involved in a domestic too!

She went home, hoping he would call but thinking it would be best if he didn't.

Frank ordered another vodka and coke and went to sit down at one of the tables. "Fucking women!" he shouted and got his phone out to put Ava's number in.

Darcy can go fuck herself; she was only good for one thing and he wouldn't be letting her go there again. The mood she was in Darcy would probably bite my cock off anyway, he thought, and laughed out loud.

He typed in Ava in his contacts and stored her number in his phone. He would definitely be calling that beauty.

Chapter 28

Martha kept looking at her phone. Toby hadn't rung or texted, like he said he would, and she was feeling a bit upset. He didn't actually say he would call on Saturday but he did say sometime over the weekend.

She didn't understand why she was feeling upset, they had only gone to the cinema once. Okay, he had bought a bottle of prosecco for her and the girls, which was a random gesture but such a lovely thing to do, but then why had she not heard from him?

It was Saturday evening. She had been to see her nan in the hospital with Steve. The doctor had said they were really pleased with how she was responding and she could probably come home on Monday, as long as someone was there to look after her. They just wanted to keep her in a couple of more nights to make sure they didn't miss anything, especially as she had sustained a head injury.

Linda immediately volunteered herself and said she could have it all under control; she just might need a little bit of help from her husband and her two kids.

They had all agreed and would do whatever they could to help.

They sang 'Happy Birthday' and gave her cards and presents round her hospital bed. She had laughed when she had opened Steve and Martha's. "A bloody day too late," she had said, and they had all laughed with her.

As Martha was due to be out on Saturday night celebrating her nan's birthday, she probably wouldn't have given Toby as much thought as she was doing now, but as she was staying in he was all she could think about.

Her phone rang and she jumped up. Steve's name showed up on her screen.

"Hi Steve," she said, feeling a little disappointed.

"You okay, Martha?" he asked. "You don't sound very pleased to hear from me."

She quickly changed her mood. "No, sorry, I'm fine, just a bit bored as we would have been getting ready to go out to dinner with Nan so I am at a bit of a loose end." She sighed into the phone.

"Great that Nan didn't break any bones though, Martha," said Steve, trying to lighten things up with a positive. "I'm going for a drink with Toby if you fancy coming?" he said, not thinking she would.

Martha wanted to scream and say, "I'd love to," but thought better of it. What if Toby wasn't happy with her gate-crashing their cosy twosome?

"No thanks," she said reluctantly. "I doubt Toby would like me tagging along."

"I'm sure it would be okay," said Steve. "I could call him if it would make you happier. Not sure why you think he would have a problem?"

"I just think he will," she said, trying to brush it off.

Steve frowned. "You had a good time when he took you to the cinema last week, didn't you? Toby said he really enjoyed it and that you were very funny."

Martha's face lit up. "Well, if you don't mind asking him that would be great." She smiled into the phone, hoping Toby wouldn't have a problem but thinking he probably would, and he was only saying he had a good time to Steve.

Did he think I was funny ha, ha or funny peculiar, she thought?

"Give me about ten minutes and I'll get back to you."

"Okay," excitement and worry showing on her face at the same time.

Martha paced up and down her kitchen waiting for the phone to ring. She picked up a magazine and started to flick through the pages but she was unable to concentrate so started to pace again. Twenty minutes later, when she had had given up all hope and convinced herself that Toby was not happy at all with her coming out, her phone started to ring.

She saw that it was Steve and just let it ring a couple of times, as she didn't want him thinking she was waiting for the call, waiting whilst pacing, waiting whilst inwardly screaming, she thought.

"Hello," she said, trying to sound calm.

"Hi sis, yeah, Toby is absolutely fine with it, said it would be good to see you again."

Martha was ecstatic but played it cool so as not to give anything away to her brother.

"Oh, okay then, will you pick me up in a cab on the way?"

"Of course, be ready at eight p.m. and I'll get the taxi driver to toot his horn."

Martha put the phone down and jumped in the air, punching it. "Yes, yes, yes," she said, doing a little dance in her kitchen on the spot where she stood. "Shit, what the fuck am I going to wear?"

137

Panic set in as she went running into her bedroom and opened both doors of her wardrobe. She stood there staring at all the clothes hanging on the rail. She had two hours to make herself look absolutely stunning for Toby.

She decided on a cream pair of straight leg trousers and a cream fluffy jumper that she could wear off the shoulder and her diamond strapped bra. She had just purchased a beautiful pair of gold shoes with a peep toe and four inch heels. She curled her hair, which fell in soft waves over her shoulders and down her back, sitting just above her bottom. She made her face up with perfection and applied her favourite pink Dior lipstick.

She had a three quarter length cream coat that set the whole outfit off nicely; when she looked in the mirror she was pleased with what she saw. Hopefully Toby would be pleased too. She was starting to get nervous as Steve would be here soon.

She decided to have a small glass of red to steady her nerves, being careful not to get any on her cream outfit.

She heard a toot, grabbed her metallic leather clutch bag that her mum had bought her for her birthday, set her alarm and shut the door behind her, ensuring she double locked it.

She didn't realise that Toby would be with Steve in the cab and she saw him standing there with the door open.

"Your carriage awaits," he said, laughing. "You look like an angel." Toby couldn't help himself; she was stunning and he was amazed by her beauty.

Martha blushed and laughed. She couldn't think of anything to say except "thank you" as she slid across the passenger seat so Toby could get in. Steve was in the front seat next to the driver. Martha felt a little awkward.

"Hey, sis," said Steve, smiling, "glad you are coming out with us, wouldn't want you staying in on your own bored." He laughed.

Martha was mortified. Did Toby think she had no friends to go out with? She had loads of friends, he had seen that the other evening when he had sent over the bottle of prosecco!

They drove for a while in silence. She could feel Toby's leg brushing the side of hers so she continued to look straight ahead.

Toby coughed. "We thought we would have a drink in Horatio's, if that's okay with you, Martha," he said, rather formally.

"Oh, that place we had a drink in last week after the cinema?" she said, still looking straight ahead and not really thinking.

"I didn't know you went out for a drink after the cinema," said Steve. He had turned his head to look at them both. Martha and Toby blushed.

Toby was about to say something but Martha beat him to it. "It was just a quick drink after the film. I didn't want to go home straight away, you know what I am like after watching a scary film, and Toby suggested Horatio's," she said, looking at Steve then at Toby.

Steve turned back to look ahead of him, happy with the answer she had given.

They arrived at Horatio's and clambered out of the taxi. Steve paid and Martha said she would give him some money later.

"No problem," he said. "It's been ages since I have taken you out so tonight's on me."

Martha smiled. Her brother was very generous with his hard-earned money; Steve was the one that usually paid when they went out to dinner or for a quick drink. I must buy him a present, she thought, glad that he had asked her out.

They walked in to Horatio's, which was heaving with people. The bar was extremely busy but Steve managed to squeeze his way in and catch the attention of the barman.

His badge said his name was Mario and Steve ordered himself a beer and turned to ask what Toby and Martha wanted.

Martha had already had a small glass of red so thought she would stick with the same. Toby ordered a beer like Steve and Mario went to get their drinks. He came back shortly and looked straight at Martha. Wow, he thought, what a stunner. Toby saw that he was looking at her and the hairs on the back of his neck came up. He took the drinks and softly pushed Martha back towards a table that was free to the left of the bar area.

They all sat down but were unable to hear what each was saying as the music was quite loud and the crowds were noisy.

Martha took a sip of her wine and began to follow Toby's gaze across to the bar area. She saw he was looking at the blonde who they had seen on the last two occasions they had happened to be together.

She was in deep conversation with the barman, Mario. She was wearing a short pink leather skirt, with a tight black shirt that had been unbuttoned to show a very full cleavage, and very high black patent heels. Her legs looked amazing. Her blonde hair had been straightened and was flowing behind her as she kept putting her hands through it when she spoke and shaking her head. She looked stunning, thought Martha, in a totally different league to me.

The men at the bar were also giving her admiring glances.

She could see Toby was beginning to look uncomfortable. "Shall we finish these drinks and head on somewhere else?" he asked. "It's so busy in here we can hardly hear ourselves think, let alone talk. Let's find somewhere quieter."

Martha felt sick. I wish I hadn't come, she thought. She noticed that the blonde was whispering in the barman's ear and he roared with laughter; she giggled back. Maybe she was doing that to make Toby jealous, she thought; it looked like it's worked judging by the look on Toby's face.

Toby stood up, thankful that Steve hadn't seen Katie at the bar flirting with Mario, and finished his drink. "Come on," he said to both Steve and Martha, "let's get out of here."

Steve wasn't too bothered where they went. He wasn't really in the mood for drinking but didn't realise that until he had got to Horatio's and his beer wasn't going down too well.

He had been worried about his nan last night and seeing her look so frail in her hospital bed upset him. Also seeing his mum cry broke his heart and he hated the thought of her being upset.

"You okay with that?" Steve said to Martha, always being the caring brother.

Martha wasn't sure what to say. She knew that there had been something going on with the blonde and Toby and she didn't feel like going anywhere else except home.

"I think I might go home, actually," she said, looking at Toby.

"No!" said Toby, more forcefully than he intended, which surprised both Martha and Steve.

"What's the problem with Martha going home?" said Steve, looking at his friend.

"There isn't a problem at all," said Toby, trying to lighten the situation. "I just know that you are both worried about what happened to your nan and think you should unwind with a drink, that's all."

Martha looked at Toby. He was so handsome, she thought, such a gentleman. There was obviously history with him and the blonde but at least he wanted to get out of the same place she was in which was good, right, she asked herself.

"Okay," said Steve, "what about going to The Feathers? It's not far and better than waiting for a cab in the cold, we could walk there."

"Great idea," said Toby, relieved that they were getting out of Horatio's and Steve hadn't seen Katie. Even better, he thought that she hadn't seen him.

They walked the short walk to their local and found that it was much quieter and they managed to get a seat at one of the high tables near the bar.

140

Martha walked towards the bar. "It's my shout," she said bossily, "I won't take no for an answer." The two boys laughed. "Ok, miss," they both said, as Martha got out her purse.

She was still thinking about the blonde when the barman came over to take her order.

Steve had decided to go on the red wine and Toby wanted a vodka and coke; they both wanted a change from the beer.

She ordered a bottle of red for her and Steve and a large vodka and coke for Toby.

She took the drinks back to their table and started to pour the red into the glasses. She was looking at Toby, who seemed to have forgotten about the blonde and was happy chatting to her brother. She realised that Steve and Toby were in the middle of a conversation about Steve's date.

How long have they been split up for, she thought, looking at Toby's deep blue eyes that were giving nothing away.

"I was supposed to give Katie a call to let her know how nan was but she didn't exactly seem bothered about her, only seemed to be bothered about herself," Steve said to Toby.

Toby looked at his friend. He still hadn't had the conversation about Katie and was so glad that he hadn't seen her at the bar flirting with that Mario. She had gotten under Steve's skin for some reason and Toby was not happy about it.

"I really like her though, Tobes," he said. "She is so sexy and hot, she does things to me that I haven't felt in a long time and she's great company." He took a long gulp of his wine.

Martha hadn't met the lovely Katie but Steve went on about her quite a bit so she knew she had made an impression on him; she sounded nice.

"Why don't you call her now, see if she wants to join us?" said Martha, looking at Steve.

Toby was just about to say something when his friend piped up. "I don't think I would have the energy to satisfy her tonight," he said, laughing out loud.

"Too much information, Steve, thank you," said Martha. "I don't need to know about your sex life."

"Not when yours is non-existent," Steve said, and Martha went bright red.

Toby was pleased to hear that Martha's sex life was non-existent. He looked at his friend, thankful that he was tired and didn't want to call Katie. Toby didn't want Katie anywhere near Steve if he was honest. She was playing around with him and probably wasn't aware that he was falling for her; she was too busy shagging other men.

"Do you mind if I head home?" he asked both Toby and Martha. "You seem to be getting on fine with each other and I really have had enough."

Toby looked at Martha. "I don't have a problem," he said, trying to read her face.

"Me neither," said Martha. Her stomach was doing cartwheels.

Steve said his goodbyes and headed for the door, leaving Martha and Toby sitting there.

"Well," said Toby, "I think I'll get myself another drink. Do you want one, Martha?"

Martha still had the bottle she had bought for her and Steve earlier. Although Steve had had a couple of glasses she hadn't drunk much and there were still a couple of glasses left.

"No, I'm fine," she said. "I'll stick to the red, thank you."

Toby went to the bar to order another vodka and coke. In through the door walked Katie and Mario, laughing. He had his hand round her shoulders. Toby looked to the sky. No, he thought, and saw that Martha was watching him.

He got his drink and went over to Martha.

"Is she your ex?" asked Martha, looking like she was going to cry.

"My ex?" said Toby, not quite believing what she had said. "Why on earth would you think that?"

"Every time I have seen you, she has been there. It's like she is stalking you. Did you finish on bad terms?"

Toby sat down. "She is nothing to do with me, Martha, honestly, and believe it or not it's not what you think at all. That's Katie!"

Martha couldn't believe what Toby had said. "Steve's Katie?" she shouted, louder than she realised.

Toby pulled his chair round to get closer to Martha. "Be quiet," he said, "not so loud."

Katie and Mario had got their drinks and were sitting at a table over the opposite side.

"So all those times that you have seen her it's not because she is your ex?"

"No, not at all. Don't get me wrong, I did find her attractive when I first saw her, who wouldn't?" he said. Seeing the look on Martha's face and realising how that must have sounded, he decided to be totally up front with her. He didn't want to play games with this one.

"Martha, I really like you. I have had a great time since we went to the cinema and I have thought about no one else since."

Martha looked at him, shocked at his statement and dumbfounded at what he had said. "I like you too, Toby," she blushed.

He leant over and kissed her very softly on the mouth. She responded and gave out a slight moan.

Toby leant in and began telling Martha the whole story about Katie and all the men he had seen her with, and how much he wanted to tell Steve but hadn't had the right moment. He didn't want to blurt it out on the phone, he told her. Steve deserved more than that. Martha agreed. He also mentioned to her that he was worried that Steve was falling for her in a big way and he needed to say something sooner rather than later.

Martha was shocked and also relieved. She really thought there had been something going on with the two of them. Katie always seemed to be there. Now she realised why Toby always seemed to be looking at her; he was as disgusted as she was with Katie's antics.

She looked over at her. "Bitch!" she said quietly, "how fucking dare she mess my brother about!"

"My thoughts exactly," said Toby, glad he was able to tell someone, even if it was Steve's sister. Hopefully they could speak to him together.

Chapter 29

Lexi woke up on top of her duvet, still in the clothes from the previous evening, and suddenly remembered what had happened.

"Oh my God," she said out loud; she got off the bed and looked at her face in the mirror. Her mascara was all down her cheeks and her eyes were puffy from crying so much. She still didn't feel great, better than when she was at work but now she had something else to feel sick about.

Lexi had made her decision. Katie Fox was no friend of hers. The sooner she could leave the apartment the better. She has no thought for anyone; it was pointless carrying on living with someone so shady.

Frank was an idiot too. Katie would just throw him away when she had had enough; she did it to them all. She was surprised that she herself hadn't been thrown away by Katie!

There was a knock at her door. "Lex, are you up?" Katie was outside the door in her dressing gown.

Lexi shouted out, "Go away, you bitch, I have nothing to say to you."

She saw the door handle being turned but it was still locked from the previous night; thank God, thought Lexi.

"Open the door, Lex please, I need to talk to you," Katie whined through the door.

"I have nothing to say to you, so just leave me alone!" Lexi screamed at her.

Katie tried the door again. "Please let me in, Lexi, I want to explain."

"Explain!" Lexi screamed. "What could you possibly say to me, Katie, that would make this situation any better? I saw what I saw and you can't fluff it up to suit your version of events, not this time!" Lexi was fuming with her.

"Frank would have been no good for you, Lex, I did you a favour," Katie said, trying the door handle again.

"So you keep saying, Katie, but that was for me to find out, not you. Please go away," she said, in a softer voice.

"I'll go and make you a nice cup of tea and we can have a chat, meet you in the kitchen."

She heard Katie move away from the door.

She wanted to take a shower but needed to know Kate wasn't standing outside the door. Lexi had an idea; she would call her mobile and that would determine where she was.

Katie heard her mobile ringing and got up from where she was sitting outside Lexi's room. She was trying to be very quiet so Lexi would think she had gone elsewhere in the apartment.

Lexi heard her answer the phone and opened her door and went into the bathroom, where she locked it so Katie wouldn't come in and try and talk to her there.

Katie saw that it was Lexi on the phone. "Hello, Lex?" she said, confused. She was not on the other end of the phone and Katie went towards her bedroom and saw her door was open. She heard the shower in the bathroom and tried the door; it was locked.

Stupid bitch, thought Katie, let her wallow in her own self-pity; she'll come round eventually.

She went into the kitchen and filled the kettle up with water and got the milk from the fridge. I will make us both a nice cup of tea and when she has had a shower she will feel better and hopefully want to talk; then we can sort this mess out and get back to normal. Katie felt happier with what she had decided to do

Lexi let the hot water cascade over her body. She still didn't feel well and her anger at what Katie had done was making her feel a whole lot worse.

Frank had been such a gentleman at the restaurant. He had been kind and funny. How can one person be so deceiving to another, she thought, as tears streamed down her face.

"Why the fuck am I crying?" she said out loud, getting water in her mouth. She washed her body with the lemon smelling shower gel and turned the shower off. She wrapped a big white fluffy towel around herself and cleaned her teeth. She looked in the mirror. Her eyes were very puffy but so what. Time to face Katie, she thought, as she unlocked the bathroom door and went back to her room.

Lexi decided to put on some clean pyjamas. She had no intention of going out and she wanted to be comfortable. She could hear Katie clanging about in the kitchen and decided to go and face her.

Katie looked up to see her flatmate standing there. "Lex," said Katie, "I've made you a nice cup of tea." She put the cup down on the breakfast bar in front of her.

"I am really sorry, Lex," Katie said, looking a little sheepish. "It was just one of those things that happened. I had no control over it."

Lexi looked at her friend. "You had no control, you couldn't say no?"

"It wasn't like that," whined Katie. "It all happened very quickly. He called me yesterday morning after you had gone to work and asked if he could come round."

"So how did he get your number?"

Katie looked at her and bowed her head. "I gave it to him last night when he was flirting with me." She took a sip of her tea.

"How was he flirting with you exactly, Katie? Would that be when you were in the hall with nothing but a small hair towel wrapped round your naked body, showing off your massive tits to a virtual stranger?" Lexi was starting to get angry.

"I didn't know you were bringing someone back," she said, starting to get angry herself. Lexi needs to get over herself, this is not my fault.

"He asked for your number and you gave it to him, even though you knew I had been on a lovely date with him and had had a good time, even though you could see that I liked him?"

"You never said you were going on a date with anyone, first I knew was when the two of you walked in the apartment together," said Katie, starting to really get annoyed with her friend's sarcasm. "For all I know you could have met him at a bar that night whilst you were out with your work mates."

Lexi was disgusted that Katie would even think she would behave like that.

"We are not all like you, Katie, picking up the first guy you see and shagging his brains out, normally in this apartment when we agreed that you wouldn't bring random men back!"

Katie looked at her innocently. "It's not as if I do it all the time, Lexi, just now and again."

"Why do you think I never said anything to you about going on a date with Frank?"

Katie shrugged. "How would I know that?"

"Because I didn't want you to know about it, that's why!" She was shouting at Katie.

"Why would you not want me to know you were going on a date?" Katie was becoming confused. They were friends who spoke about everything; why would Lexi not tell her about her date with Frank?

"Because you thought nothing of giving him your number and having sex with him the following day, that's fucking why, Katie!"

146

Lexi was beside herself. Was she really that stupid? Did Katie really think it was okay to behave in the way she had? They were supposed to be best friends. All the times she had helped her and this is how she behaves, by betraying her, shagging her date within less than nine hours of them saying good night to each other!

"Why Frank, why could you not have chosen anyone else? You were shagging random men two at a time the other month!" Her head was pounding; she hated arguing, she hated confrontation. She needed to lie down.

"That was a one off, Lexi, and you fucking well know it!" she screamed at her. "Why do you always bring it up?"

Lexi stormed out of the kitchen, leaving her tea on the breakfast bar.

"Fuck you, Katie, fuck you!" she screamed and walked into her bedroom and slammed the door.

Katie was fuming. How fucking dare she bring up the threesome again? She was always going on about it. How many times did she need to apologise? She was sorry that Lexi had caught them all at it but again how was that her fault? She was caught up in a moment, having had far too much to drink; it was also something she had always wanted to try and had loved every second of it. She would never let on to Lexi, though.

Katie had had enough of trying to explain to Lexi that she had done her a favour, and couldn't understand why she was angry with her. She should be telling Frank all this!

It's not as if she and Frank had been seeing each other for a while; it was one fucking date. What was her problem?

It was now past five p.m. and Katie had spent enough of her precious weekend trying to speak to Lexi. She wanted to see Steve, carry on where they had left off last night, before his bloody Mum phoned and interrupted their lovemaking.

Why did she need all the family there? Surely it could have waited until the morning. She hadn't even got his jacket off, let alone his trousers, and by what she had seen around his crotch area she was sure he was very well endowed. She licked her lips as her nipples hardened and her breasts began to swell at the thought of him.

She wondered if she should call him herself but that was not what Katie liked to do. She expected all the men to do the chasing, not the other way round, it wasn't right.

She hadn't heard from him and decided that she wasn't going to sit around waiting for him to call.

Katie decided on taking a long slow shower with her water resistant vibrator. She was totally wound up by Lexi shouting at her. She needed to release some of her pent up frustration.

She touched her nipples, which immediately went hard. She imagined Steve's soft lips sucking her right nipple gently. Her hand wandered down between her thighs and she reached for her vibrator, putting it inside her slowly, bringing it in and out as the water cascaded over her body. She rubs her finger against her throbbing clit, spreading the lips of her wet pussy, and moans gently. She imagines Steve is standing by the bath, fully naked, watching her expertly play with herself as she climaxes and thrashes around in the shower, feeling her juices flow out of her.

It was some time before Katie got out of the shower. She really needed to see Steve, to explore his gorgeous body and feel his cock deep inside her. She had never thought about someone as much as she thought about Steve. She couldn't believe that they had been on two dates and she hadn't had sex with him yet. Fucking mother, she thought again, spoiling our fun.

She dried herself quickly and stood looking at herself in the full length mirror. This is what he saw on Friday night, this is how he saw me, she thought, bringing her hand up to touch her left breast that was still swollen from her time in the shower. "I think I look fucking amazing," she said out loud. "I'd fuck me," she laughed.

Her thoughts went back to Lexi. It would be great if we could just move on from this and get back to normal. Why does she have to be so angry with me?

She put on her dressing gown and padded out of her room towards Lexi's. She knocked softly on her door but there was no sound. She opened the door and was thankful it wasn't locked. She saw Lexi asleep in her bed with her eyes all red and puffy from the constant crying.

Katie felt extremely sorry for her. "Bloody Frank," she whispered, as she moved a strand of hair that was across Lexi's face. She stirred and opened her eyes to see Katie standing over her.

"What are you doing in my room?" she asked, a lot more calmly than she had spoken to Katie previously. She still wasn't feeling great and didn't have the energy for round two.

Katie saw this as a sign that Lexi had forgiven her. "How about you get yourself dressed and we go out on a girly night together?" she said, smiling at her flatmate.

Lexi sat up in the bed. "You have got to be kidding me," she said, looking daggers at Katie.

"Kidding you, no why would I be kidding you? I thought we could just put this behind us and go out and enjoy ourselves together for a change." Katie sat down on the bed next to Lexi. "You're always out with your work mates or at your uncle's; how about we spend some time together?"

Lexi couldn't believe what she was hearing, did she have no compassion? Did she feel no guilt?

"Get out of my fucking room, Katie, now!" she shouted.

Katie jumped off the bed. "For fuck's sake, Lexi, get a grip, will you? It's not as if you were seeing him for a while. It was one fucking date, hardly the great romance of the century."

Lexi started to cry, big racking sobs. She could not hold it in any longer. Katie looked at her and felt absolutely awful.

"I am so sorry, Lexi, if I'd known he meant this much to you I would never have gone there." She started to step away from Lexi's bed towards the door.

Lexi couldn't speak, she just wanted Katie out of her space and somewhere else. It wasn't about Frank, she felt absolutely nothing for him; it was Katie's betrayal that had really upset her.

She didn't think she would ever be able to move on from this and call Katie her friend again.

She had made a decision to take Jo up on her offer and move in with her whilst her flatmate was travelling. She knew Jo would be thrilled with this, as she had often asked her, as she knew all about Katie.

She would call Jo later when she had calmed down.

Chapter 30

Ava Green woke up with Frank on her mind. She lay in her double bed with her head on the soft pink cushion that smelt of fresh washing. She was always getting her mum to put it in the machine as it was her favourite thing to snuggle up to.

She was thinking about Frank and wondering if he would call her, wondering if she would agree to go out for a drink with him if he did call.

He was the best looking guy she had ever laid eyes on. She was very attracted to tall men and although that Darcy girl had said he was her boyfriend Frank had vehemently denied this; was he single, she thought?

She had arranged to meet her best friend Tiffany that day for lunch. Tiffany wanted to know everything on how her date went with Rob.

Wait until I tell her that Rob never showed but I may have met my future husband, she thought with a giggle.

Ava worked in a call centre. She had been there since she was eighteen and was happy with her job and the friends she had made. It was easy work and she loved getting paid at the end of each month and buying new things. She still lived at home with her parents, as she didn't see any point in moving out. It was cheap, comfortable and she got on well with them. A couple of friends had often asked her to flat share but she had always declined.

Ava was a virgin. She had never had full blown sex with anyone, even though she was twenty-two years old. She had decided when she had reached the age of consent that having sex with multiple people just wasn't for her, and when she finally did find her Prince Charming it would be for life and she would save herself for that person. She thought it was extremely romantic that she would only ever have one actual sex partner throughout her life. Her friends thought she was crazy and said they wouldn't have the willpower to stop when it came to the crunch, although secretly they were a little envious of her keeping herself for her future husband.

Ava knew how attractive she was. She knew that she turned heads and had a lot of admirers, but flirting and going to bed with them was one thing, actual penetration was another.

She had dated a lot of guys. The opposite sex found her instantly attractive with her long blonde hair, deep blue eyes and a body to die for and she was always being chatted up in bars and flirted with. Ava was happy to flirt back, happy to let them explore her body, but she was not going to allow any of them to penetrate her.

She had always made this quite clear and even though some thought that when they managed to get her into bed she just wouldn't be able to resist; Ava was able to resist.

She had dated Josh for quite a while. He was a trader in the city and had the money to wine and dine Ava at the swankiest restaurants. He lived in a huge apartment overlooking the river. Ava had no problem in staying over; she did have a problem with the constant whining from Josh with regard to his pulsating manhood and her wanting to keep her virginity intact.

"Why can't I just go inside you?" he would constantly ask.

"You know why, Josh," she would say. "I am saving myself for my wedding night."

Josh found that Ava would get him so worked up that he sometimes thought of asking Ava to marry him just to get inside her properly. He doubted Ava would have said yes as she didn't seem as in to him as he was to her. She was absolutely gorgeous and her body was amazing.

She also gave amazing head and he would be totally under her spell whenever she went down on him but she never ever let him put his cock inside of her. He really didn't understand how she always had the willpower to stop him from doing this.

He knew she was turned on when his tongue was deep inside her pussy, his thumb kneading her throbbing clit, and he could hear her moan with delight while her fingers would pull roughly through his hair and she was writhing around on the bed, but as soon as he tried to enter her she would stop him. How on earth did she manage to resist time and time again, he often thought.

Ava always managed to have multiple orgasms and was satisfied with only allowing Josh to use his tongue. Josh, however, even though she always made sure he climaxed, was never satisfied.

"How can you expect me to not want to be inside you?" he would always ask.

"Josh, you know how I feel about that; we have spoken about it so many times it has become boring," she would tell him as she stroked his cock and snaked her tongue up and down his shaft.

"I don't understand why you are happy to let me do everything else?"

"For fuck's sake, Josh, I just want to be a virgin on my wedding night. It's something that is very important to me; you have always been aware of that fact!"

She would get very angry with him asking all the time. "If you want to go and find someone else who will let you penetrate them then please do but you won't be seeing me as well," she would often tell him, after they had the same conversation over and over again. He always said that it wasn't what he wanted.

Ava did stop seeing Josh when she went to surprise him one night at his apartment. She found him naked, ramming his cock deep inside one of his female work colleagues, who was also naked and bent over his island in the kitchen. Ava remembered meeting her at one of Josh's office parties and hadn't liked her then either!

They had both looked over to see Ava standing there watching them both. Josh had immediately pulled out of her and put his hands to his face. "I am so sorry, Ava, this wasn't supposed to happen."

"Save it," she had said as she walked out the door, slamming it hard. She had blocked his calls and never spoken to him again.

She had arranged to meet Tiffany outside the shopping centre in town. As she walked along the pavement she received some admiring glances and a few toots of horns from passing vehicles.

Ava was never fazed by the opposite sex. She was confident in their company and was a very determined young lady.

She saw Tiffany waiting there for her. "Hi, been waiting long?" she asked her friend.

"Just got here. Well, how did it go?"

Ava laughed. "Let's do some shopping first and we can sit down and have a bite to eat and I will tell you all about it," she smiled at her friend.

"Can't we have lunch first? I am dying to know," her friend asked, with pleading eyes.

"It's only just gone twelve," she said, "I'm not really that hungry yet and want to look in a few shops. I may need a special outfit."

"A special outfit for what?" Tiffany asked, needing to find out exactly what happened.

"Oh come on then, we can go for a coffee first and I will tell you."

Tiffany punched the air. "Great idea," she said, and linked her arm through Ava's.

Ava and Tiffany were best friends. They had started in the call centre on the same day and had been inseparable ever since. They went out together and were both single and enjoyed winding up the men that tried to chat them up.

Tiffany was only five foot two and had short brown hair with dark brown eyes. Although she was a size twelve she was extremely voluptuous and men were very attracted to her very large breasts. She wore clothes that accentuated her curves and showed off her figure to perfection.

They found a table at the far end of the coffee shop and ordered two skinny lattes. "Well, come on then, how was it, did you go back to his?"

Ava laughed out loud. "Actually, Tiff, Rob didn't show up. He blew me out, can you believe that!"

"No way," said Tiff. "He has been after a date with you for ages, what the fuck happened?"

"I don't know, he never even bothered to call. I felt like a right twat sitting in Lloyds."

"Lloyds, you were meeting him in that dive?" Tiff said, with shock on her face.

"Yeah, tell me about it, but am I glad I did." She gave Tiffany a slow smile, waiting for her to reply.

"Why are you glad you did, what happened?" Tiffany looked confused.

"Well," said Ava, "I met this other bloke, Frank. Tiff, he was absolutely gorgeous, he must be six foot seven!"

"Blimey," said Tiff, "that's a giant!"

"I know, but oh my God, he had the best body and his face was amazing. He had these grey eyes and the longest darkest lashes I have ever seen on a man. He was absolutely gorgeous!"

"Are you seeing him again?" Tiffany asked eagerly.

"Well, he took my number and I hope he calls." Ava hoped he would as she had decided to accept.

"I am sure he will, Ava, you are stunning, how could he resist?" Tiffany said, meaning every word. She thought Ava was so beautiful and was envious of her long blonde hair and her five foot six slim frame. Tiffany had always wanted to be tall, which was why she was constantly wearing heels; she hated how short she was.

She saw Ava looking a little concerned. "What's the problem? Your face looks a little worried."

"Well, there was this girl in the bar. Her name was Darcy. She said that Frank was her boyfriend." Ava waited for her friend to reply.

"Oh, was she?" Tiffany asked, worried that Frank was already starting to sound like a rat.

"Frank told her to stop calling him that, that he wasn't anyone's boyfriend."

"There you go then," said Tiffany, smiling at her friend. "He should know, surely."

They both fell about laughing. "She was probably stalking him if he is as good-looking as you say," said Tiffany, unable to believe that Rob had stood her friend up.

With that Ava's phone rang. "Shit, it's Frank," she said to Tiff, holding her phone in her hand like it was a bomb.

"Well, answer it," she said, pushing the phone towards Ava.

"Hello," said Ava in her sweetest voice.

"Hi Ava, it's Frank."

"Oh, hi," she said, shaking.

"It was lovely meeting you last night and I wondered if you fancied coming out for a drink with me later?" Frank had decided that Ava was too beautiful to play the long game with. He wanted to take her out and hopefully see more of her without her clothes on, preferably before the night was over.

"I would love to go out for a drink with you," she said, looking at Tiff, who was smiling.

"Great," he said. "Shall I pick you up?"

Ava didn't want to be picked up; she didn't want her mum and dad asking too many questions.

"I could meet you in town somewhere," she said, hoping that he would be okay with that.

"Do you know Partners on West Street?" he asked, glad that he didn't have to pick her up. He wasn't sure where she lived but it meant getting the cab to go to her house first, which would cost more.

"I love it in there," she said, happy that he didn't ask her to meet him at Lloyds. She hadn't been at all happy in there and also didn't want to bump into that Darcy.

"I'll meet you in there at eight p.m. if you are okay with that?"

"I look forward to it," she said, beaming down the phone and finding it hard to contain her excitement.

They both said goodbye and she sat there holding the phone and just staring at it.

"Well," said Tiff, "are you going on a date?"

Ava looked at her friend. "I so am, and it's tonight, so I need to find something great to wear," she said, finishing the last of her latte.

The girls picked up their bags and went towards the shops, chatting about Frank and the evening ahead.

Chapter 31

The cab driver pulled up outside Martha's house. "Do you want to come in?" she asked Toby, who was in the taxi with her.

They had left the bar, having ordered another couple of rounds, and both were feeling slightly drunk.

"I would love to," Toby said, looking at her intently.

He paid the driver and walked behind her as she put her key in the lock. Martha was feeling extremely nervous, as she didn't expect Toby to say yes. She knew her house was tidy, as she always left it like that. She couldn't go out with a single thing out of place; it would play on her mind for the whole evening if she ever did.

She opened the door and he walked in behind, her shutting it. He pulled her towards him. "You are gorgeous, Martha," he said, making her blush.

He put his arms over her shoulders and kissed her, very gently at first then forcing her lips apart and putting his tongue into her mouth. She responded, kissing him back and moving her body closer into him as their passion increased.

She had not enjoyed a kiss so much in a long time and she could feel her stomach contract as his kisses became more demanding.

She sighed, feeling her nipples harden as his hands cupped her breasts outside her jumper, which had fallen further down her shoulder.

"You look absolutely stunning," Toby said, taking a step back to look her up and down. "Women are mostly in black so it makes a nice change to see a light colour," he said, his eyes still on her.

Martha was thrilled he thought she looked good. When she saw Katie in her short skirt she felt very dowdy in her trousers but now he made her feel amazing and she was glad she had chosen to wear something that wasn't black.

"Thought you might prefer a woman in a short skirt?" she asked, touching his face.

"I don't like the tarty look," he said honestly, and smiled.

"Do you want a coffee?" she asked, still feeling aroused from his touch.

"Have you anything a little stronger?" he asked, still not able to take his eyes from her face.

Toby was very attracted to Martha. She made him laugh and didn't seem to be as high maintenance as other girls he had dated. He loved that she was into scary movies and he was very taken with her. He would tell Steve as soon as possible about Katie and about him and Martha; it was just finding the right time.

She led him through to the lounge and asked him to put on any tunes he liked while she went and got him a drink.

"Beer or wine?" she shouted from the kitchen.

"I'll stick to the wine," he shouted back, as he found a jazz complication CD to put on the stereo.

Martha returned with a bottle of red that was half full and two glasses.

"I see you like red wine," he said, beckoning her over to the sofa.

She sat down next to him and poured the wine into both glasses. "It's my favourite," she said, looking at him.

"Mine too," he said, taking the glass from her hand and putting it back on the table.

He leant in and started kissing her with force.

She moaned again as his tongue played with the inside of her mouth. She felt her nipples harden and he saw this through her thin jumper.

"Pleased to see me?" He smiled, really wanting to take this further.

"I am very pleased to see you," she said, feeling brave and putting her hands on his crotch. She could feel him swell beneath the black jeans he was wearing. "Looks like you are very pleased to see me too," she said, smiling.

"Martha, you are one very sexy lady." He couldn't help himself. He really liked her and he knew it had only been a short while since he had spent time in her company but she was so beautiful. He had feelings for her already and hoped she felt the same.

"I think you are very sexy too, Toby," she said in almost a whisper.

"Would you like to take this in the bedroom?" he asked, suddenly not caring if it was a little forward.

She got up and reached out for his hand, which he took and followed her into her bedroom.

Martha's bedroom was quite large and, although she had a massive king-size bed that was over on the far wall, there was still room for more furniture.

She had a charcoal grey chaise-longue which sat at the end of her bed with small encrusted artificial diamonds in the button holes. Martha had fallen in love with it as soon as she had seen it in the shop, whilst out with her mother, one afternoon after she had exchanged contracts on the house and decided to buy the house a present.

The room was all different shades of grey and she had chosen mirrored furniture for the whole room. She had mirrored wardrobes that were built in and went right up to the ceiling. The walls were light grey and the curtains were floor to ceiling, giving the room an intimate feel.

"Wow," said Toby when he walked in, "this looks amazing."

Martha was pleased with his reaction. She had loved dressing the room when she had first moved in and knew exactly the look she had wanted. She had been to many show homes and had taken some of their ideas and, putting her own twist on things, she was very pleased with the results. Toby had been the first man she had invited back to her house and definitely the first man she had invited into her bedroom! She was never comfortable letting other men see where she lived but Toby was different. She was starting to have feelings for him already. She had never believed in love at first sight and had always thought this was another name for desperation but she understood now.

He walked over to the bed and looked at her. "You don't have to go through with this if you are not happy," he said, genuinely meaning it. He didn't want to push her into something she wasn't comfortable with; he felt too much for her and was happy to wait. "We can slow things down a bit if you would prefer?"

Toby melted her heart, what an absolute gentleman, she thought. "I am fine with how this is going," she said, and pulled her jumper over her head and unhooked her bra. He looked at her longingly, not quite believing what she had just done. Her breasts were surprisingly large and her nipples were like small pink bullets which he was desperate to suck.

He pulled his polo shirt over his head to reveal his six pack. Martha took a sharp intake of breath; he looked fantastic and she was desperate to feel him.

He unbuttoned his trousers and pulled them down, revealing his Calvin Klein boxers. She loved a man in boxers, she wasn't at all keen on Y-fronts; they didn't have the same look and Martha thought they were just for small boys not grown men.

She stood there watching as he removed his boxers, revealing his manhood. It was just as she had expected, except much larger. It was hard and the head was thick and purple as it jutted towards her.

She could not believe how turned on by this she was and felt her wetness through her trousers. She quickly unbuttoned them and pulled them

158

down, standing in nothing but her cream lacy knickers. She had stepped out of her shoes along with her trousers.

"You look amazing," he said, as he walked towards her, taking one of her pink nipples and putting it in his mouth while softly playing with the other one with his fingers. Martha moaned. Toby was having the desired effect on her and she became moist down below.

He pushed her down gently on the bed and hooked his fingers into her lace panties. They are so sexy," he said, as he pulled them down over her feet. He then spread her legs wide and opened her sex to reveal her throbbing bud that was waiting for him to touch it. He rubbed his finger along her clit and she gasped as he pushed his finger inside of her wetness. She moaned, feeling the thickness of his digit, his thumb rubbing onto her clit sending waves of excitement through her whole body.

She moaned louder as he pulled out of her and straddled her and she looks at him, wondering about using a condom. It's as if he can read her mind and he hesitates. She points towards the mirrored bedside drawer, which he opens and sees she has quite a few condoms in there along with a pink vibrator.

"Dirty girl," he says, smiling, pleased that she is sensible and has what he needs to be able carry this further. Toby always used condoms but wasn't into random sex so never really saw the need to take them out with him.

"I always promote safe sex," she says, smiling at him, and is pleased that he thinks the same.

He ripped the condom from its packet and rolled it onto his erect penis; she watched as he did this so expertly. "You know how to put one of those on," she said in a whisper.

Toby blushes, he really likes her and is glad that he didn't just plunge into her without thinking first.

The condom was on and he spread her legs even wider, thrusting his cock inside her. She let out a scream as his teeth bit her nipple. He slowly pushed himself deeper and then withdrew almost completely, sliding his penis from her deliberately.

She was feeling the effects of the best orgasm she had had in a very long time and wrapped her legs around his back. Toby was able to thrust deeper inside of her and she let out a soft moan as the tension within her mounted rapidly. Her breathing was shallow and her mind thinking of nothing except what she is experiencing at that very moment as she climaxes.

Her action made Toby even harder and he exploded deep inside her, filling the condom.

They both lay there for a while, panting, as he pulled out of her, taking the condom and wrapping it in a tissue from the box on her bedside.

He pulled her up towards him and wrapped his arms tightly around her. "That was so good, Martha," he said as he caressed her left breast. "I am so sorry I came quickly but you were making me so horny." He looked at her. She felt so happy lying in his arms and was happy that they climaxed together.

She rubbed her hand over his chest. "I really enjoyed that too, Toby." She smiled into him.

He moved his hand to her chin and brought her mouth up to his where he kissed her lightly on the lips. "You are so sexy," he said again, as they both lay there, deep in their own thoughts.

They fell asleep and woke up, Toby's arm still holding her close, with the birds tweeting outside Martha's bedroom window with the light streaming in.

He looked down at her and she smiled as he started to kiss her softly and she moaned. "Round two," he said, unable to stop his hands from exploring her body once again.

They stayed in bed for most of the morning, getting to know every inch of each other. Martha was so happy. He really was a great bloke and knew exactly what he was doing between the sheets. She had had multiple orgasms, each taking her to new sensations she had rarely felt with a man.

They got up and had breakfast together when his phone started to ring. He saw that it was his mother calling and he looked apologetically at Martha as he answered.

"Hi Mum, how are you?" he said down the phone, smiling.

"Hi Toby," said his mother. "Is Ava with you?"

"Ava?" said Toby, looking confused. "No, why would she be?"

"Sorry," she said, "only she didn't come home last night and it is very unlike her not to let us know if she is staying out."

Toby looked at Martha and held his hand up. "Mum, I am sure she is okay. She is twenty-two and can look after herself; she isn't a baby anymore."

"I know that!" said his mum, a little harsher than she meant to, "but she never stays out without telling us first."

"I am sure she is just over at Tiff's, you worry too much."

"Yeah, I suppose you are right," his mum said.

Toby could hear the concern in her voice. "Do you want me to call her?" he asked, trying to help.

"I have tried," she said, "but it just goes to voicemail."

Toby didn't think too much of this and advised his mum that he was sure she was staying over at her best friend's house and she would be home soon.

They hung up and Martha looked at him. "Everything okay?" she asked, as she poured them both coffee.

"Oh, just my mum being overprotective about my sister," he said, taking a sip of his coffee.

"That tastes good," he said, as he planted a kiss on Martha's lips. She straight away responded and he laughed.

"You are one bad girl," he said, pulling her onto his lap.

"You are one bloke worth being a bad girl for," she said, putting her arms around his shoulders.

She was feeling very happy at having Toby in her house the morning after. She had had her fair share of boyfriends but never felt this way before. She never invited anyone back to her house and when she had gone back with whoever her boyfriend was at the time had always liked to get back to hers as early as possible. She wasn't someone who wanted to stay in bed all day or hang around with them in their apartments but Toby was making her feel different. She didn't want him to go, ever.

The sex they had had when they had woken up was so gentle and erotic he had made her feel all tingly inside.

"What are your plans today?" she asked, taking a bit of his toast.

"Hey," he said, "that's mine," but smiling and loving that she had stayed on his lap.

He too had really enjoyed her last night and this morning, he thought with a grin. He had not felt this way about anyone since Penelope, and she was a nightmare compared to Martha, he thought.

"I haven't got any plans," he said to her seriously. "What about you?"

"Not really," she said, "although I would like to pop to the hospital to see how my nan is doing."

He thought that was a good idea. He knew about her nan's fall and felt sorry for the old lady. She was a tough cookie and was surprised that she hadn't broken any bones when she had fallen.

"Say if you don't want to," he said sheepishly, "but I know you have your beloved Miss Ellie outside." Martha laughed. "I do," she said, "and yes, I do love her." Toby laughed. "Well, how about you drop me off at mine, go to see your nan at St Mary's and pick me up on the way back? I could get some clothes for work tomorrow and come back with you and we can have a repeat performance of last night and this morning?"

161

Martha blushed but was thrilled with his idea. She didn't want him to go; she was enjoying his company too much.

"That sounds like a great idea, Mr Green," she said, and hugged him.

"I have had a really good time with you, Martha," he said seriously.

She smiled at him and kissed him full on the mouth. "You turn me on, Mr Green, and I don't want you going anywhere," she said, loving the feeling of his arms around her body.

They both showered and Toby got back into his clothes from the night before. Martha put on a pair of jeans and a pink vest top and threw a sweatshirt over her shoulders. "You look lovely," he said, looking her up and down and feeling his groin stir again.

Martha laughed. "It's a pair of old jeans and a vest top," she said, unable to keep the sarcasm from her voice.

"Well, I think you look gorgeous whatever you wear," he said. "I particularly like your birthday suit," he said, laughing.

She swatted him from behind. "Cheeky," she said, but loving their banter.

She drove him home and went on to the hospital to see her nan. She was surprised to see Steve there.

"Hello," she said, "didn't know you were visiting."

"He has come to see his old nan," said Violet, as Martha went round the bed to give her a kiss.

Steve was pleased to see Martha too; it meant he could leave as he didn't want her on her own without any visitors and he wanted to call Katie.

"How was it when I left last night?" he asked. "Did Toby see you home all right?" He noticed Martha looked different; her face was glowing and she had a spring in her step.

Martha blushed. "Yes," she said, "he made sure I got a cab okay." It wasn't a lie, Toby did make sure she got a cab all right; he just came with her and spent the night, but Steve didn't ask that so she didn't volunteer it either. They would speak to Steve together about their relationship. She wasn't really sure where it was going herself, as it was early days, but she hoped it was going all the way to the altar. She was shocked at her thought process but was smiling nonetheless.

"You look happy," Steve said, not quite being able to put his finger on why she looked different.

"Do I?" she said, knowing full well that she was glowing after the sex she had had with Toby only a couple of hours before.

"She always looks lovely," said her nan, smiling at her.

"How are you doing, Nan?" said Martha, trying to stop Steve asking any other questions about last night.

"Bit fed up to be honest," her nan said, "looking forward to getting back to my own home." She gave out a sigh. "Hospitals are okay for sick people," she shouted, "but for those of us that are not sick they are awful noisy places and I haven't had a wink of sleep!" She was hoping that one of the nurses would hear her as she didn't want to spend another night there.

"They are only making sure everything is okay, Nan," said Steve, feeling sorry for her. "You had a nasty fall and banged your head; they are just doing their job."

"Steve is right, Nan," said Martha. "Only one more night. The doctor said you could come home tomorrow, so not long now."

Their nan looked at them both. "You are lovely kids," she said. "We are all very proud of you both."

Steve and Martha both went to hug her. She was an amazing lady and they both had a very close relationship with her.

"Right, now you are here, Martha, I am off," said Steve. "You don't mind, do you, Nan?"

She didn't mind at all. She was grateful he had visited her and had been there for over an hour.

"Where are you off to?" said Martha, making conversation.

"I'm going to give Katie a call, see if she is free tonight for a drink," he said, smiling at his sister. "The last time I saw her I had to leave due to Nan having her fall, so I thought I would take her out for a nice intimate dinner," he said, looking at them both.

"Sorry love," his nan said, feeling guilty. "I didn't mean to scupper your plans."

"It's no problem, Nan, honest. Katie was fine about it, but I think I need to make it up to her." His groin stirred at the thought of Katie and he smiled. Steve didn't think Katie had been fine about it at all, which was why he wanted to take her out.

She didn't want Steve taking Katie out, especially for an intimate dinner, as she knew full well what that would lead to, but she couldn't think of anything to say. She would speak to Toby. He needed to speak to Steve as soon as possible, not just about Katie but about them as well; she smiled at the thought of Toby.

Chapter 32

Katie knew there was no point in even trying to get Lexi back on side. She would take a few days to calm down and then they could have a proper talk, hug it out and everything would go back to normal.

She was pissed off that Steve hadn't bothered to call and decided that she wasn't going to sit in her bedroom for the rest of the night.

She wouldn't be able to go into the lounge, as Lexi would probably be there, and the atmosphere wouldn't be a good one. No, she was better of going out, she thought.

She dressed to impress in a short pink leather skirt that had cost an arm and a leg in a little boutique she knew that did one off pieces. Katie didn't like to have the same clothes as everyone else as it could be embarrassing if you walked into a bar and someone was in the same stuff, although it would always look better on her, so she was doing people a favour. They should probably pay towards it then, she thought, laughing.

She put on a black lace plunge bra that really showed off her cleavage to perfection and a tight black shirt that hugged her figure. She unbuttoned the shirt quite a way down so her bra and breasts could be seen by whoever was looking. She put on very high black patent heels and looked at herself in the mirror. She had bronzed her legs earlier and thought they looked very shapely in the short skirt and high heels. She kissed the mirror. "Sexy girl," she said out loud, looking at her reflection. Someone is going to be a very lucky boy tonight. Steve's loss, she thought, annoyed.

Why the fuck had he not bothered to call? His nan must be okay now, surely? Her fingers hovered over his number on her phone but she decided against it.

No, if he can't be bothered to call then I will certainly not go chasing him, she thought, although secretly she wished he would. She didn't know why she couldn't shake him from her thoughts but she really did want him to take her out again. Not before she had given him a hard time about dumping her for his nan though!

She called a cab to pick her up and decided she would go to Horatio's. She had had a great time when she was last there and was hoping she might bump into Mario again. She may even knock on his door if he wasn't working and surprise him. Her nipples went rock hard at the memory of the sex she had had with the good-looking barman and he knew exactly what to do to get her to orgasm, so a repeat performance wouldn't go amiss. She was moist down below as she remembered his large cock delving deep inside her and wiggled the tops of her legs.

She heard the buzzer go and shouted out to Lexi, "I'm going out, Lex, hope you are okay and we can speak tomorrow when you have calmed down." The door slammed.

"When I have calmed down!" shouted Lexi back, but Katie was already running down the stairs past Wilbur.

The cab pulled up at Horatio's and Katie got out, showing her knickers as she did. A couple of guys that were walking past stopped and stared at the blonde beauty showing what she had.

"Very nice, darling,'" one of them shouted at her. She paid the driver and turned round. "Thanks," she said, enjoying the compliment, and walked into the bar.

It was very busy but she made her way to the bar area and immediately saw Mario. She went up to him and he looked pleased to see her; she smiled.

"Hello," she said, "what's a girl got to do to get a drink round here?" Mario laughed. "Well, if you come back up to my room I'll show you," he said, feeling aroused.

She looked absolutely gorgeous and he could see her large breasts pushed up by her bra. She was a bad girl, he thought, a very sexy bad girl.

He went and got her a glass of wine and put it down on the bar beside her. She leaned over the bar and whispered in his ear. "What time do you get off?" she asked him. "In about five minutes," he said, and she squealed with delight, pleased that she had decided to go out.

Mario asked her to wait there and went to speak to one of the other barmen.

He sidled round to her side of the bar and put his arms around her and pulled her close. She could smell his aftershave. She loved a man's smell; it made her very horny.

"Do you want to stay down here for a drink or go straight up?" he asked her, hoping she would opt for the latter.

Katie looked at him. "I'd love to go straight up," she said, in a slow sexy voice.

Mario took her by the hand. Fuck she was sexy, he thought, and ran up the stairs two at a time, dragging her with him.

They fell through his door and he couldn't wait to take her. He put his hand up her skirt and pulled down her knickers. Katie squealed. "Steady on, tiger," she said, but loving that he wanted to take her there and then.

He pushed her over towards the bed and told her to bend over. She did as she was asked and he pulled her skirt up over her buttocks, taking in the gorgeous sight of her pert arse.

"You look fucking amazing," he said, as he unzipped his trousers.

She wiggled her ass in front of him, feeling the air on her intimate parts. "Hopefully I will feel fucking amazing in a minute," she laughed, as she waited for him to enter her.

He didn't straight away. He started caressing her cheeks and was teasing her with his fingers, pushing them in and out of her pussy, feeling how moist she was. She loved the feeling and moaned in appreciation of what he was doing to her from behind and opened her legs wider.

His trousers were down at his feet and he stepped out of them, again wearing nothing underneath, and pulled his T-shirt over his head. Katie smiled as she felt him rub his hands all over her arse.

"You have a way with your hands," she moaned, not wanting him to stop touching her. Her nipples were rock hard from the anticipation of what he was about to do to her and her breasts swelled, trying to get out of the confines of her bra and tight shirt. She spread her legs wider as he found her clit and rubbed his thumb up and down. She could feel his large cock on her cheeks and moved her arse further into the air. Mario was so turned on by this that he thrust his cock straight into her tight wet pussy and she screamed as she felt him go deep inside of her.

He is fucking amazing, she thought, as he was ramming in and out of her, pushing her forward and bringing her back so she was practically ramming herself onto his cock. "That feels so good," she told him. "Keep doing it, keep it going, I love that feeling!"

She ripped her shirt open and pulled her bra straps down so she could get her breasts out of their confinement. She reached for her nipples and started to pull at them hard, squeezing so it was painful, as he was in and out of her with such force that she exploded with him and cried out.

"That was fucking amazing," she shouted, still pulling at her nipples. Mario was grunting very loud as he shot his full load inside of her.

They stayed in that position for a while, both panting as her hands steadied herself on the bed. He was holding her round the waist so she wouldn't fall in a heap and slowly pulled back as she moaned once again as his cock left her wet pussy.

They both flopped down on the bed, still panting, still trying to catch their breath from their joint orgasm.

Katie wriggled out of her shirt and undid her bra and was then fully naked lying beside him.

He reached over and started to caress her breasts with his strong hands. "Your tits are fantastic," he said, and leant down to suck on one of her nipples that were still rock hard from her orgasm.

"Bite me," she said, grinding her teeth. He bit her nipple and she cried out. "I love that," she told him as he bit harder.

She reached down to find his cock. It was flaccid but it immediately went hard at her touch. Mario moaned.

"You really are a very bad girl," he said, giving her his sexiest smile, "and I love it."

Katie giggled as she took his full erection in her mouth and began to suck him hard.

They had sex another three times before they were both spent and fell asleep in each other's arms.

Katie woke up to the sound of running water. She didn't know where she was and had to take in her surroundings before she remembered. "Mario's," she said out loud and reached her hand out to an empty space.

She sat up and could hear him in the shower.

She looked at the clock and saw it was only eight a.m., why was he up so early on a Sunday, she thought?

Mario came out of the shower, his hair and body dripping with water. He hadn't bothered to dry himself and she thought he looked very sexy.

She pulled open the duvet to reveal her naked body and opened her legs wide.

"Come get me," she said, licking her lips.

"Baby, I would love to come get you but I need to be at work," he said, with a sad face.

Katie sat up. "Work, on a Sunday?" she cried, looking forlorn.

"Yep, I need to clean up from last night and get the bar ready for lunch time," he said, roaming his eyes over her body.

"Can't you just come here just for a minute?" she said, in her sweet voice.

"I wouldn't get up again and you know it," he said, laughing.

167

She started to play with her nipple and reached down and put her finger in her pussy. "I'll just have to service myself then," she said, opening her legs wider.

Mario groaned. "Babe, stop," he said, as he was becoming aroused at what she was doing.

Katie always got her own way and that wasn't about to change now; she started to moan as her fingers started working her body.

Mario couldn't resist and he jumped on the bed and started kissing her with force.

She smiled. "Putty in my hands," she said, as she started to caress his wet body.

Chapter 33

Lexi woke up and felt a little better than she had done the last couple of days. She was still angry at Katie and would be for a long time to come. Her headache had gone and her body felt a lot better too.

She hadn't heard Katie come back last night so presumed she had stayed out, probably with Frank, she thought with disgust.

She jumped out of bed and thought about the day ahead. First thing I need to do is phone Jo. She found her mobile and found her number.

"Hey chick, how are you?" said Jo, in a friendly voice.

"Hi Jo, I'm okay. Things have come to a head here and I was wondering if the offer of me moving in was still on the table?"

"You bet it is, Lexi, you're finally doing it. How come?" said Jo, pleased with what her work mate was saying but concerned all the same.

"I am Jo, things have happened that you would not believe, but let me get myself sorted and I will come over later on this afternoon with as much stuff as I can carry and tell you all about it."

"I could drive over in my flatmate's car if you want? She didn't need it to go travelling with so I bought it off her. She sold it to me really cheap as she needed the money."

"That would be great, if you don't mind Jo, thanks." Lexi was thrilled with her offer and she could get a lot more stuff out of the apartment than she first thought, which would save her having to keep coming back.

"I have already made arrangements to go out tonight for a drink with a few friends, but you are welcome to come," said Jo, feeling bad at leaving Lexi on her own in the apartment on her first night.

"Oh, sorry, have I messed up your plans?" Lexi said, feeling guilty. "I could move in next weekend if it's a problem," she said, not really wanting to breathe the same air as Katie for another week.

"No, no, it's fine," said Jo. "It was only a spur of the moment thing. I can go and meet them another time."

"Really?" said Lexi, grateful for having met Jo. She was such a kind soul and they had hit it off from the first day Jo had joined Prospect Law.

Lexi had already been at the firm for a couple of years, and although she had made a lot of friends there, it was she and Jo who had bonded the most.

They agreed that Jo would give her a few hours to sort herself out and pack, and she would be round with the car at two p.m. Lexi thanked her again.

She pulled a couple of suitcases out from under her bed and started to go through her wardrobe. There seemed to be things missing, she thought, wondering where her new suede jacket was.

I am sure I had it in here, I haven't even worn it so it should still be in the suit carrier, she thought.

"Katie!" she said out loud, and went storming into her bedroom. Katie wasn't there, which she was thankful for, but her room was a complete mess, with underwear and towels everywhere, bottles of moisturiser with lids off and tissues all over her dressing table. She stepped over some of the mess and opened her wardrobe.

There amongst Katie's clothes was her suede jacket. She also spotted a few other items that belonged to her. "My leather coat," she said. "Oh my God, that's my waistcoat," she screamed, and wondered what else Katie had of hers.

She looked at the bottom of the wardrobe and saw her red wedges, her blue Manolo Blahnik shoes. "What the fuck?" Lexi let out a loud scream. "That fucking bitch has most of my wardrobe in hers!" Lexi was fuming. "How fucking dare she!"

She grabbed all the clothes and shoes that were hers and took them back to her room as she started to pack. There was no way on earth that she would be changing her mind, she thought, as she pulled clothes from her wardrobe and opened all her drawers.

This was the very last straw, and she hoped Katie caught a sexually transmitted disease from all the men she had been shagging of late; would serve her right, she thought.

She had three suitcases waiting at the door and five large boxes and two smaller ones that housed her make-up, books, lotions and potions and other things that she had collected over the years.

The rest of the stuff can stay here until I know what to do with it, she thought.

They had bought a lot of household things together when she and Katie had first moved in, but Lexi wasn't bothered about those. She knew Katie never had any money and she probably wouldn't get a penny out of her even if she did.

She went into the kitchen and switched on the kettle. Jo would be here in half an hour and she wanted to go round the place to make sure she hadn't left anything she thought she might need.

She heard Katie's key in the door. "Shit," she said out loud to herself.

Katie came through the door and saw the suitcases and boxes lined up in the hallway.

"Lexi," she called out. "Lexi, what are these all doing in the hallway?" Katie was confused and walked into the kitchen, where she saw Lexi sitting at the breakfast bar drinking coffee.

"Hi," she said, frowning. "What are all the suitcases and boxes doing in the hallway; is someone moving in?"

Lexi couldn't believe that Katie could be so stupid. "No Katie, no one is moving in. I'm moving out!" she shouted at her flatmate.

"What?" said Katie. "Why?"

"Why!" shouted Lexi. "Why, do you really need to ask that!" she said sarcastically.

"For fuck's sake, Lexi, I said I was sorry. There is no need to take it this far and move out." Katie couldn't believe it. "How the fuck am I going to afford the rent on my own?"

"...and there it is," said Lexi, "back to Katie!"

"What do you mean, back to Katie?" she said, looking even more confused.

Lexi couldn't deal with this. She looked at her flatmate in her short skirt and tight shirt that was showing most of her bra. She was disgusted with her and couldn't believe it had taken her this long to realise what a mean selfish person she was, not to mention deceitful and shady!

She walked towards the hallway and decided to start taking her cases down to the main hallway ready for when Jo arrived. She couldn't stand being in the same room as Katie; she really had had enough of her!

Katie followed her. "Where are you moving to?" she asked, her voice a little softer. She couldn't let Lexi leave, she had to stop her going. How the fuck was she going to afford the rent on her own?

"Lex, please," she said, in a whiney voice. "Let's sit down and talk about this. I really am sorry. I didn't realise Frank meant so much to you. I promise it will never happen again." Tears started to prick her eyes and Lexi noticed.

"Oh, for fuck's sake, Katie, not the waterworks, it really won't wash with me. I am going and that's it and if you think that this is because I am upset about Frank then you do not know me at all!" she shouted at her flatmate, beginning to feel her headache come back.

171

"Well, if you are not upset about Frank, what are you upset about?" Katie was even more confused as she really didn't have a clue as to what Lexi's problem was.

Lexi opened the door and carried a large box out. She started to go down the stairs when Katie came to the top of them.

"Lexi, please, come back and speak to me, let's sort this out!" she said again, getting a little angry and wiping away her tears. Wilbur looked up looking a little scared, due to the shouting.

Lexi ignored her and continued down the stairs, being careful not to step on Wilbur and fall down them.

She put the box down and heard a toot outside. She opened the door of the building and saw Jo in a cream Mini in the road right outside the main door.

Lexi waved as Jo got out of the car. "Hi Jo, thank you so much for doing this, you are a star."

"No problem," said Jo, and picked up the box that was on the floor next to Lexi.

"This one to go?" she said, starting to walk towards the car.

"There are a few more, too," she said, looking sheepishly at her friend.

"It's quite a large apartment," said Jo, "so bring whatever you want, it's no problem."

Lexi looked at her gratefully. She had never been to Jo's apartment but had heard a lot about it.

Lexi and Jo started to walk up the stairs to get the rest of Lexi's possessions, and saw Katie standing on the second flight.

"Who is this?" asked Katie, looking at the attractive older woman.

Jo was in her early thirties and was a very striking brunette with a feisty personality, who didn't suffer fools gladly. She had a slim figure and large breasts from a boob job she had had done a few years ago. Her breasts had never kicked in like the other girls' and she had remained flat-chested, something that she hated. She always wanted to have the operation. It was on the very top of her bucket list and finally for her thirtieth birthday she decided to treat herself. She loved her new look and it gave her the figure she had always desired. Her boyfriend loved them too.

"I'm Jo," she said, "and you must be the famous Katie."

"Famous?" said Katie. "I'm not famous," she said, looking at Jo oddly.

"It's a figure of speech, love," said Jo, and carried on up the stairs, pushing past the not so famous Katie.

"No need to be so rude!" shouted Katie up the stairs to Jo's back.

172

"I was not being rude," Jo said, turning round to stare at Katie. "If I was rude you would know about it."

Katie was shocked at this venomous woman; who the fuck is she!

They all went back up to the apartment and Jo and Lexi started to take the boxes and suitcases down one by one. Katie retreated to the kitchen, feeling a little intimidated by Jo, and thought she would put the kettle on to try and appeal to Jo's better nature.

Katie was upset and angry at the same time. Lexi was being totally childish, she thought, as she put the tea bags in the cups.

Lexi wasn't happy that Katie was around and started to feel sorry for her. Jo noticed a tear roll down Lexi's face.

"Hey chick, no need to cry, you are doing the right thing. She will never change," and put her arm around Lexi to comfort her.

Lexi nodded and looked at the boxes. "We are not going to fit everything in, are we?" she said, still looking sad.

"We can do a couple more trips. We'll leave the stuff in the lobby and come straight back after we have unloaded at the other end," she said, feeling sorry for her friend. She knew that she was doing the right thing. Lexi had a big heart and didn't like to upset anyone but Katie had brought this on herself and it served her right that Lexi had finally seen her for what she was and moved out.

They left a suitcase and a couple of the larger boxes and squeezed the rest in on the back seat and in the boot.

They arrived at Jo's apartment and Lexi thought how nice it was. Jo was right; it was huge.

The apartment was on the second floor of a big Victorian mansion. It was a red stone brick building and looked very pretty from the outside and had large sash windows. Lexi loved it.

She loved it even more when she had walked into the apartment.

There were quarry tiles in the hallway and a Victorian arch that led through to a large spacious lounge with comfy sofas and a fireplace as a focal point. The kitchen was enormous and had flagstone tiles, an Aga and even a butler's sink. The cupboards were sage green with an oak dresser that housed wine glasses and plates; the island in the middle that was made of solid beech wood gave it a cosy country feel.

All the walls were in a soft cream and it had very high ceilings with a ceiling rose and cornices in every room

Jo showed Lexi into her room. "It's beautiful," said Lexi, as she saw the large white Victorian bed frame with real brass detailing and finials that had a thick mattress and a patchwork blanket over a white duvet with tiny daisies all over it.

"How did you find this?" asked Lexi, looking all around her.

"One of my sister's best friends is an estate agent. She knew I was looking and came up with this." Jo was very proud of her apartment and had enjoyed making it her home.

"It's beautiful, Jo, thank you for letting me come and stay," and she started to sob.

Jo quickly ran over to her and gave her a hug. "Come on, Lex," she said, "that girl does not deserve you and you have done the right thing."

Lexi looked up at Jo. "I feel so awful though, she won't be able to live in the apartment on her own. She can't afford to." There were tears streaming down her face.

Jo reached for a tissue that was in a box on the bedside table and handed it to Lexi. "She should have thought of that before she started being so selfish. She has no one to blame but herself," she said in a soft voice.

She knew it must have been hard for Lexi to make the decision to move out but she had definitely done the right thing and Jo was very pleased she had. That girl was not a friend and Lexi was better off without her, she thought.

Jo helped Lexi bring the suitcases and boxes in and they left to do another trip. When they had reached the apartment they didn't bother going up. They just put the rest of Lexi's belongings in the Mini and drove away.

Katie had seen the Mini pull up and expected Lexi to come up and say goodbye, but she didn't and Katie sobbed for hours afterwards.

She didn't hear her mobile ring as she was too busy wallowing in her own self-pity.

Chapter 34

Steve got out his phone as soon as he had left the hospital. He thought his nan looked a lot better than she had on Friday and was pleased Martha had arrived, as he didn't want to leave her on her own.

He dialled Katie's number but it just rang and rang. It then went to voice mail and he didn't want to leave a message. I'll call her again a bit later, he thought, feeling disappointed.

He decided to go home and get changed and go and have a workout at the gym. He had been feeling a little sluggish lately and he hadn't been in a few weeks, and he always felt better after.

He got back to his apartment and Ralph was straight round his legs. "You want feeding," he said to Ralph, knowing that his cat would never turn down a meal.

He got his gym clothes and sorted Ralph out and tried Katie again. The same happened but he still didn't want to leave a message; he hated doing that and wanted to speak to her in person.

He did an hour's workout and did feel much better after. He got out his mobile to call Katie; third time lucky, he thought.

She answered on the third ring and sounded like she was crying.

"Hi Katie. It's Steve, are you okay?"

"No, I am fucking not okay!" she screamed down the phone.

"What's happened?" he asked, concerned.

"My flatmate has moved out and left me with paying all the rent, which I cannot afford on my own!"

"Oh," said Steve, "what a bummer." He didn't know what else to say.

Katie lowered her voice. "So why have you called?" she asked, a lot less irate.

"I wanted to take you out, you know, to make up for the other night, but you don't sound like you are in the mood."

Katie was always in the mood. "I'm okay and I would love to be taken out, just what I need," she said, smiling.

"Okay," said Steve. "I was thinking of tonight?"

"That would be fantastic, Steve," she said, beaming down the phone. "Where are you taking me?"

"I am happy to take you to dinner, unless you just want to go for drinks?" He thought he would leave it up to her.

"Drinks would be good. I'm not feeling that hungry, not for food anyway," she said, smiling down the phone at him.

Steve coughed. "Okay," he said. "Shall I pick you up about 7.30 p.m.?" He had heard what she had said and his groin stirred.

"Perfect," said Katie. "I'll be ready."

They hung up, looking forward to the evening ahead.

Steve punched the air. "Third time lucky," he shouted out, and another guy who was in the changing room with him looked over and smiled, knowing exactly what he meant.

Steve quickly finished getting changed and went home to get ready for his hot date with the gorgeous Katie later.

He had decided to take her to The Feathers. It was his local and he knew the bar staff in there and felt very comfortable. He had taken her to two quite expensive places and thought he would be himself and make sure that the evening wasn't interrupted. They could have a couple of drinks and then who knows, her place or mine, he thought with a smile.

He dressed in black skinny jeans, a pink Ralph Lauren polo shirt and some Vans. He also had his black leather jacket, as it was quite cold in the evenings.

He ordered the cab and it arrived ten minutes later. He gave the driver Katie's address and they set off.

"Busy place," said the driver, looking at Steve.

Steve didn't understand what he meant and didn't reply. He was looking forward to the evening ahead, determined to enjoy all of Katie tonight. He was buzzing at the thought.

His phone rang and he could see it was Toby. He declined the call. He can wait, he said to himself, I'm busy.

The cab arrived at Katie's apartment and he got the driver to toot his horn.

The door opened a couple of minutes later and Katie ran down the stairs. She was wearing a pair of very tight denim jeans with a lime green vest top that showed some of her toned stomach and brought out the emerald green in her eyes. She had a white fluffy jacket over her shoulder and cream high heels. As she got in the taxi he could see that her nipples were hard through the material of the top.

His cock stirred as he smiled appreciatively at her. "You look absolutely gorgeous," he said, unable to keep his eyes off her body.

Katie smiled and leant over to kiss him on the cheek. "Thank you," she said, beaming at him.

She had put on more make-up than usual as her eyes were red and puffy from crying earlier, but she was such an expert with her brushes and concealer that no one would have even noticed.

"Where are we going?" she asked, putting her hand on his thigh and starting rubbing her hand up and down, getting closer to his groin area.

Steve was completely caught off guard and got an immediate hard on in the taxi.

Katie licked her lips. "So," she said again, "where are we going?"

Steve looked at her, wishing they weren't going anywhere but to bed. "I thought I would take you to my local bar, The Feathers. Do you know it?"

"I have been in there a few times, it's quite nice." She was happy with going there as they could just have a couple of drinks and go back to his; she wanted to see where he lived. She had made a mental note that she couldn't stay over the whole night as she needed to be in work early. She had phoned in sick on Friday and didn't want to piss them off any more than she had to.

The taxi pulled up and they both got out. Steve put his hand on her arse as she got out of the cab and Katie smiled. So this is how things are going, she thought, and felt the sexual tension between them.

The Feathers was quiet, which Steve was pleased about. He didn't want to have to fight to get a drink and he had already decided they were only going to have a couple. I need to get this very sexy lady back to my apartment tonight with no interruptions, he thought, and hoped Katie was on the same page.

They had both had a good night on Friday and he had thought about nothing else but her gorgeous body and those amazing breasts with the large nipples. He stirred again, fuck, he thought!

Katie decided to have a mojito as she had had enough of drinking wine and champagne and needed something to refresh her palate. Steve ordered himself a beer and they found a table over in the corner to sit down at.

She took a sip of her drink. It was stronger than she had expected but thought it tasted nice. She found the mojito moreish and had finished her drink before Steve. "Another?" he asked, pointing to her drink.

"Yes, please," she said, looking at him intently. She was really looking forward to seeing him in the flesh, as they had not managed to get that far previously. She thought of Mario and his toned, well-endowed body, and hoped Steve was just as athletic.

He came back with the drinks and she drank this one just as quickly. "Blimey," said Steve, "you're a thirsty lady. Do you want another?" Katie didn't know why she was drinking so quickly; maybe it was to do with all the upset from earlier. She was going to call Lexi in a few days when she had calmed down and hopefully get her to move back in, but for now her thoughts were with the gorgeous man to her right.

"Yes please, if that's okay?" she said, putting her hand back on his thigh.

Steve didn't want to move but he didn't want her to not have a drink either. He went back up to the bar and ordered another mojito and a vodka and coke for him. I think I need to keep up with her, he thought.

He came back with the drinks. "So why did your flatmate move out?" he asked, taking a sip of his vodka and coke. Katie took a large mouthful of the mojito. The alcohol was starting to go to her head and she felt quite drunk.

"We had an argument and she decided she wanted to leave," Katie said, not giving too much away.

"What was the argument about?" asked Steve, not really bothered but trying to make conversation so he could concentrate on that rather than where her hand was heading.

"Just something and nothing," Katie said, looking at him intently.

She didn't want to talk about Lexi. She had more important things on her mind and wanted to get down and very dirty with Steve. She had had great sex over the last few days, with men who knew what they were doing, and they had made such a lasting impression on her body that she was still feeling very aroused.

"Shall we go?" asked Steve, licking his lips and looking at her nipples that were like bullets protruding through her top.

"I'd like that," said Katie in a low voice.

"I'll order us a cab and we can go back to mine, if you're happy with that?" he said, putting his arm around her chair and moving in closer.

"I am very happy with that," she said, smiling and looking down to his groin area.

She could see that he was hard and that he wanted her. She loved the lead up to sex, it gave her an adrenalin rush.

They walked outside of The Feathers to wait for their cab and the cold air hit Katie. She wobbled and Steve took her arm to steady her.

"You okay?" he asked. "I think you drank those mojitos a little too quickly," he said, as his arm brushed against her nipple.

Katie laughed. "I'm fine, just a shock coming out into the cold," she said, trying to steady herself. She felt really drunk and her vision was a little blurred.

The cab pulled up. They both got in and she put her head on his shoulder, still feeling dizzy.

The cab arrived at his apartment a short while later. As Katie got out she still felt a bit wobbly but was very happy to be going back to his gorgeous apartment. She could see herself living there.

He paid the taxi driver and held onto her as they went into the main doors of the building.

He had his hand round her waist as they went slowly up the stairs. She was still feeling a little dizzy but was trying to ignore it and hoped she would feel better once she was able to sit down.

They walked into his lounge and she went straight over to one of the sofas and practically fell down on it. Her head started to pound and she didn't feel great at all.

Steve looked at her. "Are you feeling okay? Would you like me to take you home?" he said, hoping she would say no.

"I'm fine," she said, not convincing him.

"Can I get you some water?" he asked, thinking that she was starting to look a little pale.

Katie ran from the sofa into the bathroom where she immediately threw up. She felt absolutely awful and her head was throbbing.

He came into the bathroom where she was sitting on the floor with her head over the toilet bowl. "You are definitely not okay, Katie," he said with concern. He knew she could take her alcohol, as she had drunk so much at Papa's and was perfectly fine. She had only had three mojitos.

"I'll be fine," she said, looking up at him a little embarrassed. "I am so sorry, could you get me some water, please?"

He walked back into the kitchen, got her a bottle of water from the fridge and went back into the bathroom to give it to her. She was being sick again and he put the water down by the side of her and shut the door. He wouldn't want anyone watching him being sick and he didn't think she would either.

It was some time before Katie came out of the bathroom. She still felt a little wobbly and her head was pounding.

"Do you have any headache pills?" she asked, as she walked back into the kitchen where he was sitting.

He went to the drawer and pulled some out. "I think I should call you a cab," he said, worrying about how she was feeling but also a little pissed off that the night hadn't again gone as planned.

She swallowed the pills and drank the whole bottle of water. She really needed to lie down.

"Would you mind if I went and lay down on the sofa?" she asked him.

"Why don't you go and lie down on my bed? I am sure you would feel a lot more comfortable."

She smiled at him and was grateful that he was attempting to look after her. She didn't know why she was feeling so rough; maybe because she hadn't eaten and had drunk the mojitos very quickly. What with all the upset with Lexi no wonder she wasn't at her best. Katie was never sick. She had always managed to handle her drink, irrespective of the amount, and very rarely suffered from hangovers. She had to go to work tomorrow regardless, she thought.

Steve showed her to the bedroom and shut the curtains. He put a light on by the bedside and pulled back the duvet.

"Thanks," she said, as she started to undress. He watched her step out of her heels and slowly peel her jeans down. She had a cream lace thong that just about covered her sex. He felt his cock stir as he watched her. God, she was beautiful, he thought, as she pulled her top over her ample breasts. She wasn't wearing a bra and he immediately became hard at the sight of her large nipples.

Why the fuck did she have to be sick, he thought, as he watched her get into bed completely naked.

She watched him watching her and felt slightly aroused herself. If she hadn't felt so bad she would have put on a very sexy show for him, but her head was thumping and she needed to close her eyes. Maybe once the pills had kicked in she would feel a lot better and they could really enjoy each other's bodies.

As soon as she closed her eyes she fell asleep, exhausted from the last couple of days. She had hardly had any sleep and it was all starting to catch up with her.

Steve just stood there watching her sleep, listening to her heavy breathing. There was no way that they would be having sex tonight, he thought; not when she was feeling so rough. He walked out of the bedroom and shut the door behind him. He would leave her to sleep. He could always go into his spare room. He needed to get his head down himself, as he had an early presentation to deliver to a new client and he wanted to be on top form.

Katie woke up and looked at the clock on the bedside. It was five a.m. and she wondered where she was; she then remembered Steve.

Shit, she thought, what he must think of me throwing up and then falling asleep. She jumped out of his bed and went into his en suite. She didn't look great at all. Her face was grey and her hair was all over the place, she had mascara all down one side of her face and her eyes looked bloodshot. She still had a slight headache but nothing to how she was feeling the night before.

"Are we doomed?" she said out loud, looking in the mirror. This had been the third date and they still hadn't managed to swap juices.

She tidied herself up and put toothpaste on her finger and started to rub it over her gums and teeth. That will have to do until I can get home and sort myself out; I need to get into the office today or Miss Dawson will have a right go at me, she thought.

She found her clothes that Steve had put neatly on the large leather tub chair that was over in the far corner of his room. Bless him, she thought, as she retrieved her jeans and started to get dressed.

She went into the lounge and found her handbag and got out her mobile to call a cab. It was very early, so she didn't think it would be too long before the cab arrived and there would be no traffic.

She looked around Steve's apartment. I wonder where he slept, she said, walking into the hallway. There was another door, which she presumed was a bedroom and went inside. He was fast asleep in the bed, looking very sexy, but there was a cat curled up by the side of him. Katie wasn't too keen on cats and this one opened its eyes and started hissing at her. Katie sighed. We really do need to sort out some unfinished business, she thought, standing over him and staring at his naked torso, and trying to avoid the vicious cat.

Steve stirred and woke to see Katie by the side of the bed and Ralph with his teeth showing.

"Stop it, Ralph," he said, and pushed him off the bed. Ralph scurried out of the room.

Steve turned his attention to Katie. "Sorry about that," he said. "He isn't usually like that. How are you feeling?"

"I am much better, thank you, I am so sorry," she said, looking down at him and feeling aroused.

Steve sat up. "It's no problem, one of those things," he said, looking at her body in the tight top and jeans.

"It's only five a.m.," she said, sitting down on the edge of the bed. "Go back to sleep. I have called a cab, it should be here very soon."

"I need to get up," he said. "I've got a major presentation to do and have to get to work early."

"Poor you," she said, shifting on the bed. He wasn't wearing anything on his top half and she could see his ripped muscles and wanted to touch him.

He got out of bed and was wearing only his boxers. He had a tight little arse but packed the boxers very well indeed, she thought.

"Looks like we have unfinished business to attend to," he said, pushing his hand through his hair.

"Yes, we do," she said, licking her lips.

He was aroused and would love to take her now, but her cab would be here in a minute and he had to get himself sorted and get to work.

"What are you doing later?" he asked.

"I don't think I have any plans," she said, trying to wrack her brains to think if she had or not.

"How about I cook for us, here in the apartment?" he asked her, looking her up and down.

"That would be lovely, Steve," she said, as she heard a toot outside.

"Come over around seven thirty p.m. and we can make a full night of it. Anything particular you fancy?" he said, walking towards her.

"I could think of quite a few things," she said, watching him walk over to her with a very noticeable bulge.

He smiled and put his hand to her face. "I'll look forward to finding out what they are," he said, as he pulled her face towards him and planted a soft kiss on her lips.

Katie let out a soft moan, her nipples immediately became hard. "You turn me on, Steve," she said, as he kissed her harder.

He could feel her nipples on his bare chest and immediately became hard, which she noticed and reached down to touch his erection that was fighting to get out of his boxers.

The cab tooted again and they both groaned.

"I'll see you later," she said, walking away from him towards the door.

"You most certainly will," he said, following her out.

After Katie had gone Steve went to find Ralph, who was cleaning himself on the sofa.

"Ralphy, what was all that about?" The cat looked at him as if he didn't know what he was talking about. "You never hiss at anyone," he said, picking the cat up. Ralph nuzzled into his neck and Steve went into the kitchen to sort his beloved cat out with some breakfast.

Chapter 35

Ava was really looking forward to her date with Frank. She had bought a lovely short black dress in a small boutique that was down one of the back streets and Tiffany said she had to have it.

"You look amazing," said her friend, slightly envious that Ava would look good in a black bin liner and the fact that she had a hot date lined up.

Ava was pleased with her purchase and also bought a pair of high black peep-toe patent shoes to go with it.

She wore a chunky silver necklace with a large diamante heart that looked great with the low neckline of the dress. She had put on a diamante bracelet and had small diamante stud earrings which she thought went well with the necklace.

She had a small black clutch bag with a diamante clasp and she ran down the stairs into the kitchen, where he mother sat reading a magazine.

"Hi, Mum," she said as she entered. Her mother looked up. "Wow, Ava, you look beautiful," she said, feeling proud of her daughter. She was a good girl and had always paid her way since she had landed the job at the call centre, never really giving them any problem, and she enjoyed having her still living at home. She knew one day Ava would leave the nest but for now she was happy having her around. She was still her baby.

"Where are you off to?" she asked her.

Ava didn't want to tell her about her date with Frank as she had only just stopped asking why she wasn't seeing Josh anymore. Her mum had liked Josh; she thought he was well mannered and had a good job with lots of prospects, was earning a lot of money. She could see them settling down together and was upset when Ava had told her that the relationship was over. She hadn't gone into details and just said it had run its course and she was happy being single.

"I'm going to meet Tiff and a few friends in town," she lied, hating herself. Her mobile pinged, letting her know the taxi was outside. She had booked the cab earlier when she was getting ready.

Her mother smiled at her. "Have a good evening and make sure you get in a cab home together," she said, always worrying about Ava getting into random taxis on her own.

"We will, Mum," she said, as she went round to kiss her. "You have a good evening too," and grabbed her coat and walked out the door.

She arrived at Partners and hoped that Frank would be there as she hated walking into bars on her own. She was devastated at the time when Rob hadn't turned up and she still hadn't heard from him. His loss, she thought, as she pushed open the doors. The bar was heaving and she looked around, trying to find Frank.

She spotted him at the far end of the bar, speaking to an attractive girl who was serving behind the bar.

She walked straight up to him. "Hello," she said, looking at the girl, who blushed. Frank had been getting very animated with her about what he would like to do to her and she was surprised at the interruption, hoping the pretty blonde hadn't heard what he was saying. Even though she was working she still was happy to flirt with the handsome customer.

Frank turned to Ava. "You look gorgeous," he said, kissing her on the cheek and ignoring the girl behind the bar, who was standing there looking awkward.

"Thanks," said Ava, who thought Frank was a lot more mature than Josh.

"What are you drinking?" he asked her as he looked her up and down. She really did look a very sexy sight in that short black dress. I hope she isn't wearing any knickers!

"I'll have a dry white wine spritzer, please," she said, feeling his eyes looking over her body.

Frank turned back to the girl behind the bar. "A dry white wine spritzer and a bottle of Budweiser, please," he said, giving her a smile.

She walked away immediately to get their drinks and took the money from Frank. His fingers lingered a little too long when he gave her the money and she giggled.

Ava didn't notice this and took her drink from the bar.

"Shall we find a table?" Frank asked, putting his arm around Ava.

She smiled. "There's one over there," she said, pointing to the other side of the room.

They walked over to the table. Frank had his arm quite tightly around Ava's waist as they sat down. He pulled his chair very close to her and slotted his knee in between her legs. Ava jolted as she felt his jeans touch her upper thigh.

"You look very sexy tonight," said Frank. "Did you dress for me?" he asked, as Ava blushed bright red. This is going to be so easy, thought Frank, as he could see she was opening her legs wider.

Ava was totally turned on by what Frank was saying to her and having his knee touching her crotch. She was moist down below and could feel his knee moving forward and back, making it difficult for her to concentrate on what he was saying. Her face was flushed and there were people all around them.

"Would you like to finish your drink and go somewhere a bit quieter?" Frank asked her.

Ava was shocked. She had only just arrived and already he was asking to take her somewhere more intimate. She had no control, he had taken over. "I would love to," she heard herself say, looking at him intently. "Where did you have in mind?"

"My place," he said, taking a sip of his drink and pushing his knee further in her private area.

Ava let out slight whimper. "Okay," she said, unable to move.

Frank was about to get up and she put her hand on his arm. "There is something I need to tell you," she said.

"Go on," he said, sitting back down, intrigued.

"I'm a virgin," she said, blushing. "Although I am happy to play around I am not happy with full sex." She felt so stupid saying this to him but she thought she should and wanted to make it clear before they got back to his flat. He was very much in control but she felt she should tell him.

"Really?" said Frank, not sure if he had ever taken anyone's virginity before. "Why are you still a virgin?" he asked, a little confused but becoming very aroused at the thought. She was stunning and he was sure that many men had taken her to bed. Surely she hadn't stopped them from going the whole way?

She coughed. "I'm saving myself for my wedding night," she said, looking at him sheepishly. She had never felt embarrassed or bothered when telling any of the other men she had gone to bed with before, but Frank was different.

Frank laughed very loud and Ava looked at him, shocked. "What's so funny" she said, starting to get a little annoyed as Frank continued to laugh.

Others in the bar turned round, smiling, as laughter was infectious. "I really don't know what to say to that," he said, still laughing very loudly.

Ava went to get up, she felt stupid.

Frank grabbed her arm. "Where are you going?" he said, trying to stop laughing.

"Home!" she said. "You are laughing at me and I don't particularly like it!" She raised her voice.

"Please don't go," he said. "I am sorry but no one has ever said that to me before and I thought it was funny. I am not laughing at you, I am just laughing, sit down."

Ava did as he asked and he put his hand on her chin and pulled her towards him. He kissed her very softly on the lips and she responded, kissing him back.

"Let's go," said Frank, getting aroused by this gorgeous sexy virgin sitting at the table with him. He couldn't wait to get inside of her!

Chapter 36

Lexi started to unpack her things in her new room. Although she still felt really bad about Katie she was happy to be away from her and was loving her new surroundings. The room was much bigger than the one in the apartment and had so much more space to put her things.

Jo said she should make herself completely at home and they would have a chat about the rent in a couple of days when she had settled in. The bathroom was just outside of her door. Jo had the en suite but said it was probably better for Lexi that she didn't have that bedroom as it was bigger than Jo's small bathroom, which only had a shower.

The bathroom next door to Lexi's room was quite large and had a huge Victorian freestanding roll top bath, as well as a separate power shower and his and hers sinks. Lexi was amazed at the size and Jo said to treat it like it was hers. She did not have a problem with people using both bathrooms when they entertained, which she must get round to sorting having a few friends round to welcome Lexi.

Lexi blushed at Jo's kindness. She was pleased with her new surroundings and thankful she had savings. She would probably still have to pay the rent on the apartment while Katie was looking for another lodger as well as paying Jo. She hoped it wouldn't be too expensive but Jo's place was enormous compared to where she had left and that meant the rent was probably enormous too!

Lexi sighed as she started to hang her clothes in the wardrobe. She spotted her new suede jacket and saw that it had a small stain on the sleeve. "That bloody girl!" she said out loud. Was she just going to put it back in my wardrobe and think I wouldn't notice, she thought.

She pulled the jacket off the hanger and threw it over into the corner of the room. That will need to go to the cleaners and I hope they can get the stain out, she said to herself.

Jo knocked on the door. "Hi, how are you getting on?" she said, walking into Lexi's room. She had put some of her stuff out and it was starting to look very cosy.

"I wondered if you wanted to have a break and come through and have a coffee or a glass of wine?" Jo asked, picking up a large silver frame with a picture of a dog holding a ball in its mouth.

"That's Jude," said Lexi. "He is my uncle's dog and is so adorable." She smiled as she thought of Jude. If he was here now he would be snuggled up with her taking all her troubles away, she thought, and walked over to Jo to look at the picture.

"He is gorgeous," said Jo, putting the frame back on the bedside.

"He is," said Lexi, "better than any man!"

Jo laughed and Lexi laughed with her; they were going to get on fine.

They walked through to the kitchen and sat at one of the cream leather stools that were dotted around the island.

"What would you like?" said Jo.

"I'd love a glass of wine," said Lexi, feeling very relaxed in Jo's kitchen.

"White okay?" she asked, as she pulled a bottle from the fridge.

"Perfect," said Lexi, as she watched Jo pour out two very large glasses.

"It's a school night, remember," said Lexi.

"This is medicinal," said Jo, and they both laughed.

They had a good evening together. Jo had called her sister Faye to advise that she wouldn't be joining her and her friends for drinks but would definitely catch up soon.

Faye was fine with this and kept Jo talking for a little longer. She came off the phone and saw Lexi sitting on the sofa.

"You okay, Lex?" she asked.

Lexi looked at her friend. "I'm fine Jo, thanks. I really appreciate you letting me come and stay."

Jo sat down next to her. "It really is no problem. I told you my flatmate was away travelling, so you are doing me a favour too," she said, smiling at her friend.

They had always got on and enjoyed each other's company. Lexi had met Jo's boyfriend, Billy, and he seemed nice. He was a policeman and Jo was always threatening to set Lexi up with one of his friends but it hadn't happened yet.

Lexi wasn't too bothered about this, as she would find it embarrassing having a date set up for her. She was happy being single and could find her own men, thanks. Her thoughts turned to Frank. He came across as being a perfect gentleman, but look what happened as soon as he saw Katie; bam!

Lexi was not at all bothered about Frank. She was glad she saw him for what he was before she had gotten deeper into the relationship. If Frank had not been so shady and had carried on being like he was on their date then she probably would have fallen for him, who wouldn't?

She shook her head to get the thoughts of Frank from it. "Fucking idiot," she said out loud.

"Who is?" said Jo, who was in the kitchen pouring them another large glass of wine.

"Oh, just that Frank," she said to Jo. "I'm glad I found out what he was really like, rather than seeing him for a few dates and things going further, if you know what I mean."

Lexi was thankful that she hadn't slept with Frank. She wasn't sure how many women he had slept with and if he was quick to jump into bed with Katie like that then he was quick to jump into bed with anyone and she doubted he practiced any kind of safe sex. She knew Katie never did, something she was always harping on about to her as she knew she was promiscuous. Maybe Steve will change her, she thought, she seems smitten with him. Maybe she will settle down and stop having random sex with guys, but her words didn't convince her.

"God, Lex, you had a lucky escape there," said Jo, coming back with their glasses full. "In a way Katie did you a favour, although it must have been a shock catching them like that!" Jo pulled a face.

Lexi laughed. "What's that face about?" she said.

"Catching two people at it is bad enough, but when you know the two people then that is disgusting," said Jo, pulling another face. "She never seems to shut her door. Remember when she was having that threesome and you walked in on them because you thought Katie was in pain! Oh my God!" said Jo. "I would have run for the hills then!"

Lexi agreed with her friend and stifled a yawn. She really didn't want to think about Katie with the two guys. "Sorry, Jo, it's all catching up with me."

"No problem at all, go to bed whenever you want, it's not a problem."

"I feel really bad if I go now," said Lexi. "You cancelled your night out to stay with me."

"It was only with Faye and her friends," she said. "I can go another time."

Lexi was so grateful for Jo's kindness. It made a change for her flatmate doing something for her, as her previous one only thought about herself!

She finished her wine and thanked Jo again and went to bed. She would do some more unpacking tomorrow when she got home from work, but she had sorted enough of her clothes out and would find something to wear in the morning.

She snuggled down in the thick duvet and looked at the picture of Jude. She smiled and went to sleep.

Chapter 37

Martha left her nan with her mum. Linda had arrived and was happy to see that Martha was visiting her nan. "Steve was here earlier, too," Martha told her.

Linda smiled. "You two are just great, thank you," she said, with a lump in her throat.

"He was trying to organise a hot date with someone," Vi said.

"Really!" said Linda. "Who?" She looked at Martha.

Martha didn't know whether to tell her mum about Katie; it was Steve's business and she wasn't in the habit of telling tales.

"Oh, just some girl he met. They have had a couple of dates, I think, nothing serious." Martha decided not to say anything.

"He talks about her a lot," said her nan. "I think he is quite taken with her, actually."

Martha hoped not; from what Toby had said she would be nothing but trouble and Steve really didn't need to go back into being with someone who wasn't faithful. He really didn't deserve that, especially when she and Toby knew the truth.

Linda looked at them both. "Who is she then, how come he hasn't said anything to me about it?"

Martha just shrugged it off. "It's probably early days yet, Mum, you know what he is like. After what happened before he keeps a lot of things close to his chest; he doesn't want to get hurt again."

Linda nodded. "Yes, you are right, and I don't want him to get hurt again. It took him a year to get over that Grace. I thought they would get married, but it wasn't to be."

"He has never had anyone serious since her, has he?" said Vi. "Such a shame, as he is such a good-looking boy."

Linda and Vi looked at each other. "You seeing anyone, Martha?" her mum asked. "Are any of my children going to settle down?"

"Mum, we are not even in our thirties yet, give us a chance, there is plenty of time." Martha laughed at her.

She didn't want to tell them about Toby. It was very early days and although they had come a long way in a short time she didn't want to jinx anything.

Martha got up from her chair. "I'm off. Got a few errands to run and I don't want to get home too late. Work in the morning and a busy day ahead, and while we are on the subject, Nan, how about I look at some warden assisted properties for you to go and view? That house you live in is far too big for you to rattle around in."

"It's your inheritance!" she said, looking shocked at her granddaughter.

"Who cares about that?" said Martha. "Live for the moment. Don't worry about us, we have enough money."

Linda agreed with her daughter. "I think there would be no harm in going to have a look, Mum," she said. "You never know, you might be pleasantly surprised. Why don't we get Martha to organise a couple of viewings in a few weeks; it'll be a day out and we could stop and have lunch, too."

"I'll let you know," said Vi, looking at Martha, who was always trying to get her to move.

"I'm not trying to force you into anything, Nan," she said. "It's just I think you would be more comfortable and your bills would reduce in a smaller place."

"I said I'd think about it!" Vi snapped at her.

"Ok, Nan, no pressure."

Martha went over to kiss her mum and then her nan. "I'll come over to the house tomorrow after work to make sure you are okay and have everything. Call me if you want me to bring anything with me."

"I've got it all under control," said Linda, walking over to give her daughter a hug.

"Take care, Martha. If you need anything, let me know, and don't work too hard, take some time out for yourself."

"I'm fine, Mum, I like working hard." She laughed, and walked out of the ward.

She had enjoyed visiting her nan and seeing her mum, but now she was looking forward to picking up Toby. She smiled, she thought of him.

She dialled his number and he picked up straight away. "Hello, sexy lady," he said, and Martha laughed.

"Hello, sexy man," she said, in a deep voice just like his. Toby laughed back.

"Are you coming to get me? Not changed your mind?" He really hoped she hadn't.

"Yes, I'm just leaving the hospital now, and no, I haven't changed my mind. Why would I?"

"Good," he said, looking forward to seeing her again. It had only been a couple of hours but he found that he missed her. He decided to tell her; he didn't feel he needed to hold anything back.

"I missed you, Martha," he said seriously.

"I missed you too, Mr Green," she said, just as seriously. "I'll be there in about twenty minutes; be ready."

"I'll always be ready for you," he said, smiling down the phone.

"Mr Green!" She pretended to be shocked.

"You love it, Martha, you love it," and he laughed as they finished their call.

Toby got back to his flat to pick up some clothes. His phone rang and it was his mum. He answered the call and she didn't wait to say hello.

"Toby, I still haven't heard from Ava, have you?"

"Hi, Mum, no I haven't, are you still worried about her?" Toby knew his sister and she wasn't normally this disrespectful in not letting his parents know what her plans were.

"Her phone is still going straight to voicemail. You don't think anything has happened, do you?"

"I don't, mum, no. She is probably just out enjoying herself, although it is unlike her to stay out all night and not let you know where she is." He was starting to get a little worried himself.

"Oh thank God, Toby, she has just walked in the door. I will call you later."

Toby was relieved. He didn't want to think the worst but his mum was such a worrier that it had a knock on effect.

"Okay, Mum, glad she is home. Tell her from me to let you know next time."

"Will do," said his mum, and hung up.

Toby was looking forward to seeing Martha. He was missing her, which he thought stupid, but she really was leaving a huge impression on him and he couldn't wait to get her in his arms again. His groin stirred at the thought of their lovemaking, and he surprised himself that he had called it lovemaking rather than sex.

"Could I be in love with Martha already?" he said out loud.

His phone rang and Martha's name came up. His heart started racing. "I could," he said, as he answered the phone.

She sounded so sexy, he just wanted to be with her. He couldn't think of anyone or anything else; he just wanted to be back with her.

When he had put the phone down he rushed round his flat, putting his clothes for work in a big duffle bag.

Should I pack for a few nights? Would that be taking the piss, he thought.

He decided to take his suit, a couple of clean shirts and some jogging bottoms. He also put in a pair of jeans, just in case, he thought.

He picked up his razor and deodorant from the bathroom, along with his toothbrush, and put them in his small overnight bag. He waited for her to arrive; it seemed like forever before she pressed the buzzer.

He ran down the stairs and opened the door. She looked amazing and he put his arms around her and kissed her straight away. She responded and put her arms tightly around his neck. They were kissing for a good couple of minutes when Mr Leeson, Toby's neighbour, walked past them. "Love's young dream," he said, as he went up to his flat. Martha pulled away and blushed, and Toby laughed. "It certainly is, Mr Leeson, it certainly is."

He took Martha up to his flat, which was a small one bedroomed that Martha thought could only be described as a bachelor pad.

It had black furniture, a huge black leather sofa and a big red chair in the shape of a hand over near the window.

"This is such a man cave," she said, laughing as she looked around. He had some really cool stuff and she liked the end wall that was a huge mural of the New York skyline.

"Wow," she said, "that looks amazing. I love New York," she said, going over to the wall and touching it.

"Thanks," he said. "I love New York too, maybe we can go together sometime."

Martha blushed. "I would love that," she said, walking back towards him and giving him a soft kiss on the lips. He responded and took her in his arms. "I think I am falling in love with you, Martha Chance," he said, blushing at not quite believing he had said it out loud.

She hugged him very tightly. "I think I am too, Mr Green," she said, as they stood there hugging each other tightly in Toby's man cave.

Toby picked up his bag and followed her out of the door, ensuring he double locked it behind him.

They got into Miss Ellie and Martha drove home, smiling all the way.

They decided to order Chinese, as they were both hungry and hadn't eaten at all that day. When it arrived they got out the plates and cutlery as if they were an old married couple. They suited each other and worked together well.

"We need to sort out Steve," Toby said, starting to feel anxious. He was dreading telling him about Katie and he also needed to speak to him about Martha. How was he going to react to both conversations?

"I think it would be better coming from you with regard to Katie, as you are the one who has seen her with these other men."

"You saw her with one of them, actually the same one I had seen her with, the night we went into Horatio's after the film," he said, not looking forward to telling Steve.

"How many has she had?" asked Martha, beginning to get annoyed. She really didn't want her brother falling for a slag like that!

"As far as I know only two, but it was with one of them twice so that could be counted as three really," said Toby.

Martha looked at him. "And that's what we know about. There could be others that we don't know about," she said, looking worried.

"Shit, I never thought of that," said Toby. "So glad I didn't meet her first," said Toby.

"Actually," said Martha, "we should be thankful that he did meet her or he wouldn't have cancelled our movie night and you wouldn't have taken me and..."

Toby silenced her with a kiss. "Let's not think about what ifs," he said. "I will definitely call him in the morning and make arrangements to meet up in the week. Maybe it will be best to tell him one thing at a time." He looked at Martha.

"What, tell him about Katie first and then about us another time?" Martha wasn't sure.

"It might be too much, telling him both," said Toby, putting a prawn ball in his mouth.

"You might be right," Martha said, agreeing with her new boyfriend.

"Let's finish up and talk about this in bed," Toby said, winking at her.

"I'm not tired," said Martha, joking with him.

"Neither am I," said Toby, grabbing another prawn ball and popping it in his mouth.

Chapter 38

Katie left Steve's and went home to get ready for work. She was happy to be going back to his place after work; she felt at home there and wondered what he would be cooking.

She mainly ate in restaurants. She wasn't a great cook and found that there were too many pots and pans to use and hated clearing up after herself, so she generally left the cooking to Lexi.

That won't be happening for a while though, she thought, as she looked in her wardrobe for something to wear. It was only six a.m. and she really would be way early for work but she felt she needed to make a bit of an effort and try appeal to Miss Dawson's better nature.

She selected an outfit that wasn't so revealing. She was also going back to Steve's straight after and didn't want him thinking she was a tart. She chose black straight leg trousers with red boots that were not too high and a black wrap-over top that had white ribbons sewn into it on the sleeves. She thought she looked good enough to eat, and smiled. Hopefully Steve would be eating her later, after she had eaten his food and him, she thought, and laughed out loud.

She jumped in the shower and washed herself thoroughly, doing her ablutions whilst she was at it. She liked to be smooth all over and Steve was definitely going to be all over her tonight, that was for sure.

She sat on the bed with one of her big fluffy pink towels wrapped around her. She lay down for a minute and fell asleep, waking up two hours later.

She looked at the clock. "Shit," she shouted out loud. "Shit, shit, shit, shit!" Why the fuck did I lay down!

She raced around drying her hair and putting her clothes on. It was eight thirty a.m. before she left and she knew she wouldn't be in the office by nine a.m. Monday morning traffic was a nightmare!

She finally made it to the office at nine twenty a.m. Tracy on reception gave her a glare. "Late again, Katie," she said with a sneer.

"What's it to you, Tracy?" said Katie, sneering back. She walked straight past her, throwing her bag over her shoulder. Stupid bitch, she thought, as if it's any of her business what time I arrive!

Katie scurried past Tracy, through the double doors. She always hated the fact that her desk was over the far side of the office, as she often felt like she was doing the 'walk of shame' whenever she was late in, which was more often than not.

She could see people starting to turn around to look at her; she glared back at Vicky Smith and her stupid friend Laura. "What the fuck are you two staring at?" she hissed at them both.

They both gave her a dirty look and turned back to their screens.

Katie could see Miss Dawson coming towards her. "Oh fuck," she said out loud. She heard a few giggles behind her.

"I need a word, Miss Fox, in my office now, please," said Miss Dawson in a very stern voice, as her beady eyes glared down at Katie.

"Can't I just get a coffee first?" pleaded Katie.

"No!" shouted Miss Dawson. "You certainly may not."

Katie scowled and followed Miss Dawson into her ugly office. She sat down on one of the chairs as Miss Dawson went round to her desk.

"I see you were off sick again on Friday, Katie," she said, not looking at her but looking at the sheet of paper in front of her. "How many sick days have you had this year?" she asked, taking her beady eyes from the sheet in front of her and looking at Katie.

"Too many," said Miss Dawson. "Far too many."

"You have also had written warnings as well as verbal, yes?" Katie nodded.

"Well Katie, this was your very last chance. You have obviously no time to come into work, what with your hectic social schedule, so I am terminating your contract of employment as of now. You will be paid until the end of the week but you leave today."

Katie looked at Miss Dawson in horror. "You can't do that!" she screamed. "What am I supposed to do without a job? I have bills to pay, you know!"

Miss Dawson was flabbergasted. "Katie, you should have thought of that when you were being given all the warnings with regard to lateness and rudeness and taking time off sick!"

"Your work colleagues have always had to take up the slack and quite frankly I think the whole office is sick of carrying you. Why should you get paid for doing nothing when others are doing your work? It just isn't fair at all, Miss Fox!" Was the girl stupid, she thought?

Katie stood up and started to scream at Miss Dawson. "You fucking bitch, how fucking dare you fire me!"

Miss Dawson stood up. This one could turn out to be a problem, she thought, and started to go round the desk towards the door.

Katie followed her and they were now both in the main office area.

"The bitch just fired me!" Katie shouted to the whole of the office.

Some were on the telephone and were concerned that the customers may have heard. Miss Dawson reached for the phone on one of the desks to call reception and asked Tracy to send down for security to escort Miss Fox off the premises.

Tracy was happy to do so. They were all sick of carrying Miss flaming Fox. Serves her right, she thought, as she picked up the phone to dial the main reception.

Katie by now had moved over to her desk and started to clear out her drawers. "Fucking bitch!" she screamed, as she saw two burly uniformed men coming towards her.

She stuffed the contents into her bag and started to walk towards them. "I'm coming!" she shouted, and walked through the double doors to reception. The whole room went quiet except for a phone ringing in one of the offices.

"Bye Katie," said Tracy, with a big grin on her face.

There would be a lot to talk about in the office that day, though Tracy was happy to see the back of her.

"Fuck you!" said Katie, and pressed the button for the lift. The security men escorted her out of the building.

Out on the street tears streamed down Katie's face. What now, she thought. I have no job, no flatmate and no money! She knew that she had been late a few times but not that often; why all the drama?

She wiped her tears away and headed towards the shops. It was only ten a.m.; I have no work, she thought, so I may as well play. She hoisted her bag over, she thought. Who cares, I have the whole day to myself!

Katie went to the shopping mall and looked around the shops but she wasn't in the mood to buy anything. Her conscience kicked in and she was worried. As Lexi had moved out how she was going to pay for the apartment without a monthly salary coming in? How was she going to pay for a lot of things, she thought?

She wasn't like the perfect Lexi, always having savings. "Fuck Lexi!" she said out loud, as a woman with a small child walked past her and gave her a filthy look.

She went into a coffee shop and ordered a skinny latte. I can at least afford that, she thought, and got them to put it in a take-away cup.

She walked outside and sat down on one of the seats in the mall. She really didn't know what to do and it was now only eleven a.m. She watched as an old couple holding hands walked past her. She thought it was really sweet, and would love to grow old together with someone. Maybe Steve was someone to grow old with, she thought.

She pottered around the shops some more, not really looking at anything in particular, and decided to go into Horatio's to see if Mario was working. It was now noon and she knew the bar would be open.

As she walked in she saw him cleaning some glasses at the bar. He looked up and smiled when he saw her.

"Hello, gorgeous," he said. "How are you?"

"Hi, Mario," she said with a sad voice. "I have just been sacked from my job." Katie started to cry. It had suddenly hit her, Lexi moving out and now Miss Dawson terminating her employment. What was happening to her, how come everything was starting to go wrong?

She sobbed loudly and Mario came straight to her from around the bar.

He put his arms around her and she sobbed into them, great big racking sobs that she couldn't stop.

She was there for a full five minutes. His T-shirt was soaked.

"I am going to have to change," he said, pulling himself away from her.

She had mascara running down her face and her eyes were bloodshot. She managed a smile. "Sorry," she said, giving a huge sigh. He took one of the napkins from the table and handed it to her.

"Here," he said and she took it.

"Why did you get sacked?" he asked, not even knowing where she worked. He had explored the whole of her body and done intimate things with this girl but he didn't know a thing about her, he thought.

"I need to go and change, come up to my room." It was a request not a question, as the few people that were in the bar were starting to stare, including Mario's boss.

He asked her to wait there a minute as he went over to speak to his boss; he was back in seconds. Mario was a good worker and was always putting in extra hours when the bar was busy and staff hadn't turned up. They only had a handful of customers; he could spare him for half an hour or so.

Mario led Katie up to his room and took her bag from her shoulders. She sat down on the bed and started to cry again.

"This is so unlike you, Katie," he said, going to the bathroom to get her some tissues.

199

"Mario, I have had an awful few days. My flatmate walked out and now I have lost my job." She started to cry again and he went and sat down next to her.

He let her cry. He didn't know what else to do. Once she had got it all out of her system then we would talk, he thought.

She soon stopped crying and he went to the small fridge that he had in the corner and took out a small bottle of wine. He poured it in a glass and handed it to her.

"There you go," he said, and she took it from him.

"Thank you," she said, smiling.

She took a few sips of the wine and she could feel it go down her throat into her stomach; she hadn't eaten a thing again and she wasn't hungry now.

They both sat on the bed in silence for a while until Mario broke it by saying, "I have to go back down to the bar. It's my shift but I finish at six. Why don't you stay up here and relax for a few hours and I will see you later?"

Katie was grateful to Mario. She didn't want to go home to be on her own, and knowing he was just downstairs would be a comfort.

She nodded and lay down on the bed, putting her wine on the table that was by the side.

"Thank you, Mario," she said.

He looked at her and went over and gave her a kiss on her cheek.

"No problem, get some rest and I will see you soon."

Katie nodded and Mario closed the door quietly behind him as he went downstairs to work.

Katie didn't hear him come back up to the room at six; she was fast asleep and he decided to leave her there. Her phone beeped a couple of times but he was sitting on a chair reading his book while she slept. She obviously needed the rest.

Chapter 39

Steve had had a very hard day at the office. The presentation didn't go as well as he had hoped and he thought that might have been because he had Katie Fox on his mind.

She was gorgeous. He had felt so sorry for her being sick in his apartment. She must have felt really embarrassed, he knew he would if he'd thrown up in hers!

She had had a hard time of it late, what with her flatmate moving out and our dates not going to plan, he thought. He really wanted to make it up to her, show her that he did care, and hopefully they would have the best sex later on that evening; if she was feeling better, of course, he thought.

He had finished with his clients and it was now three p.m. He advised one of his work colleagues he was off out for an hour. He wanted to go and sort the food out for later rather than rushing after work, and he didn't know what time he would be finished. As long as it was before seven p.m. That was his cut off point.

He had decided to make her spaghetti Bolognese. It was easy to do and he didn't need to follow a recipe, as he had made it loads of times before for his family, and they had always commented on how good it was. He also didn't want to be spending too much time in the kitchen; there were other things to do, he thought, smiling.

He went to the delicatessen to pick up his ingredients. He didn't want to go to the supermarket; he wanted the best.

He arrived back at the office forty-five minutes later with two large brown carrier bags. He had gone completely overboard getting good red wine, olives and focaccia; he hoped she liked them all.

He was feeling extremely excited and sat at his desk to get through his emails. He decided to send her a text to set the ball rolling for later.

Hi Sexy lady ☺ looking forward to seeing all of you later S x

He sent the text but couldn't concentrate on his emails as he kept looking at his phone, hoping she would reply.

An hour went by and he hadn't heard from her. Maybe she was busy, he thought.

By five p.m., after continuing to look at his phone every other second, he decided to text her again. Maybe she didn't get the one he had sent earlier.

He sent the exact same text as before, but this time sent two kisses.

Hi sexy lady looking forward to seeing all of you later S xx

He got through all of his emails and when he looked at the clock it was six thirty. He still hadn't heard from Katie, which he thought a little strange. Maybe she wasn't feeling well again and had gone home; no reason for her not to answer his text, though, he thought.

He finished the last of his work and decided he would go home and start on the meal. At least it would be cooking when she arrived.

He ordered a cab so he could get home quickly. He couldn't be doing with buses and there was never any point in bringing his car in, which was parked in the road at home. He very rarely used his car and didn't know why he bothered with it. He needed to sort that out too, he thought.

He arrived home to a spotless house. He didn't realise his mum would be at his apartment today, as he knew his nan was coming out of hospital. Shit, maybe I should have gone round there, he thought, panicking.

Ralph was straight round his legs. "Hey, mate," he said, "how was your day? Did Mum feed you?" Ralph purred around Steve. "Sounds like she did, great," he said.

He put his bags on the counter and started to unpack, looking at all the ingredients he had bought at the deli.

He got his phone out of his jacket pocket. Still no text from Katie, but he saw a missed call from Toby.

It was seven p.m. Maybe this was all part of her game, he thought, leave me hanging and then turn up in the most amazing outfit, ready for me to peel it off her after dinner, or before dinner, he corrected.

Steve started to work his magic in the kitchen. The smells were delicious and Ralph was hovering around, hoping to get some of whatever was going on in the saucepan on that stove.

Steve had chopped onions, garlic and tomatoes. He had put in quite a lot of red wine, as he felt that gave it the awesome flavour, and he had bought some very expensive mince and stock, which he left on the stove to simmer. He could sort the pasta out later.

It was quarter to eight by the time he had finished and tidied up the kitchen, and he was getting a bit concerned.

"I will give her a call," he said to Ralph, who was sitting on the sofa cleaning himself.

Her phone went straight to voicemail. He decided to leave a message, something he rarely did.

"Hi Katie, it's Steve, just wondering if you were on your way over. Give me a call as soon as you get this message as I am excited to see you." He then laughed into the phone and hung up.

He always felt stupid leaving a message on an answerphone as he usually got tongue tied and went on more than he intended, which is why he rarely left them. He was fine with Toby, as they had always called each other back whenever they saw they had a missed call. Steve hadn't called Toby back though, for probably the first time ever. Toby was starting to get on his nerves a little bit lately. He had been acting shifty and Steve couldn't put his finger on it as to why.

He wanted to call him but thought better of it, just in case Katie was trying to get through.

He seemed to be pulling out all the stops for her, something he hadn't done in a long time for a woman, not really since Grace. He then shook his head. I don't want to think about Grace, and banished her to the back of his mind where she would probably always sit, only coming to the forefront of his mind when he was very drunk.

I wonder if I will always think of her for the rest of my life; maybe when I find the right woman the ghost of Grace will be banished. He laughed at his thought process and went to pour himself a glass of red wine.

He had bought the bottles of Chianti as the woman in the deli had told him it was delicious and would complement his Bolognese perfectly. He took her advice and had decided on buying three bottles. She had looked at him and asked if he was having a few friends over?

"No, just the one friend," he said, and winked at her. She had laughed as he walked out of the shop.

It was now eight thirty and he was starting to get a little pissed off. He hadn't heard from Katie and thought it was rude of her not to at least text.

He decided to turn the Bolognese off. It would spoil if he kept it simmering, and if she turned up a little later than expected he still wanted to eat, although he was losing his appetite rapidly and poured another glass of the Chianti.

Steve woke up on the sofa with Ralph by his side at three in the morning. He looked straight at his phone. There was nothing from Katie and he even sent himself a text to make sure his phone was working; his text came pinging back immediately.

He picked up Ralph and made his way into his bedroom. His bed was still unmade from that morning and he could see where she had lain.

He went and slept in the exact same spot Katie had and he got a faint smell of her perfume. He must ask her what it was, if he ever saw her again, he thought, as he drifted off to sleep.

Chapter 40

Toby's mum quickly put the phone down from speaking to her son and went into the lounge where she had seen Ava go. She appeared to be crying, and she looked at her husband, who was sitting in the armchair, with concern.

"Ava, are you okay?" she said. "Have you been crying?"

Ava looked at her Mum with sad eyes. "No, I'm fine," she lied.

"Why didn't you let us know you were staying out all night, we have been worried, haven't we Charlie!" Ava's mum, Beth, looked at her husband for some support.

"I don't have to tell you everything I am doing, Mum!" she suddenly screamed and ran up to her room and slammed the door.

"What the hell was that about?" asked Beth, looking at her husband.

"Not sure," he said, "but I would leave her for a while. Wait until she has calmed down a bit, then we can talk to her." Ava's dad was ever the peacekeeper.

Ava threw herself down on her bed and started to cry. He knew I was saving myself, she thought, why did he have to keep going on and on and on?

The evening with Frank had started brilliantly. They had gone back to his bedsit and sat listening to music, drinking wine and slowly exploring each other's bodies. Frank's touch was amazing, she thought, and the way he got her clothes off by asking her to slowly strip for him was so erotic, she thought.

He had talked her through it while the music was playing softly in the background, and he was telling her which way to turn, which item to take off and what he thought of the piece of her flesh on show when she had taken it off. She found herself being completely turned on by his low voice telling her exactly what to do and continually complimenting her.

When she had been fully naked standing in front of him he slowly took his own clothes off, asking her what she thought of this muscle and that thigh. It was a game she had never played and one she had enjoyed. It was extremely erotic and she found herself very aroused throughout the whole ordeal. When he had fully exposed his naked body she gasped at the size of his manhood; can someone be that big?

They had been at this for hours and it was early in the morning by the time he had lifted her up and taken her to his bed. He had slowly made his way down to her pulsating sex and had parted her pussy lips and found her clit with his tongue and she was spread open like a flower while his other fingers dipped inside, stroking her. She let out a very loud moan. He could taste her and he knew she had climaxed; he knew now was the best time. He immediately pulled away from her and climbed on top of her and was about to enter her with his fully erect penis when he heard her scream, "No, what are you doing?" She quickly closed her legs and moved from under him and was standing next to the bed.

"Frank, what the fuck do you think you are doing?" She was angry and very upset that he was about to enter her.

"Baby, you were begging me to fuck you, you wanted me inside you, I could tell," he sneered at her.

"I never asked you to fuck me, I wouldn't do that!" she said, with tears streaming down her face. "I told you I was saving myself for my wedding night, I specifically told you. I thought you understood and were okay with it?"

"Come on," he said. "I thought that was just to get me turned on?"

"No, it wasn't to get you turned on. I said it because I meant it. I am saving myself!"

"Who the fuck does that? You were loving what I was doing to you!" He was starting to get angry now; he needed to be satisfied and he was going to be. He grabbed Ava by the arm. "Come back here, come see what Frank has for you," he said, looking down at his erect penis. "You know you want it, Ava," he laughed at her.

She pulled away. "I said no, Frank, and if you can't respect me then I want to go home." She was disappointed with him now but also a little scared.

"Come back to bed," he said, "and we'll talk about it while I feel your body."

She didn't feel like going back to bed, she wanted to go home. "I'd rather go home if that's okay," she said, still a little upset and still a bit frightened. Thank God she had managed to stop him, as she was in a very erotic place and could have easily succumbed to his advances.

"I don't want you to go home," he said, in a much more forceful voice.

Ava started to cry. "What the fuck are you crying for?" he said. "I don't get it, you were loving what I was doing to you with my tongue, why can't I do it even better with my cock?"

"But I told you, Frank, before we left the bar, I told you!" She had stopped crying and was getting angry with him and her voice was getting louder.

"I know you told me, Ava, but I didn't think you actually meant it!" He was starting to get a little pissed off with her now and he needed satisfying and if she wasn't going to do it then he needed to sort himself out!

She looked straight at him; he really was a very good-looking bloke. "I'll come back to bed if you promise you will behave and won't try to enter me?"

"Okay," he said reluctantly, "if you give me a blow job." Ava didn't have a problem at all with that as she knew she was good at giving head and she loved hearing a man moan when she had control of his penis. She got back in bed and Frank started caressing her breasts. She started to melt at his touch once again and he knelt beside her and pointed his large erect penis in the direction of her mouth. She put it in and started to suck.

"That's it baby, good girl, yeah, that's right, suck me really hard, keep going." He had his hand on the back of her head and was forcing her right down onto his erection, forcing her to take in the whole of his manhood.

She started to gag and he was enjoying his cock in the warmth of her mouth, not caring that he was too much for her. Ava was not enjoying this at all and was glad when he exploded, although she would have rather he not climax in her mouth. He didn't even ask if he could shoot his load, he just went ahead, and Ava started coughing and gagging as his juices filled her. He pushed her away when he had got rid of every last drop and she went into the bathroom.

He felt better for finally climaxing and he started to relax. She came out of the bathroom and still wanted to go home but he beckoned her over. It was eight a.m. and neither of them had slept. "Come over here, gorgeous," he said, smiling at her. He was feeling aroused once again at the sight of her naked body.

She reluctantly went over and got into bed beside him. "I am really sorry," he said, looking at her, "you turn me on so much I just got carried away." He had decided to play the long game with this one as she was very sexy and he was turned on by the fact that she really did want to stay a virgin until her wedding night. He saw this as a challenge and if anyone could crack the nut Frankie could, he thought, giving her one of his innocent smiles.

207

"It's okay," she said, pleased that he had apologised. "I am not doing it to be difficult. I understand that people get carried away, you saw what I was like when you were doing what you were doing," she blushed, "but I am not going to change my mind, Frank. It really is important to me and I want you to respect my decision."

Frank looked at her. She was so beautiful when she was being serious, he thought.

"I do, Ava, again I am sorry," he lied. There was no way he was not going to go the whole way with this little beauty, or my name is not Frank Boyle, he said, smiling to himself.

They both fell asleep entwined in each other and didn't wake up until two p.m.

"Shit," said Ava, looking at the clock. "I really do need to go home." She hadn't bothered to phone her parents as she hadn't expected to be at Frank's all night. Ava always told them what her plans were and if she intended to stay out all night; this usually meant staying over at Tiffany's.

She got out of bed and looked around for her clothes. They were all over the bedsit and she needed to find them and get out.

Frank was still fast asleep and snoring. When she had found her clothes she decided to leave him a note rather than wake him. She didn't think he would let her go home and would probably try it on again with her.

She found a pen and a piece of paper and wrote

Thanks, sorry had to go

A x

She left the brief note on the pillow by the side of him and walked out of the door, closing it quietly. All the way home she was thinking about the events of last night. She was shocked that he had tried to enter her and take away everything she had believed in. She also had not enjoyed giving him a blow job. He was extremely rough and she didn't feel like she had control like she did have when she was doing the same to Josh. Maybe Josh wasn't so bad after all, unlike Frank, she thought.

She got two buses home and her phone told her that she may be in a bit of trouble, as there were loads of missed calls from her mum and three from Toby! She felt so bad for not contacting them but the evening had just run away with her, and Frank had been so attentive at the beginning.

She finally arrived home and knew her parents would have been worried. She had tried to hide her upset on what had happened with Frank but her mum had picked up on it straight away.

She had hoped they would be out so she could just go up into her bedroom and shut the door without them seeing her straight away but they weren't, so she had to face them.

When she did finally escape to her bedroom she knew that she would have some explaining to do to her mum and dad at some point and she hated lying to them, but there was no way she was going to tell them about Frank.

She wasn't sure if she wanted Frank to contact her or not, but she was so tired that she fell asleep on top of her duvet, not even bothering to remove her clothes.

Chapter 41

Lexi woke up with a start. She didn't remember where she was and looked around her. "Jo's," she said out loud and snuggled back into the duvet.

What a lovely room, she thought, as she carried on looking around her. She was going to be very happy here but her heart was thumping at the thought of Katie.

I wonder what she is doing now; would she have spent the night in the apartment on her own? Lexi didn't think so. Katie hated being on her own.

She looked at the clock. It was early and she could easily have another hour in bed but decided to get up and do some more sorting. She didn't like her stuff all over the place and liked to be organised and tidy at all times.

She knew she would have a busy day ahead and was up for the challenge. She turned to look at Jude. "I will come see you soon, just stay being gorgeous," she said, starting to make her bed.

The bed had been really comfortable, and Lexi had slept very well in her new surroundings. Jo had put bedding on and she felt the crispness of the cotton as she had snuggled down, smelling the lavender, her favourite.

She heard a knock on the door and Jo came into her room. "Sleep well?" she asked, smiling at Lexi.

"I slept like a log, thanks. What are you doing up so early?"

"I just wanted to make sure you were okay, that's all," she said, smiling at her friend. "Coffee?"

"That would be lovely, Jo. Are you going to do this every morning for me?" Lexi said, laughing at her.

"Probably not," said Jo, "so enjoy it while you can," and left Lexi to carry on with unpacking and went into the kitchen.

Jo was so pleased that Lexi had come to stay. She knew she had been having a very hard time of late with Katie and things were getting worse. The last straw was catching her with Frank. What a bitch, Jo thought.

Just as the coffees were ready Lexi walked into the kitchen. "This is such a cool place, Jo, I love it," said Lexi, sitting on one of the stools at the island.

"Martha knew what I was looking for," she said, "she really is very good at her job. You should meet her, she is such a lovely person. I'm sure her brother lives in one of the apartments in the building too."

"I might have to when your flatmate gets back from travelling. She would be hard pushed to find me a place like this that I could afford," said Lexi, taking a sip of her coffee, which was delicious. Katie had never been up this early making her coffee, that's for sure.

"It's not that expensive," said Jo, "you will be surprised."

Lexi was pleased. She really needed to have a chat with Jo about the rent but now wasn't the right time. Maybe after work, if Jo hadn't got anything planned.

Both girls got ready for work and walked out the door together.

"This is really odd," said Lexi, "having someone to go to work with."

"I know," said Jo, "we could almost be a married couple." Both girls laughed as they went down the stairs and out onto the street to get the bus to work.

Lexi's day went without complication and she got completely up straight and was really looking forward to getting back to the apartment.

She had a new apartment, new friend to share it with and her job was going very well. She had received a lot of compliments with regard to her efficiency on a particular client she had managed to placate, and her boss was very pleased with how she handled things. Lexi got a buzz out of pleasing people.

The day seemed to be over quickly and Jo popped her head round her office door at six p.m.

"Are you ready or shall I meet you at home?" she asked, smiling at her new flatmate.

"I'm ready. Would you like to go out for something to eat on me, so I can say thank you?" Lexi said, beaming at her friend.

"That would be lovely, Lex. Billy is on some course for the week so he won't be around, but you really don't have to."

"I know I don't have to, I want to," said Lexi, getting her bag and walking towards the door where Jo was standing; Jo was thrilled at being treated to dinner.

"There is this little Italian place I know called Papa's. Frank, believe it or not, took me there and I had the most wonderful meal. The pasta is to die for."

"Sounds absolutely amazing, I love Italian food," said Jo, licking her lips.

"Great," said Lexi. "I'm sure we will get a table, seeing as it's early and a Monday night."

Lexi took out her phone. "I will order a cab, as it's on the other side of town and the weather looks awful outside, so we can wait here, you okay with that?"

"Perfect," said Jo, feeling her tummy rumble. She hadn't eaten anything apart from a yoghurt and banana this morning due to her workload. She was famished.

The taxi arrived within ten minutes of Lexi ordering it and they both got in behind the driver.

"You off to Papa's?" he asked, pulling away.

"Yes," said Lexi, "have you ever been?"

"No," said the cab driver, "but I have taken quite a few people there. It's a very popular place at the moment. I think word has got out."

Jo was pleased with hearing this. "Must be good then," she said, looking out the window at the people walking. The weather had turned quite nasty and the rain was lashing down. People were having trouble holding on to their umbrellas as they fought with them to keep dry.

They arrived at Papa's and Lexi was thrilled that they were not too busy.

"Do you have a table for two?" she asked the waiter, who was standing at the door holding it open for them to get in out of the rain.

"We do at the moment," he said, "but we are fully booked from eight thirty p.m. so if you think you will be finished by then I can seat you no problem?"

Lexi looked at Jo. "I'm sure we will be finished by then," she said. "That gives us nearly two hours."

The waiter showed them to a lovely table over the far side of the restaurant. The candles were flickering and it looked very cosy, Jo thought. "Loving this place, Lexi. See, Frank was good for something."

Lexi laughed out loud. "He so was," she said, and sat down at the small table, still thinking, what an arsehole!

Another man came over. "Good evening, ladies, my name is Paolo and I will be your waiter this evening." Lexi recognised him as the waiter who had served her when she was with Frank.

"Hello, Paulo," she said, smiling.

"Hello miss, no boyfriend tonight?" he said, smiling and looking at Jo.

Lexi blushed. "He wasn't my boyfriend, we were just on a date and I won't be seeing him again." Lexi couldn't believe she was telling the waiter this.

Jo laughed. "She's much better off without him," she said to Paolo and looked at Lexi.

Lexi was so embarrassed and knew her face was bright red.

Paulo saw this and asked them about drinks. "What can I get you two ladies to drink?"

"Do you think we'll drink a bottle between us, rather than a couple of glasses?" Lexi asked Jo.

"I can drink anything on a Monday night after a hard day, Lex, so whatever you think is best. I am happy with either as long as it's wet and alcoholic."

Lexi smiled. "We'll have a bottle of that Pinot Grigio I had last week," she said, "it was really lovely and not sweet at all." Lexi hated sweet wine, the drier the better for her.

"Good choice," said Paolo, as he handed them the menus and went to get their wine.

"It all looks so lovely, Lex, there is so much to choose from. What are you having?"

"I'm not sure," she said, looking at the mouth-watering dishes on offer. "I had the linguine di mare last time, which was absolutely delicious. It came with king prawns, clams and squid, all done in a garlic and white wine sauce. It really was lovely and I didn't leave any on my plate," she said, remembering the taste. "I think I might go for the spaghetti alle vongole this time. I love clams," said Lexi, feeling her tummy rumble. She too hadn't eaten since breakfast, due to her workload, and was starving.

"That looks so good, I'll have the same," said Jo, "clams are my favourite too."

"Do you want a starter?" asked Lexi, "or shall I order some focaccia to have at the same time?"

"I am happy to have the bread with our meal," said Jo, loving the ambience and décor of Papa's. "What a fantastic place, Lex. I can't believe I have never been here; you would think Billy would know about it," said Jo.

"You should get him to bring you here for a romantic meal." Lexi sighed, wishing she had someone who she could be romantic with.

"What's that far away face for?" said Jo.

Lexi took a sip of her wine. "Just thinking that I would like a Billy to be romantic with, that's all."

Jo laughed. "I will sort you out, we will go on a double date with one of Billy's mates. You can't go wrong with a policeman; they are such gentlemen."

Lexi was warming to the idea of Jo setting her up with a policeman. She didn't like meeting random men in bars or clubs or even the gym, she thought, thinking of Frank.

"Yeah, whenever Jo, no rush," she said, closing the menu having definitely decided.

Paulo came over and took their order and filled up their glasses. When he had left them Lexi turned to Jo. "Right, we need to talk money," she said sternly.

"There is no need yet," said Jo. "Abbie has paid up until the end of the month; you won't have to start paying until then."

"Well, I think I should. How is that fair on you or Abbie? I should at least give Abbie some money; there are still two weeks to go yet!" Lexi looked pleadingly at her friend.

"There is no need, Lex, honest. Abbie has enough money and she won't mind at all. She will just be grateful that I got a sane person to share with. Abbie is a bit protective of me, you see."

Lexi laughed. "Well, if you're sure. I am not a charity case and I do have money, so I can pay my way. It really isn't a problem."

"I am very sure," said Jo, "you have had enough on your plate of late. Don't worry about it and this meal I know will be delicious. The wine is going down very well so I am thankful for you taking me out. We are now all square." She raised her glass to chink with Lexi's. "Cheers; to new beginnings," and laughed at her flatmate.

Lexi was very grateful to Jo. She was also pleased she had taken her out to dinner on the spur of the moment. She would make sure she bought her a big bunch of flowers to say thank you too; they would look lovely around the apartment.

Paolo brought over their meal. The smell was amazing and both of them didn't leave a single thing on their plate. He topped up the rest of their wine and asked if they required another bottle. "No thank you," said Jo. "It's a school night and we have had three glasses each. I think that's enough, don't you, Lexi?"

Lexi smiled. Jo was not the kind of person who took advantage; she was happy that she didn't go for the most expensive item on the menu and knew when she had had enough to drink. Whenever she had gone out with Katie she had racked up the bill with cocktails and expensive meals that she hardly ever touched, and Lexi was always having to stump up for the bill as Katie either forgot her purse, or would give her share to her at the end of the month when she got paid. Lexi never saw the money and didn't want to ask, as Katie was always banging on about how skint she was.

They ate their meal slowly, savouring all the flavours, and when Paolo came over to take their plates they told him how delicious it was and they would definitely be coming back.

Paolo was pleased they had enjoyed their dish. Papa's was having a reputation for good food and word of mouth was free advertising to the restaurant, which was like gold dust.

Neither of them wanted a dessert; they were completely full and agreed to coffee back at the apartment. They ordered a taxi from the table and paid the bill and put their coats on. It had stopped raining but it looked quite cold outside. They were glad they had ordered a cab ten minutes ago; it should be here any moment.

They went to wait near the door when Lexi noticed a striking looking couple walk through. Jo squealed. "Martha, how lovely to see you, how are you?" said Jo, hugging the pretty woman.

"Hey Jo, I'm fine," said Martha. She looked a little awkward. "Er, this is my friend Toby, this is Jo, Faye's sister, you know, one of the girls I was with the other night at Horatio's."

"Hello," said Toby, "lovely to meet you." He looked at both women who he thought were extremely attractive.

"We have just had the most gorgeous meal here," said Jo. "This is Lexi, my new flatmate."

"Hello," said Lexi, thinking Martha looked familiar.

"Hi Lexi," said Martha. "What a pretty name."

Lexi blushed. "Thank you. It's actually Alexandra but I have always been called Lexi by my mum and it has kind of stuck," she said, trying to think where she had seen the very pretty woman. "I love the apartment that you found for Jo; it's stunning," still trying to rack her brains as to where she had seen her before.

"Glad you like it. My brother also has one of the apartments in the building and he is always thanking me for finding it for him," she said, thinking what stunning eyes Lexi had. "How long has Abbie gone for?" asked Martha. She knew Jo's flatmate had gone travelling, as Faye had filled her in and advised that Jo was looking for a new person to share the apartment.

"She says six months but I know her, if she knows I am happy with a new flatmate she will stay for longer, I am sure of it," said Jo, looking at Toby and thinking how handsome he was. They looked great together.

Lexi was pleased to hear this as six months would fly by. She was enjoying living with Jo already and didn't want to have to move again.

"That's good that you are happy, Jo, I am pleased for you." Martha smiled and looked at Lexi; she thought she was absolutely stunning and loved the cream shirt she was wearing. "Well, lovely to meet you both. Enjoy the rest of your evening and we'll catch up soon." Martha gave Jo a hug.

"Lovely to see you too, Martha. Take care and I am sure Faye will organise something or another you know what she is like, ever the party animal," hugging Martha back.

They said their goodbyes and Lexi and Jo went out get in their taxi as Martha and Toby were shown to their table.

It was eight forty-five by the time they opened the door to their apartment and both Jo and Lexi yawned. "A quick cup of coffee then off to bed I go," said Jo, taking off her shoes and walking to the kitchen.

Lexi did the same and followed her. She had had a lovely evening and would definitely be going back to Papa's sometime very soon.

They chatted for a while, then each went into their respective rooms and were fast asleep by nine thirty p.m.

Chapter 42

Martha woke up before her alarm went off, and saw Toby cuddled up next to her. She smiled. I think I love him, she thought, how is that possible!

Toby stirred, as if sensing that Martha was awake. "Morning, gorgeous," he said, looking at her and pulling her in closer towards him.

"Morning gorgeous yourself," she said, loving his strong arms around her naked body.

He started to caress her nipple and she gave out a soft moan. "Toby, you are so sexy, do you know that?" She smiled down at him, loving the feeling he was giving her.

"I have been told that most of my adult life actually," he said, grinning at her as he stroked her breast harder.

She laughed out loud and could feel his erection against her thigh. "I think we need to get up and get ready for work, don't you?" she said, hoping he would disagree and carry on with what he was doing.

"I think we need to make passionate love first," he said, climbing on top of her and kissing her full on the mouth.

Martha gave a very loud sigh. "I think I wouldn't be able to stop you," she said in a low voice.

They made love slowly. Martha's alarm went off in the middle of it but they didn't seem to notice, both caught up in the moment of their orgasm.

When they had finished, they both got in the shower together, washing each other's juices away and enjoying yet another erotic moment. "All this before work," said Marth. "I won't get anything done."

Toby bent down to kiss her full on the mouth. The water was cascading over both their naked bodies and she responded, pulling him closer into her and loving the way his tongue felt in her mouth.

They dressed slowly. They were like a well-oiled machine and felt as if they had been together forever.

"Are you still up for dinner with the Americans?" he asked, as he put his shirt on and started to button it up.

"Of course," she said. "I have no plans at the moment, when do you think it will be?" she asked, thinking he looked totally sexy in his white Ralph Lauren shirt.

"Not sure, they were due to fly in at the weekend. I will speak to my boss today and let you know."

"Ok," she said. "What are your plans for later?" she asked shyly, thinking would he want to spend another evening with her, and hoping he would.

"I don't have any," he said. "I would love to be with you again though," and walked over to her.

She was applying her mascara at her mirrored dressing table in a lacy black bra and matching thong. She stood up as he approached.

"You look very sexy in that underwear," he said, as he started to stroke her back.

"You make me feel very sexy," she said, and kissed him softly on the lips, putting her tongue into his mouth. He gave a very loud moan and she felt his erection through his trousers.

"I am never going to get to work at this rate," he told her, pulling her closer to him and moving his hands down to her pert bottom and squeezing her cheeks gently.

Toby loved a woman in a thong and Martha looked amazing in hers.

She sighed in his arms. "I have had the best time," she said, looking straight into his eyes and loving what he was doing to her cheeks.

"Let's hope we can carry this on," he said, his face showing concern.

"Steve," she said, as if reading his mind.

"I hope he doesn't have a problem with it," said Toby, moving away from her and doing up his tie.

"Is it really any of his business what we get up to?" she asked, hoping he would say no.

"No, I suppose it isn't, but he is my best mate and I really don't want to piss him off."

"He is my brother, Toby, and I don't want to piss him off either, but I wouldn't want him to think he can stop us seeing each other!" Martha was starting to look worried.

Toby grabbed her. "It won't come to that, babe," he said, hoping he was right. Would Steve really not be happy about him being with his sister?

They both got ready for work and Martha said she would drop him off at the station. She had a few viewings that morning and needed Miss Ellie.

He went to get out of the car and turned to her with a very serious look. "I've loved being with you these past couple of days, Martha," he said.

"Ditto, Mr Green," she said, and kissed him on the lips.

They said a reluctant goodbye and each went to their work place.

Martha arrived in very good spirits and she saw David's car on the fore-court. It would be good to catch up with her boss; there had been a lot going on since he had been in two weeks ago.

"Hi, David," she said, seeing him at one of the desks as she walked in.

"Hi, Martha." He looked at her. "You look glowing." He was pleased to see her. He knew she had been working extremely hard the last few weeks whilst he had been away and had done a fantastic job taking over.

"Do I?" she said, blushing. Must be on account of all the sex I've been having, she said under her breath, still blushing.

"You do, Martha. I hope you haven't been working too hard while I have been away and you have had time to play," he said, not realising.

"I have had time to play, thank you, David," she said, still blushing and laughing out loud.

David was pleased to see her happy. "I must go away more often," he said, laughing back at her and not knowing why.

Martha sat down at her desk. She had a lot of emails in her in box and wanted to get them sorted straight away. David was kind enough to make her a coffee, as he could see how busy she was, and the other employees started to arrive.

"How was your holiday, David?" Jed, one of the negotiators, asked.

"It was lovely," he shouted from the kitchen. "Coffee?"

"Love one," said Jed, "white, no sugar, thanks."

Jed sat down at his desk next to Martha. "You missed a very busy week-end," he said, looking at his colleague, thinking how pretty she was.

"I was busy myself," she said, not believing she had blurted that out. "My nan had a fall and has been in hospital." Martha was relieved she didn't say "having sex" at the end of her earlier sentence. What was wrong with her, she thought?

"Oh, sorry to hear that," said David, as he came back in with the coffees.

"She didn't break anything, luckily. My nan is a tough old bird, but she did bang her head quite badly and they kept her in over the weekend. She is coming home today and Mum is going to look after her," she said, taking the coffee from David.

"Well, give her our love, and you know if you need any time, Martha, you just take it. It's not a problem."

"Thank you, David, means a lot," she said, as she went back to her emails.

Martha had been engrossed all morning, catching up with all the view-ings that went on at the weekend and booking in new houses to look at before they could take prospective buyers round. She liked to see for herself exactly what a property was like so she could describe in detail when she was asked by clients.

Her mobile rang and she saw it was Toby. She smiled as she answered her phone. "Hello," she said, grinning like a Cheshire cat.

"Hey, beautiful, guess what?"

Martha smiled down the phone. "Hey yourself, what?"

"The Americans are not coming to town. Something about their dog being run over and my client's wife said she is too upset to travel."

"Oh," said Martha, "that's sad."

"Yeah," said Toby, "but on the upside my boss had already booked a restaurant for us and says that we may as well go anyway, so how about it?"

Martha laughed and Demi, the office junior, looked at her, thinking how happy she seemed today.

"So when are we going and where?" she asked, enjoying the conversation.

"Tonight if you are free, to Papa's, that gorgeous little Italian just outside of town that I have always wanted to go to. I have heard great things about it; the food is supposed to be delicious and it's all on the company," said Toby with excitement.

"We were going to take Nan there for her birthday, it's supposed to be lovely."

"So, is it a date?" he asked. sounding like a little boy.

"It's a date," she said, laughing again.

"How about I meet you at yours after work and we can call a cab from there? I was a little cheeky and packed a bit more than just for one night, hope you don't mind."

Martha didn't mind and she would show him later how great she thought that was; she blushed at her thoughts.

"I look forward to it. I should get back around six thirty; is that okay with you?"

"Perfect, and I look forward to seeing all of you later too," he said, feeling his cock stir at his desk.

"Ditto," she said again, although she wanted to say a lot more, but felt she had an audience listening in to the conversation.

She hung up and looked up. Jed, Demi and David were all looking at her and smiling.

"So who was that?" asked Jed, laughing.

Martha went bright red. "Were you all listening in on my conversation?" she said, unable to stop smiling.

"We couldn't help it," said Demi, "you sounded so happy. So who is he?"

Jed and David also wanted to know, but were glad Demi asked the question.

"If you must know he is my brother's best friend. It's early days but I really do like him." There, she had put it out there; it was up to them what they did with it.

"Aww," said Jed, "how cute. What does Steve think about it?"

Martha knew this was an innocent question but she started to worry. Her face fell.

"He doesn't actually know about it. As I said, it's early days." Martha's face fell.

"Why would he have a problem?" said Demi. "I'd have thought he would be pleased that his best mate and his sister were getting it on. I know my brother would be."

"Really?" said Martha, perking up. "I am not sure how Steve will react. I hope he is okay with it." She looked at Demi for more reassurance.

Demi was their office junior and she had been at Poole's for over a year, having joined them straight from school at seventeen. She was a lovely girl, had a great work ethic and was always helping everyone out with their massive workloads, as well as doing her own. She was a definite asset to the company and Martha didn't know what she would do without her. She was glad the agency had recommended her. They had increased her salary by five thousand pounds six months after she had joined and she cried when they told her. She couldn't thank them enough and made sure she worked even harder to show her gratitude.

"My brother is very protective of me and has always vetted my boyfriends for suitability," she said, looking at Martha. "If I was going out with his best friend there would be no vetting to do, as he already knows that he is a good bloke or he wouldn't be his best friend."

Demi did have a point and when she put it like that Martha felt a lot better.

"That's very profound, Demi. I will let Toby know. It might make it easier for him when he finally gets round to telling Steve. Thank you."

"No worries," said Demi, and carried on with her typing.

The day flew by. Martha didn't have time for lunch after her viewings and wanted to get straight back to the office to ensure she was up straight with everything. She knew she would be eating later, so grabbed an apple

221

that was in the bowl which was always brimming with delicious fruit. Martha had introduced it a few years ago to stop her going for chocolate when she was peckish. It worked very well for them all and everyone thought it was a great idea.

She managed to put a call in to her mum to see how her nan was and Linda had told her that everything was under control. Nan was back home and she was comfortable. "Do you want me to come over later?" she asked her.

"Steve said he would pop in," said Linda, "so how about you come over tomorrow? She is quite tired from the journey, so it would probably be best."

"Okay," said Martha. "If you are sure." She was pleased that she had the whole evening to concentrate on Toby, as her nan was in good hands.

She would get her some flowers, to take the following day, from the florist's a couple of doors down. They always did amazing bouquets that seemed to last a lot longer than other shops she had gone to.

She got in her car at the end of the day looking forward to the evening ahead.

Chapter 43

"Why the hell didn't you wake me last night at six?" shouted Katie to Mario, when she woke up that morning and realised she had slept all night. "You said you would."

"Sorry," said Mario. "You were sleeping soundly and I knew you must have been exhausted from being sacked and the worry so I decided to leave you," he said, trying to calm her down.

"I had things to do," she said angrily at him. She was running around his room trying to find all her clothes, that he seemed to have taken off her at some time during the night, and she was naked except for her thong.

"What things did you have to do?" he said, getting annoyed. "You had just been sacked and you can't look for jobs at six o'clock at night!" he said, shouting.

He thought he was being kind by letting her sleep. He wouldn't have bothered if he knew she was going to shout at him, although she was very sexy when she was angry, he thought.

"Well, you should have woken me!" she said, pulling on her trousers and doing up her bra.

"Don't get dressed," he said, his anger subsiding, "come back to bed. I don't have to be at work until noon, I could show you a good time." He smiled.

"I can't, I have things to do," she said, not looking at him and wrapping her top around her.

"Okay. Well, will I see you later?" he asked, thinking how gorgeous her breasts looked in that wrap around top.

"I'm not sure," she said, putting on her red boots and standing up.

Katie needed to call Steve and apologise. I bet he hates me, she thought. She needed to sort this out; she didn't want to piss him off. This was not her fault.

She grabbed her bag. "I'll call you," she said, not committing to anything with Mario.

"When?" he said, sounding needy.

Katie hated needy men. He was lucky he had had her in his bed as many times as he had. She really wanted Steve, but he hadn't been available and Mario was the next best thing, after Frank of course, she thought, and her nipples hardened at the thought of all three of them. Wouldn't that be a challenge!

Mario noticed and went over to her. "I can see you are aroused," he said, putting his arm around her to pull her closer.

Katie was not in the mood for Mario and shrugged him off. "I'm sorry," she said. "I have to go."

She walked out the door and down the stairs, leaving him staring after her.

Katie felt mean at what she had just done to Mario but she needed to speak to Steve and wanted to keep Mario at arm's length. The last thing she needed was Mario thinking they were an item. They were not an item; they were just fuck buddies, just like all the rest. It was Steve she wanted and she was damn sure that she was going to have him without any interruptions!

She ran out of the side door of Horatio's and stopped to get her phone out of her bag. She saw that she had a couple of texts from him and a missed call and she could see there was a voicemail. She looked at the texts first. They both said the same thing, but were lovely, she thought. She dialled to listen to it, hoping it wasn't Steve leaving a nasty message. He sounded so sexy and she was annoyed that she had missed the evening with him, as she knew that they would have had an amazing time. She had really wanted to see him. "Thanks, Mario!" she said out loud, really annoyed with him leaving her sleeping.

It was ten a.m. and she called his number. It went straight to voicemail. "Fuck!" she shouted out loud, as a passer-by looked at her with daggers. Why is it so hard to get hold of that man, she thought?

If she knew where he worked she would have just barged into his office and made him fuck her over the desk, regardless of who was around!

She decided to go to the taxi rank and get a cab home. She didn't have much money but enough to pay for a cab; fuck public transport, she thought, that would just take too long!

She tried his number again; straight to voicemail. "Shit," she said out loud, as she was walking. She got some more filthy stares. Katie didn't care; her life was a mess and she wanted to see Steve more than she had wanted to see anyone in her life!

Chapter 44

Steve was fuming with Katie. Why the fuck had she not bothered to call, he thought, as he dressed for work early the next morning.

The Bolognese sauce was still in the pan on the stove and Steve could smell it all around the apartment. He didn't have time to sort it out as he wanted to get into the office, so he sent a text to his mum.

*Hi Mum, not sure if you are coming to apartment today as I know you are busy with Nan, just to let you know that there is a Bolognese on the stove if you wanted to take it for you and Dad.

Send love to Nan and I will pop in and see her later

Love you

S x*

He got his coat and bag and walked out of the apartment, giving Ralph a stroke of his fur as he went.

He ran down the stairs and saw the brunette who he had often seen coming out of her apartment. She had a friend with her, who looked gorgeous.

"Morning," he said, as he passed them. Jo and Steve had only ever said those words to each other, as one was either coming or going and that had been the extent of their conversation.

He walked out of the main door of the building and decided he was going to walk to work. The rain had stopped and the clouds had made way for the sunshine. It was a crisp, fairly cold morning but Steve loved walking in this type of climate, it gave him energy.

He still had Katie on his mind but didn't think it was up to him to call her.

He still got to work on time and managed to bypass Debbie the receptionist, as she was busy looking at something on her screen.

He sat down and looked at his phone. Katie had not even bothered to text, let alone call, he thought, and carried on with his work, but still not being able to stop thinking of her.

She really had got under his skin and he didn't like that. She was messing him about.

He was called into a meeting that went on for a few hours and left his phone on his desk. When he returned he saw that he had three missed calls from Katie.

About fucking time, he thought, and dialled her number.

She picked up immediately. "Steve, I am so sorry." She didn't want to play games and went straight for the apology, hoping she could see him later that evening. "You wouldn't believe what happened to me yesterday. I walked out of my job after an argument with my boss and then I fell asleep and didn't wake up until this morning. I slept through the whole afternoon and night, I must have been exhausted." She didn't want to tell him she had been sacked as she didn't want him to think she was a failure.

She spoke so fast he couldn't take it all in. "Slow down, slow down," he said. "You've walked out of your job, why? Have you anything else lined up?" He started to feel sorry for her. She must have had a very hard time of it lately, what with feeling unwell and the sickness and now walking out of her job. How sad, he thought.

"I am so sorry, Steve," she said again. "I was really looking forward to you cooking for me and spending time together." She pretended to cry.

"Hey, it's okay, please don't cry." He pushed his hands through his hair. "Where are you now?"

"I'm at home," she said, pleased that he wasn't angry with her. "Can you come over?"

"No babe, not at the moment. I have just come out of a long meeting. I have shed loads of work to do and I have to go and see my nan later."

His fucking nan again, she thought, but didn't let him hear that she was pissed off about her.

"Well, when can I see you? I really miss you," she said, in a small voice.

His cock stirred and he held on to the phone tighter. He wasn't sure what to do. He couldn't not go and see his nan; she had just come out of hospital.

"How about tomorrow?" he said, thinking that was the earliest.

"Why can't you come over tonight?" she said, in her sexiest voice.

"I would love to but I am not sure how long I will be at my nan's and don't want to come over too late. I do have a big presentation in the morning." He really did want to see her but he knew he wouldn't get any sleep if he went over there later and he needed to be on his A-game for the presentation tomorrow.

Katie was fuming with him. Fucking Nan, fucking work, she thought, what about fucking Katie!

"Can we definitely make a date for tomorrow night? I don't care where it is, I just want to see you," she said, trying to keep her anger down.

"I promise," he said. "I will call you tomorrow when the presentation is over and we can arrange where and when. I may be able to leave work early and surprise you," he said, smiling.

"I'd love you to surprise me," she said, in a very low sexy voice. "I would surprise you right back!"

He moaned down the phone, feeling his cock harden. "Miss Fox," he said, "it's a fucking date!"

"A fucking date it is," she said, laughing out loud down the phone, excited for tomorrow.

They both hung up, deep in their own thoughts about the following evening.

Chapter 45

Katie went into the kitchen. The apartment seemed empty without Lexi and she wasn't looking forward to spending the evening in on her own.

Who could she call? It's not as if she had to get up for work in the morning. She really did need to sort out what money she had and what she was going to do with the apartment. Lexi hadn't bothered to contact her at all, which surprised her; she thought they were friends. "Obviously not," she said out loud, as she went to the fridge to find the wine.

I wonder if Frank is available, she thought wickedly, and picked up her phone to find his number.

"Yo," he said, as he answered almost immediately. There was a lot of noise going on in the background and she presumed he was at work.

"How are you?" she asked him, very slowly.

"I am fine," he said, just as slowly, feeling his cock harden at the thought of Katie's tits. "What do I owe the pleasure?" he asked, adjusting himself.

"I wondered if you fancied doing anything later?" she asked.

"I fancy doing you," he said, laughing at his own joke.

Katie laughed back. "You could do me after we have gone out," she said.

"Gone out where?" he asked.

"Well, I am starving, so thought you might like to take a sexy lady to dinner?"

She hadn't had anything since she was sick, and that was a few days ago. She was starving and there was no way she was going to cook for herself, not when there were men to wine and dine her, she thought.

Frank was starving too; he hadn't eaten all day and she was such sexy lady, he could afford to spend a little cash on her. "How about I take you to a nice little Italian restaurant I know?" He suddenly thought of Papa's and was salivating at the thought of their fillet steak.

"I'd love to," she said. "I wasn't expecting that!"

"I like the unexpected," he said, and thought of her erect nipples bobbing about in front of his face while she was riding him. This one was worth it, as he knew she would put out at the end the evening, unlike little Miss Virgin, although Ava had been constantly on his mind and he really did want to be the one that she lost her cherry to. He definitely saw that as a challenge, one that he was going to succeed at winning.

"Be ready at eight p.m. and I'll be waiting downstairs in a cab."

"I'll be so ready for you," she said, happy that she had rung him.

She ran to her bedroom, whooping as she went and looking forward to the evening ahead. All these men, so little time, she thought, and laughed out loud.

She decided she would dress to impress, but something that was easily accessible in a public place. She thought she should give something back, seeing as Frank was paying the bill. She licked her lips. She loved illicit sex; it was the best kind. She had heard great things about Papa's restaurant. One of the girls in her office was bragging about being taken there by her boyfriend and had gone on and on about it all day. Katie had heard about all the intimate tables and the soft lighting from the candles, with tables that were hidden behind large plants. Perfect, she thought, for giving Frank a show whilst others were eating. She got very turned on having sex when there was the slight chance of being caught.

She found a black dress that was very short and showed off her legs to perfection. It had a very low neckline, and zips to the side that could be pulled down and reveal a lot more than most people would like. She was happy with her choice as she showered and pleasured herself, thinking of the evening ahead.

She really was a very horny bitch, she thought, as she came out of the shower and stood soaking wet, looking at her body in the full length mirror.

"He will love me," she said, blowing a kiss to her reflection.

Chapter 46

Martha and Toby were shown to their table. "How lovely is it in here," she said, looking around. They had been given a very intimate table over in the far corner of the restaurant and Roberto said he was their waiter for the evening.

"How lovely to see Jo," said Martha to Toby. "She is one of my best friend's sister," she said, feeling a warm glow inside at being here with him. "How beautiful was that girl she was with! I am sure I have seen her somewhere before."

"I didn't really notice. I was with the only beauty I ever want," he said, lifting her hand to kiss it.

Toby looked at her, still with her hand in his. "Why did you call me your friend?"

"You are my friend," she said, looking confused.

"I would like to be your boyfriend the next time someone asks," he said, smiling at her.

"Then that's what you shall be," she said, beaming at him as Roberto came over with the menus.

"What would you like to drink?" he asked, in his Italian accent.

Martha was about to speak.

"We'll have two glasses of champagne to start with," said Toby, being quite authoritative.

"Straight away," said Roberto, and left to get the drinks.

"What is the champagne for?" she asked, not complaining as she loved the stuff.

"I'll make a toast when Roberto comes back with our drinks," he said, picking up the menu to have a look at the many dishes that were on offer.

"There is loads of choice," she said, looking at all the pages.

"There is too much choice," said Toby. "I hate too much choice."

Martha laughed. "Shall we go through it together? What is your favourite meal?" she said to him, thinking this was a great way to find out what he liked and disliked.

"I love most things," he said. "That's why this is so hard for me." He started to frown.

"Okay, what is your most favourite?" she said, trying to narrow it down for him and her.

"I love steak, but I also love fish, pasta too," he said.

She laughed. "Are you having a starter?"

"Are you?" he asked back.

"I don't think so," said Martha. "I can never eat a starter and a main, I always leave my second course as I am too full, and I hate waste."

"I hate waste too," he said, "another thing we have in common." He smiled.

"What other things do we have in common?" she asked, trying to wrack her brain.

"We like sex with each other," he said, smirking.

Martha blushed. "We do," she said, smiling, and went back to looking at the menu.

Roberto came over with the two glasses of champagne. "Are you ready to order?" he asked, putting the drinks down on the table.

"Can you give us five minutes, please? There is so much to choose from and it all looks very delicious. I want to make sure I choose the right thing," Toby said in a pleading voice.

Roberto laughed. "No problem, sir," he said. "I'll come back in five minutes or so."

"Thank you," said Toby and Martha together.

Toby picked up his champagne to cheer Martha. "To us," he said, and she chinked her glass back. "Forever," she said, enjoying the evening so far. Toby leaned over and kissed her softly on the mouth. "I love you," he whispered. "I know it's very early days but I really think I do." He blushed.

Martha kissed him again. "I really think I love you too," she said.

Their thoughts were interrupted by two people sitting over the other side of the restaurant. Toby looked up and he couldn't believe what he was seeing. Martha looked round and saw Katie in a very short black dress walk over to a table not too far away with a very tall handsome looking man.

"Oh my God!" said Martha. "Who is she with now?"

Toby knew exactly who Katie was with. It was that moron Frank, who he had nearly come to blows with when he went for a drink in Lloyds.

"He is a nasty piece of work, Martha, he really is."

"How do you know him?" she said, trying to keep her voice down.

I met him one night in Lloyds when I was having a quiet drink on my own after work. His girlfriend, well she said she was his girlfriend, he said she wasn't, started speaking to me randomly when I was at the bar. He came in and went ballistic and I think he would have punched me if I hadn't have walked out." Toby shuddered at the memory.

"Fuck," said Martha, unable to believe that they were here in the same restaurant.

"That's the third bloke I have seen her with and not one of them has been Steve. I really do need to get hold of him and tell him; he has to know about her." Toby looked worried. He hoped to God that Steve hadn't gone near her; who knows what he may have caught!

Roberto returned to their table. They were too wound up to eat but both ordered the linguine di mare. "Good choice," said Roberto. "One of chef's specialities," he said, and asked if they wanted any more drinks.

"I'll have a Peroni," said Toby, trying to listen to what Katie and Frank were speaking about.

"I'll have a glass of dry white wine, please," said Martha, trying to do the same.

"Pinot Grigio okay for you, madam?" said Roberto, knowing that the wine chosen suited everyone's palate who liked a dry wine; it was their best seller.

"That would be perfect, thank you," said Martha, taking her napkin and putting it in her lap.

Frank and Katie were all over each other. Martha was shocked at their behaviour. He had pulled her zips down and she was revealing more breast than not. Luckily they had been put behind a large planter but that still didn't hide what they were doing. They watched while Katie excused herself and went towards the ladies, still hanging out of her dress. Frank just sat there looking at the menu.

"Do you mind if I call Steve now?" asked Toby. "I feel awful and I know he is really taken with her."

"No, go ahead, but what if he asks where you are?"

"I'll just say I am out with work," he said, but now thinking when was he going to tell him about him and Martha?

Toby hated deceit. He was a very honest person and that's what people liked about him. They always knew Toby to tell the truth and not stab anyone in the back. He was the same as a small child; his parents always knew to believe Toby over everyone else because he was unable to lie. White lies, yes, but big full blown lies; definitely not.

He got out his phone and dialled Steve's number. He picked up almost immediately.

"Hello, mate," he said. "Everything okay?"

"Hi Steve, you okay to talk?" said Toby, taking a slug of his beer which Roberto had just brought over.

"Yes mate, you sound worried, everything okay?" Steve was just leaving his nan's and had his phone on hands free in the car.

"No, not really. I do have to speak to you sooner rather than later," he said, talking really fast.

"Okay, okay," said Steve, "slow down." Steve knew when there was a problem, he had known Toby for too many years to not be able to read him.

"I need to ask you a question which is a yes or no answer first."

Steve was getting worried. "Go on."

Toby took a deep breath. "Have you slept with that Katie bird yet?"

"What the fuck, Toby; how is that any of your business?"

"Steve, I need you to answer yes or no, please!" he said with force, but trying to keep his voice down

He could see Katie and Frank practically shagging on the table. He had his hand up her dress and her hand was definitely massaging his private area, that was for sure.

"Well, if you must know I haven't managed to do the deed yet. I have come close but things haven't exactly gone our way. I don't understand why you are asking?"

Toby let out a big sigh. "Thank God, mate, thank God," he said, looking at Martha and putting his thumb up to her. She had finished her champagne and was taking a large gulp of her wine.

"Toby, are you going to tell me what the fuck is going on?" Steve was shouting at his friend now, getting really confused. He just missed a cyclist that had pulled out on him.

"Fucking idiot," he shouted. "Not you, Tobes," he said into the loudspeaker. "Some dickhead cyclist just pulled out on me, although you are starting to act like one of those too!"

"Sorry, mate," said Toby, still relieved that he hadn't slept with Katie.

"Where are you? I'll come and meet you," said Steve, stopping at the traffic lights.

"I'm actually in Papa's but it's a bit difficult at the moment. Can I see you tomorrow?"

There was no way Steve was going to wait until tomorrow to find out what was going on. "No, you fucking cannot. Either I come over to you at Papa's, who are you there with by the way, or you come and meet me, your choice but either way it's going to be tonight!" He was losing it with his friend and wanted to know exactly what this was all about.

Toby ignored his question about who he was with. He didn't want to lie to him and wasn't going to tell him he was with Martha. "Okay, okay," said Toby. "Can you give me about an hour and I will come over to yours?" he asked, not wanting Steve to come to Papa's. Although it would probably serve that Katie girl right if he did walk in he was thinking of his mate and didn't want to upset him any more than he was going to. What Toby had to tell him was bad enough without that slag rubbing his nose in it, he thought. There was also the problem about Martha, too!

Roberto brought their food, which they devoured quickly. It was so delicious that he couldn't help but steal one of Martha's prawns too. "Hey," Martha said, smiling, "get your own."

"Sharing is caring," he said to his new girlfriend, and he definitely loved sharing with her.

"Babe, I am so sorry that this evening has been ruined. I will make it up to you and take you somewhere even nicer when I have sorted this mess out with your brother."

Martha looked at him. "Toby, nothing has been ruined. I have had a great evening and I love you even more, watching you be so protective over my brother. It's very cute." She leant over and gave him a soft kiss on the mouth. "I'm not sure there is anywhere nicer, either."

"Steady," he said. "What's your name, Katie, showing us up in public," and laughed. He liked the fact that she thought he was cute though.

Roberto cleared away their empty plates and asked if they wanted to see the dessert menu. They did, but time was of the essence. Toby wanted to get over to Steve's as soon as possible, so he wouldn't get back to Martha's too late. Then they could spend some time together before bed, although bed was exactly where he wanted to take her as soon as.

"Sorry Roberto, something has come up and we are now in a bit of a rush, but I can assure you we will return. We both really like it in here, don't we, Martha?" She nodded in agreement.

Roberto was very pleased with his comments and smiled as he went to get the bill.

"Sorry," he said again to Martha. "I will make this up to you, babe."

"Stop apologising. I am just glad that you care enough to do all this." She heard a loud laugh and looked over to Katie and Frank. They looked like they had drunk a few bottles of wine in the short time they had been there and were becoming very loud.

Martha saw Roberto go over to their table, hopefully to ask them to be quieter she thought, how disrespectful were they!

Martha did not like Katie at all. Her manner was all wrong and she was nothing but a tart. Steve was far too good for her. She must have pulled out all the stops for him to have fallen for her, probably pretending to be something she wasn't, just to get her claws into him. She hated women like that, imposters. Once they had moved in or married the poor guy they changed to what they were really like and they didn't stand a chance. She was pleased Katie had been found out before this had happened. At least they hadn't had sex, although she didn't know how; Katie seemed like a very manipulative person.

Martha had been looking at her and she did have a very beautiful face and a body to die for, but underneath she was ugly, very ugly, she thought, and Steve was well rid!

She turned to Toby. He was about to save her brother from a fate worse than death, she thought, and realised that this was definitely the man she wanted to marry.

They walked past Frank and Katie on their way out and Toby held Martha all the way home in the cab, thankful that he had found someone as amazing as she was.

Chapter 47

Lexi was in the office early. She left her new flatmate a note on the island in the kitchen to tell her. She had grown even fonder of Jo since she had moved in and was very happy living with her.

Although Lexi was still very annoyed at Katie, she felt guilty for leaving the apartment as she knew Katie would hate being on her own.

She had read all her emails and put the coffee pot and kettle on and was starting to look in her in-tray when Jo popped her head round.

"Early bird," she said, smiling, "you okay?"

"I'm fine," said Lexi, smiling back at her friend. "Just needed to get in and get on top of things. You know what I am like when I'm not in control at work."

Jo laughed. "I do, chick, I do."

"I hope you are okay with me leaving before you this morning," said Lexi, hoping she hadn't offended her.

"Course, no problem. Why would it be silly? We can't be in each other's pockets all the time."

Lexi was relieved. What a refreshing change, she thought.

"I was wondering if you fancied joining me and a few friends at the Feathers later. There is supposed to be a band on that are pretty cool."

"Can I think about it?" said Lexi. She didn't know if she wanted to go out again. The meal with Jo had been lovely last night but she felt like staying in. She still had a lot of unpacking to do and it was starting to mess with her karma.

"Sure you can," said Jo, "let me know later, no pressure."

Lexi loved that Jo was so cool with everything, it made it a lot easier all round. Katie needs to take a definite leaf out of Jo's book, she thought.

The day went quickly. Lexi left the office a little earlier than she normally would and went home to start some unpacking. She had decided she would go out with Jo. She didn't want her thinking she was unsociable and she had plenty of time to sleep when she was dead.

What a funny thought, said Lexi to herself, as she unpacked the last box that had been over in the corner of her room.

It was the box with the photo frames in. Lexi loved photos. She was always snapping here and there and had them printed off, and loved looking for unique frames to put her pictures in. There were an awful lot of her and Katie, mainly pictures of Katie with very little left to the imagination. She looked awful in the one that she picked up and she put it in the drawer. She didn't want any of Katie's pictures on show. She wasn't ready to let her be part of her new life just yet.

She heard the door shut. "Hi Jo, I'm in my room."

Jo went straight to Lexi's room and opened the door. "Hi chick, want a brew?"

"I have not long boiled the kettle. You should only have to wait a few minutes and the tea bag is already in the cup."

"Thank you, Lex," she said, as she walked towards the kitchen.

Lexi followed her. "I've decided to come out with you tonight if the offer still stands," she said to Jo, getting the milk from the fridge.

"Perfect," said Jo. "You can meet all the girls."

Lexi wasn't sure if she was in the right frame of mind to meet all the girls, but she would give it a whirl and she may make some new friends.

"What are you wearing?" Lexi asked. "It's not dress up, is it?" Lexi was in no mood to dress up and just wanted to put on some trousers and a top and be happy.

"God no," said Jo, "although I am never one to just go out in scruffy jeans and a T-shirt. I do like to show I have made an effort." Lexi knew this, Jo was always smartly turned out wherever she was going and for whatever occasion.

The girls chatted for a while and Lexi went back in her room to carry on with sorting out her things.

They decided to call a taxi to pick them up at eight p.m. so Lexi had plenty of time to get sorted and decide what she would wear.

She opted for a skinny pair of black jeans with a black fitted top and her Christian Louboutin leopard print stiletto boots. Lexi had worn these only once and she had received quite a few comments from women and some men on how gorgeous they were, which had made her happy to know she wasn't the only one who liked them.

She wore a short leather jacket and a leopard print scarf to finish her outfit and Jo whistled when Lexi had joined her in the kitchen for a glass of wine when they were waiting for their taxi.

"Oh my God, they are amazing, Lexi," Jo said, drooling over her boots.

"Thanks Jo, I think they are special too," she said, laughing.

They were going out with Faye and a couple of her friends and Lexi was looking forward to meeting Jo's sister.

They arrived at The Feathers and Faye screamed when she saw her sister coming through the doors.

"So lovely to see you, it's been ages," Faye said, as she gave Jo a big hug.

Jo laughed and dragged Lexi beside her. "This is my new flatmate, Lexi. She has had a bit of a hard time of late and needs cheering up," said Jo, bringing Lexi in on the hug.

"Hi, Lexi, lovely to meet you, any friend of Jo's is a definite friend of mine, so welcome."

Lexi thought Faye was lovely and they settled down with her friends Charlotte and Lucy. Faye advised that her other friends, Martha and Lauren, may join them but they hadn't made definite plans and she wasn't sure if they were going to come.

Lexi was having a great evening. The wine was flowing but she was sad too. Thoughts of Katie kept creeping into her mind. She still felt guilty for leaving the way she did and she wondered if Katie was home alone. She doubted it very much, as Katie didn't ever stay home alone. As soon as she knew Lexi would be out she would make arrangements to be out too, as she was always saying that the apartment was too big and quiet when Lexi wasn't there.

The Feathers had a DJ on that night and the girls were shaking a few moves on the dance floor before returning to their table to talk and drink more wine. Lexi didn't know how she was going to get up in the morning but was enjoying herself.

She had decided she would call it a night when the others were talking about going on somewhere else and making a full night of it. Faye and her friends all had the following day off, and Jo was a party animal who could survive on the smallest amounts of sleep without it affecting her at work the next day; but Lexi decided that she was going home.

"I hope you don't mind, Jo. I don't like being a party pooper but I do need to get a decent amount of sleep. I have drunk quite a bit and don't want to have a hangover tomorrow, as I have a lot to do."

"Not at all," said Jo. "I am so glad you came out with us though, the girls love you and think you are gorgeous. Those boots have also made an impression."

Lexi laughed. "Yes, they are a conversation piece."

She decided to say her goodbyes and went outside to get in a taxi. There were always taxis lined up in the street outside the pubs and clubs and she hoped she didn't have to wait too long in the queue.

The girls were devastated that Lexi wasn't coming with them to their next destination but all hugged her and said she was welcome out with them anytime and they exchanged numbers.

How lovely, thought Lexi, as she went out the door of The Feathers. She really did feel she had made some new friends tonight and what with Jo being so nice and welcoming she was happy to be going home with a smile on her face. She would find out all about their evening from Jo tomorrow as she was convinced there would be a story or two to tell.

She went outside and waited a short while in the queue and managed to get in a cab within minutes of leaving the pub.

She was just telling the driver her address when a man got in the cab beside her.

"Hey!" she said, "this is my cab."

"Sorry," said the man. "I didn't see you get in." He looked embarrassed and Lexi noticed this.

The cab driver turned round to look at them both. "Make your minds up, which one am I taking?"

Lexi and the man looked at each other. "Where are you going?" he asked, looking straight at Lexi.

There was no way Lexi was going to tell this stranger where she lived and decided to fire the question back at him. "I'm not going to tell you where I'm going, you tell me where you're going and we will see if it's in the same direction," Lexi said bravely.

He laughed. "I do think you are wise, after all I could be anyone, you never know." He thought she was beautiful.

"Yes, you could be anyone, so where are you going?"

"I'm not going that far, just Blake Walk. Are you going anywhere near there?" he said, still smiling.

"Well, that is on the way to where I live so I suppose we could drop you off there and I could take the cab on, does that suit you?" She wasn't in the habit of getting into cabs with strangers but he did look kind of cute and had the most piercing blue eyes.

"That would be perfect, thank you," he said, giving her a brilliant white smile as he put his seat belt on.

The cab driver turned back to face the front. "Don't worry, love, I'll protect you." He laughed and pulled away from the kerb.

They didn't speak to each other much during the journey, each looking out of their respective windows. The driver kept looking in his rear view mirror at them both. She is gorgeous, he thought, and what a good-looking bloke; they would make a great couple.

"Did you have a good evening?" the cab driver asked, looking from one to the other.

"Fine," they said in unison, and looked at each other and laughed.

"I was out with my work friend and her sister," said Lexi. He really did have the most amazing blue eyes, she thought, as she fiddled with the strap on her bag. How awkward is this, she wanted the cab driver to step on it so she could get out of this situation. She wasn't good at making small talk.

After what seemed like an eternity they reached Blake Walk. Steve pulled money out of his wallet and offered it to Lexi. "There you go," he said, "my half of the cab fare."

"That's way too much!" said Lexi.

"Tell you what, I will pay this time and if ever I get in your cab again you can pay, how does that sound?" He grinned at her, liking what he saw.

She looked at him. "Do you make a habit of getting into other people's cabs?" She couldn't help but smile. "I would rather pay my half now; it's not fair that you should pay the whole lot."

He wouldn't take no for an answer and put the money straight back into her hand.

"Please," he said. "I'm happy to pay. I did highjack your taxi."

She smiled at him as she took the money. "Okay then but if I see you out and about I will buy you a drink." Lexi couldn't believe how forward she was being; must have been the wine she was drinking. It seemed to have given her newfound confidence around the opposite sex.

He got out of the car, happy that she had taken the money. Before he shut the door he put his head back in. "Lovely to not meet you," he said, "oh, and nice boots by the way." He looked her up and down.

Lexi laughed and said, "Lovely to not meet you too, and thanks, I rather like them myself."

The cab driver sped away. Lexi looked out of the rear window until he was out of sight, smiling. "Nice bloke," the cab driver said. "Shame you didn't swop numbers."

Lexi looked at the driver in horror. "I am not in the habit of giving random strangers my number, you know," but she was smiling as she said it.

"Shame," said the cab driver. "You make a good looking couple," and carried on driving Lexi home.

She paid the cab driver with the handsome man's money and gave the taxi driver a big tip.

"Thanks, love," he said, pleased with what she had given him. "You take care."

Lexi laughed at him. "I will. Thank you for saying you would protect me if he decided to be a nutter."

"No love, I know he isn't. I have taken him loads of places before, he is one of my regulars."

"Oh," said Lexi, "I feel a lot better now."

"Enjoy the rest of your evening," said the cab driver, and sped off to pick up his next fare.

Lexi had had a really good evening and did quite enjoy sharing the taxi with the gorgeous blue eyed stranger.

She put her key in the lock and was looking forward to her bed. It had been an eventful day and she was looking forward to the next, all thoughts of Katie banished from her mind, for now anyway.

Chapter 48

Frank couldn't believe Katie had rung. He knew she was a sure thing and decided he would take her out to Papa's. He had had a lovely meal in there with Lexi and he didn't think it was too expensive. If they just had a main course and a glass each then he could get her back to his, or hers, and get working on that gorgeous body. Shame Lexi had moved out; it would be so good to have them both sucking on his cock and playing with each other while he watched. How fucking cool would that be!

He was pleased with his decision. He was going to call Ava but he thought it would be best to leave her for a few days. She would be begging him to take her out if he played it cool with her and then he could have her properly and she would love every minute of it. She would be begging him not to stop!

He arrived at Katie's apartment at exactly eight p.m. and got the cab driver to toot his horn so she would know he was outside.

The main door of the building opened immediately and Frank loved what he saw.

"Fuck me," he said, drooling, "you look amazing!"

Katie smiled. "Thank you, I try," she said, sliding in beside him.

He put his hands straight on her upper thigh. Katie smiled. "Starting early, are we?" she said, not even thinking of taking his hand away.

Frank leant in to give her a kiss. "If I wasn't so hungry I would get out of this cab now and take you straight back up to your apartment," he said, snaking his tongue into her mouth.

Katie loved that he was all over her. Fuck Steve, if he couldn't make time for her she would find other people who would, and Frank was the perfect person, she thought, as she saw his erection in his trousers.

"You look very pleased to see me," she said, as she put her hand on his manhood.

"I am very pleased to see you," he said, as he pushed his hand up further, feeling the lace of her knickers.

"Surprised you are wearing any," he whispered, as his finger hooked inside and he heard her gasp.

"I do have some standards," she said, loving what he was doing. "Papa's is a respectable place and I am a respectable girl," she said, opening her legs further.

Frank pushed his finger inside her and rubbed her clit with his thumb. "You are so wet," he said. "I am not sure I can hold out."

"Well, make sure you can. I am famished and hate sex on an empty stomach," she whispered in his ear, rubbing his crotch.

Frank let out a moan. The taxi driver was looking in his rear view mirror. "Get a room," he said, and carried on driving to Papa's.

Frank got Katie to get out of the cab first so he could put his hand up her dress and feel her pert bottom. "Wait until later," she said, not taking his hand away.

He paid the driver and he stopped her. He put his arms around her and gave a long slow kiss outside the restaurant. She moaned as she felt his hand on her arse. "Not sure I am going to be able to hold out either, Frank," she said, pushing herself into him. She could feel he was hard and she loved that.

They finally walked into Papa's and were greeted by a waiter who showed them to their table. There were a few people in who looked at Katie admiringly. "You have the men all hot and bothered already," Frank said, as they sat down. Katie smiled.

Paulo came over straight away. "I will be your waiter for this evening," he said. "Can I get you any drinks?"

"I'll have a glass of champagne," said Katie immediately, looking at Frank as she was pushing out her chest.

Frank loved her chest and thought she could have anything she wanted. "Bring us a bottle," he said to Paolo, "and a Peroni."

"Very good," said Paolo, and left them with the menus.

Katie started to pull down the zips of her dress on either side and her ample breasts were even more on show.

"I love those beauties," he said, unable to take his eyes off her. Katie giggled. "They love it when you touch them," she said, moving in closer to him.

Paolo came over with the champagne, two glasses and a bottle of Peroni. "Would sir like some champagne?" he asked.

Frank nodded. "May as well," he said, and took a gulp of his beer while Paolo was pouring the golden liquid into two glasses.

"I will be back with an ice bucket. Let me know when you are ready to order."

Frank looked at Katie and picked up the champagne. "Here's to an amazing evening," he said, raising his glass to her. Katie's nipples hardened and were straining against the material of the dress, even though she had pulled the zips down slightly.

"God, you make me hard," he said, as he took a large mouthful of his champagne.

"You make me hard too!" she said, as her stomach started to gurgle.

Frank heard it. "Blimey," he said, "you must be starving. I heard that."

Katie laughed. "I must be," she said, and took another sip of her drink, which wasn't tasting as she thought it should. "Does your champagne taste funny?" she asked Frank.

He put the glass to his lips and took a big gulp. "Nope," he said. "Don't you like it?"

"I normally can't get enough of it," she said, looking at her glass, "but this tastes a bit off to me."

"Off?" said Frank. "Can champagne be off?"

"I'm not sure," she said, and started to look at the menu.

"What do you fancy?" said Frank, brushing her nipple with his finger as he opened his menu.

"Cannot wait to get you home and see those babies," he said, staring at her large breasts spilling out from the top of her dress. "I might tie you down again, that was so erotic."

"Down boy, all in good time." She smiled at him, remembering her body tied up and displayed in full to his watchful gaze. "I think I'll have the fillet steak," she said. "I like it medium rare," and gave him a sexy pout.

Frank thought Katie might go for the cheaper pasta dish but didn't say anything. "I'll have the same," he said, looking at her. "Do you want a starter?" he asked, hoping she would say no.

"I wouldn't mind having something to share," said Katie.

Frank laughed. "We will definitely be sharing later, baby."

They were all over each other in the restaurant. Paolo brought their starter, a seafood platter which looked delicious, thought Katie.

Frank picked up a prawn and Katie started to feel very sick. "Will you excuse me for a minute?" she said, as she made her way quickly to the ladies.

Frank looked at her face. "You okay? You have gone a bit green."

Katie felt awful and knew she was going to be sick. "I won't be a minute," she said as she fled.

As soon as she opened the toilet door she was violently sick. "Oh my God," she thought, "what the fuck is wrong with me?" She just couldn't hold it in but once she had been sick she felt a lot better.

Katie wiped her mouth and looked in her bag, where she found some mints. She always had mints, as she never knew who she was going to be kissing at the end of the night or first thing in the morning, she thought, thankful she had put them in her bag.

She looked in the mirror. She still looked a bit pale but pinched her cheeks and the colour came back.

I must have one of those bugs, probably caught it from one of those stupid people in the office that came in when they were still sick. "Why the fuck would you do that?" she said, still looking at her reflection in the mirror and running her tongue along her teeth.

She pushed her hands through her hair and pulled the zips on her dress down a little lower. There, she thought, irresistible, and she kissed her reflection in the mirror.

She got back to the table and Frank had devoured most of the seafood platter, which she was thankful for. She didn't feel like eating fish, especially after what had just happened. When you were ill the last thing you wanted was fish. She turned her nose up as he offered her a prawn. "No thanks, you go ahead and finish the rest. I'll wait for my steak."

Frank did as she said and finished off all that was on the sharing platter. "Delicious," he said. "The food in here is awesome."

"Would you mind ordering me a glass of water, please?" she said to Frank.

"Water, you okay?" he said, looking at her strangely.

"I'm fine, just thirsty," she said, rubbing her hands on his thigh to stop him asking any more questions. She had sprayed liberal amounts of her perfume as well as popping two mints in her mouth. She hoped she didn't smell of anything other than Armani Diamonds.

Frank didn't notice anything and bent his head with the menu in his hands that he had asked Paolo to leave to shield him as he kissed the top of her breast.

"They are fucking amazing. Have you pulled the zip down further, you bad girl?" he said, grinning at her and loving that her body was exposed for him to see.

"I did," she whispered to him in his ear, as he was trying to softly bite her.

Paolo came back to take the plates and top up the champagne. Katie's glass was only half empty but he topped it up anyway. Frank had finished his beer and was on his third glass of champagne.

"Come on, slow coach," he said, looking at Katie. "Get it down your neck."

"I am not in the mood for champagne," she said, "but don't worry, I'm a sure thing."

Frank was pleased with what she had said. He couldn't believe he had met such a dirty girl as this one. She was perfect. Why couldn't more women be just like her; takes all the hard work out of an evening, he thought, knowing that you were definitely going to be getting a shag at the end of it. Some of them were such high maintenance and wanted at least two or three dates before they would get naked and let him ride them. What the hell was that about with Ava too! That girl needed a good hard cock inside her, she would love it, he thought.

They received their main course and Frank looked up, to see a man walking towards him with a very attractive woman. I am sure I know him from somewhere, he thought, but couldn't place him. He watched as the girl stared at them both as they walked past.

Probably jealous, he thought, as the man passed. Katie also thought she recognised him from somewhere. Had she had sex with him? "Probably wanted us both," said Frank. "I would be up for that, the woman he was with looked all right." Katie looked at Frank. "You do make me laugh. I thought I had a high sex drive, but you!" Frank sniggered and noticed that Katie wasn't touching her main either.

"What's wrong with the steak?" he said, as he put his fork in his and it just melted through the knife.

"I am just all of a sudden not hungry," she said, starting to feel sick again.

"Well, don't waste it. I will get them to put it in a bag for me and I'll have it for breakfast tomorrow," he said, with a mouthful of steak.

Katie laughed. "You are such a cave man, Frank," as she pushed her plate away.

She really was starting to feel awful again and apologised to Frank. "I am so sorry, I am going to have to go to the ladies again."

"What's wrong?" he asked. "Got the trots?" and laughed.

"No, I bloody haven't!" she said, as she walked away from him, thinking how rude!

By the time Katie had returned he had finished his meal and had asked Paolo to put Katie's steak in a box for him to take home. Paolo was happy to do this and had taken the plate away to bring back in a take-away box. "Is everything okay, miss, steak not to your liking? I can get chef to bring you something else if you prefer?" Paulo asked her. He didn't want people leaving their plates untouched, it wasn't good for business.

"No, it's fine, I am just not hungry, thank you," she said.

Katie sat down heavily on the chair. "You okay?" asked Frank, wiping his mouth with his napkin.

"I feel a bit dodgy," she said, being truthful.

"Dodgy, what kind of dodgy?" he asked, finishing the rest of the champagne while Katie's glass remained full.

"Can we just get the bill and go, please?" she said, starting to feel funny again. What the fuck was wrong, she thought, starting to get worried. I need to make an appointment at the doctor. This virus is not going away.

Frank paid the bill and Paolo had called them a cab. It was waiting outside and Katie wasn't sure if she could make the journey home.

"I just need to go to the ladies before we go," she said, walking away.

"What, again?" said Frank. "What the fuck is wrong with you? You have spent more time in the loo than with me at the table," he shouted after her.

Katie just made it to the toilet in time before she threw up again. Her head started to throb and she felt just as bad as she had the other night when she was with Mario.

It was a while before she sorted herself out and went out to join Frank, who was waiting outside in the cab.

"Sorry Frank, I feel awful. Can you just take me home?"

"Yeah, sure," he said, "and I'll come too, we can play."

Katie really was not in the mood to play but she felt bad that Frank had taken her to Papa's so reluctantly agreed.

"Okay," she said, "but not for long."

"For as long as it takes, baby," he said, pulling her in the cab.

They arrived at Katie's and he couldn't help but put his hand up her dress as they were going up the stairs. She had started to feel a little better and was enjoying this. Wilbur was there on his step but didn't take much notice of them as they walked past.

They arrived at the door and she opened it. As soon as she had walked in Frank spun her around and pulled the zips right down. Her breasts fell out of it and he immediately bent down to suck one of her nipples very hard while pinching the other one with his hand. Katie yelped. "Ouch!" she said, "not so hard, that hurt."

"You normally love it hard," said Frank, looking confused.

Katie did normally love it hard, he was right, but her breasts were really tender and he did hurt her. Maybe Marco had been playing with them for too long, she thought, he loved her large nipples too.

He lifted her dress up with both hands and started to pull down her knickers. She helped by stepping out of them and felt the cold air hit her sex.

"I would love to bend you over your breakfast bar," said Frank, and Katie pulled him by the hand and took him into the kitchen.

"This is where we first started off," he said to her, as he pushed her onto the cold granite top and lifted her dress up from behind. He looked at her pert arse naked in front of him.

"You look fucking amazing from the front and from the rear," he said, as he started caressing her cheeks and slowly putting his finger into her moist sex.

"That feels so good," she moaned, forgetting about her earlier sickness and putting up with the fact that her nipples were hurting on the cold granite.

He unzipped his trousers and let them fall to the floor. He pulled down his boxers and she felt his erection nudge her thigh. "Love it that you are hard," she said, wiggling her arse.

"Love it that you are bent over," said Frank, as he pushed his cock deep inside of her.

She moaned very loudly and he pushed in and out of her, bringing his full erection back out to the tip of her pussy and then thrusting it back in. She was moaning very loudly. "You like that?" he said, and she moaned her appreciation.

"Take your dress off and stand in front of me," he said, getting more aroused at the thought of seeing her naked. He loved her big tits with the erect nipples and her shaved pussy; he was happy she called.

She did as he asked and stood there with her hands down by her side. "Open your legs for me," he commanded, as she did again what she was told. "You look fucking amazing," he said, standing looking at her while stroking his cock.

She started to play with her nipples and he moaned. "You look very sexy doing that," he said. He walked towards her as he removed his shirt. Frank was now fully naked in front of her and Katie smiled. "You have an amazing body too," she said, as she put her hands up to touch his torso.

Frank was totally aroused and wanted her to go down on him. "Suck me," he said, and she sank straight to her knees.

He didn't know why, but this girl was having an effect on him. He loved that she was doing everything he asked without hesitating.

She sucked him deep and took the whole of his erection in her mouth, making him get harder. He pushed her head onto his erect penis and she took him in deeper and deeper. He moaned very loudly as she started to squeeze his bottom cheeks and slide her finger deep inside his arse. He became tense; the feeling he was getting was immense. "That feels so good baby, keep going, keep going, that feels amazing." He climaxed fully in her mouth and she sucked up all his juices. He was in his element, not a moan or gag from her, she loved it, he thought, as he looked down at her and smiled.

She got up from her kneeling position and stood there. "You liked that?" she asked, putting her hands down to feel how moist she was. Katie loved giving head. She knew that she had a way with her tongue that sent the men wild and it was her speciality. She loved to hear them moan.

"How about I do something for you?" Frank asked.

"Let's go over to the sofa," she said, as she grabbed hold of his cock to pull him over to the sofa.

Frank laughed. "You are leading me astray," he said, as he went to the sofa with her.

She sat down and spread her legs very wide. He knelt on the floor and pushed her legs over his shoulders and kissed her belly button. He loved that she had a piercing there and saw that it was a rose dangling on a chain. He licked her navel and started his descent. She moaned in anticipation as he found her intimate part and he opened her pussy lips to reveal her pulsating bud. He flicked her bean with his tongue and she moaned louder as he pushed his finger deep inside her.

"That feels so good, Frank," she said, as she pushed herself onto him. His hand pulled her open like a flower and he sucked and sucked until she was screaming. Writhing around with his face buried in her she climaxed, soaking him. He looked up at her. "You taste amazing," he said, as she looked at him with glassy eyes, feeling the full effects of her orgasm.

"You are amazing," she said, as she got up and led him in the same way towards her bedroom.

"I want you to fuck me hard now," she said, which was music to Frank's ears.

This was what he wanted Ava to say to him and she would one day soon, he was sure of it, but for now he was about to make Katie beg him for more.

He lay down on the bed and she straddled him, her large nipples bobbing about near his face as she mounted him. They both moaned together as the size of him filled her completely. He sucked hard on her nipples, taking each one and giving both the same amount of time as the other. He held onto her waist and pushed her up and down onto him. She was like a rag doll and he was in total control. She felt waves of excitement as she reached fever pitch and there was nothing she could do but just go with it and enjoy being fucked into oblivion by this gorgeous man. Her breasts were on fire and the pain she was feeling was extremely uncomfortable but she put up with the pain as she felt pleasure elsewhere.

They both climaxed together and her piercing scream showed him how much she was enjoying what he was doing to her. He couldn't get enough of her amazing body and he gave a final grunt as all his juices shot into her. They lay there panting, each lost in their own thoughts of the raw unbelievable sex they had just experienced.

Frank spoke first. "That was amazing, you are one very sexy lady," he said, kissing her.

Katie looked at him and was just about to say something when she felt bile rise in her throat. She jumped off the bed and ran for the toilet, just managing to make it before she was violently sick yet again.

"What the fuck!" she screamed out loud. Her stomach was now completely empty and as she lay in a heap by the side of the toilet she could hear Frank snoring loudly not far away.

Chapter 49

Toby dropped Martha off in the cab and went straight round to Steve's. He was very nervous but was just going to tell him like it was. That was how Toby liked to do things but he wished he had managed to speak to Steve sooner; he had tried.

He rang on the bell and Steve buzzed him up. The door was open when Toby got to the top of the building and walked straight into Steve's apartment, closing the door behind him.

Steve was sitting in the kitchen nursing a beer, looking straight at Toby when he walked in.

"So?" said Steve, with questioning eyes.

"I am just going to come out with it, mate. I have to tell you this and I know you are going to be pissed off, probably very angry, and it will hurt but I want you to know I am doing this because I care. I care very much about you and I don't want to see you get hurt, ever!"

Steve looked at Toby nervously. What on earth had Toby got to tell him. He presumed it was to do with Katie, but what? "Okay, I'm listening. Do you want a beer before you start?" Toby thought this was a great idea and went to the fridge to help himself.

He needed to ask Steve a couple of questions first so that he could fill in when he had been with Katie and Toby could tell him what he had seen.

"Hear me out, mate. The first date you arranged with Katie, did you see her?"

Steve looked at his friend. "Yes, we went to Partners. She looked fucking gorgeous, mate. I couldn't take my eyes off her but I put her in a cab at the end of the evening, as I had a big presentation the next day and wasn't sure if she would want to sleep with me on the first date, although the whole evening was one big head fuck." He smiled at the fond memory. "Seeing her there in that dress, it was mind blowing, but I thought with my head that night due to the presentation, which we won by the way." He smiled at that.

Toby took in a deep breath. Here goes, he thought. "That was the first night I saw Katie with another bloke."

"You couldn't have. I just told you I was with her. That was the night you took Martha to see the scary movie."

"Yes, I saw her after the movie. I took Martha into Horatio's, she wanted to calm down after the film, and she was there, she was flirting with the barman and she went out the back with him. I watched her, Steve."

Steve put his hand through his hair. "Are you sure, Toby?"

Toby was very sure. He then relayed the whole series of events as they happened, right up until tonight, when he had seen her with Frank in Papa's and how they were all over each other.

Steve couldn't believe what Toby was telling him, but he did believe his friend, as he knew he always had his best interests at heart. They had always looked out for each other. "Thank God I went to see Nan," Steve said, pulling at his hair now. "I didn't know what time I would be home and I knew that if I saw her I wouldn't get any sleep. I have a new client coming in tomorrow to present to, otherwise she would be in my bed now! How fucking lucky am I!" he said to Toby, shouting.

Steve wanted to kick something, he was so angry. "Thank fuck I didn't have sex with her. Someone has definitely been watching over me, that's for sure," he said to his friend. He felt sick.

He relayed in his mind all the times he had been with her and pieced together what Toby had told him. She had practically got out of one bed and into another without a thought for any of us. Do the others know, he wondered?

"I am supposed to see her tomorrow. I said I would get off work early. We would probably have had sex for twelve hours straight." He shuddered at the thought. "That is not going to happen now!" he said to Toby, who could see his friend was still fuming. "She was so up for it, as was I. We were both so sexually charged, it was an amazing feeling. You should see the body on it, I am sure the wait would have been explosive but now I cannot even think about going anywhere near her. How fucking stupid have I been?" A silent tear slid down his cheek.

Toby felt sick for his friend. She really had got under his skin!

Steve wasn't sure what to do next. He wanted to delete her number straight away but Toby told him not to; at least he would know it was her calling or texting when she did, as he knew she would, and he could decline. Either that or block her number, which was another option, he thought.

"I am never going to speak to the bitch again!" Steve shouted, wiping the tears away. "Why do women do this? As if Grace didn't do enough, Katie comes along and gives me another head fuck!"

"I don't blame you, mate." Toby felt really sorry for his friend. This wasn't the right time to tell him about Martha, he had had enough shocks for one night. He needed to tell him soon though, as he wanted to shout it from the rooftops and Martha wasn't happy about keeping it from her brother.

"I'm going to go, mate. Will you be okay or would you rather I stayed?" Toby did want to get back to Martha but if Steve asked him to stay he would.

"No, mate, I still have to get some kip for tomorrow. There isn't anything you can do and I don't want to keep going over and over it with you. She so isn't worth my thoughts anymore."

"Okay, if you're sure. Give me a call tomorrow. We could always have a drink after work if you want."

"Thank you so much for this, Toby. I know it must have been hard. I know it would for me if I had to tell you something like this." Steve hugged his friend with true feeling. "Let's hope I never have to."

"I am just glad you believed me," Toby said, looking at his best friend with pride.

"I always believe what you say, Tobes, you know that. We have been mates a long time and I know you have my back, just like I have yours." He walked Toby to the door.

"I'll speak to you tomorrow. Don't waste any more energy on that slag, Steve. She so is not worth it and you can do much better than that!"

"I know mate, lucky escape," said Steve, but still feeling wretched.

"Deffo, Stevie boy, deffo."

They hugged again and Toby got into the cab that was waiting outside.

They both waved and Steve went back up to his apartment. Fucking bitch, he thought, and shut the door quietly.

It was the busiest day Steve had ever known, which he was grateful for. He really didn't want to waste time thinking about Katie. She had betrayed him and she wasn't worth it, but she kept popping up in his brain regardless. He could see the texts she was sending and he left her calls to go to voicemail. He didn't listen to them, he just deleted everything. He wanted nothing to do with her.

He didn't finish work until gone seven and decided to put a call in to his mum. "Hi, Mum, just checking to see how you and Dad are and how Nan was getting on?"

"Hi, Steve," said his mum. "She is good, actually Martha has just been round, how are things with you?" He swallowed a lump in his throat. "They are okay," he lied. He was still angry with Katie and didn't want to see her, but she was still there playing on his mind. He had received a call from her earlier but he just let it go to voicemail. She was probably ringing with regard to later, but that wasn't going to happen, he thought.

When Steve was down he needed to be with his family; he wasn't great at being on his own.

If he was stressed, and he had practically moved back in with his parents for a while when he had caught Grace with her boss, it had taken him a long time to get over her.

"Do you think Nan would mind if I stayed at hers tonight? I still have my keys and I have some clothes there in the spare room," he asked, hoping his mum would say it would be okay.

"What's wrong, love?" She immediately knew there was something up.

He laughed, trying to shield his sadness. "I'm fine, Mum, I just love that big comfortable bed that Nan has in her spare room. I have never slept in a bed like that one," he said, trying to smile.

His mum was not convinced but decided to leave it. "It's not a problem. I could go and be with your dad for the night if you're coming over, no point in the both of us being here. She is back to her old self and doesn't want me fussing over her. You know what she is like."

Steve laughed down the phone. "I know exactly what she is like, can I speak to her?"

Linda passed to phone to Vi. "Hello love," she said. "If you are coming over I don't want you fussing over me either, your mother won't leave me alone and I can do things for myself now. I'm not an invalid and am back to my fighting weight," she half joked down the phone.

"I am going out for a couple of drinks first with some friends." He lied about the friends. "I have my key so I'll come and give you a goodnight kiss later."

Vi was thrilled to have her grandson to stay. She would make him his favourite breakfast of pancakes and maple syrup with crispy bacon in the morning to set him up for his working day. Steve loved pancakes. Ever since he had returned from a trip to LA he talked about nothing else and was in his element when his nan had surprised him and made them for him one day. "Nan, these are amazing, better than the ones I had in LA. You are the best," he had said, with a mouthful of pancake and syrup running down his cheeks.

"I'll see you when I see you. The room will be ready, you know it always is."

Steve felt a lump come to his throat. What he would do without his beloved family he didn't know. They were the best, and he was looking forward to going home to someone that night.

Vi passed the phone back to Linda. "Take care, Steve, and don't leave it too late to come back here," his mum said. He heard his nan shout in the background. "You leave it as late as you want. I have had an afternoon nap so I will be wide awake way after midnight," she shouted.

Steve laughed. He was aware of his nan's nocturnal traits. She would sleep for a couple of hours during the day and be up most of the night reading or watching her favourite programmes that she had recorded on her TV.

"I won't be too late," he promised. They all said their goodbyes and Steve picked up his bag and decided to head for The Feathers. He liked it in there and he knew the bar staff.

His phone pinged; it was another text from Katie.

Hi Steve, I thought we had a date!

He deleted the text straight away. She had already rung his phone umpteen times that afternoon and left a stroppy voicemail, which he only half listened to before deleting. He could hear she was irate but let her be; he couldn't care less about Katie fucking Fox.

He walked into The Feathers and went straight up to the bar. He saw a couple of Martha's friends sitting at a table but he just waved in acknowledgement and decided to stay at the bar. He was in no mood to speak to anyone. He just wanted a couple of drinks, then get a taxi back to his nan's for the evening and spend a night in her amazing comfortable spare bed.

Steve and Martha had shared this bed when they were young and you never heard a peep out of them all night, as they both slept so soundly. His nan always enjoyed it when her grandchildren came to stay; they were never any trouble and played so nicely together.

He had nursed his beer for quite a while, watching as The Feathers started to get busier. He liked it in his local, he felt at home with its rustic charm and familiar faces.

He had ordered another pint when he noticed a beautiful dark haired girl with stunning blue eyes and leopard print boots walk over to Faye and Charlotte. She looked familiar but he wasn't sure where he had seen her; he turned his attention back to his beer. The last thing Steve wanted was another woman in his life to think about. Katie had been exactly the same as Grace and although they had only been out a few times he really had liked her. He thought she was someone he would be with for a long time; she turned out to be fake.

Thank God for Toby, he thought, cringing. He would probably be in bed with her at this very moment, and although he practiced safe sex he doubted she did and knew now that she was wrong. Looks and personality can be deceiving, he thought, and she certainly deceived me. I thought she was a good girl but she is nothing but bad to the very core. He shook his head, enough of thinking about Katie. As he heard the DJ cranking up the music he watched as the girls moved over to the dance floor.

Those boots were truly amazing, as was the girl in them, he thought, as she swayed in time with the music, her firm breasts jiggling about and her black jeans showing off her long legs to perfection. "Stop," he said to himself, as one of the bar staff came over.

"Hi, Steve, how are you?" It was Steve and Toby's old friend from school.

"Hi, mate, I'm good. How are you? Still working here I see." He took a sip of his beer that wasn't really going down well at all.

"I am, Steve. The pay and the chicks are too good to leave." He laughed and went to clear some glasses.

It was a lot later than Steve had thought. He decided he was going to make his way back to his nan's and have a cup of tea with her, while she fussed over him. He should really do the fussing, he thought, but he knew his nan well; she had probably been lying down for too many days and wanted to get back to her usual routine.

He decided to finish his beer and go and get a taxi outside. He hoped there would be one in the street waiting.

He jumped in the first one he saw and there was the gorgeous woman with the amazing eyes and even more amazing boots sitting in the seat. He was shocked to see her and even more shocked when she said it was her cab; he really hadn't seen anyone in it.

She was very sexy and he was glad he had managed to persuade her to let him share the ride home, even though it was a little awkward. He really wasn't in the right frame of mind to be his usual flirty self so he found himself staring out the window for the duration of the journey. She had said that she was out with her work friend; how did she know Faye and the others? He wanted to tell her that they were his sister's friends but didn't want to get into a full blown conversation.

He had also wanted to tell her that he had seen her in the bar on the dance floor but thought it may come across as if he was stalking her and that wasn't the case at all. He really didn't realise she was in the cab.

He thought he should pay, as it would have cost him that anyway had he been on his own, and when the taxi arrived at his nan's he handed her the money. She was quite a feisty one, he thought, but a beautiful feisty one. He was pleasantly surprised that she had thought it too much. Normally women always expected the men to pay but she seemed a little different for some reason, and when he got out of the cab he had wished he had asked her name and got her number. He stood standing staring at the taxi as it sped off and he wondered why he didn't.

He had managed to tell her that he thought her boots were nice though, and he laughed.

Not at all on form, Stevie boy, he said, as he put the key into his nan's door and called out, "Hi Nan, only me."

Steve thought the girl in the cab looked stunning but the last thing that was on his mind was to ask anyone out on a date; that was not going to happen after Katie. Why did women mess him around so much? What was their problem, he thought. He was definitely going to just worry about himself, not waste any more time on the opposite sex; it hurt too much.

He went through and saw her making tea in the kitchen. "Kettle's on, love," she said, as she walked towards him for a hug.

"Everything okay?" she asked, looking directly at him.

"Not really, Nan, but I'm too tired to talk about it and would just like to go straight to bed, if that's okay?"

His nan knew that Steve would tell her when he was ready. He always confided in her and she gave him the space to do it in his own time.

"No worries, love, you go and get yourself comfortable and I'll come and tuck you in."

Steve laughed. "You don't need to tuck me in, Nan. I'm a big boy now."

"You will always be my little soldier, Steve," she said, and shooed him towards the bedroom, where she had already put the light on and shut the curtains ready for when he got there.

"Thanks, Nan," he said, and hugged her. "I will tell you all about it soon, but for now I just want to sleep and forget."

"Whatever you can cope with, Steve," she said, and kissed him on the forehead.

Chapter 50

Toby felt sorry for his friend as he got out the cab and knocked on Martha's door. She opened it immediately.

"Did you tell him, how was he, what did he say?" she asked, even before Toby had managed to walk through the door.

Toby looked very sad. "He took it well, to be honest, a lot better than I would have if I'd found out you had been sleeping around while I thought we were dating, that's for sure."

He walked in and flopped down on the sofa.

Martha felt so sorry for her brother and wanted to go round there and give him a hug.

"Do you want a beer?" she asked, walking over to the fridge

"No, I'm good," said Toby, kicking off his shoes and getting comfortable. He patted the seat beside him. "Come here," he said, staring at Martha.

She went straight over to him and sat down. He put his arms around her and gave her a very long slow kiss. She responded without hesitation and gave out a slight moan.

"Thank God I have you," Toby said to Martha, pulling away. "I really cannot believe what that bitch has done to him. He's really only just got over Grace and now he lets some slag into his heart and she treats him like that!"

He told Martha the whole series of events and she was extremely pleased that Steve and Katie hadn't had sex.

Martha snuggled into Toby and put her arms around his waist. "I know he has only just got over Grace, but let's be thankful that they hadn't slept together properly. He must be relieved about that," she said, hugging him tightly. "I feel so sorry for him."

"Do you think he will be able to cope with yet another woman betraying him?" Toby asked.

"He is a very tough cookie, my brother, as you well know, and I am sure he will be okay. It's not as if they lived together or had been seeing each other for months. It had only been a few weeks so I think he will re-cover a lot quicker than he did with Grace," Martha said, kissing Toby softly on the lips.

"Look at us though, Martha. We have only been seeing each other a few weeks too, and we have already said the 'L' word."

Martha looked at Toby. "You are right," she said. "I can understand how people fall for each other quickly. I was a definite non-believer before, but you have changed how I see things." She looked up at him.

Toby looked back at her. "How about I take you and your gorgeous little body to bed and show you how much I really do love you?" he said, giving her a slow sexy smile.

"I would love that," she said, and blushed. He had such a way with words that always made her feel so good inside.

They would talk to Steve tomorrow, separately of course, but he did need to know sooner rather than later about their relationship. Martha didn't want to leave it long, as she wanted to be up front with her brother and show him how much she cared for his best friend. She hoped Steve would accept them as a couple.

She walked into the bedroom and Toby started to undress her very slowly, kissing every part of her exposed body as he did so. She was in heaven. She had never felt this way before about anyone. "I would never cheat on you, Toby. You are too special to be messed about and I don't do that kind of thing," she said, loving how he was making her feel.

"I believe you, Martha, I really do," he said, as he removed her bra and took her firm breasts in his hands.

"You have the most amazing body that I could look at all night," he said, as his thumb and forefinger rolled her nipples around.

"Toby, you make me feel so sexy and I love your touch, it's so gentle." She sighed, not wanting him to stop.

"I can be rough too, you know," he said, pinching her nipples a little harder and making her jump.

"I like that you can be both," she said, reaching down and feeling his erect penis through his trousers.

"I like that you want me to be both," he said, as he removed the rest of her clothes. They made love for hours, feeling completely satisfied in each other's arms and looking forward to a long life together.

Chapter 51

Lexi paid the cab driver with the handsome man's money and got her key out of her bag. She was glad she had come home early, she needed some space. Meeting the gorgeous bloke had been a bonus too, she thought, as she smiled and closed the door behind her.

She was happy in her own company and didn't have a problem at all. She would have loved to have a dog like Jude to come home to, but she was happy with Jo, she laughed to herself.

She kept thinking about the guy in the cab. How weird that that had happened, she thought. He did have the most amazing blue eyes and seemed really nice. She sometimes wished she could be as forward as Katie around the opposite sex but she became quite shy and standoffish sometimes and felt she didn't show them her true self.

She was a fun loving individual with a heart of gold, who would make the right someone a lovely partner one day, she said out loud. Listen to you, Alexandra Barratt, boasting about your good points, she thought, and walked into her bedroom, laughing.

She loved how it was coming along. She only had a couple more boxes to sort and she would be done. Her clothes were colour coordinated in the large wardrobe and all of her things had been put away in the drawers and on the shelves, making the room have a cosy warm feel to it. She had put her prized shoe collection neatly in her suitcases and pushed them under the bed. They would be safe there, she thought.

She yawned and stretched her tired body. It was lovely meeting Jo's sister and her friends. They were a great bunch of people and she wouldn't hesitate in going out again with them, should she be invited.

She undressed and got into the big bed. She felt happy here in her new home and fell asleep, dreaming of coming face to face with Katie in her bathroom and Katie taking too long in the shower, stopping Lexi from getting ready for work and would be late; the bath was full of goldfish so she couldn't get in that either. Lexi was never late for anything.

She was woken by herself shouting, "Get out of the fucking shower, Katie," and sat up with a start. What was that about, she thought, bit random, as she looked at the alarm clock which was just about to break the silence of the morning.

She jumped out of bed and went into the shower, thankful that there was no Katie or goldfish in there. She washed her hair and spent a little more time than she normally would under the powerful jets. It was warm and very relaxing and she was so happy she could scream.

She got out of the shower and wrapped a large fluffy grey towel around her body. She heard her phone beep in the bedroom and went to see who the text was from.

*Hi Lex, sorry didn't make it home last night, Billy came back early from his course so ended up staying over at his, hope you are ok, see you at work

Jo x*

Lexi smiled as she read Jo's text. How thoughtful of her to let me know. Katie would sometimes go missing for days and would never call or text even though she knew Lexi would be worried about her. It was like living with a very small child, she often thought.

She was enjoying having the large apartment to herself. She got ready and made herself a cup of coffee and stood at the island, looking around the apartment. Jo had made it really nice and she felt completely at home.

She went to work with a spring in her step and had a very busy but eventful day.

Jo had said she was staying at Billy's again that night if Lexi didn't mind, so she was home alone again.

"Why would I mind, Jo? I am pleased you have someone to snuggle up with," she said, although feeling little envious.

"I will get something nice to eat on the way home and watch some TV. I have no problem whatsoever being on my own." Jo was very pleased to hear this, as she often stayed over at her boyfriend's house and was glad there was someone in the apartment looking after it.

Lexi left the office dead on five p.m. and decided to go to the delicatessen round the corner and see what they had to tempt her palate.

She decided on one of their pre-packed chicken Caesar salads, which was filled with croutons and parmesan cheese. Lexi loved cheese; the stronger the better for her.

She also bought a bottle of Pinot Grigio and decided to set up her meal on the sofa and catch up on some TV. The perfect evening, she thought, as she started to go up the stairs of the building. The door opened and there was a man about to shut the main door when she shouted, "Hang on, leave it open." She looked up and there he was, the handsome stranger.

"Oh," she said. "Hello?" looking very confused at seeing him.

The stranger smiled. "Hello," he said. "What are you doing here? Are you stalking me?"

Lexi looked horrified. "No!" she said. "I live here!"

He smiled at her, still holding the main door open. "I live here too," he said, looking at her intently.

Lexi blushed. "Seriously?" she said, still looking confused and not believing he was standing there.

"I was just going out to get a bottle of wine. I finished work early and nothing is cold enough," he told her.

"Well, I have some cold wine in my bag and seeing as you paid for the taxi the other night I am happy to share mine with you." She couldn't believe what she was saying; there was this guy who she had randomly met and now she was asking him to share her wine. Lexi Barratt, she thought.

He looked at her. "That would be lovely," he said, not believing he was accepting her offer. She really was very beautiful, he thought, and she did live in the same building. "Are you sure you don't mind?"

"I live on the second floor, 2b," she said, still blushing. "Of course I don't mind." Lexi couldn't believe how confident she was in his presence.

He was still holding the door and could see her blushing and thought it was cute. "I'm on the top floor, 5A," he said, thinking how weird that 'A' wasn't on the ground floor.

Lexi climbed the stairs and stood next to him at the door. "Well, now I know where you live I won't worry about inviting you in," she said, walking through the open door.

"My name is Lexi, by the way." She still could not believe how forward she was being.

"What a lovely name," he said, standing quite close to her as she was fiddling with the key in the lock. "I'm Steve." He heard her groan.

"You don't like that name?" he asked.

Lexi did like the name but it reminded her of Katie; she couldn't believe that of all the men in the world he was called Steve, too. Lexi smiled. "No, sorry, your name is lovely," and she opened the door to her apartment.

"My name is lovely," he said. "No one has ever said that before." He smiled at her, following her into the kitchen.

Steve gave a long slow whistle. "How nice is this," he said. "I love what you have done to the kitchen, that island is huge. Your apartment is much bigger than mine," he said, looking around at the décor.

"I have only just moved in, this is all the work of my friend Jo. She has to take the credit for how lovely it is." She smiled, feeling proud for Jo that he liked what he saw.

Lexi liked what she saw too and realised how tall he was. He was wearing a nice black suit and his shirt was pink and his blue eyes were twinkling.

Lexi put her bags down on the island and went to the dresser to get two wine glasses. "I'll be mum," she said, and poured the cold wine into them and handed one to Steve.

"To strangers," he said, and laughed out loud. Lexi laughed with him.

"This is so weird," she said, "but the cab dropped you off at Blake Walk. I thought you lived there in one of those big houses." Steve took a sip of his wine, which was delicious. "My nan lives there. I was staying over with her for the night. She had a fall a couple of weeks ago but is on the mend and I thought it would be nice to see her; also I love how comfy her spare bed is," he said, taking another sip of the delicious wine.

Lexi thought this was sweet, that he went to stay with his nan. "How lovely of you to spend time with her," she said, looking at him. He really was very handsome, she thought, as she took a sip of her wine. The cold liquid went down her throat the wrong way and she started to cough.

Steve went straight over to her and patted her back. "Are you okay?" he asked, as her face went bright red.

When she had recovered she blushed. "Sorry about that, went down the wrong hole," she said, feeling stupid.

"No problem. Thank you for inviting me in, this wine is so nice."

"I like it too," said Lexi, clearing her throat.

They drank some more of the wine and seemed at ease in each other's company, chatting about families and films they had seen, music that they were into. Lexi had forgotten all about her chicken Caesar salad and before long they had drunk the bottle of wine.

"Shall I go and get some more?" asked Steve, hoping she would say yes.

"I think there is a bottle in the fridge. It belongs to Jo but I am sure she won't mind and I will replace it tomorrow," she said, going to the fridge and retrieving the wine.

Lexi was starting to completely relax in Steve's company. She secretly thanked Katie; if she hadn't have moved out she wouldn't have met this gorgeous man and he wouldn't be here drinking their second bottle of wine together.

"It's not the same wine," she said, "but I know it is cold. This fridge is great for keeping things very cool."

"I am happy with whatever," he said, "just as long as it's cold and not too sweet I am not fussed."

"I hate sweet wine too," said Lexi, feeling the wine starting to take effect. They moved towards the sofa and she heard a phone beep.

"Is that you?" she asked.

Steve looked embarrassed. "Yes, sorry, I'll turn it off," he said, getting the phone out of his pocket and seeing Katie had sent him yet another text.

Lexi could see his face change. "Everything okay?" she asked, sitting down on the comfy sofa.

Steve followed her and sat beside her. "Yes, nothing I want to be bothered with," he said, as he switched his phone on silent.

They clinked glasses and Steve made a toast. "To perfect strangers," he said, laughing as he took a large gulp of the delicious wine, which tasted slightly different from the Pinot but just as nice.

Lexi laughed. "I am not perfect," she said, "but I am a stranger to you so I'll drink to that," and she clinked her glass with his.

"Okay then," said Steve, "to not so perfect strangers," and they both laughed as they clinked glasses again.

They had both had a really enjoyable evening and when Lexi looked at the clock she was surprised to see it was past ten.

"Oh my," she said, looking at him, "where has the time gone?"

"I've really enjoyed your company, Lexi," he said, looking at her. "How would you like to come out to dinner with me tomorrow evening?" He really liked her and they had got on so well that he didn't want the evening to end, but knew it had to so he went for the next best thing.

"I would love to," she said, blushing at this handsome man's offer. He really was great company and she hadn't laughed like that with the opposite sex for ages.

"It's a date," he said, not quite believing he had asked her.

Katie had been phoning and texting all bloody day. He really was not at all interested in her and was pleased he had met Lexi on the doorstep. He wasn't looking forward to being in on his own.

He walked towards the door. "I'll knock for you about eight p.m. Are you okay with that?"

"Perfect," she said. "Gives me a chance to get home from work and shower and change," she said, looking at him awkwardly as they reached the door.

They both stood there in silence and Steve decided he had to kiss her. She was so beautiful that he couldn't resist, and bent down and planted the softest kiss on her rosebud lips.

Lexi couldn't believe that this was happening but she was powerless to stop herself and responded by kissing him back just as softly.

"You have the most beautiful lips," he told her once he had pulled away.

Lexi blushed and her cheeks went pink "thank you" she said as she bent her head and looked at the floor.

"I look very much forward to seeing you tomorrow night" he said hardly believing that he was going on a date.

"I'll be ready" she said still blushing as he opened the door and went up the stairs.

She closed the door behind her and put her fingers to her lips "What on earth just happened there, Lexi Barratt what is happening?" she said completely out loud in the hallway.

She could not believe it when she had seen him coming out of the door, was she hallucinating, was she believing she was seeing the handsome stranger from the taxi the other night but really it was just the old gentleman who lived in the ground floor apartment?

She was still standing in the hall when she heard her phone beep, she walked into the kitchen to get it out of her bag and saw she had a text from Jo.

*Hi chick, sorry about leaving you on your own, really hope you are ok, am awake if you fancy having a chat if not see you in work tomorrow and we can have a catch up.

Jo xxx*

Lexi smiled a big beaming smile and texted back

*Hi Jo, I am ok really

I have had the best evening, will tell all tomorrow

Sleep tight

L X*

She put the phone down and went to clear away the glasses as her phone beeped again

*I look forward to hearing all about it????

XX*

Lexi laughed a big loud laugh and continued to do so as she put the empty glasses in the dishwasher and the empty wine bottles in the recycling and she walked to her room to get ready for bed feeling so happy that she had met Steve and couldn't wait for their date tomorrow, what on earth would she wear?

Chapter 52

Ava couldn't believe that Frank hadn't contacted her. It had been a few days now and she really was annoyed. Just because I wouldn't let him go the whole way, she thought; he knew the score, why on earth was it such a problem for men. They should be thankful that there are girls out there who want to save themselves for their husbands. We are not all promiscuous!

She looked at her phone, willing it to ring. "Please call, Frank," she said out loud, as she sat on her bed listening to music. She had enjoyed work that day and had filled Tiffany in on everything that had happened with Frank, including her stopping him from taking her virginity.

"I don't know how you do it, Ava. Whenever I am having sex with anyone I am lost and there is no way I could stop them from carrying on!" She looked at her friend and was envious of her willpower and that she was still intact.

Tiffany wished she had thought of saving herself for her husband. She lost her virginity at the age of sixteen to a random guy who she really liked, but as soon as she had had sex with him he didn't speak to her again and went off with someone else. Tiffany felt very used and was devastated that her first time was not as special as it should have been.

Ava was just about to phone her friend when her phone beeped. She saw Frank's name come up on her screen.

Yo beautiful, remember me

Ava smiled, at last, she thought.

*How could I forget you *

*Fancy a fuck? *

*Not gonna happen unless you want to marry me? *

*I'm not the marrying kind *

*Well I won't be the fucking kind *

Why don't we meet up anyway?

Love to, where?

*My place *

When?

266

*Now! *

Ava was turned on by his texts alone, regardless of what he had in mind when she got back to his bedsit.

She had been thinking about him for a few days and realised that she did definitely want to see him again. They could get over the small problem of penetration. Their foreplay was amazing and he did fantastic things with his tongue; she wasn't about to say no to that.

*I'll be over within the hour *

I will be waiting x

Ava felt her nipples harden and felt a trickle of her juices moisten her knickers. That man does good things to my body, she thought. She loved the texts, too!

She knew that she would not be back home tonight if things went as planned, as long as Frank understood that there was no way she was going to allow him to take her virginity, not in a million years!

She had a quick shower and got herself ready. She decided on wearing very little under her coat to surprise Frank; when he opened his door she would whip her coat off and have nothing on underneath, except a very small black thong and her heels. He would appreciate that, but she needed to make sure that she got out of the house without her parents seeing her as they were always interested in what she was wearing.

She decided to go downstairs in an outfit first so they could see what she had on.

"Hi, Mum," she said, as she walked into the kitchen where her mother was preparing dinner.

"Hi, love. Decided to come down from your room? Haven't seen you since you have been home from work."

"Well, you won't be seeing much of me now. I am on my way to Tiff's and am going to stay there the night. We'll go to work together tomorrow."

"Okay, love," said her Mum. "Maybe you can find time to have dinner with us one evening and we can have a catch up?"

Ava kissed her mother. "No problem," she said, and hesitated.

"I have a new boyfriend." She decided to tell her mother. She knew she would sooner rather than later and she wanted to be able to speak about him.

"Oh," said her mum. "Finally decided not to go back to Josh?"

"You know what he wanted, Mum. He wasn't going to get it and I was bored with telling him no, that ship has sailed. I have a new man now."

Her mother smiled. She knew Ava was saving herself for her wedding night and she couldn't be happier about it. "Why don't you bring him over for dinner one night, be great to meet him?"

"I might do that, Mum," she said, thinking about it, and went upstairs to put her clothes she had on in the bag and put her coat over her nakedness. Let's see how much willpower Frank has, she laughed, as she looked at her reflection in the mirror.

She went in and kissed her Dad goodnight. He was watching the TV, waiting for his dinner. "I'll see you tomorrow, Dad," she said, hugging him.

Ava shouted to her mum and went out the door, relieved that they didn't want to see what she had on under her coat; they would have both been shocked.

She drove her car over to Frank's rather than get a cab. She could always pick it up tomorrow after work and didn't want to get a cab. She had her flat ballet pumps on for driving and decided to change into her black heels when she arrived at Frank's. She was very excited on the drive over.

She arrived outside his block ten minutes later. The traffic had been light, which she was thankful for, as she pulled up virtually outside his door. She changed into her heels and put her flats in her overnight bag where she had her outfit for work tomorrow and other bits and pieces, such as a toothbrush and toothpaste and her hair straighteners. She didn't want to go into work with her hair all over the place. People would talk and Ava didn't like anyone being the centre of attention or the talk of the call centre.

She walked into the dimly lit hallway of Frank's building and was glad she was inside. There was the faint sound of someone's TV and a baby crying coming from upstairs. She walked towards his door and removed her coat. She was outside, naked, in a thong that showed off her pert bottom to perfection and very high heeled shoes that elongated her legs. Her blonde hair was in curls down her back and her nipples were erect at the excitement she was feeling. She knocked on the door. She could hear Frank say "about fucking time" and as he opened the door she dropped her bag and stood there in all her glory. Frank was speechless and just stood there and looked her up and down, drooling, unable to believe what he was seeing.

"Fuck me, darlin', you look amazing," and he walked straight up to her and put his hands to her breasts while she was still standing in the hallway.

Ava didn't care; she was totally turned on by the look on his face and she knew that she had floored him.

"You are a very bad girl," he said, as he snaked his tongue into her mouth and kissed her hard. "I love very bad girls," and he picked her up and carried her into his room and threw her down on the bed. He removed all of his clothes and stood there as she spread her legs open. She parted her pussy lips and looked at him. "Taste me," she said, staring at his large erect cock.

Frank did not need to be asked twice. He got down on the bed and immediately his tongue found her throbbing clit.

"That feels so good," she told him, as she heard him sucking her most intimate part. "You are so good at that," she said, in a very low soft voice as she brought her own hands up to caress her erect nipples. She was feeling the heat rise within her and she was totally at his mercy. She moaned very loudly. "Why didn't you call me for a few days?" she said, writhing around the bed as he brought her to climax.

"Don't go asking stupid female questions," he said. "You are here now, let's enjoy it," and he carried on with what he was doing.

She reached an explosive orgasm and she could feel him smile as he sucked her dry. "You taste amazing, baby," he said, as he carried on licking her juices.

She lay there for a while as Frank looked at her, his swollen cock even stronger than it had been at watching her play with herself.

She looked at him. "Thank you for not trying to enter me," she said, as she moved her hands up and down his pulsating erection.

"It's not because I don't want to, Ava," he said, watching her fingers wrap around him.

"I know it must be hard for you, God, it's hard for me too, but you know how important it is to me and it means a lot that you haven't tried this time." She kept her fingers moving up and down his shaft and she could hear his heavy breathing.

"Suck me, baby," he said in a gruff voice, and lay down on the bed.

She got to her knees and straddled him so that her bottom was in his face. "That looks gorgeous," he said, as she started to take him in her mouth.

He could see her pussy still glistening from the juices of her climax and he began to put his finger inside while she had taken his full erection deep in her throat.

"Oh baby, that is so good, keep doing that, keep doing that," he said, as she opened her legs wider. His thumb found her bud and he also pushed two fingers into her. She moaned very loudly with his cock still deep in her throat.

Frank shot his full load into her mouth and she sucked every last drop up. He was in heaven and he decided that she definitely gave the best blow job he had ever had. He thought Darcy was good but this girl was amazing. She had a way of putting his cock into the corner of her mouth without her teeth touching him and wrapping her tongue round his entire erection, which made it extremely tight for him as she moved her mouth up and down.

"Come here," he said to her as he pulled her close towards him. "That was fucking awesome, you dirty girl, fucking awesome."

Ava smiled. She was so pleased that even though he was fully turned on he hadn't disrespected her and tried to mount her again to take her virginity. She sighed in his arms. "You are amazing, Frank, really amazing," she said, as her eyes closed and she fell asleep, pushing herself as close to him as he could.

Frank lay there, thinking, why did he not try to mount her? She was really turning him on but the head she was giving him was so tight he didn't feel the need to. He was happy where he was and she saw how happy he was when he exploded inside of her mouth.

That was awesome, he thought, and seeing her when he answered the door was unbelievable. He thought she looked amazing standing naked in nothing but a tight little thong and those heels. She really did have a great body and she had never been fucked. That was so cool, Frank thought.

Darcy wasn't a patch on Ava, even Katie had her rough edges, but Ava, the fact that she was still a virgin, made him feel very aroused indeed. That was a definite plus, the fact that no other man had ever had her before. Frank wanted to be the first man. He would be the first man to enter Ava Green, he thought, with a big beaming smile.

He leant down and started to kiss her softly while massaging her nipples and cupping her breasts in his hands.

She moaned as he brought her out of her dreamless sleep and he felt her respond, putting her tongue in his mouth and exploring, her legs spread open like a flower, and she reached down and started playing with her own clitoris. He loved what he was watching and became hard all over again.

They had explored each other for most of the night and when the alarm went off at seven a.m. Ava woke. Her body ached as she saw Frank lying there beside her completely naked and she never felt so happy.

She would definitely ask Frank to dinner to meet her parents. She hoped he would say yes, as she really wanted to show him off.

He stirred as she got out of bed. "What time is it?" he asked, looking at her swollen breasts and becoming aroused.

"Seven a.m. I have to go to work. You stay in bed and I'll call you later," she said, brushing her hand over his torso and feeling his muscles.

"You were awesome last night, baby," he said, as he rolled over to be nearer her. "Why not come back tonight for a repeat performance?" he asked, hoping she would say yes.

"I'd love to," she said. She could then speak about him coming over to dinner to meet her family; she would love it if Toby was there too!

He pulled her down and gave her a hard kiss on the mouth as he squeezed her breasts. She moaned. "I need to go," she said ,wishing she could stay.

Frank opened his eyes fully and took in her natural beauty. "You are one very sexy, naughty little lady," he said, "and I am going to make you explode when you come back after work. Try and greet me the same as you did last night, I loved it!"

Ava was ecstatic, she was so glad he had called her. She had had the best night and couldn't wait to tell Tiffany everything.

Chapter 53

Katie woke up feeling awful. She looked around and could see Frank had gone. His clothes were not on the chair where he had left them. Why didn't he bother to say goodbye, she thought, rude bastard!

She suddenly remembered she was meeting Steve later. Good job she felt better; maybe she was reaching the other side of her virus, and now that she had got rid of every morsel of food that she had had over the last few days she must surely have fought it off.

She reached for her phone. There were no messages or missed calls. Lexi had not even bothered to see how she was; she hadn't heard from her since she had left with that Jo woman, another rude person, she thought!

She put the phone back on her bedside and decided to take a long hot bath. She would put in her favourite bubbles and stay there for a while, relaxing in the hot suds.

She started to run a bath and looked in her wardrobe to decide what she would be wearing to meet the delicious Steve. Whatever it was, it wouldn't be on for long, she thought with a smile.

No distractions, please, she said, putting her hands together and looking up at the ceiling. This is date number four and although he has seen me fully naked and I am sure liked what he saw, I haven't seen any flesh of his at all and cannot wait to have him penetrating me. I have a feeling he will be very well endowed, judging by his Adam's apple, she thought, as she licked her lips.

She stepped in the bath that was full to the brim and lay down. She felt the soothing hot water engulf her body and she began to relax.

Just what I need, she thought, as she saw her erect nipples bobbing about in the water. We could have a bath together. Sex in water is such a turn on. That would definitely be a plan for tonight; Steve would love it. When he calls I will ask him to come here. We can christen every room, even Lexi's, she said, laughing out loud at the thought.

She drifted off in the bath and was woken by her phone ringing. "Shit!" she said out loud, and jumped out, splashing water everywhere.

She missed the call but could see it was Mario who had rung. He hadn't bothered to leave a message but there was no way she was going to call him back. Maybe she never would, as after tonight who knew what would happen between her and Steve. He may never want to leave her if things went how she expected. He would never be going home again and they would live happily ever after in the apartment and she could be a kept woman. She never enjoyed work anyway. She could learn how to cook and make homemade meals in nothing but a skimpy apron and her heels for when he walked through the door every night and took her there and then while the dinner was cooking in the oven. She would cater to his every need and he would cater to hers. She became moist down below and looked at herself in the mirror. Her breasts were huge, she thought, the biggest they have ever been!

Maybe it was due to Steve and the excitement that was building up inside of her at the thought of seeing him later. She couldn't wait to get him inside her apartment and make him orgasm like he had never before. She would also make him turn off his bloody phone!

She looked at her reflection as her nipples hardened. "You are one sexy lady," she said to herself in the mirror, as she began to circle them with her finger and reach for her wetness below.

She couldn't seem to get enough sex these days. She lay on her bed, spent, after pleasuring herself and thought about all the men she had had in the last month or so.

There was that lovely threesome that she had been enjoying immensely until Lexi had walked in and caught them; fucking bitch, she thought. Then there was that manager of a club that she had stumbled upon one night when she had been out drowning her sorrows after yet another argument with her flatmate, who had taken her to his office and fucked her senseless across his desk while the music that the DJ had been playing was pumping all around his office. The next would have been Steve but he had put her in a cab home and she had gone to Horatio's to meet Mario and then it would have been Steve but his bloody nan decided to throw herself down the stairs so she could get all the family round!

She thought again. Oh yeah, Frank, that was nice, illicit sex was the best and he pressed all her buttons, and then it would have been Steve again but that idiot Mario didn't wake me and then it was Frank again; she remembered throwing up in the restaurant. No, that wasn't good at all! Her thoughts turned back to Steve. I wonder if he is feeling as turned on by this evening as I am. She looked at the clock on her mobile; it was after one p.m. She thought she would have heard from him by now, as he said he would leave work earlier. She wanted to know what the plan was, although she already knew what the plan was; he was definitely coming to hers straight from work, no ifs or buts, he would be there and she would be waiting for him to arrive.

She decided she would send him a dirty text just to get the party started.

Hey sexy man, looking forward to seeing all of you later and you hearing me moan!

She smiled as she pressed the send button. She expected him to reply straight away but he didn't, and she hadn't heard from him an hour later!

"Tut," she said, looking at her phone and checking that she had a signal.

She decided to send another text. Maybe he was in a meeting and his phone was in his jacket and he had it on vibrate. That would be cool if it was in his trouser pocket and vibrating near his manhood. She smiled as she sent another text.

Really looking forward to swopping juices with you later baby x

She put the phone down on the pillow beside where she was lying, still naked; again no reply from him. She sat up. Maybe he was with clients and couldn't reply, she thought.

She sat on her bed for another hour and still had not heard from Steve. She decided to call but it rang a few times and then went to voicemail. She decided to leave a very sexy message in the hope that he would call her when he had heard it.

"Hello gorgeous," she said down the phone. "I am lying here naked on my bed, thinking of you standing there watching me play with myself while I suck your cock. Look forward to seeing you later, big boy," and blew a kiss before hanging up. That should do it, she thought.

After making herself some brown toast, she didn't want anything else as her tummy was still a bit fragile, she put on the radio and listened to the random songs that were being played, humming along to some, singing to others. It was now five p.m. and she still had not heard a word from Steve. What the fuck was going on, she thought, he cannot be in a meeting for this long.

She decided to get ready in what little she was wearing just in case he just turned up at her apartment. She put on a tiny pair of white shorts that went right up the crack of her arse, showing off her bottom cheeks to perfection, they were that small. She could feel the material against her sex as she didn't bother with any knickers. She had a small navy and white striped top that just about covered her ample breasts and she pulled it up further so the bottom half of her breasts were on show. Men were very turned on when they saw this and she knew Steve would be no different.

She put on some high black heels that had a thin silver chain around the ankle. She had her hair in a high ponytail that cascaded down her back in big curls; she had spent quite a while with the tongs earlier that afternoon.

She licked her lips as she looked at her reflection in the mirror and immediately her nipples went hard. "How on earth is he going to resist that?" she said, brushing her nipples with her hand. They were still quite tender.

She looked at the time. It was six thirty p.m. and still no word from Steve. She decided to leave him a stroppy message on his voicemail as this was beyond rude, she thought.

"Hi, Steve, haven't heard from you. We had a date arranged and I am in my apartment waiting for you and dressed in something I know you will like. Please can you call me the minute you receive this message, as I am waiting here for you, baby, and want to see you."

There, she thought, that should do it.

She expected her phone to ring immediately but it didn't and she just sat there on the sofa staring at it every two seconds. "What the fuck is going on," she shouted at the TV, and decided to send him another text.

Hi Steve, I thought we had a date?

She was really getting angry now and decided to leave another voicemail but couldn't help but rant down the phone. "What the fuck is happening, Steve? I have been waiting here for hours for you to call and I haven't heard anything. Can you please get in touch as soon as you get this message, as you are starting to piss me off!"

She had started to pace the apartment, still in her heels, and the chain was rubbing against her ankles with the sheer force of the way she was walking.

She really didn't understand what was going on. Why is this man messing her about so much, why is she letting him mess her about so much?

She picked up a cup and threw it at the wall, screaming, "Steve, will you fucking call me!"

Her phone started ringing and she ran to the kitchen where she had left it on the breakfast bar. She saw it was Mario again and she jumped up and down, stamping her feet. "Wrong fucking man!" she shouted to the phone, "not the one I want to hear from." She let the call go to voicemail but there was no message left.

She didn't know what to do. She was so upset that yet another date with Steve was ruined and he hadn't even had the decency to call her or text her. What a bastard, she thought, and then said out loud, "But a very sexy bastard." Katie hated not getting her own way. Steve was definitely an itch that she needed to scratch, but things hadn't been at all easy since they had met in the coffee shop that day.

Why me, she said to herself, why me?

Chapter 54

Toby put a call into Steve at work. "Hi, mate," said Steve, seeing Toby's name come up.

"Hi," he said, feeling a bit nervous.

"What's up?" said Steve, immediately picking up on it.

"I need to see you, but this time it's different," said Toby, holding the phone really tightly.

Steve groaned. "What the fuck now?"

"Can you meet me later? I want to see you face to face, not over the phone, and I'm in the middle of something but popped out to make a quick call to you, as it's important."

Steve felt the hairs on the back of his neck prickle.

"I do have somewhere to be at eight p.m.," he said to his friend, which was not a lie; he did have to be home, home to knock for the pretty girl who lived downstairs from him.

"How about we meet in The Feathers after work or I could come to yours; that way you will be home by eight p.m." Toby wasn't really interested in what Steve was doing, he just had to speak to him and tell him about him and Martha. It was really important to him that his friend didn't find out from anyone else.

"I can meet you in The Feathers at six p.m. if you like, does that suit?"

"Great," said Toby, "see you at six."

Toby put the phone down and went back to his meeting; at least that was sorted, he thought.

He was in the meeting in body but his mind was elsewhere. He really didn't know how Steve was going to take this and wondered how he would feel if it was on the other foot and Steve was telling him that he and Ava had fallen in love. He pondered it for a moment; would I have a problem with it? He thought again. No, I probably wouldn't. At least I know him and know that he is a great bloke and wouldn't treat my sister like shit and would look after her. He felt a little better. Maybe Steve would have the same thought process. Then he thought again but what if the relationship

277

went tits up, how would that be? What if he left Ava heartbroken and she was devastated that they were no longer together, that would not be cool and he would not like that!

"Shit," he said out loud, as he made another excuse to leave the meeting to go to the toilet.

He really was starting to sweat at the thought of meeting Steve. How is he going to react, he thought, as he shook his hands under the dryer. This isn't going to go well, he knew that!

The rest of the day dragged and Toby couldn't get out of the office quick enough. He decided to leave at five fifteen p.m. and get in The Feathers early and have a beer for Dutch courage.

He had already told Martha of his plans and she was pleased he was telling Steve; this meant that he was serious about her and she gave a little whoop when she put the phone down.

He ordered himself a beer and drank it quite quickly. "Thirsty?" said Levi. "Dutch courage, mate," said Toby, ordering another one.

He was about to order his third pint when Steve walked in and saw Toby at the bar.

"What can I get you?" Levi said, looking at them both. They didn't look their normal chirpy selves and Levi looked at his friends with concern. "What's up with you two?" he asked, as he put two pints of beer down on the bar for them.

"You tell me, Levi," said Steve, taking a sip of his pint and looking at Toby.

"Steve, let's sit down. Sorry, Levi, this is rather sensitive and I need to speak to him alone."

"No problem," said Levi, as he cleared away Toby's empty glass and went to serve another customer.

Steve and Toby found a table over the far corner of the bar and they both sat down.

"How are you, after the bombshell I dropped on you the other evening?" said Toby, really concerned to know that his friend was okay.

"I'm okay, actually, just really disappointed. There's no need to look after me, I'm fine." He thought about Lexi and smirked. He would tell Toby about her but it was early days and he had already embarrassed himself by falling for Katie; he was taking this one very slowly, although she was absolutely gorgeous and they had had a very enjoyable evening that he had replayed over and over in his mind all day.

"Here we go again," said Toby, nerves kicking in, and Steve noticed his hands shaking when he picked up his drink.

"What could be worse than the other night, mate, come on spill, I am all ears, you look petrified!"

"Sorry," said Toby, "but this is important. I have put it off for too long."

"What have you put off for too long?" Steve was a tiny bit intrigued. What had his mate got to tell him now? He was also a little scared.

"It's Martha."

Steve stood up from his seat. "What about Martha, what the fuck has happened to her?" Steve started to look worried. What did Toby know about his sister that he didn't know? He thought they spoke about everything.

"No, no, nothing bad, um, it's just, well."

"For fuck's sake, Tobes, just say it, will you? You're starting to worry me." He sat back down.

Toby took a deep breath. "Okay," he said, quicker than he wanted, "the night I took her to the cinema to see that scary movie we had a really good night. Remember, that was the first night I had seen Katie go round the back with the barman when she had had the first date with you."

"How could I forget?" He took a long gulp of his beer. "Bitch. You should have told me then," he said, looking accusingly at Toby.

"We've been over that, mate," he said, looking sheepishly at Steve, glad that his friend hadn't blamed Toby for not telling him sooner.

"Anyway, I then had to take this client out who was in from New York with his wife, and my boss said to take a woman with me so I asked Martha to help me out. I wanted to ask you but I didn't see it as an actual date, more like her doing me a favour."

"Go on," said Steve, not looking too happy at what his friend was saying.

"Well, the Americans cancelled, something about one of their beloved dogs getting run over and the wife couldn't bear to make the trip when she was so upset."

"Yeah," said Steve, looking a little confused.

Toby was starting to sweat. "I had the restaurant booked and the meal was on the company so I took Martha anyway. It was Martha I was with in Papa's when I phoned you and came round to tell you about Katie."

"So what's wrong with that?" said Steve. "I would have done the same, did Martha enjoy the evening?"

Toby blushed. "We both had a really good evening," said Toby, his breathing getting heavier.

"Well that's good, so what are you saying?" said Steve.

Toby decided to go for it. "That me and Martha have been seeing each other ever since and it's going really well." There, he had said it.

"You and Martha are going out?" said Steve, looking at his friend, not happy with what he had just been told.

"Well, yes, we are and I really like her, Steve, and I hope that we have your blessing and that you are okay with us as an item."

Steve was shocked. His best mate and his sister going out together, what the fuck. "How long has this been going on for?" he asked, still unsure if he was happy with the situation.

Toby didn't like the look on Steve's face. If he knew that he had already slept with Martha before Papa's he would probably hit the roof, but the discussion just had not presented itself, much as Toby had tried.

"I know it must seem a little strange to you, but I really think I am falling for her. Actually," he said, "I have fallen for her. I am in love with your sister and she feels the same." There, he had said it, he had told Steve; now for the shit to hit the fan.

"In love with my sister!" shouted Steve. "What the fuck, Toby!"

Toby felt awful. "I am so sorry, we didn't plan it, it just happened. She is a fantastic girl and we have so much in common; it just feels right."

Steve put his hands through his hair. He just wanted to have a normal day, where he wasn't told things that he should have been told a lot earlier, and to look forward to his date with Lexi, without having to go through more crap and now Toby was telling him this!

Toby didn't know what to do. Should he just walk away and talk to Steve tomorrow, when he had time to digest all the information that he had been told over the last few days, or should he just be a man and take whatever Steve wanted to throw at him?

Steve ordered another drink, not bothering to get Toby one, and downed it quickly at the bar. "So you're telling me that you have been taking my sister out behind my back and you are in love with her and she feels the same?"

"Yes," said Toby rather sheepishly. "I promise I will take care of her, I won't let her down ever and I would be the best brother-in-law!"

"What!" said Steve. "You have asked her to marry you?"

Toby laughed. "No, I was just saying."

Steve didn't know what to think. Really, what business was it of his what Toby and Martha got up to? "I suppose you can't help who you fall in love with," he turned to Toby. "Does she really feel the same?"

"Yes," said Toby, letting out a sharp breath, "we get on really well."

"Have you had sex?" Steve asked, although again it was none of his business.

Toby blushed.

"I don't want to know the answer to that," said Steve, putting his hands over his ears.

Toby laughed. "She is a great girl, Steve."

"I don't want to know that either, Tobes, she is my fucking sister and that's too much information!"

Toby went up to the bar and asked Levi for two bottles of beer, which he gave him immediately. He could see there was some kind of confrontation going on and that Toby didn't even have a drink!

Toby took a long glug of the beer and walked back to the table where Steve sat.

"I know she's your sister, mate, and I totally respect that and her. It's not as if you don't know me; we have been mates for a long time and you know I will treat her right."

"I suppose," said Steve, still finding it hard to take in what he had just been told. "Do my mum and dad know?" he asked.

"Not yet," said Toby, "we wanted to run it past you first."

"Oh," said Steve, "and if I am not happy with it you would stop seeing her?"

Toby looked at his friend, not really believing Steve would be so nasty as to say something like that; he let out a big sigh. "If you were really uncomfortable with it, Steve, then I would have to speak to Martha and tell her what you had said and probably not go there." Toby couldn't believe he was saying this, but he didn't want to upset him any more than he had already and if he really wasn't happy with the situation then he would stop seeing her. As hard as that would be, his loyalty was with his best friend.

Steve looked at Toby. He could see that his face was sad at him asking this question; he also knew that Martha would never forgive him and would probably never speak to him again, not to mention what his mum, dad and nan would think!

He carried on looking at his friend. "If you promise me that you would never shit on her, that you would always put her first, then I don't have a problem with it."

Toby looked at his friend. "Fuck me, you had me going there, mate," he said, as he patted him on the back. "I really like her, Steve, we have had such a great time the last couple of weeks."

Steve smiled. "Get me another drink so we can celebrate." He was conscious of the time and didn't want to be late getting to Lexi nor did he want to be pissed. "Actually, I'll just have an orange juice," he shouted over to Toby as he was ordering the drinks from Levi.

Toby saluted. "Yes, sir," he said, laughing.

They clinked their drinks together. "Mates," said Toby.

"To treating my sister with the utmost respect at all times," said Steve, as they both fell about laughing.

They finished off their drinks and Steve said he was going to go home. He had had enough talking for one evening and needed to save his chat for Lexi.

Toby was relieved at how the conversation had gone and said he wanted to call Martha straight away. "I'll go and get a cab," said Steve, "and we'll catch up in a few days."

They both hugged and Steve went out to get a cab to take him home for his date with Lexi.

Martha screamed down the phone, "That's fantastic news, Toby, well done!" She was so proud of him for having the balls to tell her brother. Now they could be a normal couple and not skulk around. She wanted to tell her parents and her nan straight away and decided to arrange a big dinner at her house for them all, including Steve.

Toby couldn't wait to get home to Martha and take her in his arms. Everything was going to be okay and he needed to tell his parents as soon as possible, too.

Things are looking up for the Greens, he thought. Ava has a new boyfriend and I have Martha. He smiled as he went outside to get a cab to take him home to Martha. He stopped on the way and bought her the biggest bunch of roses he could find to surprise her with.

He was feeling great and it showed.

Chapter 55

Lexi had been looking forward to seeing Steve all day. She had told Jo all about the gorgeous man who lived in 5A.

"That must be Martha's brother," she said, willing her friend to go on with her story, as she could see that Lexi had a twinkle in her eye at the mere mention of his name.

"Isn't it weird though, that his name is Steve. Katie is going out with a Steve." Her face clouded over when she thought of Katie. She hadn't bothered to phone or text her, she did wonder how she was.

Jo noticed Lexi's face. "Come on, Lex," she said, "don't go all maudlin over that one, she isn't worth it. There are loads of guys with the same name, this is just a coincidence. I know hundreds of Billys," she said, bringing Lexi's sparkle back.

"You are right, she is so not worth my time. Why should I bother phoning her? It wasn't me that slept with her date or brought guys back to the flat for me to catch them at it, and left all her shit over the place for me to clean up!"

"And breathe!" said Jo, laughing.

Lexi looked at her friend. "How was I ever so lucky to have found you?" a tear forming in the corner of her eye.

"Come on, chick, you have a hot date tonight. We don't want all puffy eyes and red noses for the handsome one, do we?"

Lexi laughed. "No, most definitely not. Are you coming back to the apartment?"

"I wasn't going to, if that's okay. Billy is on another course from tomorrow, he won't be back for three days and I would like to spend the night with him."

"Not as if I am going to be on my own, is it?" said Lexi, smiling at her friend. She was so glad she had Billy and Lexi didn't mind in the slightest. Even if she hadn't have been going on a date with Steve she still wouldn't have minded, as she had settled into the apartment well.

The girls chatted for a while longer and Lexi went back to her office, too wound up to make any kind of dent in her work but she ploughed through what she could.

She hadn't a clue where they were going but decided to play it safe and put on a pair of skinny jeans and a smart pink striped shirt. She had her stiletto peep-toe pink Dune shoes that she put on to give her some height and confidence and was ready when there was a knock on the door.

Steve was standing there looking absolutely gorgeous in a light blue shirt and dark jeans. He wore a pair of Vans and his eyes looked so blue she nearly melted when she saw him.

"Hi," she said shyly. "Would you like to come in or get going straight away?" He was bang on time and punctuality to Lexi was everything.

"If you don't mind I'd like to get going straight away," he said, smiling at her. She looked gorgeous and he was a lucky man.

"Don't you think you should get a jacket?" she said, noticing that he didn't have one.

"I'll be fine," said Steve, waiting while Lexi went to get hers.

"Ready," she said, wondering where he was taking her.

"After you," he said, turning to the right. Lexi looked confused; the door of the main building was to the left and she pointed that way.

"I have cooked dinner for you in my apartment. I hope you don't mind."

"Cooked dinner for me," she said, "how lovely." She didn't mind at all and was thrilled that he had gone to the trouble.

She was sick of going out and loved nothing better than home cooked meals.

"What are we having?" she said, as she walked up the stairs to his apartment.

"Wait and see," he said, loving her inquisitiveness and her pert bottom in front of him as she went up the stairs.

His door had been left ajar. She walked in and the smell of garlic and herbs hit her senses immediately. "Smells delicious, whatever it is." She turned to him and smiled.

"If I forget to tell you," she said, "I had a lovely evening tonight, Steve," and walked through to the kitchen. A cat got down from the chair and immediately wound its body round Lexi's legs. She immediately bent down and picked the cat up to stroke him, and he nuzzled into her.

Steve loved her little comment and was pleased to see Ralph immediately take to Lexi. "That's Ralph, my inherited cat," he said, understanding why Ralph was hissing at Katie. The clever cat knew before any of them what she was really like. She must have given off an awful scent he thought, laughing, and going over to Lexi to stroke Ralph too.

She loved his apartment. It wasn't as big as Jo's but he had decorated it well and she felt at home immediately. "I love the red sofas and that red wall is striking," she said, looking around her. He was right, it wasn't as big as Jo's apartment but he had decorated it tastefully and was quite minimalist, which made it feel spacious and cosy at the same time.

Steve was pleased with her comments and was glad she liked the apartment and Ralph. His cat was important and Lexi was so ticking all his boxes at the moment.

"What would you like to drink?" he asked her. He watched as she put Ralph down gently on the chair where he had come from. "What have you got?" she said in an American accent, which made him laugh.

"Anything you want." He couldn't help teasing her back but his face was serious.

"Dry white wine?" she asked, hoping he had it.

"Coming right up," he said, as he went to the fridge to get the Pinot Grigio, which was the exact same bottle she had poured him in her flat yesterday.

He passed her the glass. "Thank you," she said, taking a sip straight away and smiling.

"Yes, it is," he said, before she could ask, and they both laughed.

"So what culinary delights have you made for me?"

"I have made a lasagne," he said, blushing.

"From scratch?"

"Yep," he said, thinking how stunning her eyes were and loving her pink shoes.

"You're a clever cookie," she said, smiling straight at him.

"I can be," he said, smiling straight back at her.

"I did cheat with the garlic bread though, hope you don't mind."

She laughed but decided to tease him further. "You went to all the trouble of making the lasagne but couldn't be bothered to make the garlic bread!" She feigned horror.

He looked at her a little sheepishly. "I know, it's bad of me."

Lexi laughed and went over to him. "I was only joking," she said." I am very impressed that you made the lasagne. I can't wait to taste it."

He had to stop himself saying, "I can't wait to taste you"; that would definitely not be appropriate, he thought, so he bent down and kissed her on the lips instead. She was a little shocked and stepped back.

"I'm sorry, Lexi, I couldn't help it. You look stunning in those jeans."

She was a little surprised at the kiss but when he gave her the compliment she was thrilled.

"I liked it," she said, and leaned in and kissed him again. He responded and also put his strong arms around her. She was so tiny, he thought, and she felt good in his arms. He pulled slightly away and looked down at her. "I am sorry for being so forward. I just couldn't help myself."

Lexi blushed. "It's okay" and reached for her wine glass to try and cover her pinkness.

The lasagne was delicious. He had laid the table and put out red napkins and a red candle that glowed in the middle of the glass table, making shapes all around the kitchen. Lexi thought it looked lovely and knew he had gone to a lot of trouble, which she loved.

He was a proper gentleman and they were very hard to find in this day and age; she thought of Frank and she frowned.

"Your face has changed. Everything okay?" he asked, taking another mouthful of his lasagne which he thought had turned out great. His mum had given him the recipe a while ago and he made it for his family quite a lot, so he knew what he was doing.

"Oh nothing, I was just thinking what a gentleman you are and then thinking of someone I knew once who definitely was not!" She felt like it was a long time ago that she had gone on her date with Frank but it had been less than a month.

"Thank you," he said. "My parents instilled good manners in me and my sister and we will do the same with our children, as it's extremely important to have them and treat a lady right."

Lexi was gobsmacked. "Sounds like your parents love you very much and want the best for you both." She thought of her dad and a tear ran down her cheek.

Steve got up immediately and went round to her. "Why are you crying, what's wrong?"

Lexi felt stupid and wiped the tear away quickly. "Sorry, what you just said made me think of my dad, that's all. He was killed in a car accident when I was ten. I am okay about it now but at the time we were all devastated and listening to you made me sad."

"We?" he asked, thinking she had brothers and sisters.

"Me and my mum. I'm an only child and we went to live with my uncle and aunt. Mum was in no fit state to look after a ten year old so they practically brought me up. Mum has not been well since, really." Lexi looked sad.

"Don't be sad. I have a sister and she is lovely. I am sure she will be happy to be your sister, too. I can introduce you to her if you like?" trying to stop her feeling upset.

"I think I have met your sister, is her name Martha?"

"Yes," he said. "How did you know that?"

"Small world but Martha got Jo her apartment. My flatmate's sister is Faye, one of Martha's best friends, and I met her briefly last week when Jo and I were in Papa's restaurant. Do you know it? It's absolutely lovely in there, we had a fantastic meal and both cleared our plates." Lexi had also cleared hers again tonight. The lasagne was delicious and she told him so. She had also brightened up, feeling a little embarrassed at letting a tear go.

"Oh, I see, yes it is a small world. I know Faye quite well, actually, all Martha's friends are great, just like her." He smiled when he thought of her and then remembered about Toby.

"Shit," he thought.

"What's up?" she said, looking panicked.

"Oh, long story." He decided to tell Lexi all about Toby, his best friend, and his sister, and how they are now 'in love'. "I literally just got told not three hours ago. How weird is that; my best friend and my sister," he said out loud, as if to make it real. He shook his head, not quite believing it.

Lexi thought it was a lovely romantic story; she was definitely a hearts and flowers kind of a girl.

They talked for another couple of hours, both not coming up for breath, and enjoying each other's company. They told each other where they worked and spoke about the gym and working out. The time had gone far too quickly and when Steve looked at the clock it was past midnight.

Steve was sad to see Lexi go; he really liked her. He couldn't help himself, she was so easy to talk to and they seemed to have a lot of common interests.

"How about I take you to Papa's one day when you are free, my treat?" said Lexi.

"I'd love that," he said, as he walked her out of his apartment and down to hers. Ralph came too. "He is a lovely cat," said Lexi, giving him a stroke. Ralph purred around Lexi's legs. "He really likes you, I can tell," said Steve, as they stopped outside her door.

"I have had the best evening, with the best food and wine, thank you so much." Lexi looked up at him.

"Ditto," he said, as he bent down to kiss her, softly on the lips at first but it then became more forceful. Lexi moaned and Steve grew hard at hearing this.

"Thank you, Steve," she said again as they pulled apart and she opened her door. Ralph walked straight inside.

"Cheeky," he said, and walked in to get his cat. "Sorry," he said, and picked him up and walked back to the door.

"You are welcome to have a nightcap if you want?" said Lexi.

"I would love to, I really would, but it's late and I have a very early start."

She totally understood, and didn't feel embarrassed that he had declined. She didn't see it at all as a knockback; she felt totally at ease in his company.

"Are you free on Friday? We could go to Papa's then?"

"I could be," she said, "but remember I'm paying to say thank you for tonight."

"There is no need to say thank you; I had a very enjoyable evening, with a stunning looking lady who my cat seems to be smitten with." Ralph was still in Steve's arms and purring, looking at them both, and decided to jump down.

Steve kissed her again, only for longer, and they put their arms around each other tightly.

"I look forward to seeing you Friday. Can I get your number, too?" he asked, and she was happy to give it to him.

They both said goodnight and Lexi shut the door behind her, looking forward to Friday at Papa's with the handsome not so stranger anymore, she thought.

Steve went upstairs and Ralph followed back to their man cave to tidy up.

Within five minutes Lexi's phone beeped. She had a text but it showed only a number. She guessed it was from Steve, and she was right.

*Hi, I had a lovely evening, thank you but I cannot let you pay on Friday as a lady never pays, especially on a Friday

S x*

Lexi smiled and immediately added his number to her contacts. She put his name in as 'Steve x' and replied to his text.

*Hello, thank you for a wonderful evening, not sure I have ever tasted lasagne quite so good before, we will see about Friday

L x*

He smiled when he got her text. "I think Friday will be a hit for sure," he said to Ralph, who was snuggled up on the bed next to him.

He drifted off to sleep, thinking about Lexi and how beautiful she was from within and without, all thoughts of Katie Fox banished from his mind.

Lexi got into bed and sighed. How lovely was Steve, she thought, and drifted off to sleep thinking that Friday couldn't come quick enough.

Chapter 56

Frank walked into Lloyds with a spring in his step.

"You look happy, Frank," said the barman.

"I am happy. Pint, please."

Frank was just about to take a sip of his beer when he felt a hand on his waist. "Hey, Frankie Boy, how's it going?" It was Darcy, and as soon as she saw him walk in she started walking over.

"Hey Darc, how's it going?" He looked down at her breasts spilling over her top and he thought she looked cheap.

"Haven't seen you in a while, thought you might have called," she said, trying to push her ample breasts towards him. "I did text you a couple of times but you didn't reply."

"Been busy, work and shit, you know how it is." He was trying to turn away from her.

"Too busy to see me?"

"Yeah, I'm not your boyfriend, Darc, you need to understand that. We just had sex a couple of times."

"We had sex more than a couple of times." She was sensing something different with Frank and it worried her.

"Okay, a couple more times, but it's not going to happen again," he said, moving his whole body back so there was a gap between them.

"Why, have you gone off me?"

"I was never on you, Darc. You gave good head, that was it, and it's over, so go find someone else to wrap your lips around."

"Are you seeing someone else?" she asked, tears welling up in her eyes.

"I am seeing lots of people, Darc. I always was; you were just too stupid to notice."

She thought he was being really cruel and started to cry in front of him.

"Save the fucking waterworks, why do women do that?" He looked at the barman, who shrugged.

Darcy ran to the toilet. She was devastated. She and Frank went way back. What has happened for him to be so nasty? She had always been there for him whenever he wanted. She allowed him to do whatever he wanted, even though sometimes he hurt her, but she still let him. She sobbed in the cubicle.

Frank drank his beer and asked for another one. He knew he was being cruel to Darcy but he needed to do it. She was never his girlfriend; he had told her that time and time again, so why she was getting upset was beyond him, fucking women!

The door swung open and in walked Ava, in jeans and a tight-fitting T-shirt with the word 'Ready?' emblazoned across the front.

He looked round and saw her coming towards him reading the slogan on her top.

"Hello beautiful. I sure am." He smiled and bent down to kiss her full on the lips and she snaked her arms around his neck.

Darcy at that point had tidied herself up, and came out of the ladies to see this. She felt bile rise in her throat. She ran back to the ladies and threw up in one of the sinks, coughing and spluttering as she did so.

Frank ordered Ava an orange juice. This time he didn't put a vodka in it and they went to sit down at one of the tables.

"How was your day?" she asked him, wrapping her leg round his and sitting very close to him.

"Busy, loads of cars, but managed to get through them all, which pleased the boss. How was yours?"

"Good," she said, "you were on my mind for most of it." She kissed him on the mouth.

"Was I?" he said. "Fancy, and what bit of me was on your mind, Sexy A?" That was what he had started to call her and she loved it.

"All of you," she said, biting his lip.

He responded, loving that she was all over him in a public place. He thought she was the most beautiful woman he had ever seen, and to know that she was a virgin and he would be the first to pop her cherry was such a turn on for him.

Darcy had cleaned herself and the sink she had just thrown up in and was watching them from over the other side of the bar. She was mortified that Frank was in here with another woman and practically eating her in front of the whole bar! How could he, she thought. Why is he being so cruel, flaunting her in his local, knowing that I am here!

She watched as they finished their drinks and headed for the door.

She shouted out, "Frank," and he looked over to her and just waved.

Darcy was devastated, how could he do this?

291

She ran back in the toilets and was sick again all over the floor. She sat in the corner of the ladies, sobbing.

Frank and Ava went to the taxi rank. "Would you like to come to my parents' for dinner?" she asked.

Frank felt very uncomfortable. He didn't do parents and was not used to being asked. "Why would I want to do that?"

"I really would love you to meet them. I have told them all about you. They think you sound amazing and they want to put a face to the name."

Frank did not think this was a good idea. "Eh, not something I am comfortable doing," he said, putting his arm around her. She really was so cute; he was definitely liking this one a lot, but without the parents.

"Frank, please," she whined, stopping. "My parents are really important to me, as is my brother, and I would love for you to meet them. We are going out together, aren't we?"

Frank hated the term girlfriend. It made him feel trapped, which is why he didn't want one, but Ava was a very special lady and he wanted to please her. She had pleased him enough, he thought with a smile, what harm could it do?

He suddenly found himself agreeing and he heard her give out a loud whoop and grab his face and kiss him full on the mouth on the pavement.

"Steady," he said, laughing.

"You will love them, Frank, you really will. They are so easy-going and my mum is a fantastic cook."

"I love home cooked meals," said Frank, feeling suddenly glad he had decided to accept.

"I will arrange it with Mum and let you know a date. Now can we hurry and get back to your place, please? I have a very large cock that I want to play with."

Frank laughed. "Yeah baby," he said. He put his arms around her and lifted her off the ground as they went to get a cab.

Chapter 57

Katie woke up the next morning fuming that Steve hadn't contacted her. She got out of bed and felt really dizzy, then bile came up in her throat and she ran for the bathroom.

She had nothing left inside her and was just retching over the toilet bowl, her hair going down the pan.

She sat there and began to sob. "What is wrong with me?" she cried through her tears. I can't still have a bug; I haven't eaten anything properly for days so there is nothing for it to feed on.

She got up and went to find her mobile.

"Hello, can I make an appointment to see the doctor, please?"

She made an appointment for that morning. There was nothing else she was doing and the sooner the better that she saw someone and got some tablets to make her stop being sick.

Katie walked around the apartment feeling very sad. She couldn't understand why Steve had not called or even texted; what was his problem?

She felt very alone and her heart hurt. She had lost Lexi, she also hadn't been in touch. "Bitch," she said out loud. And then there was Steve; maybe his nan had taken a turn for the worse but that's no excuse for him not to call, she thought, walking into Lexi's empty bedroom.

She went and lay down on her bed and looked around; it was devoid of any life. Lexi had taken most of her stuff. There were a few pictures against the wall on the floor and she had left her bedding and most of her fluffy cushions but that was about it; it was if she had never been there.

Katie let out a wail and tears streamed down her face. What the fuck is happening, she thought. No Lexi, no job and it looks like no Steve, although she wasn't giving him up without a fight.

She left Lexi's room with a big sigh and got into her shower. The hot water was scorching against her body and she touched her nipples. "Ouch," she said, "that's sore!" Her breasts seemed larger and her nipples were extremely sensitive, even moving about in the shower.

293

Those boys had given them a good going over, she thought, raising a smile thinking about Frank and Mario. They both loved it rough, although Mario was a lot more sensitive than Frank. I wonder what Steve would be like?

She washed herself carefully and stepped out, trying not to press down too hard on her breasts, to dry herself.

She dressed in Lycra leggings and a T-shirt. She put a sweatshirt over her shoulders and went out of the apartment to go and see her doctor. Wilbur was there preening on the stairs and Katie walked slowly past him. He stopped what he was doing and started hissing at her. She moved quicker and got to the bottom of the stairs from where he was sitting and looked back. Why don't cats like me, she thought. She remembered Steve's cat hissing at her too!

She walked round to the doctors' surgery and gave her name in at reception. "Take a seat," the stern lady behind the counter told her. There were a few people in there sniffling and coughing, so she avoided where they were sitting and went to sit on a small chair in the children's end of the surgery away from the ill people. Katie was not ill and she didn't want to catch anything from them either.

After half an hour her name was called. Why do they keep you waiting so long, my appointment was nearly an hour ago. She stomped into the doctor's surgery.

"Hello, Miss Fox," a very handsome doctor said to Katie. Her angry mood suddenly subsided. "Please take a seat." He moved his hand towards the faux leather chair that was at the end of his desk. "What can I do for you?"

"I think I have a virus," Katie said, looking intently at the handsome doctor, who she had never seen before. I wouldn't mind him putting his stethoscope on me, she thought.

"What makes you think you have a virus?" he asked, looking at her notes on the computer.

"Well, I keep being sick, and even now when I have nothing else inside of me I am retching and just bringing up bile." She grimaced; why would she even be telling this handsome man all this?

He looked at her and frowned. "And are your breasts tender?"

"Yes, they are," she said. "Have other people been in with the same symptoms?"

He looked at her. "Have you put on a little weight?" he asked her, still looking at her notes.

"Not that I am aware of, but now you mention it these leggings do feel a bit tight around my waist." She looked down at herself.

"I think we need to do a pregnancy test, Miss Fox, to at least rule it out."

Katie screamed. "A fucking what?" she said, getting up out of her chair. She felt bile rise in her throat again and he handed her a plastic kidney-shaped bowl.

She retched and a little water came out of her mouth as tears slowly ran down her face

"I can't be pregnant, I'm on the pill and I take it regularly!" she shouted at the doctor, as if it was his fault. Katie took her pill when she remembered, not regularly, sometimes three at a time if she had missed any.

"Well, that's good, let's just do a pregnancy test to rule it out and then we can go from there. Wait here and I will go and get a nurse."

The handsome doctor left the room and Katie was left standing there, dumbstruck. There is no way I could be pregnant, could I, please God no, please God do not make that stick be positive, please, please, please; her voice was going round and round in her head. She put her hands together and looked up to the ceiling. "Please, please, please," she said out loud, as the doctor came back with the nurse.

"Hi, Miss Fox, can you take this in the toilet and just do a sample on it and then we can go from there," she said, handing Katie a pregnancy test.

"I cannot be pregnant," she said angrily at the nurse, as if to blame her too!

"It's best if we can rule this out and then I can give you the right anti-biotics to help your symptoms," said the doctor. "If you are pregnant then I won't be able to prescribe much except advising to eat little and often. Try dry crackers or bread, drink lots of fluids and get as much rest as possible," he said, looking at her kindly.

"I am not fucking pregnant!" she shouted at them both.

"There is no need to be rude," said the nurse. "If you continue to do so then I will have you removed from the surgery."

Katie walked out the door. "Fuck you both!" she said, as tears pricked her eyes and she walked out of the surgery into the street.

"Fucking doctors and nurses!" she screamed at a passing car, which tooted.

She could not believe what they had said. Of course she wasn't pregnant, she was on the pill, how stupid could they get, the pill is a safe form of contraception, everyone knows that! She mumbled as she walked along the street.

She passed a chemist and decided to go in and get a test just to prove them wrong; then she would take it down to the surgery and show them.

She got to the counter and the woman told her that would be £9.99. "How much?" said Katie, looking at the woman. "Are you sure?" The woman held up the box and showed it to Katie with the price sticker on the back. It's one of those digital ones that shows you how many weeks pregnant you are, too, which is why it's one of the dearer ones. Do you want a cheaper one, that just shows you if you are pregnant or not?"

"No, I'll take it," she said, handing the woman her card and hoping that it didn't decline. She wished she had got them to do it in the surgery now; at least it would have been a free in your face rather than a £9.99 one!

She went straight home and ripped the contents from the packet and went into the bathroom. I will show them, she thought, as she did what she had to do the stick.

She put it on the sink and waited three minutes, as the instructions had told her, sitting on the toilet tapping her foot.

She looked at the stick. It said in clear black letters **pregnant 2-3 weeks**.

Katie threw up on the bathroom floor and screamed very loudly. She was devastated. How the fuck did she get pregnant, she was on the pill!

She was beside herself and then it hit her like a truck running straight at her; who the fuck is the father?

She threw up again. It could be a number of people and she didn't have a clue who it was, but one thing she did know was that it definitely was not Steve's and that was the person she would have preferred it to be out of all of them.

She wailed on the floor in the bathroom, not able to control her distress. She was in absolute shock!

She lay there in the foetus position, curled up, with her hair splayed in a tangled mass on the floor, her eyes tightly shut, feeling very lonely and totally devastated.

Chapter 58

Martha was thrilled that Steve had been cool about her and Toby. She could now tell the rest of her family.

She walked into the bathroom to take a shower. Toby was on his way home and she wanted to ensure she was clean and fresh for when he arrived. It had been a long day at the office and she was looking forward to seeing Toby's parents again and meeting Ava's new boyfriend. His mum had phoned him to ask if he was free and he had said he was but can he bring someone. His mum had said as always the more the merrier which was why Martha was getting ready to go and meet them all.

If Steve had not accepted them she would never have forgiven him, but he had been the kind caring soul that he always was. He had rung to congratulate her and asked that she let Toby out with him whenever he wanted. Martha had laughed and assured him that he wouldn't be losing his friend. Their relationship was moving very fast, not something she ever thought would happen to her.

Toby used his key she had given him to let himself in. He thought it felt strange that he and Martha had fallen into quite a routine with each other so quickly but he wasn't complaining, he really did love her and he knew she loved him.

He heard the shower on and smiled. I wonder if she would mind if I joined her, he thought, and started to unbutton his shirt. He was fully naked in a matter of minutes and opened the bathroom door slowly. Martha looked amazing with the water running down her body. She had her face to the wall and he could see her very pert bottom through the steam. He closed the door very quietly and got in the shower, putting his hands round her small waist and moving them up to caress her breasts from behind. She turned into him. "Hi, what a lovely surprise." She put her arms around him and pulled him into her naked wet soapy body. "You look fucking amazing. I could have stood there and watched you all night, but I couldn't resist getting in," he smiled at her.

"I have never had anyone join me in the shower before," she said, laughing and enjoying him being there with her.

"A shower virgin," he said, as he bent down to suck her nipples. They immediately became hard in his mouth and she moaned into him, "That feels so good Toby, keep doing that." He continued to suck and caress her breasts and he became hard, which she noticed. She got straight to her knees and took his erection in her mouth and Toby pushed himself forward so she took him deeper.

He heard his phone ringing in the other room but he was too engrossed in what Martha was doing with her tongue to bother, and he let it ring. They both swapped juices and let the shower wash it away as they soaped each other and laughed together, having fun with each other's bodies and spending quality time together. They had no inhibitions and Martha was up for anything.

When they had finally finished they dried each other with a towel and padded into the bedroom. Toby flung himself down on the bed and got his phone out of his trouser pocket. It was a missed call from Steve. He tried to call him back but it went straight to voicemail; he didn't leave a message.

He turned to look at Martha, who was standing naked, combing her hair. He thought how beautiful she looked and his cock stirred again at the sight of her.

"You look beautiful standing there combing your hair," he said to her, with a serious look on his face.

She turned to look at him rather than down on the floor. "Thank you, Toby, you say such lovely things." She saw his cock stir under the towel and she smiled.

"Come here," he said. Martha couldn't resist those two words and went straight over to the bed. He pulled her down and gave her a long slow lingering kiss as she leant over him.

He pulled her on the bed and had his arm round her so her head was lying on his chest.

Martha sat up, still naked, Toby touched her breasts with both hands. She smiled at him and carried on talking, loving the feel of his hands on her naked skin. "I wonder what Ava's new man is like?" she said, still enjoying the feel of his hands.

Toby carried on circling her nipples and cupping her breasts in his hand, loving the look on her face. He smiled. "I am sure he is a good bloke, she wouldn't go for anything else. Do you know she is still a virgin and saving herself for her wedding night? I think that's an awesome thing to do, not to mention hard core willpower. I know I couldn't," he said, pulling her towards him so he could lick one of her pink nipples.

Martha moaned into him and found his lips and kissed him very hard. "I love that you love to do that," she said, "please don't stop." Toby pulled the towel away, revealing his erect cock, and Martha gasped as if she had seen it for the very first time. "You are one sexy man, Mr Green," she said to him, taking his cock in her hand and moving up and down his shaft.

He moaned very loudly and he moved her on top of him and slipped inside her with ease. She was so wet and he held onto her waist while making her move up and down on his member. He enjoyed watching her firm breasts bob up and down in front of him. She climaxed very quickly and he watched as her eyes rolled and her head went back in total abandonment.

"You are gorgeous, Martha," he said, as he climaxed inside her and he gave out a very loud groan.

Martha was so happy she could scream. Steve had inadvertently brought them together by cancelling her to go on a date with that Katie and he had made two people fall in love. What a very cool brother, she thought.

She was looking forward to seeing Toby's parents again. They would be shocked that their son and Martha were an item and she was looking forward to meeting Ava's new boyfriend.

"We should get dressed, we don't want to be late," Martha said, pulling her reluctant body up off the bed.

Toby swatted her behind. "Hey!" she said, "that was a bit too hard!"

"Sorry babe," he said, getting up and rubbing it for her.

"Don't start me off again, Mr Green. I cannot control myself when I am with you and we don't want to be late."

They both dressed and heard the buzzer go, telling them the taxi was waiting outside.

"Got the wine?" he asked her, pulling his jacket over his shoulder.

"Got the wine," she said, as she carried two bottles of good expensive wine that had been recommended to her by the man in the off-licence earlier that day. Martha thought it was rude to turn up with nothing, as she was sure his mum was going to a lot of trouble doing dinner for the six of them.

The taxi pulled up outside his parents' house, which was lit up like it was Christmas. "Blimey," said Toby, "looks like Mum has pulled out all the stops. Looks like every light in the house is on."

They rang on the door bell and his mum was at the door immediately. "Hi Toby, how lovely to see you." She hugged her son and looked over her shoulder to see Martha.

"Hi Martha," she said, looking confused.

"Mum, Martha is my new girlfriend," he said, blushing.

"Hello, Mrs Green," said Martha, also blushing. She wished Toby had told his parents about her before tonight. She felt very awkward.

"Call me Beth, Martha, not Mrs Green. We have known each other for years and it's wonderful to see you." She moved Toby out of the way and hugged Martha. "I always thought you were such a lovely girl and I am pleased that you and Toby are together. Come in, come in," she said, showing them into the hall.

She took their coats. "Ava isn't here yet," she said, "but I am sure she won't be long. What would you both like to drink?"

They went into the lounge and Toby's dad, Charlie, got up from his armchair. "Did I hear that you and Martha are an item?" he said, shaking hands with his son and moving on to Martha to give her a hug. "Very pleased for you, son, she is a lovely girl."

Martha went extremely red but was so happy with his dad's comment.

Toby squeezed her hand and his mum came in with a bottle of beer for Toby and a dry white wine for Martha.

They chatted about Linda and Ted, Martha's parents, and Beth told her they were all going out to some show in a couple of weeks and their friendship was still going strong.

The smell from the kitchen was making Martha feel very hungry. She loved a roast and couldn't wait to sit down to eat, as she hadn't had anything all day, partly due to nerves and partly because she had been so busy at work. She just had enough time to pop out to get the wine.

They all finished their drinks and Toby looked at the clock. "Where are they?" he asked. "I'm starving!"

"I'm sure they will be here soon," said his mum, and went to make sure the food was okay. Toby went to the loo and Martha and Charlie were in deep conversation about house prices when the doorbell rang. Beth came straight out of the kitchen to the front door to answer it. Martha heard Beth say, "Come in, come in," to Ava and her boyfriend, and they walked into the lounge.

"Hi Dad," she said, and looked at Martha, confused. "Hi Martha, what are you doing here?"

"She is Toby's new girlfriend," said Charlie.

"Really!" said Ava. "Oh my God, how long have you two been together? Why didn't Toby tell me?" She went straight over and hugged Martha. They had known each other for years and had always got on, even though there was a five year age gap.

Martha looked behind Ava and saw a very tall handsome man standing there, looking awkward. Beth was behind him. "Go in, go in," she said, as she walked into the lounge behind him.

"Everyone, this is Frank, my boyfriend. Actually, no, this is Frank my fiancé," and she held up her hand to show the biggest rock Martha had ever seen. "That's why we are a little late," she said. "Frank has just proposed!"

Toby walked through the door and was gobsmacked at what he had just heard Ava say. He took one look at the tall man standing next to his dad and couldn't believe who it was!

"What the fuck!" he said. "Over my dead body are you marrying this nasty piece of work!"

Frank walked over to Toby, punched him clean in the face and Toby fell to the ground.

The last Toby heard was screams coming from all three women as he hit the floor.

Chapter 59

Steve was in work, thinking about his date with Lexi. He had not managed to secure a table at Papa's until nine p.m. due to everyone hearing about how good the staff and food were.

He couldn't believe how easy-going Lexi was; she didn't mind in the slightest that they would be eating later.

He decided to send her a text.

Hey beautiful, just to say how much I am looking forward to our date tonight Sx

He could not stop thinking about her and found it hard the last couple of nights knowing she was just downstairs. He had wanted to knock on her door but he didn't want to come across as too pushy and frighten her away. He had really enjoyed the evening with her and his cock stirred every time he thought about it.

His phone pinged and he looked to see her name come up.

Hello gorgeous bloke, just to say back that I too am looking forward to our date tonight Lx

He laughed out loud. She really was amazing.

He had been very busy at work the last couple of days and hadn't got home until very late most evenings. Katie was constantly sending him texts and trying to call. He didn't want her to keep bothering him; he had nothing to say!

He decided to wear a suit tonight. He wanted to pull out all the stops for Lexi and treat her like the lady that she was. He was already thinking about her way too much than he should but he felt that she was special somehow and totally enjoyed her company; they got on great.

His phone pinged again.

*Seeing as we are on first name terms with each other and this is our second dateish, I was wondering if you would like to come to my apartment for pre-dinner drinks around 7pm. Lxx *

She was definitely getting him aroused now!

*I would love to Sxxx

it's another date! L XXXX
*Can't   wait,   seriously!   S
XXXXXXXXXXXXXXXXXXXXXXXXXXXXXXXXXXXXXXXXXXXXXXX
XXXXXXXXXXXXXXXXXXXXXXXXXXXXXXXXXXXXXXXXXXXXXXX
XXXXXXXXXXXXXXXXXXXXXXXXXXXXXXXXXXXXXXXXXXXXXXX
XXXXXXXXXXXXXXXXXXXXXXXXXXXXXXXXXXXXXXXXXXXXXXX
XXXXXXXXXXXXXXXXXXXXXXXXXXXXXXXXXXXXXXXXXXXXXXX
XXXXXXXXXXXXXXXXXXXXXXXXXXXXXXXXXXXXXX
* L X*

He wrapped up his work and turned off his computer. It was only four thirty p.m. but he decided to call it a day. He couldn't concentrate anyway and he wanted to get home.

"You off?" said Debbie, looking at the clock. "Bit early for you, Steve," she said sarcastically.

"I am," he said, looking at her annoyed. "What's it to you, Debbie?"

She realised he was a bit annoyed with her and tried to lighten the mood. "Sorry, I was just saying, it really isn't like you. I wasn't having a dig." She gave him what she thought was a sexy smile.

"Not that it's any business whatsoever of yours, Debbie, but I have a smoking hot date tonight with a very gorgeous lady and I want to get home, so I can shower and smell my best for her when I take her and her gorgeous body to bed later!" She had pissed him off and he wanted to embarrass her!

Debbie was startled at his comment. She wished the smoking hot date was with her. She had liked him for a long time and would love to be in his bed tonight.

"Oh, okay Steve, have a good evening," she said, blushing beetroot red and wishing she hadn't said anything.

"I will, Debbie, I will," he said, as he walked through the double doors to the lift, leaving Debbie looking longingly after him and a little embarrassed.

Fucking cheeky bitch, he thought, how dare she, when I was busy at my desk early in the morning and late at night while she was at home, who is she to look at the fucking clock! He needed to have a word with her. He was one of the directors and he worked very long hours most of the time. He didn't need digs from a receptionist when he wanted to have an early day!

He got out of the lift at the bottom and walked fast to his waiting taxi.

He was still annoyed when he walked through the main doors of his building and up the first flight of stairs. He was startled to see Lexi standing outside her apartment in nothing but a small towel and her hair dripping wet.

"Hello?" he said, looking at her. "Are you waiting to welcome me home?"

Lexi looked totally embarrassed. "Oh my God, Steve, you are not going to believe this. I heard meowing coming from outside the door. I didn't know if it was Ralph but he sounded like he was in distress. I looked outside the door and he was on the step, meowing so much that I went over to him and the door shut behind me. Now Ralph is nowhere to be seen and I am locked out looking like this!" She was panting as she was telling him the story and her face was bright red.

Steve let out an almighty laugh. "Oh my God, Lexi, how cute are you seeing if my cat is okay." He couldn't stop laughing.

Lexi was not at all happy at him seeing her dripping wet in nothing but a towel, she immediately thought of Katie.

"It really is not that funny, Steve," she said, trying not to laugh herself.

"Well, where is your flatmate?" he asked, still laughing.

Ralph had heard Steve's voice, came running down the stairs and snaked around his legs.

"I am hoping she is on her way home before she goes round to see her boyfriend," she said, looking a little forlorn, "otherwise I am in trouble!"

Steve looked at her, feeling sorry for her standing there in just her towel but loving what he saw. "Ralphy, look what you have done to poor Lexi," he said, picking up his cat.

Lexi went over to stroke him too, forgetting she just had a towel round her.

Steve took hold of her hand. "You look very sexy in your towel. I love the colour." He smiled a beaming smile at her and she blushed.

"Steve, stop!" but she didn't take her hand away. Ralph nuzzled them both, he loved to be stroked.

"How about coming up to my apartment? I could give you a T-shirt to put on while you are waiting." He looked at her with pure lust.

"If you are sure," she said, still blushing.

"Oh I'm sure, Lexi," as he turned her round towards the stairs and she started walking up towards his apartment. Ralph jumped from Steve's arms and went ahead of them as if to show her the way. Steve watched as her pert bum wiggled in front of him and he loved it.

She stood there waiting for him to put the key in the lock. "I hope I'm not putting you out," she said, feeling really stupid in her towel.

"I was only going to have a long hot shower before coming down to your apartment for those pre-dinner drinks. You can join me if you want?" he said, laughing out loud at her.

Lexi blushed again. She would love to join him in the shower but she would never have said.

"Let's get you some clothes on," he said, thinking that is not what he wanted to say to her.

He walked into his apartment and went straight in the bedroom to get her one of his T-shirts. He chose a long one as he didn't want to embarrass her any further than she was. He had total respect for her.

"Thanks," she said, as he pointed her towards the bathroom.

If I was Katie, she thought, this towel would have been dropped a long time ago, and she shut the bathroom door.

She came out with his T-shirt on, looking flushed.

"Suits you," he said, as he looked at her long bare legs.

"Thank you again," she said, and walked towards the glass table.

"Drink?" he asked, opening the fridge.

"Love one," she said, sitting down on one of his transparent chairs.

"Wine?"

"Perfect."

They both laughed at their single answers to each other.

She took a sip of her cold wine and she could feel it go down her throat into her stomach. She hadn't eaten since breakfast as she was saving herself for the delicious meal at Papa's she would have later, but didn't want to get drunk before the evening had even started so she decided she would only have the one glass.

She could feel Steve's eyes on her and she liked it.

"You keep staring at me," she said, smiling.

"I can't help it, you are stunning."

Lexi looked at him. "Really? My hair is a mess from the shower and I am sitting here in one of your T-shirts. As lovely as it is, I do feel at a disadvantage."

Steve walked out of the kitchen. "Wait there," he said, and went into his bedroom.

He took off his suit and shirt and found another T-shirt and walked back into the kitchen.

"Better for you?" he said, smiling.

Lexi laughed. "You are funny, Steve. Better," she said, liking his toned muscular legs.

305

They sat at the kitchen for a while and both heard the main door slam. "Jo?" she said and walked towards the front door.

Steve didn't want her to go. He was enjoying her company too much and she looked very sexy in his top.

Lexi came back after she had gone down the stairs to see. Jo was putting her key in the lock and Lexi sighed. Jo turned round to see her and frowned.

"Okay, I leave you for half an hour and you have nothing but a man's T-shirt on standing on the stairs. I hope you are wearing knickers, young lady," said Jo, laughing out loud.

Lexi laughed too. "Long story, involving a cat and a very handsome dude, which I will tell you about in one minute. Leave the door ajar and I will be down."

"I can't wait," said Jo, laughing as she went into the apartment.

Lexi went back up to Steve.

"It was Jo," she said, walking up to him sitting on the chair. "I am going to go down and finish getting ready and I look forward to seeing you for pre-dinner drinks at seven p.m. sharp."

He pulled her down to sit on his lap and kissed her softly on the lips. Lexi responded and put her arms round his neck.

"How sexy are you?" he said. "Especially when you are ordering me about?"

They smiled at each other.

"So I look very much forward to seeing you in my apartment at seven p.m." she said, putting her lips back on his.

Steve opened her mouth with his tongue and heard her softly moan. He put his arms tightly around her and they kissed for quite a while. He was truly aroused by this.

"I should let you go but I don't want to," he said, holding her firmly on his lap.

Lexi gave him a full beaming smile. "I have had a lovely time in your T-shirt and drinking your wine, thank you." She reluctantly got up. "Seven sharp," she said, walking out of his kitchen and through the lounge.

"Wild horses wouldn't stop me from being there," he said, smiling.

She really had got him going. He was totally aroused by her and couldn't wait for seven p.m.

Lexi jumped down the stairs and went into her apartment. Jo was in the kitchen, smiling at her flatmate. "Well chick, what's the story?"

Lexi told Jo all about Ralph and Steve and what had happened.

Jo couldn't help but laugh all the way through the very funny story.

"You know I am at Billy's tonight, don't you?" she said, looking at Lexi, who was sorting out glasses from the dresser. "So looks like you have the choice of two apartments to sow your wild oats!"

Lexi looked at Jo and threw the tea towel that was sitting on the island at her.

"That hurt," said Jo, laughing. "I'm going to pack," and skipped off to her bedroom.

Lexi decided to have another shower. Her hair had dried and there was no way it would go into the style she wanted so she thought she would start again.

Jo kissed her goodbye and Lexi saw that it was six forty-five p.m. She was ready for Steve. She had chosen to be a little more sophisticated than normal tonight. She had gone for a black leather pencil skirt and a cream wrap around mohair top, and she wore a big wide black belt with a gold buckle. She had on her black patent Louboutins to give her height; that elongated her legs and body and she felt really good. Her hair had been straightened and Jo said she looked like Cleopatra, which Lexi thought a great compliment as Cleopatra was beautiful.

Jo walked out and Lexi heard voices at the doorway. She went to see who Jo was speaking to and saw Steve standing there. "Hello," she said, liking that he was early.

"I hope you don't mind me being a little early, but I wasn't sure what the traffic would be like on the stairs down here and I had orders not to be late," he said, his eyes sparkling. "You look fantastic, Lexi," he said, looking her up and down.

Lexi thought he was funny and Jo did too. "I'll see you two love birds tomorrow," she said, as she closed the door behind her. Steve stood still, staring at Lexi in the hallway.

"You look very handsome," she said, looking him up and down and liking what she saw. He too had chosen to go smart; he wore a navy blue suit with a pale pink button down shirt. He had thought wearing a tie would be too much and he was pleased with his outfit.

He walked towards her, took her face in his hands and kissed her very softly on the mouth.

Lexi loved how gentle he was and knew that she would be having another great evening.

They walked into the kitchen. She had laid out a couple of champagne glasses, a small beer glass and some nibbles, as it was still two hours before they would even sit down at Papa's.

"I have ordered a cab to pick us up at eight forty-five p.m.," she said, as she walked over to the island.

"Oh, you have," he said, smiling and looking at the olives and slivers of cheese on the board.

"You have also gone to a lot of trouble," he said, popping a queen olive in his mouth.

"You are worth going to a lot of trouble for," she said, opening the fridge. "Beer, wine?"

"I'd love a beer, please," he said, not taking his eyes off her.

Lexi got a bottle of Peroni and a bottle of Pinot out of the fridge and took them over to the glasses on the island. She could feel him looking at her and she smiled.

"You have a very sexy smile," he said, walking towards her. She felt her legs go weak.

He took her in his arms and pulled her face towards him. He was more urgent this time, pushing her teeth apart and snaking his tongue inside of her gums with more force than before. Lexi immediately responded and kissed him longingly back. They parted, both panting.

"I wish we hadn't booked the restaurant," he said. "I am so happy with the one here." He looked at the food on the island.

Lexi blushed. She was thinking the exact same and dared to say, "We could cancel. There is still time, and it would give someone else a chance to sample the delights of Papa's. I'm sure there is a waiting list to get a table."

Steve immediately reached for his phone, so she wouldn't change her mind, and brought Papa's restaurant up from his contacts.

"Hello," he said into the phone. "I am sorry but I have a table booked for two at nine p.m. in the name of Steve Chance. I am afraid I am going to have to cancel. I do apologise for the short notice." Lexi smiled at how polite and sincere he was.

"Thank you very much, we most definitely will," said Steve, and hung up.

"Sorted," he said. "Now we have all night to amuse ourselves without having to go out."

Lexi went over to her bag, which was on the sofa. "Hello," she said into the phone. "I booked a cab for eight forty-five, in the name of Lexi Barratt, but I am going to have to cancel."

She finished the call. Steve walked over to her and took her in his arms. They stood there kissing for a long time before they pulled apart.

"You are amazing," he said, as he pulled her down on the sofa. Her skirt was quite tight around her legs and she fell on him.

"Steady," he said, and kissed her again, putting his hands down her top and feeling her nipples harden through her bra.

"This was not how I saw the evening going," he said, "not the first half anyway, but you are irresistible, Lexi, and I cannot keep my hands off you."

Lexi said nothing. She was enjoying him caressing her nipple through the sheer of her cream bra.

"I would like to take you to bed," he said, hoping that she wouldn't object.

"I would love you to take me to bed," she said, and stood up beside him and held out her hand.

They walked hand in hand towards Lexi's bedroom. The bedside lamps were both on and they gave a warm soft glow to the room. She walked in ahead and looked up at him shyly.

"I promise I won't hurt you, babe," he said, as he reached down to untie her top. She helped him take it off and stood there in her bra. She was still wearing her heels and she didn't want to take them off, as she loved the height it gave her. He unzipped her skirt, it fell to the floor and she stood there in a cream lace sheer bra and a cream matching thong.

He could see through the thong that she was completely shaven down below and he loved that. He reached round the back of her bra to unhook it and it fell away, revealing her large pert breasts. He took a sharp intake of breath as he cupped them in his hands. "They are beautiful," he said, as he bent to kiss one then the other, still holding them in his hands, his thumb playing softly with her nipples.

Lexi just stood there as he played with her breasts. Feeling her sex moisten, she sighed.

He put his fingers into her thong and slid it slowly down her legs. As she stepped out of it he knelt down, kissing her stomach and licking her navel as he went, just stopping above her most intimate part, his hair tickling her belly. She let out a slight moan and he stood up and started to unbutton his shirt. He had already taken off his jacket and hung it on the back of one of the stools earlier.

As he finished pulling the last button on his shirt out of the button hole she saw that his body was totally ripped and he had a six pack to rival the fittest of men. Her hands moved up to touch his stomach as if playing the keys on a piano.

"You have soft hands. They feel so good on my body," he whispered, and stood back to survey her beautiful curves, with her high firm large breasts, small waist and completely shaved pussy with the long toned legs. Lexi stood completely still while he looked at all of her, his eyes roaming all over in total appreciation. "You are definitely one of the most beautiful women I have ever seen," he said softly to her. She blushed slightly but was loving his compliment and even more enjoying how he was looking at her totally naked body. She was glad she had heels on, as it gave her more confidence.

He undid his belt and then his trousers, pushing them to the floor and stepping out, revealing his white Calvin Klein boxers, which he packed very well. He removed them swiftly and she took a sharp intake of breath as she saw how large and thick his cock was. She wondered how it would feel inside of her.

They now stood totally naked, their eyes sweeping over each other and both looking appreciatively at what they were seeing. He was the first to move and he lifted her up and laid her gently on the bed. Opening her legs wide, he bent down and parted her pussy lips as his tongue explored her most intimate part. Lexi gave out a very loud moan as his fingers got to work and she became totally wet from their touch. He pushed her legs open wider and his tongue found her throbbing clit. He teased it with the tip of his tongue as he heard her moan again. "Don't stop," she said, "please don't stop." He pushed his finger deep inside her as she writhed about on the bed, enjoying everything he was doing. Her orgasm was the strongest she had ever felt and she climaxed, soaking his face as he carried on licking and sucking her until she was dry.

He moved up the bed, wiping his face, and she kissed him, tasting her juices. She reached down and took his erect penis in her hands and slowly moved up and down his shaft. It was Steve's turn to moan and he loved her grip, holding him tightly as she moved up and down slowly but with force.

He had to have her. He had been forthright in bringing condoms with him. He didn't want her to feel he thought she was a sure thing but safe sex was something he thought was extremely important and he climbed off the bed to feel in his trouser pocket for what he was looking for. Lexi was on her elbows looking at him, a frown on her face. When she saw what he was doing she looked at him and said, "Such respect." He went to over to her, ripped the condom from its packet and put it skilfully on his raging hard on.

He pushed open her legs wide with his knees and entered her slowly as she gasped with total pleasure. She opened her legs wider so she could accommodate his huge member. He moved in and out, slowly at first but building up a rhythm. As she was taking him in further and deeper he got faster and she cried out at the sheer magnitude of her orgasm. They climaxed together, breathing very heavily as the last of their juices mixed together. He stayed inside her for a while as he watched her, sated on the bed, glowing in the aftermath of her orgasm, smiling up at him and wanting him even more. "That was absolutely amazing," she said in a very low sexy voice, still slightly moaning as she said it, feeling her body tingle all over. He smiled back. "You are absolutely beautiful, Lexi," he said, as he slowly pulled out of her and she gasped.

They lay on the bed naked, their bodies entwined, as he softly caressed her breasts, both loving the tenderness which they shared.

She gave out a big sigh and looked at him, never wanting this to end. He kissed her slowly but passionately and their tongues explored each other's mouths.

Lexi heard it first, a noise coming from outside, which sounded like someone was calling out "Steve, Steve." He looked at her. "What the fuck?" he said, as he got off the bed and stopped to listen again. "Steve, Steve." He could hear a woman shouting his name.

Lexi looked at him. "Someone is calling your name." He picked up his trousers from the floor and put them on, and grabbed his shirt and put it on, not bothering to do it up. Lexi jumped out of bed and got her dressing gown from the back of her door.

They both went to the front door of the apartment. His name was being screamed now and hairs at the back of his neck stood on end. He knew exactly who it was. He told Lexi to wait there as he went out of the front door and down the stairs. He opened the main door of the building and there, standing on the step with mascara running down her face, was Katie.

"What the fuck are you doing here?" he shouted at her, not knowing what was going on. He hadn't realised but Lexi was behind him and she looked straight at Katie.

"What are you doing, Katie, why are you here?" Katie looked at them both and saw Steve's shirt undone and Lexi in her dressing gown. She couldn't believe that they were both there standing on the steps of his apartment building without their clothes on!

She screamed as she lunged for them both. "You fucking bitch, you fucking bitch, you stole him away from me, how could you, I hate you Lexi, I hate you!"

Lexi stepped back and didn't know what she was talking about. "Who the fuck have I stolen from you, Katie?" Her eyes widened and she realised. Steve was Katie's Steve! "Oh my God!" she screamed. "Oh my God!"

Steve looked at them both. "Do you know each other?" he said, feeling very confused at what was going on in front of him.

Katie grabbed hold of Lexi's hair and pulled it hard. "I hate you, you fucking bitch, I hate you!"

Lexi slapped her arm away with force and Katie reeled back. "Get off me, you crazy bitch!" Lexi shouted.

Lexi then turned to Steve with horror on her face. "Why didn't you tell me?"

Steve was confused. "Tell you what, Lex, I really don't understand?"

People were starting to come out of their apartments to see what was going on.

Steve and Lexi looked at each other and he could see that her eyes were questioning him. "Lex, I did not know you knew her. I had a couple of dates with her and that was it. Then Toby told me that he had seen her out with quite a few men and getting up to shit loads so I didn't return her calls or her texts. I haven't spoken or seen her since I met you, I promise you that."

Katie was staring at them both, unable to believe what he was saying. Toby, who the fuck was Toby? Then she remembered his good-looking friend. She stood there feeling absolutely drained from the events of the last couple of days. I cannot let Lexi take him. She was consumed with jealousy at seeing these two together. The two people in the world that she realised she loved.

Chapter 60

Katie managed to pick herself up off the floor where she lay. She had nothing left in her body.

She was absolutely distraught at the fact that she was pregnant. She could not believe how that was possible; she was on the fucking pill!

She walked into her bedroom and looked at herself in her full length mirror. Her hair was all over the place and her make-up was all down her face; her eyes were bloodshot from crying and her throat was very sore from all the retching. She looked awful; she also felt awful.

There is no way I can have this baby, she thought. It wasn't a baby yet, she was only two to three weeks pregnant. "Pregnant!" she said, as she carried on looking at herself in the mirror.

Her hands went down to her stomach. "No, this is not happening!"

She went and sat down on the bed, moving her hair out of her face, and just sat there staring at the floor. She did not have a clue who the father was and she was devastated.

"What the fuck am I going to do?" she said out loud. "There is no way I can have this baby. I am too young to have a baby. I am having far too much fun. There is no way; I don't even have a fucking job!"

She immediately thought of one of the girls in her office who had discovered she was pregnant and was very upset about it. Katie had sneered at her and told her that she should have taken more care and not have been so stupid; that she only had herself to blame and she needed to deal with it. The girl had cried her heart out in the office and Katie had just laughed at her and told her she was a stupid bitch!

"I am that stupid bitch now," she said, and let out a wail and sobbed into the duvet.

What was she going to do? How was she going to find out who the father was? Even if she did she didn't want to spend the rest of her life with them, bringing up a screaming brat!

She thought of Steve. I need to see him, I need to speak to him, she thought, and got up from the bed and went in the bathroom to clean her face.

She brushed her hair and put it in a ponytail and put on a pair of jeans and a T-shirt and the highest heels she could find. She found her mobile and ordered a cab to pick her up as soon as possible.

She looked at herself in the mirror. Steve will help me, she thought, he will care for me and look after me.

She heard the buzzer go and grabbed a jacket and went running down the stairs. Wilbur wasn't there and she found herself wondering where he was.

She jumped in the cab and told the taxi driver where she needed to go. She knew what she had to do to make everything work out fine for her.

She gave the taxi driver the money and got out. She was at Steve's apartment but she didn't know what number he lived at. She knew it was on the top floor but didn't notice the number. She went up to the main doors. There were lots of buzzers there but nothing with names on, they were blank.

How fucking stupid, why has no one put their name? What if I was a postman, she thought, and then shook her head. For fuck's sake, Katie, get a grip.

She had no choice but to stand in the street and call his name. She could see there were lights coming from the windows at the top but she wasn't sure which one was his.

"Steve," she shouted, "Steve." No one was coming out of the door. "Steve, Steve." She carried on and she heard herself screaming his name. Her throat was on fire but she didn't care, she needed to see him.

The main door finally opened and there he was, standing there. His shirt opened, showing his gorgeous toned body. She looked at him and then behind him she saw Lexi in her dressing gown. What the fuck? She realised that they had been together, together shagging, her Steve with her Lexi, together!

She let out a scream. "You bitch, you fucking bitch," she heard herself shout. "You stole him away from me!" How could Lexi be so cruel; she was supposed to be her friend and she had taken Steve away from her. She probably did it out of malice, just to get back at her!

How selfish, how utterly selfish. She was consumed with jealousy and lunged at Lexi. She didn't know what else to do, she had to grab something. She felt herself pulling Lexi's hair as hard as she could but Lexi was stronger and she pushed her arm away, sending Katie flying down the steps; her heels were too high and she fell onto the pavement.

She had to stop them, she had to get him back, so she did the only thing that Katie managed to do well; she lied. "I am pregnant, Steve, and the baby is yours!"

As soon as the words were out of her mouth she regretted it, but when she saw the look on Lexi's face she knew that she could not take it back. She had hurt her just like she was hurting Katie. She cannot have him, there is no fucking way, he is mine, she thought, as she steadied herself.

She watched as Lexi ran back in through the main doors and saw Steve standing staring at her.

"You are a fucking liar, Katie. I never had sex with you and you well know it!" He was disgusted by her and he turned to walk in the same direction as Lexi but stopped to look back at her.

She screamed at him. "You are the fucking liar, Steve, remember when we had it at your apartment? Do you not remember, when you were sucking my nipples and getting really turned on and I took you in my mouth and you couldn't control yourself that you plunged straight into me with such force!" She was looking at him now with venom in her voice and a sneer on her face.

He was speechless at what had just come out of her mouth. The neighbours were looking out of their windows and some had come out of their apartments and were looking in horror at the disgusting things this young girl was saying!

Steve looked at Katie, unable to believe what he was hearing. "I didn't have sex with you, you nasty, conniving slag!" He couldn't help himself and ran up to Lexi's apartment and knocked on her door.

"She is a liar, Lexi. I promise you I have never had sex with her in my life!"

He could hear Lexi on the other side of the door, sobbing. It broke his heart.

"Go away, Steve, please, I just want to be on my own."

"I promise you, Lex, I promise you, I have not had sex with that woman!" He didn't know how he could convince her.

"Please leave me the fuck alone!" she screamed through the door.

He was beside himself and didn't know what to do. He pushed his hands through his hair and ran up to his apartment to get his phone. He slammed the door loudly behind him.

Katie came into the building and went up the stairs. She had seen Steve at the apartment door; was that where Lexi now lived, in the same apartment block as Steve? When she saw him go up the stairs she knocked on the door lightly.

"Lexi, it's Katie, let me in. I need to speak to you. I don't blame you, you weren't to know but I need to speak to you."

"Please Lex, let me in."

Lexi opened the door to see Katie standing there, looking tall in her heels with mascara running down her face.

"I am so sorry for lunging at you and pulling your hair. I realise that you didn't know that he was my Steve and I forgive you."

Lexi looked at Katie. She didn't know what was going on, her head was all over the place. but she opened the door wider.

Katie smiled. She knew that Lexi believed her and walked into the apartment, knowing that she had got her friend back. It was only a matter of time before she got Steve back too!

The End
....or is it just the beginning?

Book Two in the series:
COPING WITH WHATEVER
available soon!